"The sudden screams ... the monstrous beast.

The *kirin* burst throu... the ground under th... with the thunder of its headlong approach. Behind it came all the hunters who were still on horseback, following at full gallop, heedless of anything now except stopping its escape.

Kai ran after the *kirin*, not away. He was as determined as the samurai not to let it escape into the woods, but had no idea at all of how to stop it.

He saw a fleeing horse about to pass him. He headed for it, and with a final burst of speed caught the saddle and swung up onto its back. Taking the reins he turned its headlong flight into a controlled gallop, pursuing the *kirin* into the edge of the trees.

The warriors were trying to trap the *kirin* with snares, but that only seemed to enrage it more. It tore through the ropes and the circle of horsemen, creating more chaos as it ran for the trees.

Kai saw Yasuno go after it, alone, following it into the forest. Kai hesitated a moment, cursing under his breath, and then turned his horse to follow the maddened beast into the woods. He saw Yasuno draw alongside the *kirin* and, reaching down, drive his sword between the spine-like branches into its back.

The *kirin* swung around, knocking Yasuno from his horse with one blow of its enormous head. Yasuno picked himself up off the ground and stumbled backwards as he saw the *kirin* turn again toward him, preparing to charge.

Kai sent his horse galloping at the *kirin*. Leaning out, he managed to reach through the crooked spines protruding from its back and grab the hilt of Yasuno's *katana*. The branches tore at him, ripping his flesh and clothing, drawing blood as he yanked the sword free, but he managed to stay in the saddle. He heeled his mount around with a wild shout of defiance to confront the living nightmare head-on.

The *kirin* took his invitation, forgetting about Yasuno as it turned back to charge at him. . . .

Books by Joan D. Vinge

HEAVEN CHRONICLES

Fireship / Mother and Child

THE SNOW QUEEN CYCLE

The Snow Queen

World's End *

The Summer Queen *

Tangled Up in Blue *

THE CAT SERIES

Psion *

Catspaw *

Dreamfall *

The Random House Book of Greek Myths

COLLECTIONS

Eyes of Amber

Phoenix in the Ashes

MEDIA TIE-INS

Ladyhawke

Star Wars: The Return of the Jedi Storybook

The Dune Storybook

Mad Max Beyond Thunderdome

Santa Claus: The Movie

Return to Oz

Willow

Lost in Space

Cowboys & Aliens *

*47 Ronin**

* A Tom Doherty Associates book

47 RONIN

JOAN D. VINGE

BASED ON THE SCREENPLAY BY
CHRIS MORGAN
AND HOSSEIN AMINI

SCREEN STORY BY
CHRIS MORGAN
&
WALTER HAMADA

A TOM DOHERTY ASSOCIATES BOOK | NEW YORK

47 RONIN

Edited by James Frenkel

A Tor Book
Published by Tom Doherty Associates, LLC
175 Fifth Avenue
New York, NY 10010

www.tor-forge.com

Tor® is a registered trademark of Tom Doherty Associates, LLC.

ISBN 978-0-7653-6964-2

Tor books may be purchased for educational, business, or promotional use. For information on bulk purchases, please contact Macmillan Corporate and Premium Sales Department at 1-800-221-7945, extension 5442, or write specialmarkets@macmillan.com.

First Edition: December 2013

Printed in the United States of America

0 9 8 7 6 5 4 3 2 1

This book is dedicated with great respect to
the following people:

The Fukushima Fifty
George Takei
Stan Sakai

whose courage, honor, and compassion have shown me that certain values are universal and undying—stepping-stones on the path to wisdom. Those qualities will last forever, like the memory of the loyal 47 Ronin.

"Each one of us must make his own true way,
and when we do, that will express
the universal way. That is the mystery."
—SHUNRYU SUZUKI

The Seven Traditional Virtues of the Bushido Code:

GI (Justice)

YU (Valor and Courage)

JIN (Compassion)

REI (Courtesy and Respect)

MAKOTO (Honesty)

MEIYO (Honor)

CHUGI (Loyalty)

ACKNOWLEDGMENTS

Because sometimes truth is stranger than fiction . . .

Thanks to Stephen Turnbull, for his many excellent books on Japanese military history, particularly *The Revenge of the 47 Ronin—Edo 1703* ("Raid" series). Also very helpful were *Daimyo of 1867: Samurai Warlords of Shogun Japan,* by Tadashi Ehara; *Everyday Life in Traditional Japan,* by Charles J. Dunn, with illustrations by Laurence Broderick; *The Demon's Sermon on the Martial Arts,* by Issai Chozanshi, translated by William Scott Wilson; and *Seppuku: A History of Samurai Suicide,* by Andrew Rankin.

For words combined with pictures, thank you to *The Samurai,* by Mitsuo Kure, for its detailed photographs and text about historical reenactors demonstrating various aspects of samurai warfare; and *A Samurai Castle,* by Fiona MacDonald, with illustrations by John James and David Antram.

Also, thank you to Google.com, Wikipedia.com, and SamuraiWiki.com the "travel guides of the gods"; if they can't offer you what you need, they can probably tell you where to find it.

Because sometimes fiction is more "real" than fact . . .

Thanks to Stan Sakai, for his masterful adaptation of Samurai legend to sequential art, in *Usagi Yojimbo;* Laura Joh Rowland for her vivid, fascinating "Sano Ichiro" historical mystery series set during the era of the *47 Ronin;* Watsuki Nobuhiro for his classic Rurouni Kenshin manga (graphic novel series) and anime (animated series); Hayao Miyazaki for *Mononoke-hime* and many other timeless anime films. Also my thanks to the creators of numerous other manga and anime series, in particular Blade of the Immortal, by Hiroaki Samura, and Vagabond, by Takehiko Inoue, both set during the Tokugawa Era.

Because sometimes a picture is worth a thousand words . . .

The artists of *ukiyo-e* (Japanese woodblock prints), who captured the times they lived in and the legends of their past with such evocative beauty—in particular the artists Yoshitoshi, Kunioshi, Kunisada, Hiroshige, Hokusai (and too many others to name)—who inspired their spiritual descendants, the creators of modern graphic novels, manga, and anime, as well as artists and art lovers everywhere.

I would also like to thank my editor at Tor Books, James Frenkel; Cindy Chang, Julie Margules and Jennifer Epper at Universal Studios; and Alexander Besher and his brother Arseny Besher for details about the Asano clan, its history, clan symbols and banners, which were otherwise totally inaccessible to a hapless writer living in the United States who reads no Japanese.

It is dangerous to be right in matters on which
the established authorities are wrong.

—VOLTAIRE

We will fight, not out of spite,
But someone must stand up for what's right.

—"HANDS," BY JEWEL

You have been chosen. Walk the true path.

—*BRAVE STORY*, BY MIYUKI MIYABE

47 RONIN

PROLOGUE

Japan, circa 1680

If anyone had asked him, he would have said that he had been fighting for his life, running for his life . . . running away, all his life. Even when his battered body could not so much as pick itself up off the floor, still with all his soul and his heart he had resisted, fleeing in his dreams from the Sea of Trees and the lies they told him there, refusing to become what they would have turned him into.

But he had never been close enough, for long enough, to anyone of his own kind that they could have asked him.

And so he had waited, endured, meditating on the time when his chance would come . . . until at last it had.

And now he was running, as he had been running for days, through the darkness of the primordial trees, where sunlight barely penetrated deeply enough to tell him when day became night. He avoided any distant lights, any open spaces—a road or a village, anything at all that might deceive his eyes, and turn into a trap. He couldn't take any chances until he discovered what it was that he was really running toward.

It had begun to seem as if the mountain forests would never come to an end, just as they had threatened when they told him he would do nothing but run in circles, futilely, until at last he returned to the ones he belonged to.

But that was a lie, he knew there was more to the world

than the Sea of Trees—that somehow he would reach the Ocean-Sea, which was truly endless, at last; because the place where the Sea of Trees existed was an island called "Japan," surrounded by a sea greater than anything he could imagine. And somewhere the land at the edge of the sea waited—filled with the sunlight he had rarely seen, with blossoming trees and the rich green of rice fields . . . filled with people like him. His own people.

He had seen the proof of their existence, their land, in the stolen booty his masters had brought back to their hidden world; in the rags they had flung at him to wear, telling him those had once been worn by his own kind.

He had seen his reflection in the still water of forest pools, and he knew it was true—he was not one of them. *He was human.* He had seen other humans in painted scrolls and books, glimpsed them in the distance, even heard their voices echoing through the mountain valleys. But his masters had told him the humans did not want him—that they had abandoned him to death or demons, and he was wrong to believe they would ever take him back.

He had refused to listen, and sworn that someday he would find his way home, to a place where the people would welcome him, even after he had been lost so long.

Someday . . . maybe even today.

The forest was clearing, the light was changing, brighter now, as the trees thinned out ahead. Between them he caught glimpses of water reflecting the sky, and wide green fields, their colors vivid and shining in a way that he had never seen before.

His breath caught in his chest as he emerged suddenly from the trees, and a world he had only seen in dreams filled his vision. He lurched to a stop, shielding his eyes from the glare of full daylight. This couldn't be an illusion—even their powers could not make him see something so vast if it wasn't real.

But as he started out into the open at last, his body reeled, shocked by the emptiness around him: nothing but an open field and the sky, leaving him as unprotected as a rabbit when hawks were circling overhead. All at once he realized how unsteady his legs had become, that his body was trembling with exhaustion. His belly ached with hunger, his eyes blurred and burned, as if his arrival in the land of dreams had suddenly made his own existence all too real. Keeping his arm raised to shield his eyes from the light, he pushed himself to continue moving, to focus on the way ahead, never looking back, or down.

And so he did not see the stream bank that dropped abruptly out from under him. He lost his balance, and cried out as he fell with a heavy splash into the stream. He lay where he had landed on the hard stones, utterly spent, as incapable of moving again as a stone. The cool water flowed over his body, soothing the bruises and scratches he had ignored for too long. The harsh rasping of his breath, the blood rushing in his ears, were all he could hear.

Then, high in the air above him, he heard a hawk screech as it spotted prey. He struggled to push himself up as the need to escape, to keep running, startled to life inside him. But his shaking arms would do no more than let him flop onto his side before he collapsed again, unable to climb, to stand, or even get to his knees. Nothing he could think of was frightening enough, terrible enough, in that moment to make his body move.

He felt the sun's unfamiliar touch warm his ghost-pale face; it made the lids of his closed eyes glow like rice-paper lanterns. He lay waiting, wondering if hawk talons ripping his flesh would be the next unfamiliar sensation he felt, when he heard the sound of animals approaching—hooves clicking against stones, legs swishing through the long grass: horses? *And human voices . . .*

He lay as motionless as the dead, listening to their approach, hoping that, whoever they were, they would take him for dead and pass him by like a corpse in a ditch.

But looming shadows fell across him, as the riders stopped on the stream bank directly above him. He heard the sounds of leather and cloth and metal, as they shifted in their saddles. He opened his eyelids a fraction, trying to see who or what had found him.

The two closest riders were peering down at him from what seemed to his eyes like an impossible height and angle: two men, dressed in clothing that was both stranger and finer than any he had ever seen. Both of them wore the matched pair of swords that marked their rank as samurai—the warrior elite of the world beyond the Sea of Trees.

He felt more gazes settling on him, as other riders joined the two who sat looking down at him; all their stares combined felt like a physical weight. He lay still, barely breathing, listening to the sound of their voices, so different from the voices he was used to hearing that their murmured words were barely understandable.

". . . really a body?"

"Not from around here. Who—?"

"No . . . *what*? That doesn't look human."

"Lord Asano—?"

The older man who sat on his horse with the dignity of a lord nodded at the warrior beside him. "Oishi,"—he gestured toward the boy in the stream—"see if he's alive."

The boy's body threatened to betray him with sudden trembling, as the samurai beside the lord dismounted and started down the slope.

The lord dismounted then as well, although several voices protested. He passed the hawk perched on his gloved fist to someone else, and stood watching closely as his retainer reached the boy and caught his arm, turning him onto his back.

Still the boy didn't move, holding his breath. Through slitted eyes he saw the lord gazing down at him, his curiosity and surprise obvious, but nothing showing on his face that looked remotely murderous.

"He's not from Ako," the samurai holding the boy said, with absolute certainty. "How did he make his way here? He could never get past a checkpoint on the roads."

The lord started down the shallow bank to the stream, but the samurai named Oishi held up a hand, signaling caution, as he crouched next to the boy. The boy realized that Oishi was not much older than he was . . . but the young samurai's eyes were filled with suspicion as they peered down at his face.

Oishi reached out almost hesitantly, touching the scars that covered the front of the boy's shaven head, as if an unreadable incantation had been etched into his scalp. Then a gloved hand caught the boy suddenly by the chin, turning his face for a better look. The samurai frowned and shook his own head. "It's not . . . human, *tono,*" he said, addressing his lord again. "It's a changeling . . . a shape-shifter. It must have come out of the Tengu Forest, or from deep in the mountains—"

"It's human enough," another voice said, in disgust. The others had dismounted and gathered at the top of the stream bank. "It's a halfbreed. Look at that face—it's the get of some straw-hair from the Dutch Island. Not even a prostitute would bear the shame of a mixed-blood brat—"

Lord Asano turned toward the speaker, silencing the man with a look. Oishi bent the boy's head to the side again, studying his profile, and his own frown deepened.

And then suddenly he froze, as the knife the boy had pulled from its hidden sheath pressed his throat. Oishi held as still as the stones in the brook; now he was the one who didn't even dare to breathe. The boy's eyes glared up at him, wide open and filled with fury. His arm shook; a thin line of blood showed on Oishi's neck.

Oishi moved with the quickness of a cat, grabbing the boy's wrist, twisting it so sharply that the boy dropped the blade with a small cry, without even struggling. And then the boy's entire body sagged, going limp again in his hold.

Grimly, Oishi rolled the body onto its stomach, and pushed its scarred head under the water.

"Oishi!"

At the sound of Lord Asano's anger, Oishi let go of the

head as if it was burning hot. "My lord," he protested, daring to glance up, "it is a demon, not a child—!"

"He is a child," Lord Asano said, his voice stern, and yet filled with a compassion that Oishi couldn't begin to fathom. "Pick him up." Lord Asano reached down with his own hands to help Oishi pull the boy's body up onto dry ground. Even dripping wet and unconscious, the boy weighed almost nothing; he was so thin that his bones could have been hollow like a bird's.

The other retainers joined him as they saw the proof that this was really their lord's choice of action. They carried the unconscious boy away from the stream bank, and laid him across the back of a horse meant to carry home far less unexpected game from their now-forgotten hunt.

When the boy opened his eyes again, it was night—but a night like none he had ever seen before. Somehow he had come to be slung over the back of a horse, which made breathing difficult, and thinking even harder. The last thing he remembered was the look in the eyes of the young samurai, and a strong hand forcing his face under the water. . . .

And now, this—He raised his head, trying to make sense of what he saw as the horse stopped moving. He glimpsed the night sky dimly flecked with stars, high above a barrier of hand-cut stone topped by painted plaster walls and tiled roofs. In the flickering glow of torches, he saw the men who had captured him, on their horses . . . and now more men on foot, surrounding them. All their faces were alike in a way that was good, a way far more like his own than anyone he had ever seen up close.

As he strained to keep looking at them, they gathered around him, their faces half shadowed by helmets—so much larger and taller than he had imagined: grim men wearing the armor of guards, staring back at him with the same expressions on their faces that had been on the face of the one named Oishi, the one who had tried to drown him. Harsh, cold, contemptuous, filled with disgust and suspicion . . . as if they were looking into the face of a demon or a beast, not a human being: *not one of them.*

His heartbeat faltered; his hands tightened into fists. He knew without trying to reach for it that his knife was gone . . . just as he knew that he had no hope of fighting his way free of this stone-walled fortress, or escaping so many hostile, well-armed men. *What did they want with him? Why had they brought him here?*

". . . that it's a straw-hair's get from the Dutch island."

"—or English maybe?"

"It's a demon—"

". . . dangerous, we should get rid of it!"

Listening to the muttered voices, he realized they were ready to . . . to. . . . *At any moment one of those gleaming blades would take off his head, or strong hands would snap his neck like a stick.*

His attempt to face those stares without showing fear failed utterly. *The Old One hadn't lied. There had never been anything better waiting for him on the outside. . . .*

He struggled like a fly in the web of rope that tied him to the horse's back as panic filled his thoughts the way water had filled his lungs, until he felt himself drowning in it.

And then suddenly another face appeared before him, as unexpected as the face of the moon. A young girl, not even his own age, her long black hair like a silken waterfall . . . carrying a lantern, and dressed in flowing robes the colors of moonlight and early spring, decorated with images of blossoms and flowing streams.

The samurai stepped back, bowing their heads as though she was a goddess, while she moved between them with perfect composure until she was standing in front of him. She raised the lantern, spreading a warm protective glow over the two of them, as he looked up and she gazed serenely back at him. The fear in his eyes turned to wonder as he went on staring at her, and realized there was no fear or disgust in the way she looked at him, only a quiet curiosity, and concern that turned gradually to compassion, as if without a word passing between them, or a word to anyone else, somehow she understood everything he thought and felt.

In the light of the lantern, the boy realized that the samurai lord was still sitting on his horse in the background behind her. Astonished, the boy saw a smile come over his face as he watched them, watched the girl . . . a father's pride, and a wise man's approval.

The girl took hold of the horse's rein as the hunting party began to move forward again, toward the castle's upper courtyard. Even as overwhelming relief tried to close his eyes, the boy clung to her gaze, the otherworldly beauty of it, the gentle acceptance touched with something that was almost awe as she looked back at him. She moved alongside him as if she was guiding his fate as well as his horse now, reassuring him that no matter where they were taking him, as long as he was under her protection, no harm, nothing evil, could befall him.

Realizing he was safe for the first time that he could remember, the boy finally let his eyes close for good.

"You're not afraid of the catch from our hunt today, Lady Mika?"

Mika looked up as Oishi Yoshio, the son of her father's *karou*—his chief retainer—guided his horse carefully alongside her. She shook her head, puzzled by the question. "Why should I be?" she asked, unable to keep from raising her head a little higher, because she thought she caught the faintest trace of bemusement in his voice. "It's only a boy. Poor boy . . ." She glanced back at the small body lying motionless across the horse beside her.

Oishi would take his own father's place as *karou* one day, but right now he was hardly more than a boy himself, and still much too impressed with his newly gained status as a warrior. "The men are of the opinion that it isn't human—

that it's a beast, or demon-spawn." He shrugged, as if he believed that too, but wasn't in the least frightened by it. "Only your father, and you, seem to see nothing but a boy. . . ."

She smiled, giving her head a shake so that her long hair rippled down her back. "I am my father's daughter, young Oishi," she said, and watched him choke like he'd swallowed a large glob of spicy *wasabi.*

"But your father's retainers are concerned . . . excuse me, my lady, but we are all in agreement that it is dangerous to bring a strange creature like this into the castle itself . . . that simply his presence here could attract misfortune to Ako."

"Oh, horse dung!" she said, very distinctly, enjoying the shocked looks on the faces of the men around her, until she saw her father's face. He sent a disapproving look over his shoulder at her, and then glanced away as if he was searching for her nursemaids.

"It's just a boy." She spoke only the truth now, but she saw some of the other men glance at her, with looks either condescending or worried. "He's no different than we are." She raised her voice slightly, in response.

The looks she got this time were more pity than censure, but they irked her just as much. She knew what they meant: that a girl-child, even if she was the daughter of their lord, was a foolish creature indeed if she didn't know the forms evil could take. Feeling the sudden need to explain herself, she said, "He's afraid of strange places, and people he doesn't know. Just like we are." She glanced at the boy, remembering the stark terror in his deep brown eyes when she had first looked into them: the look of someone lost and all alone in the hands of his enemies.

And she remembered how his expression had changed, when his eyes found hers. Her voice softened, turning wistful. "And he wants to belong somewhere, with someone, more than anything . . . just like we do."

Oishi stared down at her a moment longer, his expression almost thoughtful. But he only took a deep breath that sounded more like a sigh, and rode on ahead to join her father.

When the boy opened his eyes again, he found himself in yet another world—one his returning vision could not be sure wasn't still a dream, or an afterlife far more incredible than anything he had ever imagined.

He lay on a futon, the padded mattress seeming as soft as a layer of clouds beneath him. A quilt with an embroidered silk cover kept him exactly warm enough, soothing his bruised, scraped body like the embrace of loving arms. Candlelight gradually revealed the place where he rested now—no longer surrounded by bleak stone walls, but inside a room where the floor was covered in finely woven *tatami* matting. The walls were partitions of polished wood with painted screens filling the spaces between them. The paper screens were covered with blossoming trees and exotic birds, images of the outside world far more beautiful and welcoming than any real view he had ever seen.

He was all alone in it—no grim samurai holding spears or drawn swords surrounded him; there was no sign even of the young girl who had appeared suddenly, causing the men to back away. He remembered how she had looked into his eyes and smiled at him—the first time he had ever been given a true and welcoming smile.

He wondered where she had disappeared to . . . if she had been a *tennyo,* a heavenly maiden who had been sent to bring him here. If only she could have stayed beside him for long enough to tell him where *here* was, and what he should do now. . . . Had he wakened in an afterlife more beautiful than dreams, only to find that he was still as alone in it as he had been when he was alive? He closed his eyes as he felt them beginning to burn, and let himself slip back again into the peace of oblivion.

"Sakura, sakura . . . yayoi no sora wa. . . ." When he woke again, it was to the sound of a voice singing: ". . . cherry blossoms, April brings . . ." It was a young girl's voice, so sweet and soft that it seemed to be a part of the air he breathed. ". . . *Izaya,* come with me . . . to see the cherry trees in bloom. . . ."

His forest-trained ears told him the song was not coming to him out of thin air, but from somewhere to one side. He turned his head toward the translucent rice paper-paned sliding door that stood slightly ajar beside the bed where he lay. He saw a shadow-figure beyond the wall, kneeling just out of sight . . . the shadow of the young girl singing.

An inarticulate sound escaped his throat, and he stretched out his arm toward the opening in the wall.

The singing stopped, and he was afraid the shadow maiden would vanish too, but instead she leaned forward, shyly peeking in at him through the doorway. It was the girl he had seen before, in the courtyard.

Her eyes met his, and the smile on her face was like the one she had given him then, as if she was truly glad to see him again, and awake. She reached in to touch his straining hand. Her fingers felt soft and warm, and real. In her hand was a small bundle, wrapped in an embroidered silk scarf; she dropped it quickly onto the mat beside him where he lay, before she withdrew her arm again.

Only then did he notice the other, fainter, shadows on the wall, as they materialized through motion into the forms of the young girl's attendants, who had been patiently waiting along with her, while she waited for him to wake.

He heard the women's voices urging and chiding, as they drew the *tennyo* to her feet and hurried her away across the room beyond the wall, toward another doorway. She hadn't had time to speak even a word, but through the rustle of billowing robes, he made out the voices of women saying ". . . Lady Mika . . ." and "—past your bedtime!" She managed to glance back over her shoulder at him before they swept her out of his sight and hearing.

And then the young samurai called Oishi followed them out of the room, from wherever he had been silently standing guard. Oishi paused in the doorway, staring after the just-departed daughter of his lord, before he looked back at the boy. His face was quizzical and full of doubt, as if he still couldn't fathom why both father and daughter were so drawn to a thing he could only see as a threat. But at last he turned away again, his hand dropping from the hilt of his sword as he left the room, and closed the screen behind him.

Slowly, cautiously, the boy raised himself onto an elbow and reached for the bundled scarf left for him by the girl Mika . . . *the Lady Mika*? Then she must be the daughter of the lord who had rescued him—from Oishi and his own samurai. "Lord Asano," they had called him—the *daimyo* of this dreamlike castle and the lands around it—of all the people who lived here. And would all of that come to include one nameless boy, a boy who was a total stranger in ways even he couldn't understand? Could it ever . . . ?

The boy held the soft whisper of silk scarf in his hands, staring at the embroidery that made its delicate colors even more beautiful. He felt awed by the very existence of a place where even the commonest piece of cloth seemed to have been transformed by magic.

But his nose told him there was more to this bundle of fragile cloth than dye and embroidery . . . he smelled food. Suddenly his hunger felt as ravenous as the beast the samurai had claimed he was. He unfolded the cloth with clumsy hands and began to eat what he found inside it.

He didn't recognize any of the foods except rice, and even simple rice tasted nothing like what he was used to. But as hungry as he was, and as fearful that the rice, and everything around him, would vanish like an enchantment, he realized that the food Mika-*hime* had left him had been prepared as exquisitely as everything else. The exotic flavor of each bite he took forced him to stop swallowing it whole and eat more slowly, savoring each mouthful, something he had never done before, because for all his life the food he was given had only been intended to keep him alive.

But the pleasure of eating passed too quickly, in spite of that. He could have eaten this food forever . . . he would gladly have eaten his own weight even of the food that he had choked down for years in order to survive.

But his hunger, like his fear, had had the edge taken off it, and his exhaustion outweighed even his hunger. A miracle seemed to have happened to him, even though he was sure there were no miracles.

And although he wasn't even altogether certain whether he was alive or dead, he was in a land of dreams, where the bed was soft, and the coverlet of silk as soothing as Mika's lullaby. There was no reason for his eyes to stay open now, ever watchful, ever wary. And so he let his eyelids close, willingly this time, and slept. . . .

They named the boy "Kai," for the sea, at Mika's insistence, because when he came to them he had no name at all. But the first words he had spoken, when he tried to communicate, had been about the "Sea of Trees." The Sea of Trees was a place that existed in legends and folk stories—a place no one from Ako had ever seen, or that could be found on any of the Shogunate's official maps of Japan. The rational men of Ako Castle doubted that it had ever existed, at least on the earthly plane, even if every time they looked at the boy Kai, it seemed he could only have come from such a place.

That he had lived in a forest his entire life was easy to believe; that he had lived there without parents for most of it was obvious. He might as well have been abandoned there, and suckled by wolves, because the simplest peasant knew more about proper behavior than Kai did. His Japanese was stilted and strange in a way even a foreigner would find laughable, although at least it was slowly improving.

The fact that Kai could speak at all was a wonder, Oishi

thought, as he stood with Mika-*hime*'s head nursemaid in the antechamber and waited for Lord Asano to call them in. But that didn't keep the boy from causing more trouble than a plague of insects.

Lord Asano had tried to find the boy a place among the castle's staff of workers and servants, thinking he might become a courier, or a sparring partner for the squires, because two things he could definitely do were run like the wind and fight like a devil. Oishi glanced away, his dignity restraining him from letting the nursemaid see him grimace in wonderment at the very idea.

Lord Asano was the embodiment of the perfect *daimyo,* in Oishi's estimation—as excellent in his leadership abilities as he was at martial skills, as gifted in the refined arts as any pupil of Confucius. Perhaps it was the quirk destiny demanded of any great man that caused even one who was as wise as his lord to be taken by notions that would confound the patience of a bodhisattva. . . .

Even if Kai was just a halfbreed and not a genuine demon, he would never be disciplined enough to follow the strict rules the castle's servants were required to obey, or confident enough to be sent out into the world alone as a courier.

At last even Lord Asano had finally become convinced that Kai was unfit for castle life, after the humiliating incident when the boy had usurped the official duty of a hot-headed young retainer named Yasuno. Kai had ignorantly tried to assist his lord and Mika-*hime* . . . and actually touched them. Yasuno would have killed him on the spot if Lord Asano had not stopped it. Oishi doubted Yasuno would ever forgive or forget the loss of face Kai had caused him.

That Kai clearly seemed ashamed of his failure was as surprising to Oishi as his lord's continued belief in the boy. Everyone who was born into this world had a place in it, and knew his place—except Kai. He could not even tolerate living on the castle grounds; the open space within its walls made him restless and distracted. It was Oishi's personal opinion that since the boy had been permitted to live at all only because of Lord Asano's compassion, he should have shown his gratitude by simply disappearing again, back into the forest he had come from.

But Kai seemed to have developed one identifiable positive trait—the least likely one of all, to Oishi's mind—a sense of loyalty to their lord as complete as his failure to learn any other sort of social behavior that allowed a man to call himself "samurai," or even "human."

However, the fact that the boy was fit only to live with beasts had given Oishi an inspiration he had finally summoned up the nerve to share. . . . And so Lord Asano had assigned Kai the task of cleaning out the hound kennels. It turned out to be a suitable match at last, and Oishi had gained another favorable nod from the lord who would one day rely on him as his next chief retainer.

The boy did his task unfailingly, uncomplainingly, and as diligently as if he were caring for his own family—something which made Oishi wonder if he had in fact been raised by wolves, or possibly a *kitsune*. He was as good with the dogs as he was to them, making up for the skills he lacked in his relationships with human beings. The largest and surliest of Akita—hunting dogs that could hold a bear at bay, or take a man's hand off on a whim if he offended them—wagged their tails and licked his face when he entered their pens, as docile as puppies.

Oishi sighed, shifting from foot to foot. Kai had long since finished his duties as a cleaner of dog pens by now, and was off roaming the open fields and woods beyond the castle walls. Oishi had risen at dawn to get dressed, neaten his room, and eat breakfast with his parents. Then, as his father's apprentice and assistant, he had been assigned enough paperwork, observation duty, and martial arts practice that he would barely have time to bathe, pray, and eat his evening meal—never mind share some sake and laughter with a few friends. He would not see his bed again until midnight—and even then, he was expected to meditate on the worthiness of his day before he closed his eyes in blessed sleep.

A spark of resentment caught fire behind the stoic expression he always wore while waiting to be summoned for an audience with Lord Asano. He had other duties, far more important things to attend to. What was he doing here, forced to escort the head nursemaid so that she could complain to Lord Asano about the demon dog-boy . . . ? Unthinkingly, Oishi pressed his fingers against his weary eyes.

He realized it wasn't actually Kai that Mistress Haru was concerned about . . . it was Mika-*hime,* Lord Asano's daughter, who had run off into the fields with Kai. The foolish girl still inexplicably found Kai as fascinating when he smelled of dog excrement as she had when he was merely covered in mud—

Oishi abruptly came alert, as his name was called at last from the next room.

"Kai—!" Mika called, half laughing and half pleading, "Wait!"

Kai's long strides and baggy peasant clothes always let him get too far ahead of her, and he never seemed to tire. Even her new sandals didn't help her much as she chased after him. He only stopped when he reached the top of the hill. Then finally he looked back, waiting for her to catch up.

She had kicked off her rigid wooden clogs as soon as she had escaped from the view of her desperately persistent nursemaids. Hiking up her kimono to her knees, she had run barefoot to the place where she knew she would find Kai at this time of day.

And he had been there, as usual, sitting on the bank of the stream with his chin-length brown hair and his faded clothing still damp from washing up after his work in the kennels. He kept himself as clean as any samurai could have, under the circumstances.

She wondered what he would do when the weather turned cold: whether he would break the ice on the stream to bathe, as disciplined as a monk; whether he would even make a small fire to dry off by, or would sit shivering on the bank until he froze to the ground.

Whether he sat here in this same spot, day after day, only because he hoped that she might come and find him . . . ?

Today, as she arrived, he had looked up from his somber meditation with welcome in his eyes and a smile turning up the corners of his mouth—a smile that transformed his entire face, now that she had come to know it.

When he had first come to the castle, his smile had been so uncertain that when he greeted her she was hardly sure he had smiled at all. But then one day it occurred to her that perhaps it was shyness that made his smile so hesitant . . . or, even more disturbing, that perhaps he'd never known how to smile before.

When she had realized that, the purity of his newfound smile and the look in his eyes as he saw her had been like a *shakabuku* . . . "a spiritual kick in the head," Basho, one of her father's men—a former Buddhist monk—had told her once, "that knocks your vision completely clear."

At last she felt she finally knew what Basho was talking about. It was as if her father had brought back a *tennin* to the castle . . . a heavenly being from the sutras. It was said that sometimes *tennin* became inexplicably lost, as if they had forgotten the way back to the celestial realm, and wandered the earth or sat on mountaintops, waiting for the call to return. . . .

Today when she found Kai, his smile had seemed wider than ever, almost confident, and she realized he had been especially hoping she would come—even though he had looked away from her own sudden smile as though it was too bright for his twilight eyes, like the brightness of the sun.

But then he had groped beside him on the ground, as if he had a reason to look away, and his hand came up again holding a pair of woven hemp sandals like the ones he wore . . . like the ones peasant women and virtually all the men she knew wore.

"Here," he had murmured, still looking down, but with the smile trying to escape onto his face again. "If you wear these, you can keep up better. I won't always have to wait for you."

She flushed, both indignant and delighted in the same moment as she took them from him. She pulled at her silken robes in frustration, trying to uncover her feet when even her arms were buried in long sleeves that fluttered like butterfly wings. "I can't help how slow I am. Father never lets me dress like a boy, even when I'm training with the bow or the *naginata* . . ." She found a foot, just as she glanced up and saw how her thoughts had changed his expression, along with her own. "But I'm sure these will help." She smiled again, pointing at the sandals. At least there would be no more thorns or stone bruises when she was wearing these.

She almost plopped down on the ground beside him—caught herself just in time and sat gracefully on a warm, dry rock instead. She held out her foot.

Kai stared at it for a moment, before he realized that she was waiting for him to put the sandals on for her, like a proper lady . . . though a proper lady would never let a boy, especially a commoner, touch her foot. She kept her smile to herself, imagining the aghast faces of her nursemaids . . . and prayed that they never caught her at a moment like this.

Kai took her foot and slipped the sandal onto it with more gentleness and care than he had ever shown to any of the priceless objects he had accidentally smashed while he had been in the castle. The sandal fit perfectly. He put the other one on for her and then stood up, bowed, and with the gallantry of a samurai offered her his hand.

She blinked at him, wondering as she took his hand and rose to her feet how he knew such things. Everyone in the castle said he was hopelessly stupid and couldn't be taught anything. Yet she knew he had recognized much of what he saw there, and understood it, even though he had spent his life alone in a forest. Some people muttered about how that only proved he was a demon. But she knew they were wrong.

She had realized that he saw, and remembered, what was meaningful to him, and ignored the rest. He was a *tennin,* and nothing anyone said or did could change that about him.

She looked down at her feet, remembering again where she was and the gift she'd just been given. "Oh, these are much better!" She glanced up, beaming. "How did you know the size of my feet?"

Kai shrugged. "From your footprints." He met her eyes, and a flicker of pride she rarely saw showed in his own. "I made them by copying mine."

"Really!" She laughed in surprise. "All I can copy are scrolls. I've copied the proverbs of Confucius twice . . . did you know that he says 'women should be seen and not heard'? How dare he? I am a samurai—" She broke off. *And samurai did not complain.* "But my nurse always says, 'Words, not deeds, are suitable for a lady.' So what am I supposed to do—?"

She broke off again, as she saw Kai's expression, and realized all at once that thoughtless words could be deeds—as surely as a slap in the face, or the thrust of a sword through a trusting heart. "Thank you, Kai-*sama,*" she murmured, and bowed to him in return, as if she was addressing one of her father's most respected guests. "No one has ever given me a gift before that they made with their own hands. This is the most wonderful present I've ever had."

Kai smiled again, and his pale skin suddenly turned the color of the deepest pink cherry blossoms.

Mika hid her hands inside her sleeves, clutching her arms against the sudden urge to hug him. She had learned that he did not like to be touched. "Well, then," she said in her best *daimyo*'s-daughter voice. "Where shall we go today? . . . Will you show me where you live?"

"No." Kai made a face, and she wasn't sure what it meant. He had refused to accept even a tiny abandoned cottage at the very edge of Ako village, and some of the men had joked that he should live in the kennels with the dogs. But her father had assured her that Kai had made his own house, at the edge of the forest. She couldn't help wondering what the house of a *tennin* would look like.

"Don't ask that," Kai said.

"But why not?"

"It's . . . you wouldn't—" Kai forced a smile she didn't believe at all. "There are a thousand better things to see."

"But—"

"Come on." He jerked his head, and started off without another word.

She hiked up her robes again and began to follow him along the stream.

Oishi, and Lady Mika's head nursemaid, whose name was Haru—he hoped—entered Lord Asano's chambers and kneeled before him, bowing deeply. Their lord looked at them with a hint of surprise as they raised their heads again, somber-faced . . . as if this was a pairing he had never expected he would live to see. Oishi agreed silently with his unspoken opinion, as Lord Asano gestured for them to sit comfortably.

But as they sat back on the padded matting before his low writing table, Lord Asano suddenly frowned, as if he had realized the one reason their paths might intersect. "Has something happened to my daughter?"

"No, my lord!" Oishi said, hastily and a bit too loudly. He took a breath, bowing his head again. "Forgive me, *tono*; there is nothing wrong. But . . . ah, Mistress Haru asked for an audience because Mika-*hime*'s attendants wish to express their concern about . . . uh . . ." He glanced at the head nursemaid hopefully.

"My lord," Mistress Haru said, far more subdued now than she had been with him, but still determined to have her say. "Your daughter has begun to act most inappropriately. She insists on taking long walks outside the castle walls—"

Lord Asano raised his eyebrows. "Spring has barely

bloomed, and she is in the spring of her life. Why should she not want to experience the beauty of nature? Are you women getting too old to keep up with her?" He smiled wryly.

Mistress Haru flushed, lowering her own head again. "Not at all, my lord! And please believe that we would sacrifice anything to ensure that Mika-*hime* is happy. But we have never had this particular problem with her before. Only . . . only since that—" She broke off again, as if she suddenly remembered how Lord Asano felt about the boy Kai, whatever she thought of him. "—since Kai came here. Now, whenever she can, Lady Mika slips away from us when we are out walking. She doesn't come when she is called, and she runs . . . she runs right out of her shoes!" She reached into one voluminous sleeve of her robe, and held up a small clog, obviously one of Mika's.

" 'Since Kai—'?" Lord Asano repeated. Oishi had never before seen his lord nonplussed twice in the same day, let alone in the same conversation.

"Whenever she vanishes, she goes to meet that boy!" Mistress Haru pursed her lips. "When we find her, they are always together."

"What are they doing?" Lord Asano asked, his face again taking on a concerned look.

"Well, once they were wading in the stream . . . her clothing was soaking wet, she could have become ill. Once they were tossing a muddy sandal about. And once they were sitting right on the edge of the cliff, up by the old watchtower. Their feet were hanging over! They were 'only looking at the beautiful view,' Lady Mika said."

"It is a beautiful view," Lord Asano observed. He picked up the fan lying on his desk and opened it, gazing at whatever was written or painted on the side facing him. He looked up again. "They weren't holding hands—?"

Mistress Haru's face puckered as if she had eaten a persimmon. "Certainly not! That is, I would have come to you immediately, if I even suspected—"

"My wife and I often held hands there, when we were young. . . ." For a heartbeat Lord Asano looked down at the fan again, not seeing them at all. But then he snapped it shut, his attention fixed on Mistress Haru again. "What you're saying is that my daughter has been behaving like a spoiled brat. I thought it was up to you to curb that sort of behavior. She's the daughter of a country *daimyo*—not a goddess."

"I . . . no—that is, yes, my lord, we have always tried to raise her to be the kind of daughter you wished her to be—"

"And as far as I have seen, she still is," Lord Asano said, with a smile of reassurance.

"Until now." Mistress Haru clasped her hands on her knees. "She has never defied us like this before, and it just seems to get . . ." She looked down again.

"You are not also planning to tell me that the boy is a *yokai* who's cast a spell on her . . . ?" Lord Asano's expression changed from bemused to weary before she could even raise her head again.

"No, my lord," she said, reluctantly. "But even if Kai is only a boy, and means no harm . . . he is a *hinin*."

Oishi started as the nursemaid spoke the term no one else had dared say aloud in front of Lord Asano, despite their preoccupation with the boy's strangeness. *Hinin* meant "non-human"; even if it was not meant literally, it might as well be. It was a term for the utter dregs of society: ex-convicts, vagrants, halfbreeds, outcasts of all kinds . . . the invisible people who survived in the cracks of a society where class and rank were everything—a man's identity, and his destiny. Even the beggars in Edo city had a union, with a designated headman, under the law. *Hinin* had nothing.

"The boy may not understand what that means, but Mika-*hime* does. If she is seen with him, especially without her attendants . . . he might as well be a demon." Mistress Haru shook her head, eyes closed, as if even the thought of it was too unbearable. "Please, my lord—we have tried everything to make her listen. If you would speak to her, this one time. . . . She would honor her father's wish, I'm sure."

Lord Asano's face was somber now, as was his voice when he said, "You have made your point, Mistress Haru. I will speak to my daughter. And to Kai."

"*Tono,* will he listen?" Oishi dared to ask. "Can he even understand how this could harm Lady Mika? You should send him away, to be sure that he—"

"Kai will understand. And I believe he would sooner die than harm Mika in any way." Lord Asano frowned at him. "He knows his place, better than my daughter seems to . . . even though he has the potential to be much more, someday. Remember, Oishi—*hinin* is not a caste you are born into; it is one you are thrown into, by fate. You may fall so far that you become invisible to other people, but with enough strength of will you can alter the course of destiny—you can change the outcome of your life. I believe Kai has that kind of strength. I only hope that when he proves it, you are there to see it for yourself."

Oishi bowed a last time, to hide the reddening of his face. But in his mind the rebellious thought formed that there was one thing he would never see—and that was a halfbreed kennel boy marrying a *daimyo*'s daughter. *Because no matter what Kai did to raise himself up in the world, he could never become a samurai.* Sensing that the audience was at an end, he got to his feet, masking his humiliation at Lord Asano's rebuke as he put out his arm to help Mistress Haru rise.

"Thank you, my lord," she said humbly, glancing toward Lord Asano. "Please forgive my intrusion. I am so grateful for your help in this."

They bowed again and Lord Asano nodded, making a small motion with his closed fan that hurried them on their way. Whatever was on his mind now, clearly it was none of their business.

Mika finally reached the top of the hill where the ruined watchtower stood; the view of Ako that she had been waiting to see filled her eyes.

Kai stood motionless, gazing outward beside the solitary tree that had been the only sentry stationed here for nearly a hundred years. He looked so intent that he might have been keeping watch himself. If he were any other boy, she would have thought he was pretending to be a samurai in the Age of Wars. But he was not like anyone she had ever known, and when he looked out over the land, she knew he saw things that no one else could even imagine.

Below them lay the vast panorama of Ako Castle, Ako village, and the cultivated fields beyond them extending to the distant edges of the forest. There were terraced hills, and wooded hills and valleys, and the river that circled the castle and flowed on to the limits of their sight, where the sea itself lay, and Ako's port town.

The sight made her heart ache with its beauty; she wished that it could be painted on screens and put in her room, so that sleeping there would be like sleeping in the summer grass. She would have stars painted on the ceiling in gold leaf. . . .

She shook the image out of her head. No painter could ever capture all this beauty, even on a screen of silk; how selfish she was to wish it could be captured for her alone. Her father had always said that Ako's beauty was a blessing from the gods, not to be bought and sold like a bale of rice. It belonged equally to all who lived here.

She would be content simply to have eyes to see it, like Kai was. She looked out over the fields, seeing how the view had changed, how days that turned to months had revealed the seasons, following one after another in an endless spiral. The last time they had been here, the rice paddies had been flooded for planting; they had reflected blue skies and white clouds until Ako Castle seemed to float in midair. Now they were filled with healthy, thriving plants, and the land was like a quilt dyed in all the tones of early summer green. . . .

She thought suddenly of what her father had told her, after her mother died: *People wept when they lost a loved one,* he had said, *because it tore a hole in the cloth of their own lives, and that caused them pain. But they should not grieve for the one who had died, because each ending led to a new beginning, as the eternal soul returned to the wheel of reincarnation.*

One day, he had promised her, the soul of their beloved wife and mother would come back again to this world, as would theirs, and they would see one another again. Like the seasons, their appearances would have changed—but the soul was like the land itself, reborn to a new spring after every winter, all the more beautiful because it had rested peacefully for a time.

Mika blinked and shook her head. She had not known what her father was trying to tell her, then. But now all at once it seemed as if she could see it clearly. . . . How strange it was that when she was with Kai she always saw herself, and her life, in a light like no other.

As she approached him, he turned his head and moved a few steps away, seemingly oblivious to her arrival as he crouched down and peered at the branch of a shrub.

Just as she opened her mouth to speak his name and surprise him, he suddenly raised his hand, whispering, "Stop—"

Startled, she closed her mouth and crouched down quietly beside him. He held up the branch of the bush he had been looking at. "Shh! Look—what do you see?"

She stared at it. "A branch." She stated the obvious, disappointed.

"No." He shook his head, showing her the place where the branch was broken. "It's a deer. It took this path." He pointed away along the hilltop. He raised his head, his eyes tracking something that was invisible to her. "It's hidden in . . . that thicket."

In the distance, as if it had felt his gaze touch it, a deer sprang from the underbrush and bounded away into deeper forest.

Mika watched it disappear, smiling at the grace of its effortless movements until it vanished. In her mind, the uncanny connection between Kai's spirit and those of the forest creatures seemed almost like *chi,* the mystical energy that filled the universe and united all things, from the humblest stone to the realm of the gods.

She had studied tomes and scrolls about the sacred beliefs of Shinto and Buddhism since she was small, but they had only been endless pages of text to be laboriously copied, no more. In Kai's face, so familiar and yet subtly different in ways she couldn't define, she had found a beauty she had never seen before; in his eyes there was a magical kind of knowing, something she had never found in the gaze of anyone else.

At Ako Castle, some people still whispered that Kai wasn't human . . . but if they could tell that, how could they not see it was a *tennin* who walked among them, and not a demon? The adults discussed Enlightenment, and how to achieve it, endlessly over tea or *sake* . . . and yet they sent a heavenly messenger who had come among them to clean up after the dogs. . . .

Kai had accepted the job humbly, without complaint. And instead of being afraid to go among the dogs, he had entered the territory of a pack of snarling semi-feral beasts that she was—wisely—afraid of, and transformed them into well-behaved animals that greeted him with eager barks and wagging tails.

Suddenly her eyes felt too full, and her hands tightened. *It wasn't right. It wasn't right—* She blinked rapidly, glancing down until she got control of herself.

Then she looked up at Kai, who was gazing curiously at her . . . and this time he didn't look away as he usually did. His gaze held hers, as if he had glimpsed something—her awe, her amazement, a reflection of the otherworldly beauty she found in his face, and in his soul—and held it up to her like a mirror.

Abruptly he let his glance fall again, and kept his head bowed; she began to bite her lip with concern, until she noticed that his hand was searching in the grass. He picked up a hairpin that had fallen from her hair, her favorite one, made of ivory and carved like an arrow fletched with hawk's feathers.

He held it out to her on his open palm. As she took it from him, her fingers curled around his hand, tightening.

And at that exact moment the voices of her nursemaids, frantically calling her name, reached them from down below.

The moment dissolved like her image in his eyes. She took the hairpin from him and stuck it into her hair, her face filling with frustration and disappointment.

Hastily they got to their feet, brushing leaves from their clothing. She turned to lead the way down the hill, before one of her overwrought attendants fainted from heatstroke or worry.

Turning to go, she saw her disappointment reflected in Kai's expression . . . saw the profound loneliness that always lay hidden behind his eyes.

She turned back impulsively, and kissed him. And then she left, too quickly to see his expression, or for him to see her own, as she started down the trail, as blithely sure-footed as a forest doe.

1

Japan, 1701

Kai crouched down, searching the forest floor in the maze of new growth that marked another spring's arrival. His calloused hands, years past sunburn, so tan now that they were indistinguishable from any peasant's, scooped up a clump of loose earth that some creature's passage had dislodged from among moss-covered stones and last winter's dead leaves.

He breathed in the scent of the soil and frowned. *Wrong.* He stared at the enormous indentation in the ground a few strides further on; it was a kind of imprint he had seen only once before, long before they had begun this hunt . . . far too long ago.

The faint crack of a twig made him look over his shoulder, searching the woods behind him. He exhaled, a sigh of relief. *Not a monster* . . . only a fox.

A snow-white fox. The vixen stared back at him from where she stood, one paw raised, with a gaze that met his own as if they were equals, taking each other's measure. And then abruptly she turned and darted away, vanishing into the dim green light of the forest as if he had shouted.

A white fox . . .

But then he heard the sound of hoofbeats approaching from downslope, and knew the others had caught up to him. Perhaps the fox had simply heard them coming.

He looked back down the long hill as Lord Asano and his hunting party of samurai materialized out of the morning fog: The mounted warriors in full armor were like a vision from the past, emerging from some crack in time out of the centuries of warfare when a man had become a samurai by proving his courage in battle, not by inheritance at birth.

Now, that era was already fading into legend after a century of the "Tokugawa Peace," in which the endless bloodshed had been replaced by endless laws and regulations. A rigid caste system existed under the new rule of law, which defined the nobility of the warrior class strictly by the blood of its ancestors, and established its permanent place at the top of society. Laws defining what the other classes were, were not, and could never hope to be had been enacted as well, to keep them in their places . . . invisible walls, as unbreachable as the stone walls of Edo castle, home to the Tokugawa Shogun.

Most of the men riding up the hill toward him rarely put on full armor—and then only to practice skills they might never need. But this was no ordinary hunt; when they finally caught up to their prey they would need that armor, and all the weapons they carried with them as well.

As they spotted him, the riders pulled their horses to a halt a short distance down the hill. It was only then that Kai realized he had been holding his breath; he exhaled and sat back on his heels, waiting for Lord Asano to acknowledge him.

He could spot Lord Asano easily enough, by the crest on his ornate helmet; knew the others more by instinct than by spotting any recognizable features, from this distance. It was difficult to believe that he had lived for nearly twenty years among these men and yet, just for a moment, when he saw the hunters and they saw him, he had still been thrown back into the mind of the terrified boy he'd been the first time they had come upon him, so long ago.

Now he was Lord Asano's head tracker, not a *hinin* cleaner of dog kennels. But in reality little else had changed in any meaningful way, so little that it was still possible for him to forget for a moment that his life had actually changed at all.

His brown hair had darkened until it could pass for a pureblood's, and he used the same spearmint oil to keep its stubborn waves straight that the samurai used to keep their topknots looking orderly. They all reeked—pleasantly enough—of spearmint, to the point where they had never noticed that he did too.

And yet no matter what he did to make himself fit in, at least as a commoner, in their eyes he would always be a halfbreed first. His presence—his very existence—was still as repugnant to the samurai of Ako Castle as if he actually were a demon.

But there were a few exceptions, who made the rest bearable—and one of them was the lord he served. A rare feeling of warmth and concern filled him as he focused on Lord Asano's face, seeing the combination of fatigue and resolve in the *daimyo*'s expression as he looked expectantly at Kai.

Kai raised his arm, a signal that he had found something more than just tracks—something significant, something else to repay the debt he owed to the man who had saved his life and gone on believing in him when no one else would.

The group of samurai started forward again as the porters, and the farmers who were there to beat the bushes, came scrambling up on foot.

Kai saw Oishi Yoshio riding beside Lord Asano as he always did—Oishi had become chief retainer when his father retired some years ago. He was a married man now, with a load of bureaucratic duties and a son who had recently come of age—a son barely younger than he himself had been when Kai first met him and they had tried to kill each other. But wearing full battle armor, Oishi still looked as formidable to Kai as a wall of spears.

Another samurai—the unfailingly arrogant Yasuno—

rode up alongside Oishi and bowed his head to Lord Asano. He was close to Oishi's age, but so far life had taught him nothing, at least nothing that Kai found admirable. He pointed on up the rising slope, as usual ignoring Kai's signal. "My lord, I think the beast has moved to higher ground."

The wind carried their conversation easily to where Kai waited; his mouth thinned when he heard the words. But Lord Asano only looked further up the mountainside, where the trees and undergrowth became even more impenetrable, and shook his head. "Ask Kai." Yasuno stiffened visibly, but he only bowed again in acknowledgement, before he started his horse toward Kai. "Go with him, Oishi," Lord Asano added.

Oishi nodded and followed Yasuno; he was always swift to obey his lord, but still nearly as reluctant as Yasuno to approach Kai. Kai gazed at the ground as he waited for them, centering his emotions until he was sure his face was perfectly composed.

He rose from his knees to his feet to face them as they stopped their horses in front of him. It was still difficult having to look up at them, when they looked down on him from horseback like two disdainful gods, armed with spears, bows, and swords. Nonetheless, he held their stares for another long moment before he obediently lowered his gaze.

He held out the clump of bloody animal fur, so tangled with an unnatural growth of plant matter and fungi that even when he had brushed the dirt from it, he had thought at first that he had made a mistake.

The two men looked at it, and then at him again. Their expressions suggested they weren't sure where his arm ended and the evidence he'd found began.

"There is something wrong with the creature," he said finally, nodding from what he held toward the wooded slope above them, where not even his eyes could see clearly enough to penetrate the wall of green. "It's up there on the rise—but it will come down again to hunt. It would be safer to set a trap and wait for it here."

Yasuno dismissed Kai's words, his years of experience, his unfaltering instincts, and his very existence, with a disdainful grunt. "If we wait, it will get away!" He shook his head like an impatient horse. "We have chased this beast for days—" he said, as though Kai had not been leading them the entire time, on foot. "We must kill it now, before it does any more damage!"

Kai glanced at Oishi. He found Oishi regarding him with the same dubious expression that had been on his face all those years ago, when they had first laid eyes on each other. After this much time, Kai decided that any hope the two of them might have had for coming to an understanding was long gone, if it had ever existed at all.

But Oishi studied the bloody clump of hair and unnatural plant growth again for a long moment, frowning but at least seeming to consider it seriously. He glanced up, and Kai shook his head in warning. Oishi turned his horse without a word, and rode away with Yasuno, back toward the spot where Lord Asano waited.

Kai watched in resignation as Oishi and Yasano reported to their lord, deliberately keeping their voices low, trying to keep him from hearing their words. But he already knew what Yasuno would say.

And Oishi—despite his tactical skills and dutiful weaponry practice, despite his hunting experience or even his responsibility for his lord's safety—was siding with Yasuno. He had ignored Kai's warning out of pure spite . . . or worse yet, the hunger of an unblooded warrior for a taste of the blade's edge. "It's up there, my lord. We should go after it while we have the chance."

Fool—! Kai tightened his jaw against the urge to shout the protest he was forbidden to make. *He had lived on the blade's edge for so long. . . .* But if he tried to warn those fools what they were truly asking for—what they were leading their lord into—Yasuno would only draw his untried *katana* and kill him on the spot for daring to criticize their judgment.

A samurai had the right, under law, to cut down any commoner who offended him for any reason, or for no reason at all. Kai knew that if he hadn't been under the protection of Lord Asano, one of his lord's own samurai would have long ago tried out an untested blade's edge on the halfbreed kennel boy—cutting off his limbs, or his head.

There was no point in trying, no point in dying for no reason. Lord Asano would never hear a word he had really said . . . even if it cost all of them their lives.

Lord Asano nodded and urged his horse forward, leading the way on up the hill. As the men rode past, Lord Asano glanced up at him with a grateful smile. Kai bowed in return, keeping his grim expression to himself. He looked up again as the other riders passed. Not one of them so much as glanced his way.

When they were gone, Kai threw down the clump of animal hair in disgust. He forced himself to recite a prayer for their safety, if only for Lord Asano's sake, and not the curse he would have called down on the retainers whose eagerness for slaughter might just lead their *daimyo* to a crippling accident, or even his death.

Because it was no ordinary beast—not even something as formidable as a bear, or wolves in winter—that they had been trailing for days. It was a *kirin.* Kai had never even seen a *kirin,* and he had seen more strange things than anyone at Ako Castle could imagine.

He had seen drawings made by people who claimed to have seen *kirin,* but clearly never had. The images were as absurd as they were grotesque. But he had also been told the truth about *kirin,* by ones who *had* seen them. . . . Their accounts were both awe-inspiring and terrifying, all the more so because they were true.

Kirin were rarely seen by humans or any other creature, even in the high valleys of the most remote mountains—their usual home, and sanctuary—even though their size was enormous. They were shy solitary creatures who ate only vegetation. Moving with infinite patience, they wandered the mountain slopes, meditating on the profound and unknowable, he had been told; often they moved so slowly that their fur became draped in trailing vines and branches, until they were all but invisible to human eyes. . . .

But there was more to the *kirin*'s seeming ability to vanish from sight than natural camouflage. Men were not the only creatures in this world who kept a wary eye out for the malice of other men. And like many creatures of the primeval forests and cloud-peaked mountains, *kirin* led a strange, shimmering existence, manifested partly in this world and partly on the spirit plane. The beings that humans called *yokai*—demons—were simply more powerful manipulators of *chi,* the fundamental energy that filled all existence and moved through all things, animate and inanimate.

Why did stones possess chi . . . ? He suddenly remembered the question that had been put to him as a boy. He still had the scars from failing to guess the answer. But over and over through the years, patience and endurance had kept him alive . . . and stones needed more patient endurance than most things. He could see now how all things used *chi* in their own way—how humans used it to animate their bodies, whether they realized it or not, in the same way stones employed it to remain still.

There were days in his own life—especially the days when he caught a rare glimpse of Mika, and she looked back at him—still with longing in her eyes—when he felt as if bit by bit he was becoming more of a stone than a man.

But while he had become acutely aware of his own shortcomings as a human being, he had become ever more aware of how far short most human senses fell, compared to the abilities of the *yokai,* whose awareness of *chi* let them draw on it consciously to perform acts humans called impossible, unnatural, demonic.

Humans considered all *yokai* "evil"—a term that covered many things that might truly be evil, and far more that were simply incomprehensible.

It was a rare human who could detect the presence of *chi.*

Very few could even accept the possibility that such an ability might exist. The vast majority would always remain ignorant, and fear all *yokai,* because they could never truly understand them.

But *kirin* were normally among the most peaceful of living things. Only if something violently disturbed the fragile balance of their existence would they be anything else. . . . If something occurred that did, they were among the most powerful manipulators of *chi* in the world, and their destructive fury could be unimaginable—

Kai had never heard of one that had come this far down from the mountains before, to invade the lands humans had claimed for their own . . . let alone gone rampaging through villages and fields the way the one they were tracking now had, crushing buildings and destroying crops, eating the flesh of slaughtered animals . . . and even human beings.

And why in the name of all the gods had it sought out the lands of Lord Asano—who, to Kai's knowledge, was far from the worst of men, and in his personal experience, one of the best?

Left behind with the porters and the peasants, Kai crouched silently with his eyes closed, listening, testing the feel and scent of wind, trying to force his other senses to tell him what it was impossible to see from where he had been abandoned.

Not permitted to touch a real weapon, not permitted to ride a horse, he was as helpless as anyone around him to keep a disaster from occurring up on the mountainside. None of the peasants waiting near him had ever taken part in a hunt like this one before . . . any more than the samurai had. But they'd rarely had a personal stake in the capture of the prey, either. Even so, like him, they had been inescapably assigned to their place here, just as they had in their lives, and for now they seemed content to stay in it.

The hunters neared the uneven top of the rise, entering a thick pocket of morning mist that still lingered among the dense forest growth and outcroppings of gray stone. They were forced to keep their restless horses under tight rein, holding them back to the careful walk their mounts would normally have chosen for themselves as they picked their way through the twisting, blind terrain.

A knot of tension caught in Oishi's throat, as Kai's unspoken warning replayed itself in his memory. Suddenly he was unsure whether he had done the right thing in ignoring it: The horses were more nervous and difficult to handle than the dangerous footing, or even their rider's tense alertness should account for. *"If the horses are restless, there are attackers there." Was it Sun Tzu who had said that?* Not all enemies were human. If he had let himself lead Lord Asano into danger because of his pride . . .

He could make out nothing among the moss-covered boulders, the thickets of overgrown shrubbery, and the overhanging branches of trees. All the world seeming to become an emerald blur in the shifting reality of the fog. His horse stopped suddenly, without his signal, its head high and its ears pricked forward.

All at once he heard the sounds too, somewhere ahead—sounds unlike anything he had ever heard before. Some unimaginably huge beast was snarling deep in its throat, the guttural noises punctuated by sharp cracks, as if the branches of trees were being snapped in two. *No, not branches . . . bones. It was feeding on . . . something. . . .*

He turned back to Lord Asano, trying to keep the trace of genuine concern out of his voice as he said, "Let me send some men ahead, my lord."

Lord Asano smiled at him, sensing his concern anyway, intent on laying it to rest. "You worry too much," he said, and Oishi saw the sudden gleam of warrior spirit in the *daimyo*'s eyes—his need to do battle against a truly worthy opponent, just once before he died. "Two groups," he ordered, gesturing. "Drive it toward us."

Oishi relayed his orders, and instantly the hunting party split up, some of the riders cautiously circling the thicket ahead of them. Archers unslung their bows and readied their arrows. The riders who carried straight spears and curved *naginata* adjusted their grips.

When all the hunters were in position, Oishi nodded to Hazama, his second-in-command in the field. Hazama raised an ancient bone horn with silver fittings to his lips, and blew. The horn emitted the most blood-curdling animal cry that Oishi had ever heard; the sound made him grit his teeth.

When the call and its echo at last faded away, the entire forest was eerily silent. No more unidentifiable sounds that could only be the *kirin*; not even so much as a bird call. The silence continued for what must have been mere seconds, but seemed like forever.

And then, with a deafening crash, the entire thicket-covered hillside ahead of them seemed to come alive, as a monster more terrifying than anything Oishi had ever imagined burst from cover and came thundering down on them like an avalanche.

The beast was twice the height of a man on horseback, and as massive as a fall of boulders. It had two sets of horns—one set on its forehead like spears ready to impale attackers, and a second pair on the sides of its head, with prongs like the limbs of a lightning-struck tree, curved at a perfect angle to gore anyone who attacked from the side. A blow from any of its hooves could cripple a man and his horse together; so could the lash-like tail that was longer than its body.

And there was *something wrong with it,* Oishi realized, nearly forgetting to breathe as he watched it come. Its three pairs of eyes burned red with madness, it bared fangs like knives as it charged. The hideous face was naked of fur, the skin rough and splotched with moss green and leprous ash-gray like a lichen-covered boulder, and its side-whiskers were like tentacles. Its mane was matted with filth, stained with lurid orange and rust-red until Oishi could not tell what was bloodstain and what was disease. Its whole hide was crusted with lurid orange and green scales, as if its entire body was covered in some sort of luminous blight. The creature was like the embodiment of an entire diseased forest's maddened spirit, and even finding a spot to drive home a spear seemed impossible.

He pulled his mount around in a tight circle, leaving Lord Asano no choice but turn back himself, urging his horse up a hill and out of the *kirin*'s path. The other riders were trying frantically to turn their horses, to get out of one another's way and avoid the oncoming beast, but the treacherous footing of slippery rocks and steep hillsides hemmed them in.

The archers released a hail of arrows as the *kirin* passed between them, but they might as well have thrown straw at it. The arrows had no more effect than needles, only driving the beast to greater frenzy. Oishi saw Basho, a warrior with the size and strength of a sumo wrestler, thrust the curved blade of his *naginata* into the *kirin*'s side, but the spear fell from its scaled body as if the tip had not even penetrated its skin.

Yasuno held his place at the center, and Oishi recognized too late his suicidal determination to claim the kill for himself. But he was no more blessed or cursed by the gods than any other man on the hill that day; the *kirin* changed direction, passing behind him, and he had no success in even slowing its charge.

The hunters attacked it from every side as it roared through them, using every weapon they had, but the monster swept them aside as if they had the substance of wind. And then Oishi realized that the *kirin* was coming for him . . . no, not for him, it was heading straight for Lord Asano, just beyond him, as if its obsessive madness was directed at the Lord of Ako alone.

The *daimyo*'s stallion realized it too, and reared in terror;

Lord Asano struggled to stay on its back, without a free hand even to defend himself.

Oishi drove his own rebellious horse forward as he realized the danger his lord was in. He shouted at the top of his lungs, trying to attract the *kirin*'s attention.

At the last second, the *kirin* veered away from Lord Asano and charged him instead. Oishi thrust his spear at it; the spearpoint shattered on the *kirin*'s horns. He flung it down and drew his *katana*.

But the demon didn't turn back; by then it was past him and gone, bounding over the last line of defenders in a tremendous leap, driven now only by a mindless urge to escape their trap.

Down below, Kai and the gathered peasants listened in growing disbelief and horror as the unseen battle raged on the mountain above them. Even Kai was unable to make any sense of the chaos—the shouting and crashing, the sudden screams of men and animals, combined with sounds of incredible destruction—as entire trees disappeared into the fog-shrouded blur of gray and green.

And then suddenly it was all too clear what had happened, as the *kirin* burst through the tree line into the open, and the ground under their feet trembled with the thunder of its headlong approach. Behind it came all the hunters who were still on horseback, following at full gallop, heedless of anything now except stopping its escape.

The farmers and porters who had ventured the farthest toward the sounds of the battle turned around and began to flee, but it was already too late. There were more screams as the *kirin* burst through them and ran headlong back toward the shelter of the forest below.

Kai ran with the rest, chasing after the *kirin*, not running away from it, as determined as the samurai were not to let it escape, although he had no idea of how to stop it.

Suddenly he glimpsed a panic-stricken horse about to pass him. He headed for it, and with a final burst of speed caught hold of the saddle and swung up onto its back. Taking the reins, he turned its headlong flight into a controlled gallop, pursuing the *kirin* into the edge of the trees.

Weaponless, he could only force his half-mad horse into its path, waving his arm and shouting, trying to lure it back out into the open. The *kirin* actually responded, if only because in its madness it saw something to be destroyed. As Kai emerged once more into the open field he saw the samurai riding toward him––toward the monster. He veered away, giving his horse its head, more than glad to let the ones who had asked for this battle finish it themselves.

Some of the warriors were trying to trap the *kirin* with snares, now, but that only made its efforts to escape more furious. It tore through the ropes, and then through the circle of horsemen, as it ran again for the trees.

Kai saw Yasuno go after it, alone, following it into the forest. Kai hesitated a moment, cursing under his breath, and then turned his horse to follow the madman and the maddened beast back into the woods.

Kai caught sight of them just as Yasuno drew alongside the *kirin* and, reaching down, managed to drive his sword into its back behind a pronged side-horn.

It wasn't a fatal wound—and nothing less would do anything but feed the insane rage of the creature he was attacking. The *kirin* swung around, knocking Yasuno from his horse with one blow of its enormous head. Yasuno picked himself up off the ground . . . stumbled backwards as he saw the *kirin* turn toward him, lowering its head as it prepared to charge.

Kai sent his horse galloping at the *kirin*. Leaning out, he managed to grab the hilt of Yasuno's *katana*. The prongs tore at him, ripping through his sleeve and gouging his arm as he yanked the sword free, but he managed to stay in the saddle. Armed at last, he heeled his mount around with a wild shout of defiance to confront the living nightmare head-on.

The *kirin* took his invitation, forgetting about Yasuno as it turned back to charge at him.

At the last moment before they collided, Kai swung his horse to the side. Standing in his stirrups, he leaned out further this time and drove Yasuno's sword between the knife-sharp antler prongs into the side of its neck—directly into the vulnerable spot where the *kirin's* spine joined its head.

A spray of diseased blood burned like acid as it struck his skin. He barely felt the pain, caught in the terrifying euphoria of a moment suspended between life and death. He had not used a *katana* for years, but he felt its deadly blade drive deep, severing the *kirin*'s knotted spine like lightning made of steel. *With blades of steel fit for slaying gods—* He had heard that too, from the ones who had told him how they had slain a *kirin*. Now at last he knew that every word was true.

Kai jerked back on his horse's reins until it reared, swinging it away from the spike-walled trap of the antler, but not quickly enough: The *kirin* flung its massive head to the side in a paroxysm of agony, and gored him in the back. Kai gave a raw cry as a prong caught beneath his shoulder blade, jerking him from the saddle and flinging him to the ground. He slid until he crashed to a stop against a tree; he lay there struggling simply to breathe, helpless against a further attack.

But this time the wound that the monster had taken showed its fatal effect. The *kirin* staggered and fell to its knees, unable to rise again.

Dizzy and sick with the pain in his shoulder, Kai forced himself to get to his feet. Blood soaked the worn cotton cloth of his kimono as he stumbled toward the fallen *kirin*, drawn by a compulsion he didn't understand.

He stopped before the enormous head, trying to stand

within the gaze of its three sets of eyes. The red gleam of madness was already leaving them . . . as he watched, they grew dark and quiet, and he glimpsed the depths of ages-old wisdom lying beneath their sorrow.

As its head settled lower to the ground, the *kirin* looked back at him in resignation, without rancor, as if it was recalling a peace it had known in what must now seem like another life. Despite the agony it must be in, trapped in this ravaged body, Kai could still feel the presence of the noble creature it had once been. Its mind was returning as its eyes grew dim and approaching death released it from the unspeakable curse that had been laid upon it.

Its suffering was about to end; he felt its spirit passing through him toward the great spiral of time that was always cycling into the future. Filled with compassion and remorse, Kai raised unsteady hands to its mottled forehead in a futile gesture of apology. Its dark eyes watered, almost as if it was shedding tears, as he struggled to remember the ancient words of a blessing to ease its passage out of this world, back into the spirit realm.

The *kirin*'s immense head drooped further, until it rested motionless on the ground. He saw the hideous malignancy that had corrupted its flesh and its sanity shimmer and disappear; as if everything that had occurred had been no more than a nightmare, a dream that had vanished as its life-spirit woke to an unknowable new day.

Kai glanced down as the poisonous burn where its blood has splattered him vanished. The stains on his skin and clothing turned from the color of tar to a red that shone with golden radiance—the same eerie radiance that was transfiguring the stained, wormlike snarl of the *kirin*'s mane back into a ruff of thick golden fur.

He struggled to make his own body move again, until he reached a point beside the *kirin*'s head where he could grab the *katana*'s hilt. Taking hold of it with both hands, he pulled it from the creature's neck as gently as possible.

And then, as he stood holding the sword, he finally became aware that someone was standing behind him—had been standing there for some time, watching everything he had done.

He turned around at last to face Yasuno, who looked first at the sword in his hands, and then up at his face. Yasuno's eyes burned with outrage and humiliation; his voice shook with spite as he said, "I would rather have been killed by that animal than saved by a halfbreed."

Kai looked down at the *katana,* for a long moment not even seeing it, while he considered the words. Without looking up again, he bowed deeply and held out the sword. "I did nothing." He spoke the words with uncommon feeling, making the traditional phrase of demurral into a vow of silence.

Yasuno snatched the sword from him, as if it were his own soul that Kai had been holding in his hands. To a samurai, Kai knew, they were considered to be same thing. But he didn't know why.

Yasuno's stare only darkened as they heard riders coming—the last of the samurai were approaching them through the trees. The riders circled the two men and the slain *kirin*, looking from one to another to another. Their eyes barely touched Kai, despite the fact that he was in too much pain to formally kneel down. Their gazes lingered on the dead *kirin*, before the focus of all their attention became Yasuno, who stood holding the bloody sword in his hand . . . all of them obviously assuming that he had slain the beast with it.

Lord Asano rode forward through the ring of samurai. Kai felt relief wash over him like a wave of dizziness as he saw his lord still alive and unhurt.

Lord Asano looked from the dead *kirin* to Yasuno, assuming like the rest that Yasuno had done the deed. With a warrior's grim smile, he said, "Now you have to carry it home, Yasuno."

All the other samurai burst out in laughter, in relief and triumph; all of them except for Yasuno—who bowed low to Lord Asano long enough to hide the fact that he wasn't even smiling.

"Ako owes you a great debt," Lord Asano said, speaking seriously now. He acknowledged Yasuno's bow with a nod of his own, his face filled with the same relief and admiration that showed on the faces of the other men. "We can finally welcome the Shogun without fear."

The Shogun's visit. Kai had forgotten all about it, because it had nothing to do with him personally. No wonder Lord Asano had felt so driven to put an end to the hunt today that he had thrown aside even his common sense.

Kai began to back away, careful not to stumble as he moved through the mounted samurai gathered around the dead *kirin* . . . attempting to fade back into the group of peasants who stood watching from a respectful distance, before Lord Asano ever noticed he had been there. He had won no glory this day . . . but he had not wanted to. *Not here. Not this way.* He glanced a last time at the dead *kirin*. *He only wanted to disappear.*

But in backing up he managed to brush the sheath of Oishi's *katana*. He jerked, startled, and Oishi glanced down. The chief retainer merely looked annoyed, and not infuriated that a commoner had touched so much as its sheath. But his face changed as he recognized Kai, and saw the wounds on his body, the *kirin*'s gold-tinged blood still staining his hands and clothing. Oishi's expression turned quizzical. He glanced at Yasuno, and Kai saw his expression begin to change again.

"For Ako!" Lord Asano called out, and Oishi's attention was snared in the cheering of the other men. By the time he looked back, Kai had disappeared.

Kai sat down on a fallen log, out of sight of Oishi and the rest, and let the top of his kimono slip from his injured shoulder. He used his fingers to dig loose a patch of mossy clay, and packed it into the wound where the *kirin* had gored him. His good arm could barely reach the spot; the agony of the motion made him want to retch. He bit down on the cloth of his sleeve to keep from betraying himself with any sound of pain.

It had to be done. Some of his other cuts were deep, and they needed tending, but they could wait. He hurt all over, and he had almost forgotten how that felt . . . but he knew from bitter experience that it wouldn't kill him. However, the wound on his back had already bled too much; he wouldn't survive the long walk back to Ako Castle unless he did something.

He looked away again at the *kirin*'s body, for what he wished was the last time. But he knew he would remember its death, and transformation, forever. *For Ako* . . . Carefully he pulled his kimono back into place. He was exhausted beyond belief, and he wanted nothing except to be home once more, and safe.

He turned suddenly where he sat, as he sensed eyes staring at him—not human eyes, this time.

The white fox he had seen before had returned. The vixen sat observing him from behind with an interest that seemed unnervingly sentient; he realized this time that one of her eyes was the reddish brown of a true fox-eye . . . but the other one was pale blue.

A *kitsune* . . . a shape-changing *yokai* gifted with sorceries too numerous to name, that usually wore the form of a fox. Now that he really looked at her he could see the shifting insubstantiality, almost like an aura, around her fox-shape. Her snow-white color marked her as an ancient spirit, and a powerful one. He wondered what had drawn her here—had it been the *kirin*?

The fox gazed at him a moment longer, almost thoughtfully, before she turned away and vanished into the forest, like the last whispers of morning mist.

2

The view of Honshu from the sky was truly a thing of wonder . . . and a thing no human eyes had as yet ever seen. The distant sea receding, becoming a part of the clear blue sky . . . the ever-changing green of cultivated fields and stands of bamboo, turning to a darker green as the trees of the deep forest became dominant with the ever-steeper hills . . . and beyond them, tier on tier of gray-violet mountains with snowcapped peaks.

The green of spring in the lowlands receded like the lapping waves of the ocean's distant shore as she continued to soar higher with the rising land. Occasional patches of snow showed among the trees, icy white gradually overcoming the green, and the stark grays of lifeless stone intruding more and more on the realm of living things.

By the time Kirayama Castle came into view, the stone fortress walls seemed to be the only thing any human had ever raised in the wilderness of white and gray, which was all there was to see now beneath the sky.

The sentries keeping watch from the castle's walls and towers noticed nothing as the *kitsune* arrived at her destination; only a tiny glimmer of light marked her descending arc as she arrived at the castle keep. Foxfire by daylight might have been no more than the gleam of sunlight on ice.

As it was, the sentries rarely looked up, where nothing

was ever visible except an occasional bird of prey. Living things seldom showed themselves in the lands below, either, before spring; only wild animals spent winter in these mountains by choice, and few creatures, human or otherwise, approached the castle without a good reason. As for humans, even invading the castle's domain would rarely be reason enough. The guards paid more attention to the life-giving warmth of the charcoal braziers, where they huddled, than to anything else.

And so the snow-white fox arrived in the castle unseen and unannounced, as always, trotting across the stone floor of the entrance hall, her shadow flickering in the torchlight as she moved. Every movement seemed to transform her image, but not as completely as she transformed herself, with every step she took . . . until by the time she had entered the palace area of the keep, the servants and retainers who saw her pass saw only what they expected to see: Mitsuke, the stunningly beautiful, sensual companion of Lord Kira.

They could not stop themselves from watching as she swept up the stairway leading to their lord's private chambers, her movements so graceful that she seemed almost to float above the steps. As always, she wore a kimono and outer robes of the finest fabrics, artfully patterned and detailed in the colors of the wild, deep woods of early summer: the golden-green of sunlit grass, the velvet green of mossy stones along a stream side, sky blues dappled with the leaves of overarching branches.

She might never speak a word to them, and move among them as if she was completely unaware of their presence, but simply the sight of her, a glimpse of her enchanted clothing, seemed to cast a spell of contentment over them. The colors and fragrances that surrounded her reminded them that spring would return again, even to these bleak heights—as it always did, eventually, if only they could remain patient a little longer.

She had seemingly cast the same spell over their lord—and she had changed him the most of all. When she was with him, his dour moodiness vanished and gave them a welcome respite from the violent fits of anger and frustration he apparently hid so well when he was at the Shogun's court.

The fox-witch opened the door to Lord Kira's private chamber softly but unhesitatingly, making none of the servile obeisances that human men expected from their women, and a *daimyo* expected even from the samurai who served as his retainers.

Her glance swept across the lantern-lit chamber, searching for the lord she too served, more truly and loyally and completely willingly than any human.

Her strange eyes—one colored the deep russet of autumn foliage, one as ice blue as a winter sky—found him stretched out beneath a fur robe laid down on the *tatami* and draped over the brazier that warmed the heart of the room, concentrating its warmth around his body. She moved to his side as silently as a fox, and stood gazing down at him where he lay, seemingly asleep.

His face when he was at rest was as peaceful as a child's, something it never was when he was awake, with ambition glowing like live coals in the depth of his eyes. He was the most beautiful human man she had ever seen—his earth brown eyes, his shining black hair like a raven's wing, his perfect features . . . his tender devotion when he made love to her, as if only then could he forget the almost feral hunger that gnawed his soul the rest of the time. She didn't know which of those things it was—or whether it was the rare combination of them—that had captured her heart in a net of passion. She had never even realized what she was being drawn into, because it was so unexpected, and so rare.

He had fallen under her spell the moment he laid eyes on her . . . which was her intent, and only to be expected. But then she found, to her eternal surprise, yet never dismay, that the bewitchment had worked both ways. She thought that perhaps he had been a *kitsune* himself, in a former incarnation.

And yet just as surely, the ebb and flow of *chi* that created the destiny of everything in existence, on earth and even in the realm of the gods, had predestined this. It had been beyond their fate, beyond the foreseeing of even her witchcraft.

She sighed, her eyes returning to his face as she prepared to lie down beside him and awaken him with kisses.

His eyes opened and he looked up at her—fully awake, as she suddenly realized he had been the entire time. No other human could ever catch her by surprise the way he did.

"Does Asano live?" he said.

She stood still, gazing down at him, knowing that her silence told him all he needed to know.

He pushed up to rest on one elbow, his attention moving over the exquisitely rendered map of Japan lying on the floor beside him. His fingers followed his gaze, touching one domain and then another, as he said, "Steel from Nagato may craft fine weapons, and gold from Izu buy the allegiance of men. But the fertile soil of Ako can feed an army—" His finger stabbed at Ako's location on the map, as if he could strike its *daimyo* dead simply by willing it. "Ako is the key to Japan. If a man with vision ruled it, he might even call himself Shogun one day."

He threw off the fur robe and stood up, turning his eyes on her, eyes that were more profoundly disappointed than censuring.

Helpless to look away from them, she lost all ability even to protest, let alone lash out at him for his ingratitude. This had been the most complex manipulation of the forces of earth and heaven she had ever attempted: to cast a corrupting spell on a *kirin*, and place Lord Asano's image in its mind as its tormenter; to magick the *kirin* from the deep recesses of the mountains to Ako . . . where in its frenzy, it had wreaked terrible havoc. Lord Asano himself had pursued it, as she had known he would have to. He should be dead—

"My lord," she said, "I did everything in my power." And it was true.

She suddenly remembered the peasant who had struck down the *kirin* with one blow, when even Ako's finest samurai had failed . . . who had looked into her eyes and suddenly pierced the illusion, seeing clearly all the way to *her*. She was certain he was no more than human, and not even a priest. *But still . . .*

"You failed me," Kira said, more in resignation than anger, and she trembled inside. He touched her face gently, but there was no warmth or forgiveness in the gesture.

He moved on past her to a window and slid it open, ignoring the frigid draft that entered around him as he stood gazing out at his barren lands. His hands locked together behind his back, unconsciously imitating a prisoner. "My ancestors gave their lives to put the Shogun's family in power and this was their reward," he said, his voice hardening with familiar bitterness. "Asano's gave orders from their camp stools and they were given Ako. Now he is honored with this visit, while I am commanded to attend."

His fists tightened. "Ako should be *mine*!" He broke the invisible chains with which his frustration had bound his resolve, and leaned on the sill of the window, glaring out at the windswept peaks of his sterile domain. His eyes were as cold and unrelenting as the snow-covered mountains.

Mitsuke followed him across the room and slipped her arms around him, pressing the warmth of her body against his own. His flesh felt so cold that it seemed as if the sight of his own land had frozen him to death. Pity filled her, and she held him even tighter, trying to rekindle the warmth of his hope, and his love for her. "What can I do to soothe my lord?"

He turned abruptly, pushing free of her embrace, refusing to be comforted or beguiled. "Do what I ask," he said harshly. "I need Ako, and you need to help me take it."

She met his unyielding gaze, and her own dropped away, troubled. *Destiny* . . . he was so determined to defy his own, to change it utterly if he could. Only a human would be so naïve, and so arrogant, that he would spend his entire life struggling to change what could not be altered, except by the most extraordinary events.

And yet, because of their blindness to *chi,* humans were the only creatures in existence who had the potential to create events so chaotic that they could bring about an alteration in their own fate. Like that peasant today, who had slain the *kirin* single-handed: For a human, he was truly gifted in his ability to manipulate *chi.* How ironic, how like the inscrutable will of the gods, to waste such a blessing on a creature like that.

But she was certain it was the same gift, combined with the determination to defy his future, that made Lord Kira who he was . . . the only human being she could possibly love, let alone willingly devote her powers to.

"You may not take Ako by force. Its leaders are canny, its men are fearless fighters, and fiercely loyal . . ." She hesitated. "But you can take it by breaking their spirit." She reached out and touched his cheek with gentle fingers, and this time he allowed it, even pressed his face against the warm hollow of her hand, as he looked to her for an answer.

"In three days all eyes will be on Ako," she said quietly, but with deadly promise. "If my lord wishes, Asano's hour of triumph shall be his downfall."

"How?" He straightened, lifting his head, his eyes already alight again with the flames of ambition.

Mitsuke tossed her head, her unbound hair moving sinuously across her shoulder with the motion. "Every man has his weakness," she murmured, being careful not to let him look too deeply into her eyes as her own confidence returned. "Asano has an ego. We shall challenge it. He has a daughter. The one thing he would die for." She let the faintest promise of a smile touch her lips.

Kira smiled at last in return, and put his arms around her, pulling her close against him. He kissed her then, with all the desire that she had been longing for. . . .

The hunting party returned to Ako Castle in high spirits, every man thinking that the jade green rice paddies along the valley floor and climbing terraced hillsides, the sapphire ribbon of the river mirroring the blue sky, had never looked more beautiful. Everywhere the cherry trees were covered in blooms, from the simplest five-petaled white flowers through multilayered blossoms of deep coral that seemed to glow like rubies in the sunlight. Ako itself seemed to be welcoming them home, after their triumph over the monster that had threatened both the land and the people who belonged to it.

Mika glanced up from the circle of black-robed advisors with whom she had been consulting for days as Oishi Chikara, the young samurai who was the son of the *karou,* arrived with undignified haste among the nearly finished preparations in the lower courtyard. Chikara scanned the area where an arena had been set up for the martial tournament, the main event of the festivities for the Shogun's visit, as if he was looking for someone—for her, she was certain.

Mika didn't dare call out or wave to him from the company of such excruciatingly well-mannered men, even though Chikara—so like his father had been as a newly made samurai, and the *karou*'s proud assistant—woke the urge in the country *daimyo*'s impulsive girl-child who still lived inside her. She was a grown woman now, and for her father's sake—as well as her own, as a woman—it would never do for the most sophisticated consultants money could lure here from Edo to see a trace of inattention on her part.

Keeping her smile hidden, she gracefully adjusted her sleeve, making certain that her outer robe clearly showed the golden crossed hawk feathers of the Asano clan *mon.* Chikara would spot it soon, and the glow she had seen on his face had been enough to reassure her that she could wait until then to hear his news.

One or two of the advisors glanced at her as she rearranged her sleeve to make the clan's crest more visible. Its design symbolized a proud history generations long, dating back to the days when the feather of a hawk had been presented to a man who had earned the rank of samurai for his courage in battle, or to a victorious commander in the field.

She returned her attention patiently to the seating plan the advisors had laid out for her approval. "Where have you seated the chamberlain?" she asked, as if she had nothing more important on her mind.

"Between His Highness and Lord Asano, my lady," one of the advisors said, pointing at the chart, "but we still need your father's approval for the plan—"

"It is approved," she said firmly. She held up her fan, which also bore the Asano family crest, and then shut it with an abrupt motion, reminding them that her father had left her in charge of the preparations. It was not just her father's whim, but her longstanding legal right to act as steward for his castle and lands—which the advisors knew as well as she did.

She had been granted complete authority to speak for him when he had been called away . . . to lead an emergency foray against the monster that had suddenly appeared to not only terrorize Ako's people, and wreak havoc with their crops, but also to disrupt the preparations for the Shogun's ceremonial visit.

The less the advisors knew about that, at least until they heard news of its successful conclusion, the better. If they were to hear the details any sooner, she had no doubt they would flee back to Edo and the safety of the capital, where the plans for the Shogun's visit to Ako would immediately be canceled.

She took a deep breath, and added, "Except for one detail. Lord Sakai will sit at my father's side, not Lord Kira."

"Lord Kira is one of the most powerful lords in the land—" another advisor protested.

The most influential political manipulator at the Shogun's court, she amended silently. And her father detested him, with good reason. Keeping her thoughts to herself, she only said, "Lord Sakai is my father's friend." She smiled as though that explained everything. *Her father's good friend and loyal ally in curbing Lord Kira's naked ambition.* Kira's determination to get his hands on her family's hereditary fief was hardly a secret among the *daimyo,* who were required to visit the Shogun's palace in Edo, at their own considerable expense, far more often than the Shogun ever set foot outside of it.

How a man like Kira, who barely qualified as a *daimyo,* and whose tiny, marginal fief contributed nothing to the country as a whole except a view of icy mountains, had gained such a high position at the Edo court had been a mystery to her, until she had learned to eavesdrop while she played hostess to her father's visitors. Most men spoke too freely when the *sake* flowed, and regarded a woman—even Lord Asano's daughter—as less self-aware than a piece of furniture. She had gathered that Kira combined an extremely charming personality with acute political shrewdness and the morals of an assassin.

Lord Kira already possessed far more power and influence than he should. She only wished that it would be enough for him . . . at least as far as the Shogun was concerned. But she knew by now that that was rarely the way things worked out.

Chikara appeared beside her at last as she took the seating plan into her hands and began to roll it up. He made a very low bow to them all, confident in her promise that news about her father gave him leave to approach and interrupt any consulting session freely.

"My lady," he said, his face flushed and his words almost getting ahead of him, "your father has returned."

Mika let her relief out onto her face at last, beaming at

him and the startled officials. Graciously, she excused herself from their company, happy in more ways than she dared to say when she told them that her father would want to see her immediately.

They could hear the details about Lord Asano's absence straight from him, and she was sure they would have no reason to feel anything but impressed by the outcome. Nudging Chikara away from the advisors before he could say another word, she made him take her directly to where her father waited.

Lord Asano swung down from his horse, by now feeling more relief than anything else as he finally set foot on the flagstone pavement inside the walls of the lower courtyard. His weary body felt every bit of its age, now that the hunt was truly over.

"Father!"

He glanced up, and saw Mika hurrying toward him, her face as radiant as the day, her eyes bright with her own relief at the sight of him. He was reminded for a moment of his wife, and hoped that wherever her spirit dwelled now, somehow she might see this sight through his eyes—the image of their love made visible in their lovely daughter. His aches and weariness vanished, along with his thoughts about old age, at the sight of Mika. She was the constant reminder that everything he did for Ako was worth the effort, because this was what came of honor, justice, courage, and love—a beautiful future.

Mika threw her arms around him, hugging him tightly, not even wincing at the sharp edges of his armor. She let go of him again, and stepped back to gaze at the entire party of hunters, sharing the light of her smile and her pride with them all. But she said softly, only to him, "I was so worried. We were expecting you home last night."

Lord Asano shrugged, and sighed, but his own smile remained firmly in place. "The hunt took longer than we hoped." He handed the reins of his horse to a waiting retainer, and Mika took his arm as they started away together across the courtyard.

She glanced past him, her face tightening with sudden concern as she saw some of the men who had been injured being led or carried past to a place where the doctors could tend to their wounds. "Is anyone badly hurt?"

Lord Asano patted her arm. "A few of the porters . . ." he said, looking away again in an attempt to distract her. "Yasuno showed great courage. He killed the beast on his own." He gestured toward the spot where Yasuno was being congratulated by a gathering of the retainers from the castle, trying to keep her thoughts away from the injured and focused on the positive outcome of their hunt.

Mika half frowned as she noticed Yasuno's apparent discomfort at the effusive praise and congratulations he was receiving. To see him looking abashed was the last thing she would have expected; he was one of the least modest men she had ever known. And after all, he had killed a *kirin,* of all things, single-handedly.

She looked away again, her attention suddenly drawn to a group of injured commoners.

"Who are you looking for?" her father asked.

Her breath caught at the question; his intuition surprised her more than even her own realization that she had, without thinking, been looking for someone in particular. She shook her head, glancing down, unable to meet his gaze. "No one, my lord."

"You seem upset?" It was not really a question, and she heard the concern behind it.

She shook her head again, fixing a smile on her face as she finally looked into his eyes. "I'm worried about the arrangements." She hoped that excuse would be enough to cover her distraction.

"Don't be," he said, smiling. But he took her hand reassuringly, the way he had when she was a child, as they entered the zigzag defense corridor that angled steeply upward to the gate of the inner courtyard.

As they passed through the gate and walked toward the palace buildings, she heard him sigh in contentment as he looked up at the splendid profile of the keep—the symbol of his home, his world, surrounded by blossoming cherry trees and the quarters of his highest-ranking retainers. Their way was lined with attendants and retainers, all of whom kneeled and bowed, waiting for a chance to congratulate him, or ready to do his bidding immediately—whatever he required to keep things secure and satisfactory . . . and today also to prepare for every possible expectation of the Shogun and his retinue.

"What gifts do we have for the Shogun?" he asked Mika, as they reached the door of his private chambers.

Mika turned to smile at him again, as he almost caught her still looking back out the gate, her thoughts still on the injured men in the lower courtyard. "A dozen hawks, and a *katana* from the House of Morei."

Her father looked thoughtful. "Do you think that's enough?"

Her smile widened, and irony sparked in her gaze. "Any more and the other lords might think you are trying to outdo them."

He laughed with genuine amusement and relief.

They entered his chambers, still going down the list of preparations done and undone as attendants removed his armor and took it away for cleaning. He looked relieved to be rid of it, but more relieved by her answers to his questions. She imagined how the details of the Shogun's visit must have been preoccupying his mind all through the long ride back from the hunt, once the monster itself had been slain, and its threat removed. She was both proud and pleased that she could give him the reassurance of positive answers to virtually everything, with up-to-date reports on the preparations still in progress.

"I want all our people to share in this honor—the samurai, villagers, farmers . . ."

"I've ordered stands put up all along the route," she said, with satisfaction.

"Is there anything you haven't thought of?" Her father's eyes shone with admiration as well as love. His smile and a pat on the shoulder released her at last from the besiegement of his concern. "Your mother would have been so proud."

She smiled too, glancing down with a modest bow of acknowledgement that was not entirely honest, or free of worry. She bowed again more deeply as she departed, admonishing him as she went out the door to try and get some rest.

Once she had slid the door to his chambers closed, she headed directly through his garden toward her own rooms. Her smile faded once she was out of his sight, replaced by the worried expression she had been hiding from him ever since she had seen the injured men from the hunt being taken away. There was one face she had not seen anywhere, among the injured, or with the others.

And that meant there was something very personal she still had to attend to—something she was forced to keep silent about, even with her father. She would have to wait until sundown, but that would give her time to make preparations.

Mika entered her own chambers, to see her attendants freeze in place, with their eyes wide and their hands in various positions that suggested they had been actively discussing matters more concerned with her and the return of the hunters than with thoughts about the Shogun's visit.

The all dropped gracefully to their knees and bowed like puppets in a *Bunraku* play when they saw her. Every last whisper of their murmured discussion had been stilled. Mika gestured impatiently with her fan and told them to get up, more desperate to hear what they had to say than they could imagine.

She could only ask to be notified immediately when her father returned from the hunt without raising awkward questions. But her attendants were free to mingle with the retainers who had accompanied him, begging to hear the details of their bravery with much fluttering of eyelashes and flashing of fans, as they ingenuously asked questions that would have seemed inappropriate from a man, or potentially scandalous coming from their lord's daughter . . . particularly questions about Lord Asano's halfbreed head tracker, who had identified the beast when no one else could, and then led them to its hiding place so that they could slay it.

Kai.

When she had learned what sort of creature had suddenly appeared and begun to ravage Ako, she had been incredulous, but hearing that it was Kai who had called it a *kirin*, her disbelief had turned to concern for everyone involved. Aside from her father, she had been the most fearful for Kai. Her father was not a young man anymore; but at least he would be wearing armor, carrying weapons, on horseback, and surrounded by his best warriors. As a commoner, Kai would not be permitted any protection at all.

Far too many years ago, her father had insisted that she put class and social position ahead of her friendship with Kai. He had warned her, as kindly as he could but with unrelenting sternness, that if she continued to consort with the halfbreed *hinin* kennel boy, it would not only cast a shadow over her own future, but mean that Kai would have to be sent away.

He had told Kai the same thing, she knew—explaining it as kindly as he could, she was sure, but accompanied by several of his retainers.

And so the gossamer strand of silk that had joined their lives had been severed, and whenever she even chanced to get close enough to Kai to speak to him, he had fallen to his knees and bowed until his face was in the dirt, and would not get up again or even speak until she had gone away. It had given immense satisfaction to her nursemaids, or whoever else happened to be with her.

None of them had ever seen the tears it always brought to her own eyes . . . not even Kai. Finally, she had been unable to bear watching him abase himself every time they met, and she had given up trying to find ways to encounter him face-to-face.

But none of that would let her forget him; it had only made her more achingly aware that he remained in her life, no matter how unreachable he was. She had only been free to express her true feelings to her diary, whenever she caught a glimpse of him across the castle grounds—usually carrying heavy loads with a group of porters, or working with a gang of laborers repairing the castle walls, covered in stone dust or splattered with the gleaming whitewash that protected its wood-and-plaster structures from fire.

She had watched him grow into a tall, strong young man, still as beautiful to her eyes as he had been as a boy, and composed poems about lost *tennin* that no one else understood. She had read *The Tale of Genji,* and vowed to become a nun. One night in the middle of winter, she had thrown all her bedding out the window and lain shivering on her bare futon until morning, because she had dreamed that Kai had frozen to death.

And meanwhile, her unsuspecting father had protected Kai from the abuse of his own retainers, and rewarded him for his dutiful obedience, his uncomplaining hard work—and eventually for his uncanny ability to locate game on a hunt.

Kai had been Lord Asano's head tracker for nearly ten years now, and there had never been an accident or injury. . . .

But then they had gone to hunt a *kirin.*

All through the years that Kai had spent working his way up from an outcast kennel boy into a man who held a secure, responsible position among the servants at Ako Castle, Mika had faced her own struggle to become, and remain, independent, despite the restrictions placed on her as a woman—even a samurai woman. She had finally shaken free of nursemaids disguised as attendants, and patiently assembled her own group of loyal retainers—attendants she trusted both for their intelligence and their discretion.

For the first time since her mother died she had the companionship of other women she could rely on, who shared emotions like her own . . . who understood exactly what she meant, when she asked them which they thought more beautiful, the crescent moon or the full moon? And when they answered, told them that she loved a moonless night the best, because then she could see every star.

And so she had only to look into their eyes as they rose to their feet and gathered around her now to know that her second deepest fear had been realized. *No one had been killed,* her father had said. But she hadn't seen Kai anywhere . . . not with the hunters, and not with the injured.

Now, in a rush of overlapping details, she learned that Kai had been injured badly, so badly that he had needed help returning to the castle. But he had left the hunting party before it even reached the castle gates—gone to his own cottage at the edge of the forest, like an injured animal slipping away to lick its wounds in solitude and let the gods decide whether it lived or died.

She wondered with an aching heart if the loss of their childhood friendship had made Kai feel he could never trust anyone, even her father, completely . . . the way it kept her stubbornly avoiding marriage, at an age when most women had children older than she had been then. *But would Kai truly rather die than ask anyone at all for help?*

She looked back at the earnest, expectant faces of the young women waiting for her orders.

"At dusk," she said with quiet urgency, and they nodded.

Oishi stood like a statue in the familiar surroundings of his home, too weighed down by fatigue and his armor even to speak as Riku, his wife, unfastened the pieces and took them off him, one by one. He felt stunned by the extra toll the urgency and danger of this hunt had taken on him, now that he was finally able to stop moving.

He wondered if this was what it had truly meant to be samurai, a member of the warrior class, in the days when wars were constant, and other men like himself were the target of the hunt. How had his ancestors endured being on campaign for months or years on end, never knowing when the next attack would come, or when they would see their loved ones again, if ever? Through generations of war, samurai had lived that way—unless their lives were abruptly cut short by an enemy. He thanked the gods that he lived in a time of peace.

He wondered how a man who spent all his life killing other men just to stay alive had ever had time, let alone the inclination, to work on improving himself as a human being by trying to attain the virtues of *Bushido*, the Samurai code of ethical and moral behavior. Even in peacetime . . .

The unwelcome memory of Yasuno and Kai—and the truth about which one had really killed the *kirin*—pushed to the forefront of his mind again, as it had repeatedly on the journey home.

Conflicting emotions pulled at the frayed edges of his belief in honor and justice. Yasuno had taken the credit for himself. He had lied simply by not telling the truth—that the halfbreed, not he, had killed the *kirin*. Oishi understood the crushing blow his pride had taken . . . but that didn't excuse the lie.

Should he confront Yasuno about it? He didn't want to lose one of his best men because Yasuno committed *seppuku* out of shame—or equally bad, turn Yasuno into his enemy, and cause strife among the men he trusted, if Yasuno refused to admit the truth.

He told himself the time when a halfbreed could have become Yasuno's equal simply by Lord Asano's recognition of his courage had been over for a hundred years now. Besides, the halfbreed had not even protested. Whether he'd kept silent because he was afraid Yasuno would kill him, or simply because he realized it was pointless, didn't matter.

Yasuno had taken the credit. It had been a craven and dishonorable act, the kind of thing no samurai should ever allow to go unchallenged . . . or be allowed to live down. *But if neither Yasuno nor the halfbreed had willingly told the truth. . . .*

Oishi shook his head, not even realizing that he had moved until Riku placed a steadying hand on his arm, as if she thought he was dizzy.

Now bloodlines counted for more than bloodshed; now everything was different. And no one was perfect—or what need would they have for gods, or codes of conduct either?

Oishi let his eyes wander over the beautifully painted murals on the wall screens, the time-darkened wood of the support beams of the house, all of which he knew by heart, because this was where he had grown up, in the shadow of Ako Castle's keep, within the secure walls of its inner courtyard. Memories of his youth, his parents, and his ancestors filled his mind, blotting out the days just past.

He thought about how his own son had grown up here too, surrounded by tradition. How he and Riku had taught Chikara the things he would one day need to know to assume his hereditary duties as *karou,* as the men of his family had done for generations, since long before Tokugawa Ieyasu had established the dynasty that now ruled Japan.

He took a deep breath. *He was home. That was all that mattered, now. . . .*

By the time Riku removed the last piece of his armor—patiently and lovingly relieving him of the burden of his duty, which was finally done, at least for today—he felt lighter not only in body but in spirit. He was inexpressibly glad to be a married man with a family to return to—far happier than he had ever expected to be when he was young.

His marriage to Riku had been arranged by his father, with Lord Asano's approval . . . no different than most marriages within their class, where first consideration went to rank, reputation, and strengthening political alliances through added kinship ties. Frequently, as in his case, the main participants did not even know each other.

But they had been blessed by the gods—or the wisdom of their elders—with compatible natures, to the point where he looked forward to growing old with her . . . her warm body next to his at night, her smile always welcoming him home.

He smiled at her as he stretched his arms and shrugged his shoulders, then glanced away again for a moment as he heard the clack and whack of *bokken* in the courtyard outside, where Chikara was engaging in a mock duel with another boy—*young man,* Oishi corrected himself—using wooden practice swords.

Riku looked up into his eyes, seeing that his mind had reentered their world sufficiently for conversation. Placing her hands gently on his arms, she said at last, "I was worried." Her concern showed suddenly through her fond smile.

His own smile widened. "You always worry," he said mildly. But he was grateful that, after all these years, she still cared enough about him that she did. He reached out and caressed her cheek. She kissed his palm, cupping his hand in hers.

He was about to ask her what they were having for dinner when he heard a fierce cry from outside, and they both looked toward the door. It sounded like the mock battle was becoming a real one.

Oishi moved to the entrance and slid the door aside. He realized then what he had been too tired to notice before:

That Chikara was dueling with Jinnai, who was three years older, taller, heavier, and more experienced with a sword.

Even a wooden sword could give a crippling blow, and neither of the boys—men, Oishi reminded himself silently—was even wearing protective padding. Chikara had had his *genpuku,* his coming of age ceremony, nearly half a year ago. And yet from where Oishi stood now, across the chasm of more than two decades' experience, those were still only half-grown boys. It was said among samurai that a man's soul was in his sword, and a woman's in her mirror. However, it struck him that Chikara should have taken a good look in the mirror and put on his practice armor before he invited Jinnai to spar with him. A *gembuku* did not give you a grown man's body overnight.

He watched the two of them attack and parry, impressed by the recent strides his son had made in his swordsmanship, and the confidence he seemed to have gained along with it—but still seeing that Jinnai had the advantage.

Chikara took a savage blow on the arm and dropped his guard, leaving himself wide open to Jinnai's blade. Oishi felt Riku stiffen in alarm as she came up beside him, even as his own body instinctively tensed against the pain of the coming blow.

But Chikara switched his *bokken* from his useless right hand to his left with a suddenness that startled Oishi and, with one deft sweep, knocked Jinnai's feet out from under him. He had both upended his opponent and won the duel with one decisive move—a move Oishi had never seen his son, or anyone else trained by Lord Asano's official sword master, ever make before.

"Chikara!" he shouted.

Chikara looked up, flushed with his victory, but startled by his father's tone of voice. He stood still, looking back at his father as Jinnai struggled to his feet, wincing.

"Jinnai," Oishi said, dismissing the older boy with a look before Jinnai could even speak. He waited until Jinnai was beyond hearing, Chikara and Riku waiting along with him, until at last he was free to say what was on his mind. "Who taught you that?"

Chikara hesitated, staring at him; the elation that had been in his eyes guttered out like a flame as he heard the anger in his father's question. He looked down then, silent for a moment too long, before he muttered, "No one, Father."

Oishi felt his wife's hand tighten ever so slightly, but insistently, on his shoulder—reminding him of how proud Chikara had always made them, and of how much more his son needed his encouragement than his anger.

Oishi kept his expression stern, but he let the question drop. That was swordsmanship worthy only of masterless ronin who brawled in the street because there were no real battles to fight and they had no other skills to fall back on. It was not for a retainer of high standing—or any warrior who had enough honor left to be worth defending. He took a deep breath. "You come from a family of samurai," he said to Chikara. "We do not fight like that."

Chikara's flush of pride was completely gone now, but for just a moment, Oishi thought his son was actually going to protest.

Instead, Chikara only bowed respectfully, accepting the admonishment with the dignity of an honorable man, as his father turned and went back into the house.

The sun had finally slipped down behind the distant hills when Mika and her attendants left the castle to wander in the fields, carrying lanterns, in search of fireflies . . . or so she told the guards at the gate. The hems of her clothing trailed in the mud of the path they followed out to the edge of the forest, where Kai had built his solitary home, but the state of her favorite kimono was the furthest thing from her thoughts.

She had learned long ago where Kai lived, and she had

followed this track many times, up to the spot where she could glimpse his hut at the edge of the trees. But she had never had the courage to go up to the door—too afraid until now that Kai would refuse to open it to her.

Even if she had come here, and Kai had let her in . . . if anyone ever found out, if her father so much as suspected . . . what would become of Kai then? The thought of what might happen to him—the least of the possibilities being his banishment—had always stopped her, even when her longing would have overcome the fear that he would turn her away.

What might happen to her if she had come here and Kai had let her in had never really bothered her all that much—she was a woman, and so she would not be allowed to inherit Ako. It would go to some male kin of her father, when he died, unless he adopted a male heir . . . and before that she expected she would be forced to marry someone she didn't love, and had probably never even met—used as a pawn in the ongoing match of *shogi* that *daimyo* played on a board that was all of Japan.

Fortunately her father had seemed as reluctant to make a pawn of his only child as she had been to become one. She was well beyond the age when most daughters had been negotiated for and sent away from their homes. But he had rarely brought up the topic of marriage, and her immediate and completely sincere response—that she loved Ako so much that it would break her heart never to see it again—had been enough to make him fall silent. Her father could easily understand why she loved her home so much, with its radiant beauty and wealth of tradition. And she suspected that loneliness might break his own heart, once she was gone.

That she loved Ako too much to imagine ever leaving it was the heartfelt truth. She also loved the dignity and responsibility that her father's wisdom had granted her; he had treated her almost as if someday she would be his heir. But those were not the only reasons she couldn't bear the thought of leaving.

Her father would never understand—and she could never tell him—the most important reason of all: that she loved Kai, and Kai was here. She might as well be in love with Prince Genji, the dream of a man who had lived only in the book written by Lady Murasaki seven hundred years ago.

Mika knew more about Genji than she knew about Kai, and she could no more be with Kai than with Genji. All she had been able to do for years was look at him from afar . . . and know that every time her eyes found him, his own eyes would already be gazing at her.

One of her attendants made a small startled sound, and pointed ahead. Looking up, she saw Kai's home at last. It was a tiny, ramshackle thing, more like the hut of an ascetic monk than even a peasant's cottage. But over the years he had added to the temporary shelter of his first home, with materials salvaged from abandoned houses or found in the forest . . . as if the longer he lived here, the more he had begun to believe in a future.

Just before they reached the house itself, she noticed a small devotional shrine made of stones. It had not been there before he came; only Kai could have built it. The thought that he might pray to any gods at all surprised her, she realized . . . perhaps because when they were young, he had always seemed to her more like someone from the realm of the gods, of Buddha, than merely a human boy.

She stopped, gazing down at the shrine, and then she bowed reverently and clapped her hands, a call to the compassion of Buddha, to all the bodhisattvas, to whatever gods or goddesses the shrine was dedicated to—asking them all to hear her. She humbly bowed her head and put her hands together a final time, praying silently that tonight Kai had left the door barring the way between them unlocked. She started on again, her attendants silently following, her heartbeat sounded as loud in her ears now as her clapping had.

By lantern light, Kai's home looked like something that had simply taken root here, growing out of the land itself.

But dozens of Buddhist prayer ribbons, some faded and some still bright red, covered with gold kanji—the colors of Ako—hung above his doorway, fluttering in the soft breath of evening.

"*Wabi-sabi*—" one of her attendants murmured, in wonder, and Mika's breath caught.

"Yes . . ." she whispered.

Wabi-sabi: A thing of such unexpected beauty, in its mismatched and accidental parts, that one was startled into seeing it with the soul:

Beauty was unique and born of chance . . .

. . . one must find joy in it while one had eyes to see . . .

. . . because beauty, like life itself, was ephemeral . . .

. . . and joy would vanish like sakura *blossoms . . .*

The words of philosophers and holy men echoed in her thoughts. Blinking suddenly, she wondered what it was that Kai prayed for, and whether she would ever know.

She gestured to her attendants to stay where they were; she had already cautioned them to stay silent while they waited.

To ask was a temporary shame . . . not to ask, an eternal one.

Biting her lips like a child, she set her hands to Kai's door.

3

Kai kneeled on his bed—the remains of a traveler's abandoned sleeping mat that gave him barely enough room to stretch out—where he had finally collapsed this afternoon, unable even to tend his wounds until he'd slept.

Fortunately, he supposed, the pain in his back had wakened him after only two or three hours, judging from the position of the sun. By then he realized that if he'd slept much longer, he might have been too stiff even to get up again.

He had eaten the handful of pressed rice cakes that the small group of porters and farmers had left with him, when they'd brought him here at his own insistence. That had at least given him the strength to fetch water from the stream and start a blaze in the fire pit.

Functioning more from long habit than conscious choice, he had set the pot of water to heat on the bone and antler grid above the fire, while he chose medicinal herbs from the small bundles gathered in baskets. When the water had warmed enough, he put some of it aside to clean the worst of the dried blood and dirt from his arms and upper body, while the herbs simmered into a brew he hoped would be healing enough.

He could admit to himself, now that it was too late to make a difference, that he had been foolish not to go to the castle with the other returning hunters. But the truth about the *kirin*'s death—everything about it—had festered worse than the wound on his back. He had not gone, he would not go. The best that he could do on his own would have to be good enough, as it always had been before.

At last he removed the pungent mixture from the fire, and poured most of his small jug of *sake* into it as a disinfectant. He saved the last of the cheap rice wine for a painkiller, gulping it down because he found no pleasure in the taste of it. It burned in his stomach as he carefully slipped his arms out of his kimono again, letting it drop and hang from the sash so that he could get at his wounds.

The makeshift clot of moss and clay he had used to stop the bleeding from the wound the *kirin* had given him had not held for long, and the pace the samurai on horseback had set in their haste to return to Ako had barely given him time to catch his breath, let alone take care of the wound along the way.

By this morning, he had fallen so far behind, and was falling down so often, that some of the farmers and porters—who had trouble enough on their own—had nonetheless turned back to get him on his feet and help him keep moving. He'd realized then that they were far more appreciative of his skill as a tracker, and more aware that he was seriously hurt, than the samurai who, seemingly oblivious, had ridden on ahead.

The possibility that certain samurai hoped he didn't survive the trip would not have surprised him at all. The idea that whether he lived or died mattered to people he scarcely knew—people already bearing too many burdens of their own—had surprised him a great deal. He owed them a debt; he hoped that the death of the *kirin* would at least partially repay it.

He picked up the broken mirror he kept for when he hacked off his hair: He never wore it too short, because he hated even the memory of his shaven head as a boy and the sight of his scarred scalp. But he could never let it get so long that he could actually pull it into a topknot . . . because that might be all some drunken retainer needed to justify trying to kill him, for the crime of attempting to pass as something more than he was.

Every time he looked into the mirror it reminded him again of who and what he really was, as well—one more reason why he needed to cut his unruly hair: because when it bleached out in the sun, it showed streaks of red, like a true demon's hair.

He sighed, looking away from his face. The mirror was useful at times like this, too.

He held it up awkwardly, trying to see the wound the *kirin* had inflicted, but it was impossible to force his lacerated body into a position where he could get a clear look and at the same time clean the blood-clotted gouge with the cloth soaked in medicine. Any way he tried to move made him feel as if he was being torn open by the *kirin*'s horn again.

He choked off a curse that was half pain-noise. Sitting cross-legged on the mat, he forced himself to relax and breathe deeply, to focus his will, to prepare his body to succeed at the impossible.

He raised the mirror again, ready to make himself do what he had to in order to survive.

His door rattled. He froze in mid-motion, looking toward it with a sudden frown. The door began to slide open, not even giving him time to demand the name of whoever was there.

Before he could reach for his knife, the door slid fully open. He stared in disbelief, the knife and every word he knew forgotten, as Lady Mika entered. She stopped for a moment, hesitating in the dim glow of his fire, as luminous as the moon in her mist-colored cloak. She seemed as stunned as he was to find herself here, actually facing him.

At last she said softly, "They told me you were hurt?"

He was already kneeling, and yet his arms trembled as he lowered himself in an awkward bow. He pushed upright again while he could—but that left him still sitting in front of her half-undressed, filthy and haggard, in a hovel that must seem to her no better than the dog kennels. He kept his eyes fixed on the packed dirt floor as he mumbled, "It's nothing, my lady."

But Mika started toward him anyway. He looked up and saw only deep concern, nothing more, on her face—as if nothing else mattered except him . . . nothing at all.

"Let me see," she said, kneeling down beside him. Gazing back at him, her eyes took in more than just the cuts and bruises covering his chest, his arms—she was looking at *him,* his body, his face, with something far deeper than simple compassion.

He turned away from the look, as the ache it set off inside him overwhelmed him with a worse kind of pain than any physical wound that had ever marked his flesh.

As he settled himself again, facing away from her, he heard her sharp, indrawn breath.

"Your back. . . ." Her voice was barely audible.

But then he heard the sensuous rustle of silk as she settled herself beside him on the mat. Her hand touched him, her fingertips on his skin as light as the feathers of a bird wing. He couldn't control the shiver it sent up his spine, raising gooseflesh all over his body. "My lady," he said hoarsely, half protest, half plea, "I can clean the wounds myself—"

"Not if you can't reach them." Her voice held more tenderness than he had ever heard in it, but at the same time it denied him permission to refuse her help. She was more than ever the *daimyo*'s daughter as she touched his body, defying every rule that had kept them in their places and separated them for all these years.

More embarrassed, more uncertain, and more afraid than ever that he would ruin her life simply by existing in it, Kai turned his face further into the shadows. It let her see his back as clearly as possible: Either she would be overcome by the sight of the bloody wounds and leave, or clean them as well as she could, and leave. *Anything, to get her to leave*— Because that was the last thing in the world he wanted her to do . . .

But she was samurai, in all the ways that had ever made the word worthy of respect—not simply honorable, compassionate, and just in her dealings with all people, but fearless and unflinching in the face of challenges that would make most women—and most men—lose their courage and flee, abandoning a person, or a cause, as hopeless. He should have known that his wounds wouldn't be enough to drive her away.

She took the scrap of dripping cloth from the crude pottery bowl beside him and began, with infinite care, to wash his back.

Freed of the excruciating difficulty of trying to treat his own wounds, he felt his knotted muscles slowly release their tension. He focused so deeply on the sensation of Mika's nearness, the scent of jasmine from her hair, the whisper of silk . . . her hands, so soft and so gentle in their movement that the relentless pain of his lacerated flesh and damaged tissues began to recede at last, to a place far more distant from his conscious mind than the awareness that he was sitting here in the middle of a dream.

The thought that this might only *be* a dream, nothing but delirium—and then the certainty that it was not—suddenly brought back the other, sourceless pain that had filled him when he first laid eyes on her.

Sourceless—? No, not sourceless. It was the sight of her, here, inside his world, that had caused it; and yet the ache lay somewhere unreachably deep in his soul, where there was nothing he could do to control it.

He tried again to focus on physical pain as she began to clean the area around the deepest, worst wound—the one inflicted by the *kirin*'s horn—preferring even that to what her nearness made him feel.

"Someone should have seen to this before," she said, as she began to discover the full extent of the wound. The concern that was half a question had a sharp edge of anger as well, although he knew the anger was not directed at him.

"There were others who needed attention," he mumbled, as if it was nothing, managing to keep his voice under control, just as he kept his body still despite the fact that her hand was not quite so steady now. After all, it had not been entirely the fault of the others that his wounds had been ignored. On the way back to Ako Castle he had intentionally tried to remain invisible.

Mika's touch disappeared from his skin. He waited, puzzled, while she sat behind him for a long moment . . . until he almost thought he could feel the touch of her eyes on him instead, as she studied the network of old scars and new wounds that patterned his flesh.

"Were you with Yasuno when he killed the beast?" she asked.

Startled, Kai hesitated, and then, closing his eyes, he nodded, glad that he wasn't facing her.

"They say he was very brave," Mika went on, and this time he heard a hint of doubt in her words.

"Yes," he said, the only word that he could force out of his mouth. His hands tightened on his knees, although he kept perfectly still.

"My father wants him to fight for us at the tournament instead of Hazama."

The tournament that was the main event during the Shogun's visit. Kai's body almost jerked free of his control, as anger overtook his surprise. *Of course.* Yasuno was the great hero of the hunt, to everyone in Ako—everyone but the single person who knew the truth. Kai sucked in a long, unsteady breath. It would suit him perfectly to watch Yasuno humiliated in real combat, in front of the Shogun and the most important lords in the land.

Except for the shame that it would bring to Ako.

Right now Yasuno was the least honorable samurai he knew, and far from the best fighter. But that wouldn't mean anything, even to Lord Asano, if Kai tried to denounce Yasuno as a liar. It would be his word against Yasuno's. And despite all the things Yasuno wasn't, he was still a samurai—and under the law, there was no justice, not even the truth, that could bridge the river of blood that flowed between them.

Kai realized that he hadn't answered . . . and that he couldn't sit here in silence forever. "Yasuno is an able swordsman," he said quietly, the only thing he could think of to say that wouldn't choke him to death.

"But with so much at stake," Mika persisted, "the Shogun and his lords watching—it is important we do well."

He glanced back at her, hearing the doubt in her voice clearly this time. *Why was she telling him this, in such a troubled voice—?* But he realized that this time there was no need for him to answer her, or even his own question. Nothing was all that he had a right to say . . . no matter what came of it.

Mika laid her hands on his back, as carefully as before. She finished cleaning out the wound, and then took a roll of fresh cotton bandage from inside the sleeve of her kimono. She wrapped it around his body, over his shoulder, until the worst of his wounds were protected.

He felt her fasten off the ends of the bandage, and then her hands were no longer touching him at all, at last. He got to his feet and pulled the upper part of his kimono back in place, infinitely relieved that he was no longer kneeling half-naked in front of her. "Thank you," he murmured. He waited, with his back turned, for her to rise and depart.

She sat there for another endless moment; he felt her yearning like a song without words or tune, making the truth of his own feelings resonate inside him until he could barely breathe.

"I saw the shame in Yasuno's eyes when they were praising him," Mika said at last, as if she couldn't help herself. This time, the words were a challenge.

He turned around finally to meet her gaze. Her eyes were too full, brimming with sympathy for him and outrage against the ones who had stolen his honor and nearly his life . . . *She knew. She must have realized her suspicions were true when she saw his wounds, in spite of all he hadn't said.*

"Even when you try to help them, they hate you," she said, her voice shaking. *Why . . . ?* her eyes asked, not of him but of the gods.

It was the same question that had lain in the depths of his own soul for so many years that he had finally stopped asking it, because it had no rational answer: It made no more sense than why her father could see enough that was human about him to grant him a human life . . . and yet, because Kai was not born a samurai, had refused to allow even an innocent friendship between two children to continue.

Lord Asano had told him frankly what the consequences would be for Mika . . . and for him . . . if they continued as they had, if friendship ever became something more. He had acknowledged Kai's frustration, his grief, his protests, with a patience Kai now realized was worthy of Buddha, for a samurai lord speaking to a halfbreed *hinin* boy.

But Lord Asano had also forced him to comprehend what it meant to be human, and yet not samurai. To be human—and yet not. "Your father's samurai have always treated me as well as could be expected." He looked away, hearing the resignation, the surrender, in it.

"And is that all you expect?" Mika demanded. Her eyes still burned with passion, but this time they were looking directly at him, forcing him to look back at her. *You killed a* kirin*!* they said. You, *not Yasuno. You are the one with a samurai's heart, a samurai's honor. You deserve the praise and the rewards . . . to wear the hawk's feather. To bear the name. To be my love. . . . Why won't you—?* Her hands trembled. *Why—?*

"It's all I know. . . ." He glanced down again as he spoke the words of a coward, refusing to rise to her challenge.

Her dark, shining eyes became even more luminous as disappointment rose into them like tears. "It doesn't have to be, Kai—"

He turned away abruptly, unable to go on looking at her at all, as his own need and frustration became too much to endure. "Did you come alone?" he asked, staring into the fire.

"Are you sending me away?" She answered his question with another, forcing him to make the decision, to speak the words . . . to send her away for her own good, because she would never understand.

Her honor was everything, as a samurai woman, and if she sacrificed it for him, she would lose everything. . . . If they tried to stay here, even meeting secretly, Ako itself would tear them apart. And if they ran away, there was no place they could go where retribution wouldn't find them. Their relationship was forbidden—and Mika was a *daimyo*'s daughter. If they left Ako together, word would reach the Shogunate *bakufu;* agents of the government would hound them to their deaths.

Gods, the kirin *should have killed him*— Because if he hadn't simply been wounded, she would never have come here. He would never have had to endure this next moment as he spoke the words he would rather die than say, and still go on living. . . .

He looked back at her at last. "This is no place for you, my lady," he said, the words as empty as his eyes.

She stared at him, sitting completely motionless, stunned by pain. And then, slowly and deliberately, she gathered up the muddy skirts of her silk kimono, like moonlight surrendering to darkness, and got to her feet. She walked to the door of his wretched hut with quiet dignity. "Good night," she said, opening the door. She stepped through; he saw the lanterns of her attendants glowing like fireflies beyond it, before she closed the door behind her.

Kai stood staring across the empty room at the closed door. In the fire pit behind him, a branch split and fell deeper into the fire, sending up a brilliant flare, and a whirl of sparks that faded away like fireflies, dying even as they gave off the light that called out desperately to a lover.

4

Lord Asano and his Honor Guard, headed by Oishi, stood assembled in orderly lines in Ako Castle's lower courtyard to greet the seemingly endless procession of *daimyo* and their entourages entering through the castle gate. All the nobles had come at the Shogun's invitation, or Lord Asano's own—to demonstrate friendship or loyalty, as well as to celebrate the hospitality of Ako in the full bloom of its glorious springtime.

More retinues were still making their way along the winding road to the castle, in an endless stream of colored banners and flags, for as far as anyone could see from the watchtowers or walls. The Shogun himself was not expected to arrive until somewhere near sunset; the arrival of guests might easily continue unabated until then. Mika was extremely glad that she had taken the assumed number of guests who would need to be fed and given shelter, and added half again to the number, just to be certain no influential lord, or anyone else, went hungry or was left in the open to be eaten alive by mosquitos during the night.

Mika kneeled, along with her attendants, on the cushions of a raised platform behind her father—a platform just high enough so that they could see and be seen over the helmets of the men standing in front of them, who were wearing full dress armor. She was glad for once to spend the day kneeling on cushions, dressed in airy silks, while the men below stood and bowed for hours in the sun.

The Asano colors of red and gold lent themselves well to the variety of colors she had chosen for her kimono and outer robes, and those of her attendants. Her father had been determined to spare no expense to stage this auspicious event, and so she had let herself enjoy one assignment to the fullest: choosing colors and styles of decoration for the kimono had recaptured her blissful childhood memories of dressing up in her mother's beautiful, sumptuous robes.

She was secretly pleased by the results: each of them wore a kimono elaborately patterned in the brilliant hues of a different flower, helping to bring the pragmatic, nondescript tones of the lower courtyard to more vivid life. The ladies of the court were a part of the overall effect, as much as the profusion of flowers blooming now in the upper yard; as much as the standards of the different units of Ako's samurai troops and arquebus mercenaries assembled around her, their individual flags, banners, and pennants displayed in every imaginable elaborate form, all of which transformed the dour outbuildings near the gatehouse with a display that was both proudly martial and still as colorful and welcoming as a spring festival.

Her father had even commissioned new armor for the samurai and himself. He looked splendid; even his helmet was newly made, more elaborate than the one he usually wore, which had been his father's.

Remembering how tired he had been by today, she hoped he would remember to sit on the camp stool he was allowed, as *daimyo*—at least between rising and bowing to acknowledge each new dignitary who arrived. Glancing down at him, she saw that he looked fully refreshed, and prouder than she had seen him in a long while. She felt herself shining with reflected pride, as he was honored in a way few *daimyo* ever were—especially an "outsider" lord, whose ancestors had remained neutral during the ultimate internecine battle that had won the title of Shogun for the Tokugawa clan.

Because the Asano had clan ties on both sides, they had chosen not to fight for either. But the Tokugawa had long memories, and if a clan had not fought for them to the bitter end, then they might as well have fought against them.

Lords who had opposed Ieyasu, the first Shogun, had had their lands, and usually their lives, taken immediately. But then, gradually, and on the slightest pretext, Ieyasu's descendants had begun to seize the domains of other outsider lords—ones who had simply remained neutral. Those lands had been added to the Tokugawa's already vast holdings, or given as rewards to the inner circle of *daimyo* whose clans had supported the Tokugawa takeover, and now included most of the officials who held high positions in the government.

Even Tsunayoshi, the fifth Shogun, whose arrival they awaited now, was still confiscating fiefs whose *daimyo* had done nothing but stay out of the way during the final conflict of the War That Had Ended War a hundred years ago.

The "Tokugawa Peace" meant nothing without the kind of control needed to back it up: *Only a warrior could choose to be a pacifist.* The Tokugawa had made sure they would remain in power by removing that choice from any possible competition.

And yet the struggle for power went on, as it always did. "Politics is war—" her father had told her once, "the weapons are just better concealed." Now the machinery of control lay inside Edo Castle, securely within the halls of the *bakufu,* the Shogunate government. The *bakufu* had constructed, stone by stone, an impregnable fortress of laws and restrictions so complex that the Shogun had a special counselor just for the protocol surrounding visits to and from the Shogun. The advisors who had driven her almost mad with their endless nitpicking and criticism while she tried to prepare for the visit had come from him, and they had not come without a considerable "gift" to the high counselor for sending them.

It had become her opinion that Japan must be the most over-governed country in the world.

As a result, she had come to appreciate that Ako had been doubly blessed until now—by its location on the seacoast, with wide expanses of coastal plain where the rich soil made farming good, and also because of its isolated location, a very long way from the capital, Edo, where the *bakufu*'s unsleeping eye watched everyone, all the time.

In her father's opinion, as well as her own, they were better off where they were. Ako's gifts from the natural world had not only allowed them to pay for the costly display expected in honor of the Shogun's visit, it also allowed them, year after year, to keep the people well-fed and their defenses as strong as the law permitted, while still meeting the government's ever higher demands for taxes.

Mika turned her attention back to the procession and its surroundings, as she had the sudden feeling that someone was staring at her. She glanced toward the crowd of commoners standing well back in the courtyard, searching for Kai.

But then she realized that the eyes gazing at her were not so far away. As she looked down at her father again, she saw the man who was looking up at her. From his extremely sophisticated ceremonial clothing—with the Tokugawa *mon* displayed on its belt sash—he was clearly someone highly placed in the Edo government. A very handsome man, she thought; something that would not have lingered in her mind before a few days ago, when she had said goodnight to Kai, perhaps forever.

The man was gazing up at her as if she was Kagura-*hime*—the daughter of the moon, beloved by an emperor—and he had been moonstruck.

And then she recognized the colors of his formal court garments, and the octopus *mon* on the banners carried by his retainers: *It was Lord Kira.*

Her face turned as red as peony blossoms with her sudden shame at even thinking about his appearance. Lord Kira—the Shogun's high counselor for protocol—was also the man who had been her father's patient, insidious enemy for years, a subtle knife forever lying too close to the Shogun's right hand, with its point always directed at Ako.

"Ako is as beautiful as I remember, Lord Asano," Kira said, his gaze still lingering on her face, before he bowed to her father. Mika glared back at him with barely concealed disgust. How dare he look at her like that—with the hunger of a starving dog, the same look that was always in his eyes when they settled on Ako.

"We are honored by your visit, Lord Kira," her father answered, as if he actually was. She alone recognized the tension underlying the words. Was it only his usual wariness regarding Lord Kira, or had he noticed Kira staring at her?

"It is you we come to honor," Lord Kira replied smoothly, but she felt the edge on the flawless politesse of his words. The image of the subtle knife sent a chill through her, as if it had pricked her spine.

"I hope everything is to your satisfaction." Her father smiled, his confidence paying her an unspoken compliment for all her work on the preparations.

A more visible trace of the knife's edge showed in Kira's slight smile as he replied, "Other than a few minor matters of ceremony, everything is perfect."

Caught by surprise, her father could not help but step into the trap. "Which matters of ceremony?"

Mika's breath caught with sudden alarm. *What? What was it? Where had she made a mistake—?*

"My lands may be far from Edo, but my ancestor's loyalty to the Shogun gives me a place at his side. Some fool has seated Lord Sakai closer to His Highness than I."

Her father did no so much as glance back at her, but she saw the muscles tighten in his shoulders as if he sensed her humiliation. "It was my mistake," he said humbly. "Please forgive me."

He bowed in apology, and Mika felt her own shame double. It had been her spiteful whim when she arranged the seating that had placed her father in this position. He had trusted her with the power of a *daimyo,* and she had used it like a spoiled child.

Lord Kira gestured with his fan, magnanimous in victory. "Forgive me for mentioning it. Your welcome is splendid. I look forward to the tournament." His smiled widened, almost good-natured, and she wondered what he meant by that.

Kai stood as close as he could to the front of the crowd of commoners, his weariness from the long day of standing worsened by the pain in his injured back. But he realized that this was a once-in-a-lifetime sight . . . and one he would not have been able to watch even if he'd survived the *kirin*'s wound, if Mika had not come to him and helped him treat it.

The memory of what else had occurred between them that night filled him with a different kind of pain that somehow made the experience of today seem all the more dazzling to his eyes.

He savored the wonder of its ephemeral pageantry as he did the fragile beauty of the cherry blossoms still painting the countryside in colors of spring, or the fireflies that would return, seeking lovers, as soon as twilight fell on the fields, reminding him with each brief flash of the truth of their lives . . . of all lives.

He pushed his way a little further forward, as he had been doing all day—trailing in the wake of the food-sellers, or following a handful of soldiers who weren't in the Honor Guard, who kept maneuvering for a better view while they watched over the crowd.

He spotted the deep indigo and silver, the octopus *mon,* of the Kira clan. Long ago he had learned from idle gossip that, out of envy and greed, Lord Kira had worked tirelessly to cause Lord Asano trouble with the Shogun. It occurred to Kai that for a small domain like Kira's, deep in the mountains and far from the sea, an octopus was hardly an auspicious clan symbol . . . but then it struck him that the grasping tentacles described Lord Kira's intentions all too well.

Kira was strikingly handsome, dressed in the height of Edo style, and wearing the insignia of a chancellor to the Shogun—whatever else he was, or intended to be. And Kai did not miss the fact that he spent more time gazing up at Mika than he did greeting her father.

Kai glanced again at Mika where she kneeled on the platform behind Lord Asano, enjoying this long-overdue acknowledgement of the Asano clan, and the splendor of the scene. He had not been able to catch her gaze once, all day, although whether that was intentional—or even whether it was his fault, or her choice—he wasn't sure. But his mouth pulled down when he saw her notice Lord Kira's unabashed stare and start to smile back at him.

Abruptly Kai looked away from all of them, pulling together the ragged edges of his faded cotton kimono, which he had done his best to mend and scrub clean of blood before the ceremony today. He had even covered it with the now-sleeveless vest that had once been someone's jacket, and was the only semi-respectable piece of clothing he owned. And yet he suddenly felt ashamed of his appearance in a way he never had before, as if he might as well have come here wearing nothing but a loincloth.

But he couldn't keep himself from looking back again, suddenly filled with envy for Lord Kira . . . and with helpless longing as he looked at Mika, in her exquisitely dyed silks, with her shining black hair piled high on her head and held in place by combs that dangled pearls, and hairpins carved from jade, and carnelian. Prominent among them was the ivory hawk's feather she had worn proudly since she was a girl. She was dressed in Ako's colors of red and gold, mingled with a glowing profusion of the shades in between. To see her was to see the sun rise on the first morning of Midsummer. . . .

As he watched her go on looking at Lord Kira, her face abruptly changed, as if Kira had suddenly slapped her from where he stood down below; she frowned, refusing to look his way again.

It took Kai a moment to realize why her expression had changed—that she had only now recognized her father's enemy. But before that moment passed, sudden hope at her anger had stunned him . . . letting love, loss, and frustration try to force him forward through the crowd.

The iron self-control that had been beaten into him so long ago was all that saved him—driving the blind emotions back down into the darkness where they belonged. Instead, he held himself perfectly still, holding even his breath. Not acting was all he could ever allow himself to do: *for Mika's sake, for Lord Asano's sake, for his own.*

Mika gazed toward the gates again as he looked on, as if she was suddenly impatient for the Shogun to appear and put an end to their seemingly endless day.

The Shogun did not arrive until almost nightfall. As the sun set and the shadows grew long, a guard called out from the main watchtower that he had sighted the Shogun's procession topping a distant rise in the road. Everyone shifted positions, moving as far as they dared, to catch a glimpse of gold and black banners bearing the Tokugawa *mon* in the last rays of the setting sun.

Kai managed a bare glimpse of the Shogun's procession cresting the hill, before he looked back at Lord Asano still standing in the courtyard, spear-straight, waiting at the head of the line of *daimyo,* who had all made certain to arrive before the Shogun in order to greet him with proper honor.

Kai focused again on patience, on the safe, impersonal anticipation of actually seeing the Shogun and his retinue, something he had never expected to see in his lifetime—although until now that fact had never mattered to him in the slightest. But it served well enough to keep his restless mind off himself. The unexpected, conflicting emotions he had been forced to control had pushed him closer to the edge of total exhaustion than he'd been all day. But he would have to stay, and keep standing as straight as Lord Asano himself, at least until he had seen the Shogun. Then he could leave, at last, because there was nothing more to keep him here. . . .

Hundreds of ornate lanterns illuminated the way for the Shogun's procession as it passed over the bridge and entered the castle—the pageantry of the entourage's different colors and patterns of flags, banners, and pennants, and the resplendent garments of the courtiers who began to fill the courtyard, was breathtaking. Their splendor was reflected in the castle's decorations, Ako's brilliant clan colors standing out even in lantern-light among the banners of the other attending clans.

Kai's attention wandered everywhere as he lost himself in the display again, taking in the riot of colors, the astonishing designs—flowers, trees, landscapes, exotic birds and their plumage—among the robes worn by the court lords and ladies, as well as the wives and concubines of the various *daimyo.*

He caught sight of one young woman among them who made his gaze stumble the way Mika's had when she looked at Lord Kira. The concubine's kimono and robes were dyed and embellished with subtle hints of color dappling a background of countless variegated greens that he had only seen deep in the forest—and only then on rare occasions, when something magical sent sunlight showering down through the canopy of leaves onto blooming shrubs, windswept grasses, the limpid flow of streams. . . . He felt as if he was seeing not just another woman, but a spirit of the wild places that had taken human form. There was something almost magical about her as well, to his eyes—an aura of the myriad *kami*, the spirits that all together made up the soul of untouched, ancient places like the one where he had spent his childhood.

He glanced up, and saw above her head not sky but the octopus banner of clan Kira.

As if she had sensed his stare or his fascination, the young woman looked back over her shoulder. She gazed directly at him, without hesitation, as if she knew exactly what she was searching for, and who she would find.

As her eyes struck his, her stare penetrated his thoughts clear to his soul, with the blinding impact of a black-lantern—but not before he realized that one of her eyes was brown, and the other was ice blue.

The shock of recognition broke her spell, and before his eyes shut her out, his mind said, *I know you. . . .*

When she saw his face change, she turned away abruptly. With an arrogant toss of her head, she moved deeper into the gathering of women, where he quickly lost sight of her.

Unnerved by the encounter, he looked back at Mika, and found her staring at him. For the first time all day, they had looked toward each other at the same time, and for just a moment their gazes locked.

But before he could even be sure what her expression really was, there was a sudden stirring throughout the courtyard, and Mika looked away again.

The Shogun himself had arrived, at last.

Lord Asano's Honor Guard separated, clearing a wider path for the line of horsemen that entered the courtyard. The Shogun's escort, on foot and on horseback, wore the richest, most elaborate armor Kai had ever seen, its black-lacquered plates stitched together with saffron-dyed silk, and the Tokugawa *mon* displayed prominently in gold leaf on their cuirasses. The banners and flags that surrounded the Shogun bore every imaginable variation of the Tokugawa colors, all of them prominently featuring his clan *mon* of triple hollyhock leaves inside a circle, their tips meeting like spear points at its center.

The Shogun himself was, not surprisingly, the most impressive sight of all, his black armor nearly covered in gold, with red and gold decorative silk stitching the plates together, and a tall helmet with golden rays formed like spearheads and needles transforming his *mon* into the image of a rising sun. He rode an enormous warhorse that made him seem larger than the men around him . . . larger than life.

Behind them came the Shogun's chief advisors and more courtiers in elaborately carved and decorated palanquins suspended from poles borne by servants, plus porters carrying enough baggage to outfit a small palace, with still more troops and standard-bearers bringing up the rear.

The Shogun began to dismount, and everyone standing in the courtyard fell to their knees and bowed, arms outstretched on the ground, as he stood gazing around in apparent gratification.

His adjutant dismounted in front of Lord Asano, and announced to the air above his head, "Asano Naganori, ruler of Ako—Shogun Tokugawa Tsunayoshi, Lord of the Provinces and Master of all Japan, thanks you for your welcome." He bowed from the waist, apparently the signal for everyone else to rise. Lord Asano got to his feet first, and made a return bow of acknowledgement and gratitude as the rest of the crowd found its feet, barely even daring to whisper.

The Shogun opened an immense gilded metal war fan with a red circle, also a symbol of the sun, prominently painted on it. He gestured with the fan, and retainers came forward one by one, presenting Lord Asano with a seemingly endless array of rich and beautiful gifts as a sign of his favor.

Kai looked away, finding himself oddly disappointed and unimpressed. The Shogun was a man who ruled an entire nation, but still found it necessary to proclaim his status with such an outward show of importance that his armor could have come here on its own to represent him, leaving the man in Edo.

He glanced at Lord Kira, whose face was a mask of

expressionless propriety as he watched his rival being so greatly honored.

He searched the gathered women waiting silently behind their men, looking especially for the one in green who sheltered beneath the banner of Lord Kira, with one earth brown eye, and one that was pale blue like a winter sky . . . He did not find her. Half frowning with concern, he turned and began to work his way back through the crowd, moving slowly toward the rear.

Oishi crossed the lantern-lit upper courtyard, carrying his helmet under his arm. His duties as chief retainer and head of the Honor Guard for this day were finally over, and he wanted only the sanctuary of his home and family. Everything had gone flawlessly, as far as he could tell. The Shogun and his retinue, the visiting *daimyo,* and their countless retainers, women, animals, and baggage, plus the servants whose responsibility it was to care for them, had all been properly fed, according to their rank, and then securely stowed in their designated quarters for the night.

The palace and the upper courtyard's guest rooms were completely filled, to the extent that his unmarried senior officers had had to relocate to the barracks in the lower courtyard for the duration: A place for everyone, and everyone in their place, according to the Shogun's personal scheme of things. . . .

One of the last faces he had seen tonight, although not because its owner was the least of their honored guests—far from it—was Lord Kira's. The man had smiled at him. Merely smiled . . . but there was something in the shadow behind his smile that had turned Oishi's stomach.

He had no reason for such a reaction, other than his lord's history with Kira. Perhaps it was just that he hadn't had time to eat—barely enough time for a sip of water—all day. But still, something about the encounter plagued him. He hoped that Riku would be in the mood to massage his back after dinner.

He stopped dead as he reached the entrance of his own home; his frown deepened with genuine annoyance.

The halfbreed Kai was waiting for him on his veranda. At least Lord Asano's head tracker had not dared to foul the interior of his home; but just the sight of that misbegotten wretch, here in the upper courtyard, barring his own doorway, was suddenly one thing more than he could endure.

Kai kneeled and bowed deeply, keeping his eyes downcast.

"What do you want?" Oishi snapped, as hours of fatigue and years of resentment pushed the words out of his mouth.

Kai raised his head, and Oishi's mouth thinned with impatience as the halfbreed struggled simply to find the words to address him. Kai looked as exhausted as Oishi felt—possibly worse, although probably not for the same reasons.

Oishi's eyes turned to flint as the sudden memory of the dead *kirin*, and the guilty secret not even Kai or Yasuno knew he shared with them, worsened his bad mood.

At last the halfbreed took a deep breath and said, "At the hunt last week, I saw . . . a fox. I didn't realize at the time that it was a *kitsune*."

Oishi stared at him, his expression changing for the worse. "A witch—?" he said, barely keeping the scorn out of his voice. He could have listed until dawn the things Kai was, and was not. That he was also a superstitious fool hardly came as a surprise.

There were no *kitsune* in Ako; uncanny shape-shifters who could take animal forms belonged in deep mountain forests, like *kirin*. For a *kirin* to appear here had been hard enough for him to accept. Did the halfbreed expect him to believe that seeing a fox meant Ako was being overrun with *yokai*?

But Kai held his gaze, and nodded. "I believe I saw the same creature again tonight—" He broke off, seeing Oishi's complete lack of response, as if even he realized how unlikely his story sounded. But his face only became more stubborn as he added, “She was in human form. Among the nobles' concubines.”

Oishi glanced down, considering the words, but when he looked up again, his expression was unchanged.

A spark of frustration showed in the halfbreed's shadowed eyes. “I came to you because I thought it might be a bad omen for his Lordship and Lady Asano.”

Oishi studied his face more closely this time, seeing the genuine concern on it. The one place where his life, or his mind, and Kai's intersected was in their complete loyalty to their lord and his only child. That explained why Kai had found the nerve to come here, to speak directly to him, to tell him such an incredible tale. . . . But it was still nothing more than an incredible tale.

“They say only demons have the power to see past a witch's disguise. Are you a demon—?” His voice dared the halfbreed to answer with an affirmative. There was no need to hide the contempt he felt here, now, when Lord Asano would not see or overhear it, and he could be as brutal as he had long wanted to be.

The spark in Kai's eyes turned to ash, as he suddenly realized the truth behind Oishi's seeming indifference . . . that Oishi despised him as completely as any of Lord Asano's other retainers, and always had. “No,” he said flatly.

Oishi shrugged. “Then I suggest you were simply bewitched by a beautiful girl.” He pushed past the halfbreed as if he had ceased to exist and entered his house, sliding the door shut too hard behind him, leaving Kai on his knees, alone in the silent courtyard.

5

The day of the tournament dawned as beautifully as if even Amaterasu, goddess of the sun and ancestor to the emperors of Japan, had chosen to honor the Shogun's visit to Ako with her shining presence.

The open area in the lower courtyard that was normally set aside for combat training had been temporarily transformed into an immense pavilion, open to the sky, its sections and corridors created by hundreds of *tobari* set up end to end. The six-foot-tall segmented curtains, which had traditionally been used for temporary military field headquarters, were also employed for outdoor events on a vast scale like this.

The main point of interest in the curtained-off maze was the tournament arena, which had been set up for today's duels designed to showcase the skills of the attending *daimyo*'s best swordsmen.

The *tobari* had been decorated with the Asano clan *mon* of crossed hawk feathers within a circle. The designs were printed in red and gold every few feet along the reams of pale cloth. The Asano *mon* was interspersed with, and in places supplanted by, the *mon* of the Tokugawa, printed in gold and black along the pathway that led to the covered viewing stand that had been erected for the Shogun, his courtiers, and Lord Asano's other most honored guests. It had been constructed at the point along the side of the arena that provided the best view of the duels; close by it were stands and sectioned-off areas for the ranking samurai of Ako, and for those serving the other lords.

In a tradition that still lingered from the days when *tobari* were military equipment, and the Shogun had been first among warlords, not politicians, the seating for the event remained humble camp stools, with the addition of kneeling cushions for whatever ladies might attend at the bidding of their lords.

Oishi stood alongside Lord Asano and Lady Mika as they greeted the dignitaries arriving to watch the tournament. The most highly ranked Asano officers were already seated in their private viewing area, by Oishi's order, while other samurai he knew he could depend on ringed the arena to stand guard. All of them wore the new, bright red lacquered armor that Lord Asano had commissioned just for the Shogun's visit; all of them were well-armed. Any hint of laxness in the security at Ako Castle, any incident at all that might conceivably bring harm to the Shogun, had to be prevented at all costs.

An incident would cost their lord his honor, at best . . . at worst, his lands, his life, and possibly even his daughter's life as well. The samurai of Ako would become ronin, disgraced and masterless, with no way of supporting themselves, let alone their families. Oishi was well aware that it had happened to others before, too often, for too little reason. . . .

He suddenly had another moment of sickening insight into the peril that had ruled the lives of men like him in the Age of Wars—when he would have been the commander of Lord Asano's army, not simply the head bureaucrat in an army of clerks. For all their martial arts training—even ordeals like treading water in full armor while aiming at a target with bow and arrow—the closest anyone here had ever come to the kind of danger that men knew in real warfare was when they had confronted the *kirin*.

He was still obsessed by the memory of how close to disaster they had come that day . . . how poorly they would have fared, in an age when there had been only two ways to return from battle: with an enemy's head tied to your saddle . . . or missing your own.

Gods. . . . He pressed his fingers against his eyes. *Why was he even thinking of such things now?* He cursed Kai, whose unlikely presence and unnerving portents on his very doorstep last night had left him plagued by nightmares, when he had so desperately needed sleep.

Mika glanced over at Oishi as she heard him sigh, and saw him rub his eyes; her forehead furrowed in sympathy. She looked back at her father, who still stood as straight and alert as if their ages were reversed, proudly holding a fan of hawk's feathers in his hand. She wondered how many days he would have to spend resting when the double ordeal of the *kirin* hunt and the Shogun's visit was finally over.

She looked toward the viewing stands as the Shogun and his retinue moved sedately toward their seats. Her eyes were distracted by the troupe of performers she had hired to entertain before the dueling began. The actors were performing a crowd-pleasing *kagura* dance from a *Noh* drama, the title of which she had been told when she hired them, although she had forgotten it in all that had happened since.

At least, she thought, their masks and costumes were as elaborate and beautifully made, their performance as sophisticated and richly nuanced as their leader, a man named Kawatake, had given his word they would be. His word would have meant little except that she knew his troupe had performed for the Emperor, which made her confident they were worthy of entertaining the Shogun. The Emperor might only be a figurehead with no real power now, but he was descended from Japan's own gods, and as a living symbol of their favor he held a revered, if sheltered, place at the top of society.

She spotted Kawatake himself at the front of the players—recognizing the grace and controlled flourish of his movements, even though he wore a traditional demon mask. He danced and struck poses as dramatically as if he had been born to portray the larger-than-life gods and legendary heroes that were the subject of *Noh* dramas. *Perhaps he had,* she thought . . . if, as it seemed to her more and more, destiny controlled all their lives, struggle though they might to change their fate.

She looked away from them, her eyes moving restlessly around the open arena. Now that the first rush of excitement had passed, she was as weary of standing and waiting while their guests were seated as she had become of preparations and details. But she shared her father's justifiable satisfaction at the sight of Ako's samurai, looking every inch the proud and noble men they were in their new armor . . . until the thought led her to remember the one man whose face she would not even see today . . . the one who truly deserved to be their champion on the field.

She looked up at the stands where Oishi's ranking officers sat, seeing Hazama, Isogai, Hara. She tried to imagine Kai sitting among them in fine armor bearing the Asano crest, and felt herself grow more unhappy by the moment. And then suddenly her eyes encountered the face of the captain the others all called "Basho." As he caught her eye he smiled, and actually winked at her, startling her out of her haze of sorrow.

She smiled back at him; her smile widened as she remembered their first meeting.

In her mind Mika saw her childhood self, lost in misery, sitting among autumn-bright red maple leaves on the cold flagstones of the courtyard, until it was hard to tell where her kimono ended and the world began . . . sitting and weeping, as she had done for days, deaf to the cajoling and pleading of her nursemaids, certain that nothing could ever stop her tears, or end her sorrow. She had been eight years old when her mother died, and her father had taken to his chambers, sunk in such grief that he could not even remember his own daughter's needs.

And then the warrior Basho had passed by, looking like all the rest of her father's grim, unresponsive retainers, except for his size—and the fact that he covered his head with a cowl of white cloth because he had been in a monastery until recently, and trained by warrior monks. It only made him more disturbing to look at.

But unlike all the others, Basho had noticed her weeping among the leaves, and stopped to look at her. And then, after a long moment, he had approached her, bowed deeply, and said, "Lady Mika, you are a *daimyo*'s daughter, and as brave as any warrior. Would you like to stand guard with me on the inner wall awhile?"

She had looked up at him, so startled by his presence that she hiccuped and covered her mouth. A smile came out of hiding on his face, and widened until he looked like the boy he really was. She had been as startled by his smile as she had been by his speaking to her . . . and completely nonplussed by his request. She couldn't remember what she had said in reply, caught between her grief and sudden amazement. But somehow she had found herself climbing the steps to a sentries' lookout on the high wall, with her nursemaids following behind her like anxious geese.

Standing atop the wall for the first time, she had looked out across Ako, its fields and forests, the river and the sky, from a completely new perspective. The strong breeze from the sea that set her hair streaming had made her feel like she was flying, as Basho pointed out rice paddies and farmers' villages, named trees on the hillsides by their autumn colors, and even pointed out the sea itself, which she had never realized lay so close.

And then he had turned her attention to the sky. When he was at the monastery, he said, he would lie in the grass and imagine he was at the bottom of the sky, as if it were the sea, and wonder how it might feel to float up from the depths into all that blue. . . . How sometimes the clouds drifting overhead took on the shapes of strange fish in his imagination, or rabbits, or dogs, or caricatures of people he knew, changing from one form into another like magic.

He had asked her then what she saw and, as she looked up at the clouds, helped her to imagine they were taking on the most absurd shapes her mind could think of . . . until, sometime later, she had been shocked to realize that she was laughing and pointing, no longer sitting like a stone and silently weeping. Her face and sleeves were dry of tears for the first time since her mother had died. Somehow, now, she felt as tall and strong as Basho, as if she had been transformed like the clouds into something new—something much greater and more far-seeing than a grieving little girl could possibly hope to be.

She had asked Basho if her mother might appear to her in a cloud-form. He had explained that her mother's spirit was a part of all things now: the sky, the land of Ako, and all its people both inside the castle and outside it . . . but especially a part of her own heart, and her father's.

His words had filled her with the comfort she had needed, the willingness to rejoin life, carrying her mother's love with her like a precious treasure. And as she had felt herself changed, she became determined to make her father come out of his chambers and climb with her to the top of the wall, to share what she had learned.

"Basho!" an angry voice had suddenly called out, and Mika had seen Oishi Yoshio—only the chief retainer's son, with the haircut of a boy, and the overconfidence of an almost-man, striding toward them along the parapet. "What in—"

He had stopped short as he recognized Mika, and realized that the women were all nursemaids. He made a deep bow. "Lady Mika, forgive me! I didn't . . . um, forgive me for interrupting—"

When he straightened up again, his face was bright red,

and Mika had giggled. "Oh, it's all right." She had waved a hand at him, and then directed his attention to the sky, to make him stop looking so stupid. "Can you can find the rabbit?"

She had turned back to Basho, and in front of Oishi and her shocked attendants gotten down on her knees and prostrated herself at his feet, as formally as she might have to the merciful Buddha. Gravely she had thanked him for his wisdom.

She still recalled that as she got to her feet and abruptly ordered her nursemaids to come with her to the *daimyo,* Mistress Haru—the only one of them who had not been struck speechless—had quietly asked Basho how he had brought such a change over her.

He had smiled and shaken his head, as if it was not his doing at all. "Laughing is spending time with the gods," he said.

And then he and Oishi had walked away.

Later Oishi had told her Basho was the monk-warrior's nickname; that the other men had started calling him "Basho" after the famous poet, because her father had judged his poetry the best in a contest they'd held. Why poetry was a skill so valued by samurai had remained a mystery to her, until she grew old enough to read *The Book of Five Rings*.

Mika's mind returned abruptly to the present as she remembered its author, the legendary swordsman Miyamoto Musashi . . . and thought of Kai. In her heart resentment burned over the fact that Kai was not even allowed to be here today, watching, let alone fighting for Ako.

Suddenly afraid that her resentful thoughts might attract misfortune, she began a brief, silent prayer to the Shining Ancestress, asking her to smile down on the warrior who had stolen Kai's rightful place—if only to preserve Ako's honor.

A voice interrupted her prayer before she could finish

it—a voice she recognized, but not one she had ever wanted to hear again.

Lord Kira said, from behind them, "I had no idea your concubine was so lovely, Lord Asano."

Her father turned to face him, as she turned crimson with humiliation and outrage beneath the white face powder of her formal makeup. Oishi stepped up beside her father, allowing her a moment's grace to get her emotions under control before Lord Kira could glimpse the effect the words had had on her.

"She is my *daughter,*" her father said, his voice as cold as the winter sea.

As she turned to glare at Kira, her eyes as cold as the wind off that sea, he covered his face with his hand in feigned embarrassment; it changed nothing about her expression. *If she were only a man—* Her hands pressed the wide sash that circled her waist. The *obi* was not only a lovely piece of cloth. It was also a hiding place for a dagger that every samurai woman kept close to her heart.

"Forgive me, my lady," Kira said, with a humility that from anyone else she would have sworn was utterly sincere. No wonder he was a favorite of the Shogun, and his advisor on all matters of protocol . . . she had never met a better liar. He gazed into her eyes as though they were not barring his way like a wall of ice and bowed gently to her. He glanced at her father, and then back at her. "Now that I see how beautiful you are, I can understand why your father has never taken another wife."

Even though she could find nothing wrong with the words, or the way he spoke them, Mika felt his subtle insinuation slide across her skin like a snake's tongue. She glanced at her father, and saw that his eyes had grown even colder, although he said nothing. Oishi shifted from foot to foot, glancing down at the pair of long and short swords he wore thrust through the belt ties of his wide legged *hakama.* Abruptly he pushed his closed fan into the *hakama*'s waistband, and put his hands behind his back. She watched the hands knot into fists.

She looked back at Kira, and found his eyes lingering on her face again as if he couldn't get enough of the sight of it. Her throat tightened like Oishi's hands, strangling a remark that would have cut through Kira as cleanly as the *karou*'s sword and left no more trace than Lord Kira's own poisoned barb. With her body as taut as a drawn bow, she forced herself to make a polite bow in response to the supposed compliment.

Her father stepped forward protectively this time, laying a hand on her arm as he moved in front of her. But before he could say anything, Lord Kira turned to face him, and said, "May I ask that your daughter sit with us? I should like to make up for my rudeness."

Mika saw the urge to refuse in her father's eyes, and willed him to speak the words.

But once again, Lord Kira's request had been made with such flawless courtesy, both in words and in tone, that there was nothing her father could do but accept, lest he appear pointlessly rude himself.

Oishi remained with them for as long as he could, standing by until they were all seated. Mika was forced to kneel on a cushion between her father and Kira, as if she truly were someone's concubine.

Mika wondered who Kira had been expecting to kneel there beside him. . . . Or had he actually planned this all out ahead of time, so that she would find herself forced into this trap? Was it possible for a man to be more devious than fate itself?

Finally Oishi bowed to her father, and to her, and headed away toward the spot reserved for Ako's senior samurai. Mika watched him depart, his hand resting pointedly on the hilt of his sword as he crossed the short distance to the seating for his senior officers. He turned when he reached them, looking back, keeping his eyes on his lord and lady. But

Mika felt her frustration and unease rise even more as they lost the ready presence of their watchful guardian.

Kai stood with Oishi Chikara, the son of the chief retainer, in the preparation area beside the arena. Here at least he could observe the various lords' champions loosening up and practicing their most finely honed moves before their upcoming duels. There were other Ako samurai here, ones who, like Chikara, did not have the rank to sit or stand somewhere on the field, but at least had the right to peer through the wind-slits in the *tobari* to catch a glimpse of the contest.

Because he was with Chikara, none of the other men had challenged his right to be present, at least. He glanced back at the boy, who was picking through a pile of oak *bokken,* in search of the best one to give to Yasuno. The swordsmen in the matches today were not fighting to the death, and so they were using wooden practice swords instead of *katana.* But the duelists wore full armor, nonetheless, and protective face masks attached to their helmets, because even a blow from a *bokken,* delivered by a skilled swordsman, could be fatal.

The heavy steel-tipped wood could cripple a man or even kill him—and for a blunt instrument, they were deceptively subtle in the way they did it. They couldn't cleave a man from shoulder to heart, or cause so much bleeding with a few non-fatal slashes that he passed out and bled to death. But they could splinter bones, rupture internal organs, or crack skulls . . . often leaving no more than a telltale bruise on the surface. A man might suddenly drop dead from an unsuspected injury hours, or days, later, never even realizing that he had been badly hurt.

Chikara held up his choice for Yasuno's dueling sword, with a question in his eyes. Kai crossed the yard to where he stood and took a close look at the wooden blade, studying the density and straightness of its fine grain, looking for flaws that might mean a weak point. He shook his head.

Rummaging through the swords that remained, he picked out another one—the best of the lot—and tossed it to Chikara. Chikara caught it deftly, left-handed, still holding the other *bokken* in his right; Kai's mouth turned up in a rare smile of approval. Chikara held the two swords against each other, comparing them. He nodded and laid his own choice back on the pile.

Kai considered the irony that, despite the fact that he didn't know a single man at Ako Castle whom he could actually call a friend, he had become the private martial arts tutor of Oishi Chikara, the chief retainer's son.

The *karou*'s son had come on him unexpectedly in the woods, one day in early spring. Chikara had been out wasting his arrows shooting at returning birds and wakening animals, and caught Kai practicing his sword moves with a stick. Kai had never intended for anyone to know that he could handle a sword, since he would never be allowed to touch a real one again. Yasuno had found out . . . but Yasuno would never dare speak of it.

But that day in spring Chikara had seen him, and arrogantly challenged his right even to wield a stick. Chikara had been wearing actual steel, too proud of his newly gained status as a man to leave his clanking swords home while he went out hunting birds and rabbits with a bow. Only the fact that Kai had been so deeply focused on his own movements had kept him from hearing the young idiot long before they ever caught sight of each other.

Kai had let Chikara draw his sword. And then he had knocked the blade out of the boy's hand with one swing of his stick, and upended him with the next.

And then he had picked up Chikara's sword, and placed its point against the boy's throat as he lay on his back on the ground. Pressing just hard enough to break the skin, he had ordered Chikara to swear on the samurai blood trickling down his neck that he would never tell anyone what he had seen.

He had watched the boy swallow a lump of fright as the blade pricked his skin . . . and then the defiant light had come back into Chikara's eyes, and he had sworn he would never tell . . . if Kai would teach him everything he knew.

Kai had given him back his sword without comment, and told him to go home to his father. He had known the risk he was taking—that if Chikara actually told his father what had happened, then Oishi Yoshio would come after him with steel, and the match would not be anything like one-sided. But he had no other choice.

And so the next morning, when he rose barely after dawn, he had found Chikara waiting outside his door, alone in a drizzling rain, holding two wooden practice swords.

From what he had seen since in their practice sessions, Chikara had his father's potential for wielding a *katana*. But the *sensei* of Ako Castle's sword school seemed to value form over function, to the point where he should have been teaching his students calligraphy, not how to kill.

And so Kai had begun to teach Chikara to use a sword as if he was truly fighting for his life.

Chikara gestured at the champion practicing in front of them, drawing Kai's thoughts back to the yard. "He always tries the same trick. Every time he lowers his guard he's about to attack."

Kai gave a laugh. "If you can see it, then he doesn't stand a chance."

"He doesn't stand a chance anyway, against Yasuno," Chikara said, holding up the *bokken*.

Kai looked at him in surprise, just for a second, before he remembered the truth . . . the lie that Chikara would never hear about.

Chikara began to turn away, heading off to give the *bokken* to Yasuno.

"Did you leave an offering at the shrine?" Kai asked suddenly. As he had left his hut this morning, he had stopped at the shrine he had built beside the path, to pray that fortune would smile on Ako today. But someone had been there before him . . . and left a token.

Chikara looked at him, puzzled, and shook his head. "What was it?"

"A feather." Kai shrugged as if it meant nothing. But it had been a hawk's feather. The symbol of Ako; the symbol of a warrior. *If not Chikara, then who? Mika? And if it had been Mika, what had the feather meant—to her, for him . . . ?*

Chikara grinned. "It must have been a sign from the gods. Yasuno is—" He broke off, staring as if his eyes suddenly saw something they couldn't make sense of among the tents behind Kai.

Kai turned to see what he was gaping at, and blinked in disbelief. A man in full armor had just emerged from somewhere in the *tobari* maze—a literal giant of a man, and massively built. In his armor he was nearly half again as tall as Kai, and Kai was taller than most men.

The stranger's armor was made of a peculiar blue-black metal, and constructed like none he had ever seen before—more like an insect's carapace, with subtle, wicked spikes at points that would do the most damage in hand-to-hand combat. The armor covered virtually the entire body of the swordsman; the weight of it alone would have been more than most men could carry and still move effectively, let alone fight. As Kai stared at it, its dull finish seemed to change, scintillating like a beetle's wing.

The swordsman's face mask was no mass-produced protector, either—its expression was like an agonized demon's, or something dragged up from the depths of Enma's hell in a form that was neither wholly dead nor really alive.

Kai shut his eyes, blinked them clear again—but before he could get a second look, the call of drums announced the start of another duel. The warrior was already striding away toward the arena, his movements unnaturally smooth and agile for a man so large.

An incredulous murmur passed through the men clustered

by the gaps in the *tobari*; the sounds of disbelief spread on around the field as everyone watching caught their first glimpse of the samurai in black. The winner of the previous match suddenly raised his *bokken* in a defensive stance; he began to back away as the giant moved across the arena toward him with the inevitability of death.

Sitting back on her heels between her father and Lord Kira, Mika raised her head and stopped fanning herself as the people around her began to murmur and point. Her position on the ground did not provide nearly as good a view of the field or the swordsmen fighting on it as the camp stools on either side of her. She had spent virtually the entire time staring at her hands clasped together in her lap and fidgeting with her carven ivory fan.

Usually she enjoyed skilled displays of the martial arts, the contests that were virtually the only real reminder of the samurai's proud history as warriors . . . unless she allowed herself to think about the hardships and suffering, the maiming, the constant risk of death, that the real heroes must have faced. The fact that her ancestors had found a way not only to triumph over their enemies, but simply to endure a lifetime spent on one blood-soaked battlefield after another during the Age of Wars was the real proof of their skill, their courage, and their honor.

Only that thought could have prepared her for the sight that met her eyes now. A small sound of disbelief and dismay escaped her, as she saw the giant in black armor who was the next challenger. She would not have believed a man could grow that large; she could barely believe it now, even as he stood in the arena before her. Was he truly just another man in armor—?

There were tales about Oda Nobunaga, the most ruthless of the Three Unifiers who had ended the Ages of Wars, that called him "the Demon King." They claimed that even now he plotted his revenge somewhere, because he actually was a demon, and not a mortal man. . . .

A demon. She had heard Kai called "demon" for most of her life, and known the word for what it was—an insult and a lie. But this monstrous—*thing*—couldn't be human, if it was real at all. The warrior's protective face guard hid any sign of his true appearance behind a cast-metal image that made the demon-masks worn by the actors who had performed earlier look like ridiculous caricatures. This was the true face of horror, of evil . . . a night monster . . . a *yokai*. . . .

"Who is that?" she asked. Her voice sounded unsteady as she glanced up at her father.

Lord Kira leaned toward her, with satisfaction on his face as he answered instead, "My fighter."

She turned back to look at him, stricken. Then she looked out into the arena again, as the samurai facing Kira's champion stopped backing away and readied himself to attack. He struck suddenly at his opponent, landing a hard blow on the giant's sword arm.

The black-armored warrior seemed not even to feel it. He slammed his own *bokken* against the defender's side, staggering him. Before the man could catch his balance, the huge samurai knocked him off his feet with a single sweep, then brought the *bokken* down on the man's head so hard that it dented his metal helmet.

The match was over before Mika could finish taking a breath. The other swordsman did not get up again. He didn't even move.

The audience sat in stunned silence for a long moment, before anyone at all could find a voice to speak with, let alone shout or cheer. Mika found herself with her hand covering her mouth as if she had tried to stifle a scream, not even remembering how or when.

Lord Kira leaned toward her again with a reassuring smile. "Your father's champion is next, my lady. I'm sure it will be a more even contest."

Mika locked her hands together again, one clinging to the other until her rings bruised her fingers. But that was all she could do: not looking at either Kira or her father, staring straight ahead at the nightmare in black, but seeing nothing. *Yasuno* . . . Yasuno didn't have a prayer, no matter how many gods she might ask for mercy now. Only Kai could kill a monster. *Only Kai* . . .

"Kai!"

Kai stood watching the fallen samurai's comrades drag his limp body from the field of battle. He wondered if the man was dead. He looked dead . . . and after a blow to the head like that one, he probably might as well be.

"What?" he said, distracted, as he glanced away from the arena. Chikara was hurrying toward him, out of breath and with panic showing in his eyes. "What is it—?" His own look changed to concern, as the drums began again, summoning the next fighter to appear on the field where the giant in black armor, the new victor, stood waiting.

There was no sign of Yasuno, with Chikara or anywhere else. *Had Yasuno lost his nerve?* If he had, Kai thought, he would kill him personally.

But Chikara tugged unceremoniously on his arm, and the look on the young samurai's face said something was very wrong with Yasuno, far worse than an attack of nerves.

Kai followed Chikara back to the tent where Yasuno should have stood ready in his armor by now. Pushing aside the entrance flap, Kai went inside without announcing himself—which would have been pointless, because Yasuno lay flat on his back on the ground, his eyes wide open and staring at nothing.

"What's wrong with him?" Chikara said. "It's like he's in a trance—"

Kai didn't answer, kneeling down beside Yasuno, peering into his glazed eyes. "Did you see anyone near this tent?"

Chikara shook his head. "No one. Only . . . I think I saw a fox."

"A white fox—?" Kai looked up with a sudden frown, to see Chikara nod and stare at him. He looked at Yasuno again, this time noticing a strange, unnatural white tint on Yasuno's eyelashes.

The drums sounded once more. Kai had a sudden vision of the tournament ground: the anxiety on the faces of Mika and Lord Asano; the growing impatience of the crowd . . . of the Shogun . . . as the gigantic samurai paced back and forth alone on the field, registering his scorn for an opponent so craven he wouldn't even set foot in the arena.

He looked up at Chikara, and shook his head. "Get your father."

"There isn't time!" Chikara said desperately. He looked toward Yasuno's armor, still hanging on its stand. Yasuno had never even had a chance to put it on. "If he doesn't fight we'll be disgraced—"

Kai followed his glance toward the armor, seeing the helmet with the protective faceplate that completely disguised a man's appearance, the body armor with the crest of the Asano clan proudly displayed on its cuirass. He could. . . . *No. No, he couldn't.*

As if Chikara had read his mind, the boy said, "They'll never know it was you."

Kai crouched beside Yasuno's senseless body, his hands tightening over the desire to reach out, simply to touch the armor . . . his mind torn between the truth, and the consequences if he dared—

"You can beat him, and they'll never know," Chikara insisted.

Out in the arena, the drums sounded yet again.

Kai pushed to his feet, reaching for the first piece of armor; Chikara leaped forward to help him put it on. *For Ako. For Mika. . . .*

Out in the tournament arena, the tense silence of the crowd was broken as the Shogun suddenly rose from his seat, snapping shut his fan. His gesture of impatience spread through the viewing stand like the ripples from a carp suddenly leaping in a pond. The dignitaries and *daimyo* rose in unison, bowing their heads respectfully. Kira did the same; only Mika saw the trace of smile hidden by the motion.

Just as the Shogun began to walk away, a samurai with the Asano *mon* showing clearly on his armor stepped into the arena. He started forward and then paused, looking toward the stands.

Yasuno. Mika turned to her father, sharing his sudden relief . . . missing the start of surprise that Lord Kira could not entirely conceal.

The Shogun stopped, looking back at the newly arrived swordsman, and at the victorious samurai in black. His interest rekindled, he returned to the platform and sat down again; the rest of the nobles did the same, quickly and obediently. Kira sat down again beside Mika, but this time he didn't even glance at her. He went on staring at the two swordsmen, with something in his expression that almost looked like consternation. She felt only relief that he finally seemed more interested in watching the duel on the field than in staring surreptitiously at her.

She pushed up onto her knees, gazing out at the field too, her first concern back in her thoughts again, now that Yasuno had finally appeared. At least he was here . . . but he hadn't been able to kill the *kirin*. Did he have any hope at all, against this monster?

Kai stood in the arena like a man in a waking dream, watching the Shogun and the other lords return and take their seats again. If Chikara had taken another second to get him laced and buckled into Yasuno's armor, it would have been too late.

But it wasn't, and now he was here on the field, and there was no turning back. He had never worn armor before. His body was sweating and trembling, more from the fear of what he was doing here, wearing it, than from the armor's weight. The face mask attached to his helmet was hot and made breathing difficult; his rising panic made it nearly suffocating. His heart was racing as if he'd run all the way from the forest in armor, not just the short distance from Yasuno's tent.

He looked out at the crowd, at Lord Asano and Mika. At Oishi and the samurai of Ako. To win their respect, he suddenly realized, meant more to him than the praise or condemnation of the Shogun himself and all the lords in the land—

He looked again at the swordsman who stood waiting to test him—the giant in black armor. *Kira's champion.* He remembered the white *kitsune . . . Kira's witch.* Everything that was going wrong for Ako was their doing, Kira's plan.

He stared at the strangely coruscating surface of the black armor, and the twisted demonic mask that was its face. The mask wouldn't stay still in his vision, as if it was some insidious parasite trying to work its way in through his eyes, into his brain, to paralyze him with terror. Its eyeholes were lightless tunnels; he couldn't tell if there was anyone—anything at all—looking out at him.

It seemed like forever since he had fought an actual duel. It might as well have been. *And what was he really facing?*

Kai shut his eyes, blocking everything out. *Deep breath. Hold. Center. Exhale.* This wasn't the first time he'd ever fought; or the first time he'd ever fought for his life . . . or even the first time he'd ever fought a demon. *He could do this. He would. He would win—*

He opened his eyes, and the world leaped into focus, as sharp and clear as a crystal. Suddenly he saw his opponent's eyes, as if they had been there all along, staring at him, but he had been afraid to meet them.

The eyes were sulphur-yellow.

But the eyes didn't matter. Its form didn't matter, human or not. As long as it was solid enough to hit with a sword, the thing in front of him was only a thing.

He strode out into the middle of the arena, to a place

before the stands where he could engage Kira's fighter freely, in full view of the crowd. He turned toward the Shogun, and bowed. But his eyes found Mika's face; she seemed to glow in the sunlight, in his vision. Even though she'd never know the truth, the faith she had always had in him was like a beacon, a reminder of all that mattered to him—a charm against anything that had the power to harm him.

He turned back to his opponent; they bowed to each other. Silhouetted against the sun, the samurai in black raised his *bokken*—an animate shadow that loomed over him like the darkest fear in all the world's hearts, forged into human form.

Solid human form.

The crowd was utterly silent as Kai raised his own weapon and began to move, circling like the other warrior did—like Yasuno would have done—in a ritual opening move that let each swordsman observe the other in motion.

Abruptly Kira's champion stopped circling and lunged. His *bokken* rose and fell so fast that the movement was barely even a blur.

It came down directly where Kai had been standing a second before; but Kai was no longer there, leaping aside even faster, into a counterattack.

In the stands, Mika exchanged impressed glances with her father. Maybe she had misjudged Yasuno. Maybe he would rise to this seemingly impossible challenge, after all.

In the separate area where the senior samurai of Ako sat watching, Oishi glanced over at the others and saw them exchanging looks that ranged from surprised to puzzled. He felt his own mind run the entire gamut of emotions as he watched the two swordsmen maneuver around one another, continuously in motion, feinting and striking. Every move had been inconclusive so far—although at least Yasuno had already lasted longer than the swordsman before him. His moves seemed to be what Oishi would have expected. And yet there was something he couldn't put his finger on, in the quickness of Yasuno's responses, the fluidity of his style. . . .

He watched Ako's champion stand still, after having dodged an overhead strike at blinding speed; saw him wait with unnerving calm as the giant came after him, clearly angered by the missed opportunity to fell his opponent with one blow.

Waiting . . . for the black-armored samurai to get within range. *Waiting* . . . to determine his next move. *Yasuno had never waited for anything in his life; especially for a fight to come to him.* He had always been too impulsive for his own good.

As the samurai in black crossed the invisible line that Oishi read as the point where his longer reach brought his *bokken* within striking range of Yasuno, Yasuno unexpectedly made his move. Again with a quickness and agility that Oishi had never seen before, Yasuno attacked: The steel tip of his own *bokken* shone like a blazing brand in the sunlight as he ducked under the giant's slantwise downstroke and struck at his knee—one of the few vulnerable points someone could hope to hit on a man that size, in order to bring him down quickly.

The black-armored swordsman seemed to realize the same thing—somehow he managed to block the hit. But the trajectory of Yasuno's *bokken* reversed with a speed that shouldn't have been possible, as if it had rebounded off his opponent's strike, rising toward the giant's outstretched sword arm—toward a joining-point in his armor, or his inner elbow, or the fragile bone in his forearm—

The giant moved with equal speed: His own weapon blocked the blow, and the two *bokken* collided full-force in midair.

The *crack* echoed through the castle grounds as both weapons shattered on impact. The crowds in the stands, and the men ringing the perimeter, reacted with the same shouts of astonished disbelief.

The two swordsmen were still on their feet, facing each

other, holding the remains of their swords. After a long moment in which neither of them moved, they turned slowly toward the viewing stand, where the Shogun was watching along with the cheering crowd.

A draw? Oishi thought—almost prayed—feeling hope and incredulity tighten like a twisted rope inside his chest until he could barely inhale. A draw was probably the best thing that could happen, the best that they could possibly hope for, under circumstances like these. Yasuno had been absurdly lucky so far. *If the Shogun would just let it end—*

But he saw Lord Kira lean away from Mika for once bending his head toward the Shogun to murmur something in his ear.

The Shogun sat for a moment, considering whatever the request had been. Then he nodded, and gestured to his adjutant, who shouted out an order.

As if someone had been prepared all along for the summons, two steel-bladed swords were carried out onto the field. One was a normal *katana,* which the bearer passed to Yasuno. But the sword the other man handed to Kira's champion was made of the same strange blue-black steel as his armor, and nearly the length of a spear, but all curving blade to its extended hilt.

An odachi*—?* Oishi shook his head in disbelief. *Odachi,* great-swords, had been used by horsemen to cut down foot soldiers on the battlefield. Few normal men could draw one from its sheath without help, let alone fight a duel with one. *Only a giant—*

An ordinary man with a single katana, *against an* odachi *in the hands of a giant.* This duel had just become a death match. . . . *No. Even worse: This was murder.*

His hand closed over his own sword hilt and tightened; he heard an angry muttering pass through the men seated beside him. In the dignitaries' stand, Lord Asano turned to look coldly at Lord Kira, as if he too realized that this must have been Kira's intent the entire time.

The black-armored swordsman swung at Yasuno without

even a preliminary feint, bringing his sword across in an arc meant to cut his opponent in half. Yasuno dropped to his knees and flung himself flat on his back as the sword swept over him. He was up again before anyone could blink, bringing his *katana* up with him. Its edge struck the flat of the *odachi*'s extended blade at a right angle, with a momentum that should have snapped the black sword in two.

But the blow had no effect. The *katana* rebounded in a shower of sparks. And then he was rolling to escape as Kira's swordsman hacked down at him with a move that seemed to absorb the impact of Yasuno's hit and double it.

Yasuno leaped to his feet; one foot came down on the end of the giant's sword as it struck the dirt. He took two impossible strides up the *odachi*'s length and then pushed off, leaping into the air. His *katana* struck a glancing blow off his opponent's helmet, but again to no effect. The giant didn't even shake his head; his hand rose and slapped at Yasuno like a gnat as Yasuno dropped back toward the ground.

The blow connected, but Yasuno somersaulted in midair, landing on his feet. He staggered two steps back, but even as he did he brought his sword around to catch the *odachi*'s next side-angled swing and divert it past his body. Before Kira's swordsman had recovered his momentum, Yasuno dove between his braced legs, and rolling again, slashed at his ankle.

The *katana* struck chain mail, and he barely avoided a backward kick, as the black-armored samurai swung around with furious speed, bringing his sword around with him. Yasuno threw himself against the swordsman's pivoting leg as he diverted the next strike, trying to drive his opponent off balance; but he might as well have tried to push over a tree.

He slid around to the front, forcing the giant to turn back again, gaining a split second's grace, but no accessible target for his sword before the other man's blade was coming at him again—

If the spectators had been excited before, they were left

speechless now, watching the preternatural dance of two bodies in motion around each other, to the music of constantly clashing swords, the dazzling rain of sparks from steel-on-steel—a dance of death that seemed to be taking place outside of their normal reality, as if they were witnessing a legend brought to life.

Oishi watched with the other Ako samurai, all of them sitting as rapt as the gaping nobles in the stands, but tracking each virtually invisible blow and parry with the eyes of trained swordsmen.

Motion in an unexpected quadrant distracted Oishi for a moment; he saw that a group of the Ako samurai who had been watching from behind the *tobari* had gathered at the entrance to the practice area for a better view, all of them so caught up in the duel that some were actually standing unprotected in the open at the edge of the arena. He spotted Chikara among them, saw the pride and awe that filled his son's face, along with something more than belief—

In the seats beside him, Basho shook his head. Leaning forward, he muttered, "Yasuno isn't that good a fighter. . . ." Hazama and Isogai laughed, assuming he was making a joke; Yasuno was his best friend. But Oishi glanced at Basho's eyes, and saw that he was completely serious.

And correct. When had Yasuno learned how to fly—? Oishi frowned. He'd never seen anyone this good . . . except the samurai in black armor. *This duel was impossible.* Even if Yasuno had been a far better swordsman than any of them suspected, where and when had he learned techniques like the ones he was using now? The longer the fight went on, the less the moves Ako's champion made seemed familiar, or even recognizable. Ako's sword master had never taught them to move like this; it wasn't even a fighting style Oishi could put a name to.

And yet, he *had* seen some of those unorthodox moves . . . recently. He suddenly remembered that after seeing how Chikara had ended his duel with Jinnai, he'd been keeping a closer eye on his son's solitary practice sessions.

He forced his eyes away from the match again to glance at Chikara, at the look in his son's eyes, the expression on his face. Suddenly Oishi was not only sure that the moves looked familiar, he was certain that it really wasn't Yasuno fighting out there . . . and almost as certain that he knew who had taken Yasuno's place. His hand went to his own sword again, as all trace of hope disappeared from his face.

Kira's champion swung and struck a brutal blow with his sword that Ya—*no, not Yasuno,* the one fighting in his place—parried, as deftly as before. But this time he stumbled, as if the blow had knocked him off balance. *Was he tiring?* How long could any man's strength hold out, against an enemy like that? *This was what it truly meant to fight for your life. . . .*

But as the giant lunged, following through on his seeming advantage, the Ako swordsman ducked and spun in a graceful arc, and caught him by surprise; the *katana* flashed toward the giant's unguarded flank—

As it slammed into the black armor, the *katana*'s forged steel blade shattered like glass. The watching crowd gave a collective gasp of shock.

The Ako swordsman froze, staring in disbelief at the bladeless hilt of his sword still clutched in his hands. And in the split second that he spent not in motion, Kira's samurai swung a massive, armored elbow, and caught him full in the face.

Ako's champion flew ten feet through the air toward the viewing stands before he crashed to the ground. The audience members gasped again; there were shouts and cries as some of the watchers even rose to their feet.

And then the entire world stopped.

The helmet and the dented faceplate from the armor of Ako's champion lay twenty feet away from where he had landed . . . letting everyone present see his face, and his true identity.

It was the halfbreed.

Oishi swore out loud this time, but it was lost in the incredulous voices of the men around him. Now the entire crowd was on its feet, staring. Beside the Shogun, Lord Asano was as pale as ash. Lady Mika looked as stunned as if she had taken the blow herself.

Lord Kira's face was as astonished as anyone's . . . but he looked like he'd seen a miracle.

6

Kira's champion strode toward the spot where Kai lay, stunned and motionless in the dirt. The samurai raised his blue-black *odachi* like an executioner, to end the match once and for all.

"Stop!" the Shogun said.

Kira's champion froze at the word—and then slowly, reluctantly, he lowered his weapon as the Shogun himself stepped down from his place in the viewing stand.

One of the men beside Oishi murmured, "They say our Shogun favors dogs. Maybe he'll be merciful. . . ." Several of the others snorted with suppressed laughter.

Oishi turned back from watching the halfbreed's fate play itself out. "Silence!" he hissed, his voice deadly. There was absolutely nothing humorous about this. Their lord had just been publicly humiliated at the most important moment in his life, by the mongrel outcast who owed everything to him—owed him his very life.

How and why the halfbreed had taken Yasuno's place in the tournament was a complete mystery . . . and it seemed as though the only one who knew the answer was his own son.

He watched, transfixed, as the Shogun approached Kai and leaned down to examine his face with morbid fascination.

What Oishi could see of that face looked worse than

usual after the blow it had taken from the giant's armored elbow. The impact had dented his protective face mask and knocked his helmet loose; the helmet had flown nearly to the spot where Oishi and the other samurai waited. The halfbreed was fortunate the blow hadn't smashed his skull in, too . . . although how fortunate remained to be seen. Blood ran freely from his nose and mouth, and a fist-sized bruise had already begun to distort one side of his face, coloring it red and purple.

Kai's eyes opened—or one of them did—as the Shogun took hold of his chin with a hand, turning his battered face from side to side with the casual indifference of a man studying an exotic animal specimen.

Oishi could see that Kai was conscious, though the halfbreed made no protest, not even a sound, as the Shogun prodded and squeezed his face, and pulled apart his lips to look at his teeth. Whether Kai was allowing the callous treatment or merely enduring it, at least by keeping still he made nothing worse.

The Shogun smiled in amusement and gave a slight shake of his head as he straightened up again. As he walked away, leaving Kai on the ground, he passed through the line of his bodyguards and spoke two words: "Kill it."

The Tokugawa samurai circled around Kai, drawing their swords.

"No—!"

Oishi looked back at the viewing stands as he heard a woman's voice cry out the word—a voice he knew too well. He saw Lady Mika leave her place and run from the stands toward the Shogun. She fell to her knees, prostrating herself on the ground before him.

Gods, no. . . . Oishi didn't know whether he merely thought it, or actually said the words out loud, as he saw Mika-*hime* drop to the ground before the Shogun, pleading for the halfbreed's life. Her father, still in the stands, stared at her in confusion that suddenly turned to realization—the realization that, despite everything he had tried to do, one random act of kindness had brought his entire life to this excruciating moment of grief. *That his daughter was in love with Kai. Still was. Had always been. . . .*

Lord Asano lowered his head in sorrow and resignation. The only sound that Oishi could hear was the incongruous billowing and snapping of Ako's banners in the wind.

He forced himself to move, somehow, crossing the motionless world to stand at his lord's side. Lord Asano raised his head, looking back at his *karou* with heartbreak in the depths of his eyes, and his face set with resolve.

"Tono—" Oishi put out his hand unthinkingly, in his own distress and confusion daring to try and stop his lord from what he was about to do, as Lord Asano started down from the stands toward his daughter. Lord Asano shook off his grip and walked on, hurrying protectively to Mika's side.

Oishi stole a glance at Kira. At least Kira made no further move; he stood where he was, looking on with as much genuine surprise as everyone else.

Lord Asano approached the Shogun and dropped to his knees, bowing until his forehead touched the ground. "Forgive me, my lord," he said, "but in Ako the punishment of death is reserved for men alone." He raised his head, glancing toward Kai. "Not animals."

Kai's body spasmed, and he struggled to roll over; he fell back, as if the words were the deathblow to all that had been keeping him alive. But Mika raised her head to gaze at her father, as if she realized that despite his shock and disapproval, he was humbling himself for her.

"The fault is mine," Lord Asano said.

The Shogun stared down in grave disappointment at the lord of Ako and his daughter alongside him. Behind them, Lord Kira looked on with all the other *daimyo*; his face was like a carnivore's as he savored his victory. Oishi turned away, staring out across the arena at nothing, seeing even less, unable to bear the pain of watching the scene before and around him any longer.

The Shogun turned to his adjutant, and pointed at Kai. "Strip him of his armor, and beat him."

Lord Asano bowed low again as the Shogun turned and left the arena, his guards following.

Mika raised her head again to look at her father, and then at Kai, unable to keep her eyes off him even now, when all that showed in her gaze was her anguish.

The Shogun's adjutant called out to the samurai of Ako still waiting uncertainly in the stands, commanding them to come forward and deliver the halfbreed's punishment. They obeyed silently, unable to ignore the command but uncertain about what to do. Hazama looked toward Oishi, still standing by the empty seat of Lord Asano.

Oishi stared back at him, painfully aware that everyone's attention was suddenly focused on him; feeling as if the last of his own dignity had been stripped away.

He glanced toward the place where Kai lay, helpless to defend himself; images of how the halfbreed had moved, how he had fought, flickered like lightning inside his head. No matter why Kai had taken Yasuno's place, he had fought for Ako's honor—not like a samurai, but like a demon. None of the samurai here would have stood a chance against Kira's champion, even if he hadn't been wearing armor that could shatter a *katana*. But Kai had fought him like an equal—he would have been victorious, if he'd ever had an honest chance of winning—something Yasuno could never have achieved. Kai's slaying the *kirin* had been no fluke.

It wasn't right. Nothing made sense to him: Instead of winning, Kai had been defeated, by what could only have been sorcery. Instead of celebrating the greatest day of his life, Lord Asano had been humbled in the dirt at the Shogun's feet, because the daughter he loved so dearly loved the halfbreed more. Lady Mika had thrown away her father's love, her honor, and her good name for something that wasn't even a human being. Oishi's first impression of Kai had been the right one: *Kai was a demon.*

The thought that the halfbreed could also somehow be

the best and bravest warrior in Ako made the least sense of all. *That mixed-blood bastard . . . he didn't deserve their respect, or even their pity.*

Oishi looked back at Hazama and nodded.

The Ako samurai picked up steel-tipped *bokken* from the pile brought out of the practice yard by the Shogun's men, and surrounded Kai where he lay. The samurai in black looked down at Kai a last time without ever removing his own demonic face mask. And then he stepped aside, leaving his victim to the revenge of his own people.

The Shogun's adjutant waited as well, along with a contingent of his samurai, to make certain that his lord's orders were carried out thoroughly. The other *daimyo* remained in their places, silently witnessing the public humiliation of Ako's champion, all of them aware that the stain of scandal attached to the Asano clan would last far longer.

Oishi watched, his mouth set in an expressionless line, as Kai tried to push himself up, to defend himself somehow against what he knew was coming. But a vicious blow from Hara knocked him flat again, and Hazama followed it with another—

After that, there was no escape for the halfbreed as they took out their impotent fury on the mongrel, the demon-spawn that had grown up among them because of the mercy of their lord . . . only to bring disgrace to his family's proud name, to his only child, to his samurai, and by association, all the people of his domain.

Oishi did his best to keep his eyes on the punishment being meted out by his men, but his attention kept sliding away . . . to Lord Asano, standing now with bowed shoulders, staring at the dust; to Lady Mika shuddering with every blow that fell on Kai, as if it had fallen on her; to the thinly veiled pleasure on the face of Lord Kira. . . .

Mika's eyes brimmed with tears, and although Oishi tried to hold onto his anger at her female weakness, the thought of what his wife might feel if the victim had been him somehow entered his mind.

And then he only knew more shame, as a tear escaped from Mika's brimming eyes. It ran down her cheek, leaving a sun-silvered trail; she stood frozen, fighting to hold back more tears until her unblinking eyes reminded him of the eyes of the dead. He could not remember ever seeing her weep publicly since her mother had died, when she was a young child. A samurai woman should not weep—at least not over something so disgraceful. But he could see that inside, she was drowning in tears.

He controlled his own emotions again, wondering how many of her tears were for her father's sake, and how many for Kai. Kai, who had killed a *kirin* single-handed, risking his own life . . . who had risked his life and everything that went with it again today, for the honor of his lord and his lady . . . for Ako.

Who had been secretly tutoring his own son in swordsmanship, stealing the obedience and respect of Chikara just as he had stolen the heart of Lord Asano's daughter.

He glanced across the arena to the place where Chikara had been standing, watching the duel with the pride of his secret knowledge outshining even his pride of place.

Chikara had disappeared, unable to bear what was happening now—but unlike everyone else involved, able to leave of his own free will. Oishi looked back at his men taking out their frustration and loss of face on Kai. They were going to beat him to death soon, if they weren't stopped. *Should he order them to stop? Did he even have the authority?*

He glanced at the Shogun's adjutant, still watching them with a critical eye. The man seemed satisfied with the punishment Kai was receiving, but Kai was still moving—trying feebly to protect himself—and so he was not content to call it enough.

As Oishi looked back he saw Basho, who had kept well away from the center, wary of his own strength, abruptly step forward as if he had reached some decision all his own.

The others moved aside; his mere presence was enough to make them back up, by now. He raised his *bokken,* and Oishi saw the resolve on his face suddenly turn to compassion. His mouth formed the words, "I'm sorry . . ." as he looked down at Kai.

Then he brought his *bokken* down in a precise blow that finally knocked Kai out. Kneeling down Basho began to strip the armor from the halfbreed's unconscious body, so that the punishment could end. The Shogun's adjutant did not protest, and Oishi gave the sign for the rest of his men to help.

Stripped of armor, unconscious, and covered in blood, Kai looked all too human and vulnerable as he was dragged off the field. Oishi looked away, back at Lord Asano and Mika. Mika's eyes were filled with tears again, but this time Oishi saw shame and self-recrimination there as well—things he had needed to see even more, if he was ever going to look at her again with any kind of understanding.

The guests were departing all around him now. That meant Lord Asano and Mika-*hime* were finally free to go as well; the Shogun's adjutant left to report to his own lord about the disciplining of Lord Asano's disobedient freak of nature.

Oishi stayed where he was, feeling as if his feet had taken root in the ground. He had just watched the highest-ranking, most respected of his samurai forced to commit an act only the lowest of street thugs would sink to, beating a helpless man nearly to death. Now he watched as they dropped their *bokken* in the blood-spattered dirt and headed toward him for further orders. The rest of the samurai who had been present looked on, wordless and expectant, from the places where they had been stationed.

He sent Basho and Okuda to escort Lord Asano and Lady Mika back to their quarters, warning them first in a low voice to remain at the furthest safe distance from their charges, and not to speak at all. He sent Hazama to find out where Yasuno was, and what had happened to him. The rest he dismissed to their regular assigned duties, or a well-deserved rest.

And then, finally, he went in search of his son.

By dusk, the clear bright sky that had held the promise of an equally shining day for Ako had turned gray and sullen with the clouds of an oncoming storm. The heavens were the color of a cruelly beaten body . . . the swollen clouds of indigo and dull purple streaked with deep blood red by the last rays of the setting sun.

The brilliant red that was the color of Ako's banners . . . the gold that was also Ako's color, as well as the Shogun's, had dimmed almost entirely by the time Mika finally left her chambers again.

When she had returned from the tournament she drove everyone out of her rooms, so that at last she had space to weep with grief and shame until she thought she had no tears left, and then weep some more, in remorse and sorrow. . . .

Finally she slept—and when she woke again, sent her worried attendants to find all the remedies they could for eyes and a face that were red and sore from crying. She would not deny her grief, but neither would she abandon her pride, if only for Ako's sake—no matter how she had tarnished its name today. But she had to go out, had to speak to her father . . . whether he would speak to her or not.

She searched and asked questions everywhere she thought he might have gone, once she found that he was not in his chambers. No one had seen him, anywhere she went, or they had seen him earlier, but knew nothing now . . . until she began to fear that either they were under orders not to tell her anything, or that he might . . . *might even* . . .

In despair she sat down on a bench beneath the cherry trees in the courtyard, wringing her hands more fiercely than she had knotted them together during the tournament, under Lord Kira's unwelcome scrutiny. Her fingers were already bruised from the pressure of her rings against them, but she welcomed the pain, anything to distract her mind.

She saw one of her father's samurai coming toward her in the deepening twilight, recognized him by his profile, which was like no one else's.

Basho approached her hesitantly and bowed with great deference. "My lady, *Kuranosuke* Oishi said that you were seeking your father. I saw Lord Asano recently sitting in his garden, by the *koi* pond."

He did not meet her eyes, and she wondered whether, if he did, she would see the same things she had seen in the eyes of her father's other retainers, and even the eyes of the servants. Whether their gazes held pity or censure, or both, she could not bear to see either emotion in the eyes of one more person . . . especially not this man's eyes. It was hard enough just to imagine how she would endure what lay in her father's.

"Thank you, Sir Basho," she murmured, her voice barely audible. She kept her eyes lowered as she stood up and returned his bow; cherry blossom petals slid from her silken garments and rained down silently around her.

"My lady—" he said, as she began to turn away. "The halfbreed is being cared for; a doctor has seen him. He should survive this day. . . ."

She turned back, seeing Basho's moon face without its ready smile, but still with depths of kindness in his eyes, in such contrast to his enormous, powerful body, or his monk's skill with a *bo* staff and *naginata*. "Why are you telling me this?" she asked faintly.

"Because you wish to see your father, Mika-*hime* . . ." he said, as if for once they stood not in a castle courtyard but in a monastery hall, "and he needs to see hope in your eyes, the same way he needed to see your smile, when you were a child. I thought . . . perhaps if you knew something that would bring you comfort . . ."

"Basho-*sama* . . ." She struggled to hold onto her self control, to stand straight and meet his gaze, not to dissolve into a grieving child again after all these years. "I thank you from the bottom of my heart, for my father's sake. But . . ." she bowed her head again, more in humility than gratitude, "why do only you, out of everyone here, still look at me with the same eyes, after what I did?"

He looked surprised. "You did nothing wrong, my lady. You simply fell in love with someone, someone whom your own father's kindness had saved. We love whom we love; that is our destiny . . . whether it is right or wrong." He glanced away, as if he was unsure that he had the right to express such an opinion to the daughter of his lord.

But as though his conscience would not permit him to keep silent, he pressed on, "Mika-*hime,* you speak of *wabi-sabi* like someone born with the sacred words of Buddha inscribed on her heart. Buddha once said, 'A man's true worth is not a matter of his outward appearance or rank; it lies in the breadth of his spirit.' You see the true beauty in things, and people—which is their uniqueness, as well as the fragility of their existence in this world. That is a rare gift."

He looked up at her again, his face half in shadow. "The Tokugawa *bakufu* has cocooned our country like a silk-worm, to shut out all that is not Japanese. . . . To take pride in our way of life is good, but it has its perils. Pride always does. We are not the only Children of the Gods in this world . . . any more than all the strangers we meet are demons in disguise. It may even be that the halfbreed is in every way deserving of the rank of samurai. But he was born here, and now . . . in the wrong place, at the wrong time."

Mika's hand rose to her mouth; she bit her finger, hard, to stifle a sudden noise of pain.

"Mika-*hime* . . ." Basho shook his head in gentle admonishment. "Buddha also said, 'Radiate your loving-kindness to every living being without discrimination.' In the end the kindnesses we offer, and the kindnesses we take into our hearts, are all that remain with our souls. The halfbreed's next life will be a better one, for having shared your kindness. And so will yours."

He smiled, briefly and almost self-consciously, before he bowed and left her, walking away as if he had merely delivered his message as ordered. She watched him go, for a moment wondering what had really brought him to her—Oishi's order, or the compassion of Buddha.

She turned in the opposite direction, and started away to find her father.

She discovered him at last where Basho had said he would be, sitting by the *koi* pond in the garden that he spent his free time tending, gazing down at the darkened sky reflected in its surface—the world turned upside down.

As she approached him, timidly and with eyes downcast for the first time since she was a child, one of the gold-and-silver carp suddenly leaped out of the water and landed on the stones surrounding the pond.

Her father rose slowly from the bench to pick up the floundering fish and toss it back into the water. The *koi* had done that ever since Mika could remember; as if, when they reached a certain size or age, they longed for something more than the world they had always known. And so they leaped out of the pond, into the unknown.

She remembered when she was a girl how quickly her father would move to rescue them, chiding them as if they could actually understand him, as he returned them to the place where they belonged.

But today her father said nothing, merely flung the fish into the water, as if he despised it for its stupidity. As he started back toward the bench, for the first time he seemed to Mika to move like an old man.

"Father—?" she said tentatively, taking a step toward him.

He glanced up and saw her, and suddenly his expression shut her out like a wall.

She stopped moving, as if the barely controlled outrage and grief in his look had been an actual blow.

He turned his back on her and walked away through the garden with his usual brisk stride, heading toward his chambers.

"My lord—" she called out, stumbling after him, although suddenly her whole body felt as numb as though his gaze had paralyzed her.

"Not now—!" he said, neither slowing down nor glancing back at her.

"Father, please—" she cried, reaching out to him as he stopped at his door to slide it open.

He went inside and shut the wood-reinforced screen behind him without looking back.

As Mika stood trembling outside his door, unable to force her feet to take even one step followed by another, there was a blinding flash of lightning overhead followed by the crack of thunder, and the rain began to fall.

Rain poured down, drenching her to the skin, but still she could not force herself to turn and walk away. She called out again, and yet again, hoping against hope that her father might change his mind, or his heart, and open the door to her. Her voice sounded as plaintive as the crying of sea birds, and as far away, lost in the hiss and thunder of the storm.

How long she stood there, waiting, she didn't know; time had no meaning, now. Nothing meant anything. *Kai was being cared for.* Her heart was glad, but even the thought that it mattered so much to her filled her with shame.

At last she turned away, surrendering to the inevitable, and slowly moved back across the courtyard through the cold rain, avoiding any inner hallways that could have given her shelter until she had no choice.

She entered the part of the sprawling palace where her own rooms were located, holding herself together by will alone. She'd thought she had wept all the tears that were hers to weep today . . . but she realized now that the human soul's capacity for tears was as infinite as the night sky's capacity for stars.

As she walked down the hallway, she glimpsed Basho standing with Oishi, deep in a conversation that, from the somberness of their expressions, could have been about anything from today's disastrous events to a shortage of feed for the horses.

She thought she heard Oishi speak the name of his son as she moved toward them, her eyes averted, hoping they would not even glance her way. But she was still Mika-*hime*; the two men broke off their conversation and bowed to her with the required respect.

She barely nodded in return and started to move on. But there was a trace of regret in Basho's glance, as if he hadn't expected to see her again this soon, and dripping wet with rain.

She stopped, looking back. "Sir Basho," she said, as Oishi looked on, surprised. "Do you believe that the gods, or merciful Buddha, truly hear and answer all our prayers?"

It was Basho's turn to look at her in surprise. It swiftly changed back to regret. "I do, my lady . . ." he said, glancing down. "But sometimes, the answer is 'no.' "

He bowed to her again, and she moved on as quickly as she dared, so that neither man could see her expression.

The sky was black and starless when Kai finally regained consciousness. His first thought was that he had not expected to wake up. But when he moved his head, or even tried to lift a hand to his face, the pain he felt was so intense that the arms of oblivion nearly dragged him back down into the deeper darkness, and so he decided that he had survived, yet again. *Why . . . ?*

He made a sound that was not remotely like a word, too pitiful even to be a moan.

"Finally awake?" a voice asked. It seemed familiar.

He tried to focus on whoever was speaking, barely made out the face of Oishi drifting in the lamplight above him, and a shadowy, unidentifiable space beyond.

Someone supported him as a few sips from a dipper full of water trickled into his mouth and down his throat. Then the rest of the water was dumped unceremoniously over his head, leaving him drenched and gasping.

"Throw him out," Oishi said.

Horizontal and vertical changed positions sickeningly as Kai was pulled up by two pairs of strong arms and dragged through a doorway, out into a chill drizzle that clung to his skin like cobwebs. The rain began to fall harder as the group of men surrounding him forced him to cross a vast open space toward wherever they were taking him.

At last, through a haze of pain, he heard the grating creak as the small access in the outer gate was forced open. Raising his head, he saw nothing at all beyond the pool of lantern light outside the gate, as if the world beyond it had dissolved in the rain. The men who had dragged him to this point heaved him through the gate into the world outside.

Kai landed facedown in the mud outside the castle walls. Behind him, the sound of the gate slamming shut cut through the deepening slurry of his thoughts just enough to keep him conscious. He struggled to push himself up before he drowned in mud, the mindless instinct for survival trying to get his body up on its feet . . . *just to his hands and knees . . . just—*

He pushed up far enough to raise his face from the muck and inhale. And then he rolled over onto his back and lay still, with no strength left to do anything more. The rain poured down like the tears or the wrath of heaven, to either wash him clean of his sins, or finally let him drown. . . .

7

Burning ash gleamed in an ancient bowl in Lord Kira's quarters at Ako Castle, as Mitsuke gazed into the fading embers, studying the cracked deer bones glowing with heat, revealing in the faint tracery of their patterns a whisper of the greater patterns woven by destiny's invisible hand. The moment was right—deep in the heart of darkness, when the only light that existed for her lay in the glowing signs she conjured from a wisp of smoke.

She glanced up at the face of her beloved lord, revealed by the same light, and smiled. "Asano's mind is unsettled. It is time."

As she looked into his eyes, the pupil of her own blue eye, the one gifted with the Sight, narrowed suddenly as she sensed Kira's hesitation. "What are you afraid of, my lord?" she asked softly, controlling her sudden animal urge to seize him by the throat. *Humans . . . they were all so weak. And yet—*

"Show me your courage. Give me your heart. . . ." She sidled closer to him, deftly parting his kimono and running her long-nailed hand down his chest, leaving faint lines of color on the smooth skin over his heart, feeling his heartbeat quicken.

"After this there is no turning back," she whispered.

"You are bound to me, and I to you. . . ." His eyes closed, and his lips parted in a sigh of ecstasy as she continued to caress him, loosening the sash of his kimono. "Rivers of blood and mountains will not stand in our way. Nor the tears of widows and orphans," her voice took on the sing-song quality of a chant. She felt his blood rushing through every vessel, now, saw the veins at his temples throbbing with his heart's desire. *They were so easy, humans . . . easy to manipulate, even easier to kill. And yet—*

"Find your envy and hatred—" she commanded, and her nails raked his flesh like claws. He cried out, but not with pain. She took a long pin from her upswept hair, and pricked a vein on his wrist, catching the drops of blood in her cupped hand. "—and I will give you all you desire. . . ."

The whispered words that had put him under her spell changed to another kind of chanting, as a grotesque, deep red spider began to form from the blood in her palm—the manifestation of his deepest desires, his deepest fears. The ambition and the envy that burned in his blood had been held back for too long by his human frailty. Her beloved would become Shogun, but not on his own. His spirit was too weak—he would never have the courage to act on his desires. But that was all right, because he had her, and she had fearlessness and strength enough for them both. They were perfect for each other, in every way. . . .

Lord Asano lay deep in the sleep of utter exhaustion, after a day that had strained his body and his mind to their absolute limits. He never stirred as the shadows cast by the dim lantern at his bedside began to move on the walls above him. In the darkest corner of the room, the fox-witch materialized into a creature of shadows, creeping along the walls until she was directly above him.

She descended the wall like a nightmare, until she reached a point just above his head. Then, opening her hands, she released the bloated red spider, its feet still wet with Kira's blood.

The spider crept as she willed it to, leaving traces of blood potion as it moved over Asano's lips like the kiss of Death.

Above him, watching intently, Mitsuke whispered, "*Father . . .*"

Lord Asano sat bolt upright on his futon, his eyes wide and staring with horror. His hand found his sword, lying at his bedside as it always was, as he searched the room for intruders, for any sign of movement—

But there was nothing . . . no one here but him. *It had been a nightmare, nothing more.* He rubbed his face, brushing away the odd sensation that lingered from his dream, and began to lie down again, too exhausted even to dwell on it.

But then he seemed to hear a muffled cry somewhere nearby, and Mika's voice called desperately, "Father!"

No . . . he was imagining it. It was only his own guilty conscience that made him think he heard his daughter—

"Father!"

"Mika?" That was her voice, he was sure of it. *This was no dream—* Her cry came again, and again, rising in volume and terror each time. Lord Asano got to his feet, grabbing up his sword, and left his room.

He ran through the courtyard garden, following his daughter's cries of terror and pain, shouting, "Mika!"

Inside Mika's chambers, he pulled aside the screen to her bedroom, and saw Lord Kira on top of his daughter, pinning her down, as he tried to—

With a cry of pure rage, Lord Asano drew his sword.

Kira looked up, releasing Mika as he scrambled away from her father's wrath, but a blow from the sword caught his shoulder, and he collapsed on the floor, his eyes wild with fear.

Lord Asano raised his sword over his head in cold fury to

cut down the man who had dared attack his daughter, when suddenly—

—the scene before him vanished, like a dream struck by sunlight.

He found himself somehow standing in Lord Kira's chambers, not his daughter's. Only Kira was there, cowering on the floor, his arm covered in blood, shouting, "Guards! Guards!"

Mika was nowhere to be seen.

Lord Asano turned, blinking nightmare out of his eyes, to face the courtyard beyond the open doorway as it began to fill with people. His gaze filled with disbelief as he saw Mika appear among them, unharmed, her eyes wide with shock as she saw him standing over the bleeding Kira with a raised sword.

Lord Asano lowered his *katana,* as stunned as anyone who stood there looking on . . . and far more stricken by the enormity of what he had done. He looked back at Kira, his face filled with incomprehension; he scarcely resisted as Kira's guards took hold of him and pulled him from the room.

"Father!" Mika tried to push her way to his side through the crowd in the inner courtyard, but the Shogun's guards held her back.

As Lord Asano heard her, he began to struggle with his captors, trying to reach her. But suddenly Oishi was there in front of him, holding up his hands, eyes pleading with him to come to his senses and not to resist. "Please, my lord—"

Lord Asano stared back at his *karou,* blinking as if daylight was hurting his eyes, even though it was still the middle of the night. Then, at last, he shook his head in surrender, lowering his sword again . . . feeling as if he had just stumbled out of a wilderness into an unknown world, but reassured to discover a familiar face there—the face of his second-in-command.

Oishi stood back, the fear and concern that had filled his eyes fading to relief. It died stillborn as the guards disarmed Lord Asano and led him away.

He watched them go, despair filling the emptiness inside him as he saw what had become of his lord, his mentor . . . his friend. It settled in his chest like a weight, the heaviest stone of all on top of the burden of these past days and weeks, which had slowly been crushing a part of him he had no control over, no access to . . . until finally he felt his own heart break.

The crowd around him began to disperse, muttering. He saw Mika drifting back toward her own chambers, barefoot, with her unbound hair falling around her like a dark shroud. She looked as pale and somehow insubstantial as a grief-stricken wraith. He looked away again, knowing the image would haunt him like a restless ghost, unless he could find some way to undo what had been done to her father.

Oishi fixed his gaze on Kira, as a doctor and members of Kira's retinue treated his wound. But his eyes refused to stay on the man, moving on aimlessly until they reached the Shogun, standing in the doorway of his own quarters . . . witnessing everything.

The one thing Oishi did not see, because she chose at the moment to let no one see her, was Kira's concubine, the witch with one blue eye. . . .

Kai wandered, lost once more in the twilight world of the hungry ghosts—the world he had fled, so long ago. *But that had only been a dream* . . . a dream . . . *The forsaken souls of the unwanted and unmourned still clung to him with phantom fingers of blue flame until every step he took pulled him backward. The moans for pity filled his helpless mind with visions of the wounded and dying abandoned on some forgotten battlefield beneath tattered banners of red.* . . .

The moaning ended in a sudden sharp pain-cry, and Kai woke from his delirium dream. Vertigo and confusion welcomed him back into the world, along with a sickening headache. The haunted cries and intangible flames had vanished; instead there was only the sound of the chill wind entering through crevices in the walls around him, and a single candle sitting in a cracked dish on the dirt floor. Its golden flame struggled against the draft as he tried to focus on what the light revealed; his mind struggled like the flame to make sense of what he saw.

He was back in his hut, he realized at last, although he had no memory of how he had gotten there, or when. It was night, and the embers in the fire pit had burned to ash long ago, leaving the hut's interior dark and cold. In the flickering candlelight he saw what he thought was his own hand, battered almost beyond recognition. The muddy sleeve of his kimono was torn open past his elbow; what he could see of his arm looked equally stomach-turning. And that was all. His face was so swollen that one eye was completely shut; he couldn't move his head to glimpse any other part of his body . . . if his body still had separate parts. He felt as if it had been reduced to an unidentifiable core of pain that worsened every time he tried to draw a breath, as though everything below his neck had been crushed.

The candle flame shivered in the wind; shadowplay showed the tournament yard, the samurai in black, the duel . . . he remembered being beaten like a dog, in front of the lord he had risked everything for, and the woman he loved more than his life, as they stood with heads bowed in humiliation—because of his failure. He had brought shame on Ako and the House of Asano by the shame of his very existence, and how it had been revealed. . . .

. . . he remembered the Shogun's heavy hand seizing and twisting his battered face, leather-gloved fingers probing his torn mouth as callously as if he truly was an animal . . . the animal even Lord Asano had declared him to be, repudiating his humanity before the entire world. And Mika . . . prostrating herself in the dirt to beg for that animal's life, throwing away her honor, disgracing her father's good name. . . .

Abruptly the candle flame guttered out, the firefly light of his hold on reality vanishing with it.

In the moonless depths of his mind, beyond the shores of memory or even dream, delirium once more tinged the sourceless horizon and illuminated the sea of dimensions with shimmering visions of blood-red and ice-blue, growing brighter . . . until what had been intangible and formless congealed into pitiless eyes too real to be phantasms.

I'm not afraid of you. He met their gaze, but they looked straight through him, as if he was only a phantom himself.

But as the *kitsune*'s mind blew like a chill wind through his own, she whispered, "You should be," and he cowered away from something far more terrible than merely fear of discovery: *Treachery, betrayal, a curse on the House of Asano. . . .* What curse, he didn't know; he only knew that everything he had dreamed before waking was true, and everything he thought he had known was wrong, and because he had been cursed, so long ago, there was nothing at all he could do to stop it. . . .

The death of all hope swallowed his consciousness whole, and dragged him back into the abyss.

8

Morning came all too soon, even though—after the events of the night before—it had seemed to everyone in the House of Asano that the sun might never show its face again.

But with morning came judgment, as swift and implacable as the edge of a blade.

Lord Asano kneeled before the Shogun in the Great Hall of his own castle, waiting with resignation that passed well for meditative calm while the Shogun's advisors huddled together, debating and consulting with each other as if there was really any doubt regarding the outcome of last night's incident.

At last, one of the Shogun's advisors leaned forward to whisper in his ear. The Shogun seemed to consider the words for a long moment, before he said, "The law is clear. The penalty is death."

Lord Asano almost thought there was regret in his voice, perhaps because the Shogun did not usually find himself in the position of ordering the death of the *daimyo* in whose castle he was currently an honored guest, at least not before he had even departed.

"Because of your rank, and the service you have done Ako, I will allow you to die by your own hand, so that you may show the same courage and dignity in death that you once showed in life. The sentence is to be carried out immediately."

Lord Asano bowed, accepting the verdict with all the courage and dignity he had never truly lost, even though the suddenness with which the sentence was to be carried out came as an added blow. Usually a *daimyo* was granted a certain number of days or weeks—enough time in which to set his estates in order, and prepare his family and friends for the parting—before he committed *seppuku.*

He rose numbly, and was escorted by the Shogun's guards directly to a preparation chamber that had already been set up, where he would have a brief time to compose his formal death poem, and himself, before what was to come.

The walls of the room were decorated with beautifully painted screens illustrating events from the long and honorable history of the Asano clan. He kneeled before the writing desk, where fine paper, a brush, water, and ink stone awaited his final thoughts. He sat back for a moment, gazing at the walls, comforted by the knowledge that the resolve he showed in carrying out his final act would remove any stain from that honor. *A life was but one generation; a good name was forever.* There was no honor in protesting, or claiming that what had occurred had been beyond his control. It had happened, on his lands, within his very castle walls. It was his responsibility to accept the consequences.

He had already composed his farewell poem in his mind, last night, as he lay sleepless waiting for the dawn. He committed it to paper, being as careful to keep his hand steady and his arm's motion fluid as he had when he was a schoolboy. He was leaving far too many things that were unfinished—and too many that were simply incomprehensible—behind him, but he would do nothing today that would bring further harm to Ako, or further shame to the name of Asano.

He should have used his remaining hours for meditation and prayer . . . but he had no time left for himself. He had asked the guards at the door to have his *karou* waiting there for his summons, so that he could settle as many matters as possible with Oishi, to ensure the welfare and safety of Ako . . . and Mika. They were all arrangements he should have been given the proper time to make—but perhaps he should have made them years ago, because after the death of his wife he had understood too well the fragility of all existence. *Nothing was certain but change. . . .*

Oishi was waiting, as he had requested, when he slid aside the door panel. The guards had taken his *karou*'s swords, but they permitted him to bring inside the bundled scrolls, ledgers, and other documents he carried in his arms; he had not even brought an assistant to help him fetch them to this final meeting.

Oishi looked like he had not had a moment of sleep last night, either—and obviously he hadn't. He had brought along his own lists of concerns and questions and details that he had spent the night writing down, along with all the related items that were his responsibility to maintain.

They settled the most basic matters quickly, with the ease of two men who had worked together and known each other's minds for years. Lord Asano thought briefly and fondly of the many games of *shogi* and *go* they had also played during those years—the results of which had convinced him that in another age his chief retainer and counselor would have been his most trusted general, a strategist to be reckoned with.

In the age of the Edo *bakufu,* Oishi's memory for detail, and his ability to see a hundred steps ahead even as he took the first one, had also let him excel at the job of a peacetime *karou.* He was responsible for overseeing the multitude of tasks that were necessary to keep Ako Castle, and the lands around it, secure and well-tended—and for making certain the subordinates he delegated those tasks to did their jobs well. It was a hereditary position, but one for which the history of the samurai class hardly guaranteed every man's son would be suited.

But in an age when all that really remained of the Way of the Warrior were essays written by men who had never seen battle, and good penmanship served the average samurai better than good swordsmanship, the Oishi clan was an exception, reliably producing heirs who had been able to adapt their skills to less heroic deeds that were nonetheless vital to their ancestral homeland.

Eventually the moment of silence arrived that both men had privately been dreading, as Oishi laid aside his final list and documents . . . the long pause that told them there was nothing more to be said about dry statistics, or the future one of them would not live to see. Lord Asano gazed at the painted screens that surrounded them again, gazing into the past, drawing strength from it. Oishi looked down, trying not to stare at his lord's death poem lying on the writing desk, not to let his eyes make out a single word or phrase on it before the appropriate time.

He raised his head again, and his eyes held the look of a man who would rather have been torn apart by a pack of wolves than forced to endure the helplessness he was feeling now. "This isn't *right*—"

Lord Asano met his eyes with compassion and apology. "I tried to kill an unarmed man in my own home, a guest." *A high-ranking guest, that he was known to feel enmity toward . . . and at a time when the Shogun himself had been present as well, making it a direct threat against him.* "The Shogun could have denied me the right to *seppuku,* and had me strangled like a criminal. Instead he has allowed me to take my life with honor—"

"You were bewitched, my lord," Oishi protested. "Your mind was poisoned. Give me the word and I will have horses ready—"

Lord Asano raised his eyebrows. "Would you have me run?" He shook his head wearily. "Your ancestors and mine have always served this land. So must our children. If I accept my fate, no one will question the honor of our people, or punish them for my crime." He held Oishi's gaze for a long moment, realizing that there were no words to express how grateful and how fortunate he was to have had the man who knelt before him now at his right hand for so many years. But there was still one thing he had to be certain of, before their time together ended. "Promise me you will put Ako first."

He watched Oishi fight a silent battle within his own soul, as he realized what his lord was asking and struggled to keep his emotions in check—not to protest, and not to break down. After an agonizing hesitation, he finally bowed, acknowledging Lord Asano's final command, and his final wish.

Lord Asano took a deep breath of relief. "I am ready, Oishi, and when I die, all I pray for is that I am reborn to serve this House as well as you served me." As Oishi raised his head again, Lord Asano realized that he had one request that still needed to be made. "I would be honored if you would act as my second, old friend."

Oishi nodded without hesitation.

The sun shone in a flawlessly blue sky, as it had on the fateful day of the tournament, as Lord Asano, dressed in funereal white, was led through the same ornamental garden he had run through in a blind fog last night . . . as if the maddened nightmare that had led him to such a disastrous waking had been a kind of premonition of today.

Of all the people who had loyally served him and Ako Castle for so many years, only the samurai were not present and lined up along his path to say farewell. Oishi, acting as his second, followed behind him, keeping watch over him to the end—but the rest were being held under restraint, by the Shogun's guard and retainers of the other *daimyo,* who had been his guests but were now afraid they could have been his victims—or could still become the victims of his samurai, if his men decided to try and prevent the Shogun's justice on their own.

The castle's servants and their family members bowed, or

fell to their knees, or pressed their hands together in prayer for him as he passed between them. He managed to nod farewell graciously, as well as gratefully.

And then he saw Mika waiting for him, at the end of the line. The closer he approached to her, the more clearly he saw her misery and shame, and felt her anguish reaching out to him, as she could not—

But suddenly she abandoned the social codes and laws, and the barrier of her own self-control one last time, as she left her assigned spot and ran toward him, throwing herself into his arms. He felt her tears hot on his neck; her voice was barely audible through her muffled sobs, as she said, "Father, it was my fault—"

He closed her into his arms, sheltering her for the last time from the world of men—men like himself, before he had met his wife, and met his match; before he had become enlightened to the truth that Buddha's words about "loving-kindness" did not exclude *anyone.*

That world ruled by men would break her spirit and her noble heart, if it could, and turn her from a samurai into a mere woman—a "useless creature"—something less than human, no matter how unjust a fate it would be. . . . *Exactly as it had done long ago, to the only man she had ever loved enough to willingly marry.*

He realized that all his efforts to protect her from the world they lived in had gone for nothing, because he had never been truly enlightened enough to free his mind from the rigid barriers of class that divided their society . . . to let himself see the truth about Kai that had been obvious to his daughter from the moment she first laid eyes on him.

No matter how human Kai had proved himself to be, how loyal, how hard-working, intelligent, skillful, or trustworthy, no one at Ako Castle besides Mika had ever truly acknowledged it; not even he himself. He had never even considered the possibility of betrothing his daughter to a halfbreed. He had raised Kai up from an outcast to the level of a peasant farmer—better off and better protected than most, because he was an Asano family servant.

But he had blinded himself to the possibility of anything more; even to the idea, so obvious now, that Kai was the reason Mika had always refused to discuss marriage. He had never suspected their feelings for each other still ran so deep, let alone considered that he could make it possible for them to marry, if he adopted Kai as his heir. If Kai had been born a samurai, even of the lowest rank, he would have seen the truth—and acted on it, long ago.

If only Mika had told him . . . but he knew why she had not. And now it was too late to change anything.

"Don't let them see you cry," he murmured, stroking her hair. "Let all these great lords and their samurai see that they have much to learn from the women of Ako."

Mika's arms loosened; slowly she drew far enough away from him to look into his eyes. Her hands clung to his arms as he watched her willing her eyes free of tears, so that she could meet his gaze with the same determination that was reflected in his own expression. Her hands fell from his arms, and she stood as straight as an arrow before him, with nothing but pride showing on her face.

He smiled at her, his pride becoming tenderness. "This world is only a preparation for the next. All we can ask is that we leave it having loved. And having been loved." He took her hand in both of his. "Do not give up, just because I am gone." *Never give up, if you believe your cause is just.*

Still struggling to hold back tears, Mika stepped away from him and let him pass, followed by Oishi, as ever his loyal second-in-command, his protector, and his truest friend, as he moved on toward a place where she was not allowed to go. But there was another place, beyond that, where one day they would meet again. . . . She believed it with all her heart, although she could not imagine what she would do now, how she would endure in the meantime, until that day came . . . somehow, somewhere; in the future, or in the realm of the gods.

The Shogun and his entourage of advisors and counselors, plus the train of *daimyo,* had entered the Great Hall first, to take their arranged seats, while the guards kept Lord Asano and Oishi waiting outside. More guards kept the servants—with Mika again caught among them—from waiting nearby.

The two men stood in silence together, neither one trusting himself to speak of so much as the change in the weather, their self-control pushed closer to the edge of endurance with every moment that passed. At last the solid wooden doors of the Great Hall, ornately carved with the Asano *mon,* opened again and allowed the two of them to enter.

They crossed the wide expanse of the hall under the grim gaze of the assembled nobles, to the place at its center where a single small low table sat on a layer of spotless white cloth covering a section of the *tatami.* On the table lay an ornate *tanto* bearing the Asano crest: the traditional dagger used by a samurai to take his own life. Lord Asano kneeled down as he reached the table, and placed the death poem he had written on its surface before him. Oishi went down on one knee beside and behind him, positioning himself to rise quickly, prepared for his duty.

Lord Asano paused, collecting himself, and bowed to the onlookers, before he looked up at the Shogun. He saw Lord Kira kneeling to the Shogun's right. As he sensed the triumph barely hidden beneath Kira's quiet composure, the sight of the man turned his soul to fire and ice.

Kira registered the change, and a trace of foreboding made his own gaze falter as Lord Asano picked up the shining *tanto.*

Lord Asano fixed his gaze on the Shogun again. In a voice that betrayed no emotion except conviction, he spoke the ritual words, "I open my soul before you, so that you may judge if it is clean or impure." With the final word, he plunged the knife into his belly. Through the sudden agonized astonishment his body felt at its own betrayal, he saw Kira's eyes try to look away from Death's.

But they only found Oishi's vengeful stare, as he abruptly rose to his feet, his sword drawn. Oishi's gaze turned back Kira's attention like a wall, forcing Kira to face the truth of his lord's suffering, the proof of his courage and the denial of the lies spoken against him. Lord Asano kept his head high, his own eyes fixed on Kira—a focus point beyond the excruciating pain as he drove the knife deeper, tearing flesh and entrails until his body shuddered with protest, and at last he bowed his head, the barest breath of protest escaping his lips.

Behind him, Oishi's uncertainty, his own agony of doubt, vanished in a heartbeat. He brought his sword down in the mercy stroke that with one deft blow ended his lord's life and his suffering, secure in the knowledge that Lord Asano had died as he had lived, in a way that set an example of integrity and strength no one would ever have reason to question.

Lord Asano had maintained his control to the end; the blow that separated his head cleanly from his body had been struck exactly as it should, the fountain of blood spewed into the catch-basin waiting before him, as perfectly as even a Shogun could have required. There was scarcely a drop of blood on Oishi's own clothing, but he deliberately wiped the blood from the blade of his *katana* directly onto his sleeve—knowing that he could never wear this clothing again. He had never killed a man before, and he had just killed his own lord. He would burn his clothes *or they would remind him forever of the moment just past.*

He looked up at Kira one last time as he sheathed his sword, slowly, with implacable hatred and the promise of vengeance in his eyes. He bowed formally to the Shogun and the attending nobility a final time, before he picked up Lord Asano's poem from the table, turned, and strode out of the Hall alone. If anyone saw the shine of tears on his face, he felt no shame at the thought that they might deride him behind his back for showing human feeling.

Mika rose from the spot where she sat waiting by the *koi* pond in her father's garden, as she saw Oishi come out of the Great Hall alone, carrying a single piece of paper. She saw his shoulders sag as the doors closed behind him, and he leaned against a post of the veranda as he bowed his head to read her father's final words. She could see the paper trembling in his hand. He stood that way for much longer than she would have expected, as if the blood smeared across the sleeve of his kimono had made the garment so heavy that he could barely remain upright.

Her father was dead.

Her mind tried to form a picture of what must lie in the middle of the Great Hall: a headless body, a sea of blood . . . her father's sightless eyes. She pressed her arm hard against her own eyes, trying to stop the vision forming behind them; when she finally lowered it again, her sleeve was soaked with grief.

She looked up, to see Oishi crossing the courtyard toward her—his head high again and his pace brisk, his eyes gazing straight ahead at her as he passed the samurai still watching the castle grounds, who wore the *mon* of Tokugawa, of Kira, of every *daimyo*'s retainers except his own.

Don't let them see you cry. Fiercely Mika wiped her face on the sleeve of her kimono, as Oishi approached along the garden path, not even glancing right or left at the broken promises of the newly-formed buds and fragrant blossoms on the wisteria and iris, peonies and hydrangeas lining the paved stone walkway. The guards had dispersed the servants immediately, and she had sent away her own attendants with them as she slipped off alone to sit here, in the last spot where she had seen her father before the terrible events of last night.

"My lady." Oishi kneeled in front of her, and bowed deeply, before she could quite meet his eyes. He held out the piece of paper. *Her father's death poem.* "Forgive me . . ." he said, his voice breaking, as she took the poem from his hand.

"I—"

"Forgive me . . ." he murmured again, his voice back under control as he straightened up and met her gaze. But he was still blinking as if his eyes hurt; she realized that his face was wet. "Your father has restored his honor," he said quietly. "I have never seen a man show more courage. Ako, and the House of Asano, should be proud. . . . Now I must go and ask—*demand* the release of our men. Forgive me—" He rose to his feet and turned away so abruptly that she could say nothing at all before he was walking off among the flowers.

She stood staring at the piece of paper she held in her hands. At first it might have been blank, because her mind would not register what was written there. But as she went on looking at it, she saw calligraphy in her father's style—clean, without flourish, but never graceless—begin to take form, and she read his final poem:

More than the cherry blossoms
Inviting a wind to blow them away
I am wondering what to do
With the remaining springtime.

Oh, Father. . . . She bowed her head, and more tears that would not be denied stained the page. Those had been her father's thoughts, as he faced the final hours his life . . . and yet how much greater a question they asked of those he had left behind, who must exist without him in their lives from now on: What to do, with the remaining springtime . . . ?

"Let them see they have much to learn from the women of Ako," her father had told her. But what did she have left to teach anyone? Her father had made her feel as if she was free to do or be anything. But she realized that even as she had told herself it was true, in their hearts they had both known it was a lie. *That was why she had never told him she loved Kai.*

Kai had always seen clearly, from the outside, what neither of them had ever allowed themselves to admit, for so many reasons. . . . *If you believe you are truly free, there is no escape.* Her hands tightened, crumpling the paper, as she sank onto the bench again, her body racked with silent sobs.

At last she dried her tears once more, wondering how she would ever cleanse her soul of so much grief, if her tears must always be shed in stolen moments. . . . She smoothed out her father's poem and folded it neatly, slipping it into her *obi,* before she stood and left the garden. She walked out alone across the courtyard and through its open gates, bearing herself as nobly as Oishi had before the eyes of the Shogun's guards . . . Lord Kira's spies . . . the eyes of too many strangers watching her, everywhere she looked.

Looking straight ahead, not meeting anyone's gaze and refusing to respond to any question or muttered comment, she crossed the lower courtyard to the outer gate. She needed to escape this castle, which had always been her home and meant everything to her, for now, while it was still controlled by her father's enemies and her own. Her courage would never hold unless she could see Ako, free of walls, and bring back the memory of why it mattered so much that she go on.

The guards stationed at the outermost gate demanded to know where she was going and why—treating her as rudely as if she was a woman traveling alone, stopped at a checkpoint on the Tokaido Road, and not the daughter of the *daimyo* who had been their host.

She merely stared at them, and went on staring, with the memory of her father burning in her eyes. And that was enough, as she had somehow known it would be. They fell silent, lifting their spears, and bowed to her as they cleared the way for her to pass.

She walked on, her pace quickening as she reached the bridge. She stopped at last when she reached its center, and stood looking down at the river flowing past beneath her. Faithful, eternal, it was a blessing to all who lived here, from the hills down to the sea, bringing life-giving water to the many fields and the people who tended them. It was also a blessing to Ako Castle, an ever-vigilant protector that kept the moats of its defenses filled.

Her eyes brimmed with tears again, here where she was free to let herself feel. But this time they were not tears of loss . . . they were tears of wonder, that the beauty of Ako could remain as eternal as the river. *Wabi-sabi* beauty . . . eternal only compared to the fleeting lives of human beings, eternal yet always changing like the seasons, the weather . . . eternal yet forever new each time she saw it.

What would it look like, a hundred years from now, or two hundred . . . ? If she were reincarnated then, would she still know it, by the subtle forms of the land beneath a surface that had changed beyond all recognition? Would she know her father, when their souls met again, hidden behind the masks of faces that had changed beyond all recognition? Nothing was eternal on this earth except change, her father had always said. But if change itself was eternal, and their spirits were eternal . . . how could they not look into each other's eyes again someday and feel joyful recognition?

She moved on across the bridge, with her hands pressed against the poem hidden below her heart.

. . . wondering what to do, with the remaining springtime.

As she reached the other end of the bridge the wind rose, sending ripples scudding across the river's surface, releasing a blizzard of fallen cherry blossoms along its shores—as if even the gods had been disturbed by the injustice carried out on earth today.

The Shogun and his retinue had departed almost immediately, even before the ashes of Lord Asano's cremation fire had cooled. Their other guests/occupiers departed with him, much to the relief of everyone who actually belonged there.

The Shogun's adjutant had informed Oishi—and Mika, whom he never once acknowledged beyond a courteous bow—that the Shogun would return, on his way back to Edo, after completing his ceremonial foray into the west. He was paying his respects to the lords of Ako's neighboring domains, most of whom were controlled by clans that had supported the Tokugawa in the final battle that had given them the Shogunate. As the Tokugawa regime had seized one domain after another over the past century, they had placed their allies strategically, like pieces on a *shogi* board, between the fiefs of clans that were not part of that inner circle, effectively preventing discontented *daimyo* from banding together to foment rebellion.

The Shogun would stop by Ako again in about a month, the adjutant had said—and ordered *Kuranosuke* Oishi, as acting commander in place of his *daimyo,* to make certain that things were set in order, with all the necessary documents and information brought up to date and available for inspection. At that time, he had informed Oishi, again without once glancing at Mika, the decision would be passed down about what disposition was to be made of Ako, since there was no living male heir to inherit. . . .

In so many words, he had declared this branch of the Asano clan to be deadwood, waiting to be pruned: The domain of Ako would either be added to the already immense Tokugawa holdings, or awarded to one of the Shogun's favored advisors. Lord Asano's samurai would become ronin—still samurai by blood, but in reality masterless, dishonored vagabonds, cast out to survive however they could—while Lord Asano's daughter . . . was beneath notice.

Short of informing them that they had all been condemned to death, it was the worst news they could have imagined. Benumbed with shock, they had returned his perfunctory bow of farewell and watched him ride away, watched the Shogun's retinue depart . . . seen Lord Kira looking back with more than casual interest, as he left their home and the home of their ancestors.

Oishi and Mika stood side by side, saying nothing, until the retinue had departed through the final gate, and crossed the bridge. And then Mika turned, with a choked cry, and slammed her fist with all her strength against the pillar of the veranda beside her. Oishi stared at her in disbelief, as if she had struck the blow he had intended to strike, before he could even move. She turned back, her face flushed and her hand throbbing, and spat a curse at the departing Shogun that would have made his troops blush.

"Mika-*hime*!" Oishi said sharply. But she saw in his eyes only a vast relief that she had held her tongue until the Shogun's retinue was safely out of earshot.

"I am not invisible! Or deaf and dumb!" she snapped at him. "You may be the only one who is allowed to give orders now—but you are also the only one required to listen to them," she added bitterly. "I am my father's daughter . . . and you will never be my father, Oishi Yoshio. Never speak to me in that tone again."

"Forgive me, Lady Mika. . . ." He dropped to his knees, and bowed until his forehead touched the cedar planks of the veranda floor. When he raised his head again, she saw in his eyes genuine understanding of the humiliation she had just suffered. She also saw his exhaustion, his impotent anger, and the dread he had felt as keenly as she had, when they both realized that the Shogun had left a funeral pyre of his own piled behind him at the castle gates, ready to consume Ako's future . . . and his adjutant's words had put a torch to it.

She remembered, too, how Oishi had repeatedly asked her forgiveness, as he had given her her father's death poem, there in the garden after he . . . . She closed her eyes.

"Oishi-*sama*," she murmured, "please, get up. I am the one who should beg your forgiveness, and express my gratitude that you have always treated me with dignity, no matter . . . no matter what you may have thought of me, or my behavior. . . ."

She looked away, shamefaced. "I know you have much

left to do in preparation for my father's funeral service. And I . . . I should go now, to pick my father's bones from the ashes." It was traditional for the members of the family to perform that final ritual of preparing the remains for burial . . . and she was the only member of the family left. She stepped down off the veranda and gazed into the distance.

"Lady Mika," Oishi said softly, getting to his feet behind her. "Riku, my wife, would be honored if you would allow her to help you. And . . . and there are others. . . . You need not be alone; we are all still here, the family of your father, our lord."

She looked back at him, blinking, moved beyond speech.

He managed a smile, no less kind for being uncertain. "And as for the future . . . we have a month. Today may have foretold the end of honor as we knew it, but for now our honor still belongs to us. *Inu-Kubou*'s future plans will not intrude on your father's prayer service, or our love for him."

"Thank you, Oishi-*sama*." Her own face formed a tremulous smile at his use of the scandalous epithet. The "Dog Shogun" was a nickname coined in whispers, because of the Shogun's hardly selfless obsession with the welfare of dogs. She had heard that a priest had told the Shogun the gods might grant him a male heir if he performed good deeds; he had chosen to protect dogs, because he had been born in the Year of the Dog. The smell from the shelter he had set up for them in Edo was said to be appalling. . . .

Oishi walked with her to his home, where Riku went down on her knees in front of them, and then, when Mika reached out to raise her up with her own hands, embraced the younger woman like a mother, speaking soft words of comfort and condolence. More moved than startled by the other woman's spontaneous, heartfelt gesture, Mika watched Oishi's face unfreeze behind Riku's shoulder, and felt his relief that his lord's daughter was only glad to encounter his wife's warm heart.

The traditions of burial wound on through the next two days, through a formal ceremony at the family shrine, and then the interment of her father's urn in Ako Castle's graveyard by the river, where his ancestors, and those of so many of the people looking on, had been laid to rest for generations.

Instead of feeling more alone than ever, Mika found herself consoled by the presence of an entire extended family she had never realized she possessed, all of whom became more real to her as the hours passed—both the reticent samurai and the self-conscious commoners who approached her to murmur condolences, or share a personal memory.

Death was the great equalizer, and here among so many reminders of their finite lives and uncertain futures, as well as the bonds of loyalty that had joined their ancestors and families down to the present day, she realized how sincerely they all shared her sorrow, as well as her outrage at the injustice of his death.

There was only one person whose face she did not see, the one whom she had hoped most of all would come to pray for her father . . . the one person who truly felt about him the same way that she had, and who had obeyed him far more unselfishly than she had, for so many years.

Kai. Kai had not come, even to say good-bye. . . .

As the day moved on toward sunset, she led a procession out across the fields, and up the winding path to the promontory that overlooked what was still the most beautiful view of Ako she had ever seen, extending all the way to the sea. It was the place, her father had told her, where he'd often sat with her mother, on soft spring evenings . . . the place where, in what now seemed like another life, she had sat together with Kai and gazed at the same view.

More people joined them on this journey, farmers from along the valley, and people from the village below the castle. Some had even come from the seaport to pay their respects, and recite the prayers that would lift his spirit like the rising smoke from the incense that she burned as the last of her father's remains were buried here, in a simple wooden box, to enrich the ground in this place they had both loved. What was, to her, the true resting-place of his spirit was marked only by a single large stone inscribed with a *haiku* of her composing:

Clouds gather, rain falls.
Below the mountain's summit
red blossoms and white.

Blinking too much as she turned away from the grave marker, Mika glanced at the faces around her a final time. She had clung to the fragile hope that she would find Kai here; believing he would at least come to this place, for her father's sake, even if he would not go to the castle and risk being driven off by the people who had treated him so cruelly.

But he had not come.

After what had passed between them when she had visited his home, and all that had happened at the tournament, she wondered if she would ever see his face again, even if it was only for long enough to beg his forgiveness. . . .

It was only as the sun began to set that she suddenly realized that Kai might have been injured so badly that he couldn't climb the hill, even to pray for her father. *Was it possible that no one had even told him Lord Asano was dead—?* She looked away across the evening fields toward Kai's solitary hut, but the edge of the forest lay in shadows already.

The final burial service, and the day, were over. Other people began to file back down the hill, moving carefully but quickly, before the path vanished completely with nightfall. Oishi and his family gathered solicitously around her; his son Chikara escorted her down the hill, stumbling more than she did in the deepening twilight, on what was to him an unfamiliar slope.

They made their way back across the fields, with lanterns

and fireflies to guide them home, as the last red-and-golden light of Ako's honor faded from the sky.

For the first time in nearly two weeks, Kai made the journey from his home to Ako Castle, although getting there took him half the morning, and far more than half his strength.

Lord Asano was dead . . . by his own hand, at the Shogun's order. Kai had not even learned of the death, or what had led up to it, until days later, when he had wakened once more in his hut with no idea how long it had been since his disgrace.

The last thing he really remembered was being thrown out of the castle, by Oishi's order. . . . But as his eyes slowly cleared, he saw one of Oishi's samurai in the hut with him—a man so big that he almost filled the remaining space of the hut's interior. *Basho* . . . Yasuno's best friend, and an insufferable jokester, whose jokes had been at Kai's expense more often than he liked to remember.

Basho sat in a pose usually reserved for meditation, silently reading a scroll.

"Why . . . ?"

Kai wasn't aware that he had said it aloud until Basho glanced up at him. Basho turned away and put the scroll back into the carven box behind him. Lord Asano himself had given Kai that box, to protect his small accumulation of treasured books and scrolls, after Kai had asked if he could sometimes be paid not in the worker's usual stipend of rice, but in cast-off books from the *daimyo*'s library.

"Get . . . out," Kai whispered, his voice trembling as much with outrage as weakness. "My house. Out—" He tried to raise an arm to point at the doorway.

Basho nodded placidly and said, "When I'm through."

Kai shut his eyes, shaking his head. There wasn't so much pain now, or so much fog. No rain. . . . He remembered, then, finally, that Chikara had come to find him where he lay in the mud . . . and this man had been there too. They had been trying to take him home when Oishi had caught up with them, slapped Chikara, and ordered them back to the castle. Chikara had gone, because his father was also his commander. But Basho had merely nodded, and said, "When I'm through."

And that was all . . . until now.

Basho lifted Kai's head and made him drink tea. It tasted of earthy ginseng, bitter honeysuckle, and pungent ginger . . . to strengthen his body, to ease his feverish mind, to settle his queasy stomach. He realized then that he also reeked of onions; almost his whole body had been plastered with cloth soaked in a warm broth made from boiled scallions, to take the pain out of his wounds.

"You know your medicinals, halfbreed," Basho said, looking around as if he was honestly impressed by the baskets filled with small bundles of herbs, and the plants Kai had drying overhead. "You already had everything I needed. I saw the shrine outside. Were you raised by *yamabushi* monks?"

"No." Kai turned his face away. "Why are you here?" He couldn't remember Basho ever having spoken more than two words to him before, and one of them had also been "halfbreed."

"Chikara is confined to the barracks. Someone had to come—and I have some knowledge of healing. Alone, you would have died."

Kai had tried to find the strength to ask why that mattered to Basho, or anyone. He said nothing.

"You needed to live," Basho said, as if he had read Kai's thoughts in his expression, or his silence, "for Lady Mika's sake. And for Lord Asano's. . . . He's waiting for your prayers."

Kai looked back. "What—?"

Basho glanced down. "Lord Asano . . . was forced to commit *seppuku*."

"What?" Somehow Kai managed to push himself up onto an elbow. "Because . . . of *me*?"

"No." Basho's large hand barely touched his chest; Kai collapsed under its weight. "Lie still."

And then he explained. Everything.

He had gone away, after that, leaving Kai to sip the dregs of his misbegotten life, which had left him with nothing but pain and remorse.

It had taken him more days than he thought he could endure of helplessly lying in his hut, and enduring Basho's visits, before he could even crawl again, let alone walk any distance at all. He still had not been to Lord Asano's grave on the promontory to pray for his spirit and say a final good-bye . . . to ask for forgiveness; and, if it was his right, to grant it. He didn't have the strength yet to make the climb.

But the way to the castle lay over fairly flat ground, and so at last he had made the long, exhausting trek there to pray at the Asano family shrine before the final memorial day had passed.

He entered the lower courtyard, wishing that he was dressed in the all white garments that were appropriate for the visit he was making today. But as usual he had only the clothes on his back, and though he had painstakingly mended and patched them, he suspected he could pass for a beggar, looking the way he did. He hoped that the people milling around the merchants' stalls and barracks would do their best to find him invisible, which was the usual lot of beggars.

Entering the upper courtyard was more difficult; beggars were never allowed near the official living area of the *daimyo*'s family and senior officers. But Kai was known to enough of the castle's guards so that he was able to find the shrine before he was harassed by anyone else.

He slipped inside, closing the door again as quietly as possible. The scent of incense filled his head. Mika was there, alone, kneeling with her head bowed before the statue of Buddha. A wisp of smoke from the incense rose into the still air above her.

He walked the length of the shrine to kneel down beside her, his body obeying his will well enough so that his arrival did not disturb her prayers.

Although she did not look up at him, he could tell by the

faint tremor that ran through her body that she realized who had come to pray beside her. He bowed his own head without speaking, and with all the gratitude and sorrow held prisoner inside him, prayed that Lord Asano's soul would find its reward—that he would be reborn into a better, more just world, the one he had earned, and deserved.

And then he prayed, with all of his heart, for Mika, who had lost more than he could even begin to grasp when she lost her father. No matter what else came to pass, she would never again have the comfort of someone she could turn to in times of need, for help, for unquestioning love and support . . . for the rest of her life. And he already knew that was a fate worse than death.

His memories of the tournament and how it had ended were muddled, but certain images remained, burned into his brain, that would leave scars worse than the beating he had received. *The humiliation of being treated like an animal . . . to be called an animal again, after so long, by Lord Asano himself.*

But he had brought it on himself, trying to be someone he could never be . . . and by his actions he had dragged the honor of Mika and her father, and all of Ako, down with him. Now that his mind was clear again, he understood why Lord Asano had said what he had, and so it was easy to forgive: He had said it to save his daughter from what she had done. And all that she had done was try to save Kai's unworthy life.

In calling him an animal, Lord Asano had been too kind: His body might be only human . . . but it was cursed with a demon's soul.

He finally allowed himself to turn his head to glance at Mika. His thoughts flooded with unexpected tenderness as he saw her profile, its proud spirit and beauty turned to fragile porcelain by loss—saw the translucency of her skin, the telltale redness around her eyes, the shadows beneath them that made her look as if she had not slept in days.

He wanted to take her in his arms, to hold her against his

heart, to comfort and protect her . . . to offer her the kind of shelter from life's cruelty that she, and her father, had offered him.

But he did nothing, except keep on silently gazing at her, praying that someday her heart would be whole again.

That someday she might even forgive him.

"It was my fault," Mika murmured, staring down at her father's portrait, and the offerings that lay before it: the bowls of rice and fruit, a cup of *sake,* a bouquet of fresh flowers from his own garden.

"No," Kai whispered, stunned.

"All I could think of was you." She still did not look up at him, only went on staring at the things laid out before her. He saw her eyes brim with fresh tears. "I never had the courage to tell him . . ."

She met his gaze at last. Always, secretly, he had been afraid that one day he would find he had disappeared from her eyes, but he saw the same love for him that had always been there . . . left torn and bleeding now by the knives of her guilt. "You were right," she said, her voice dreary with resignation. "You had your place, and I had mine. I was wrong to dream."

Kai reached out, only to touch her hand—but she rose and turned her back on him. She walked away toward the door as quickly as she could, before he could do anything to stop her.

He remained where he was as the door banged shut behind her. He bowed his head and pressed his hands together, trying again to pray; but no prayer would come to him now that held any meaning at all.

9

The *tobari* from the tournament had all been taken down by the time the Shogun had departed, but they had not all been stored away. A small number had been set aside, by Oishi's order.

Now they had been set up again, in the castle's upper courtyard—as *jin maku*, the walls of a makeshift field headquarters.

The silhouettes of guards holding spears and *naginata* lay reassuringly across the faintly flapping walls, as Oishi listened without comment to the final arguments of his most obstinate officers regarding the future of Ako, and their own futures as well.

The Shogun had said he would return in a month. Oishi had never before experienced a month that had passed so swiftly, and yet with such agonizing slowness.

Three days ago he had received word from a messenger that the Shogun would arrive today—and not alone.

He had finished all the preparations the Shogun's adjutant had ordered him to make before their return . . . the preparations Lord Asano had not been given time to make. He had not even needed to ask what the Shogun's adjutant had meant.

In the Shogun's mind, Ako Castle and its lands had already been confiscated.

But Oishi, with Lady Mika's approval, had made additional preparations of his own, just as the Shogun had been doing.

Their lord was dead, by the Shogun's order, making the reason for the abrupt departure and date of return equally clear: The Shogun had needed that time to conscript troops from the neighboring *daimyo*—staunch supporters of the *bakufu*—and ensure that there would be supplies available for a siege, if necessary. He intended to leave no question about the outcome when he returned to claim Ako Castle. The samurai of Ako would surrender their lord's domain to him immediately and bloodlessly . . . or they would all die.

In the chaotic era before the Tokugawa Peace, control of land had ebbed and flowed like the turning of the tide, and a samurai's duty had been clear: He lived and died serving the clan of his lord, and no one else. But the Tokugawa dynasty had its own interpretation of *Bushido*. Now a samurai's ultimate loyalty belonged to the ultimate lord—the Shogun—superseding the generations-long tradition of service to his own *daimyo*.

But the Shogun was a total stranger to most people who lived beyond an easy day's journey to Edo. Samurai who were not a direct part of the *bakufu*'s immense bureaucracy had little motivation to dedicate their lives to the Shogun—particularly if generations of their family still lived much as they always had in a remote domain like Ako, where the Asano clan's independent rule had remained largely undisturbed for the last hundred years. Officially, the samurai of Ako swore fealty to the new order, but their true loyalty to their own lord remained unchanged.

It too had remained unchallenged . . . until now.

So far there had been few desertions among the troops that Oishi had under his command, despite the fact that their lord was dead, or the reality of what they were facing. The mercenary arquebusiers had gone back to their home provinces, but they were commoners, and that was their right. He was grateful for, and encouraged by, the willingness of Ako's own troops to stay exactly where they were. Many of the peasants and villagers who lived outside the walls had joined them here; he was surprised by how many. They were being housed in the castle's keep. The original function of any keep had been as a sanctuary, not just for the nobility but for citizens of Ako who were threatened by an invading army.

In these times, when domains tended to change hands peacefully—if under duress—ordinary people had very little to lose by doing nothing, and nothing to gain by fighting back except a bloody death. Given the fact that the Shogun was expected to arrive today before sundown, Oishi realized that Lord Asano's benign rule—and the people's outrage at his abrupt and seemingly inexplicable execution—had stirred unusual feelings of loyalty and defiance in all but the most remote of them.

For the samurai it was different: "Men who served" was what "samurai" meant. The unwritten code they lived by, which had evolved through centuries of warfare and strife, put their very lives in their lord's hands, creating bonds between samurai and their *daimyo* the same way that members of a family were bound to one another, and to its patriarch. Oishi himself was a distant blood relative of Lord Asano, but there was more than one kind of blood bond, and even domains without an enlightened leader like Ako's lord, "families"—mired in resentment or led by fools—still tended to band together to defy an outside threat. "Don't rejoice over him that goes, before you see him that comes," was a very old saying.

The men who served Lord Asano were his family. Which meant they were a threat to anyone—even the Shogun—who tried to seize his domain. That was why Lord Asano had had to die first, and suddenly—so that there would be no question of divided loyalties. Left without a lord, the samurai would not be expected to resist; the Shogun was now their only lord, and to defy him was treason.

If they chose willful defiance anyway, he had gathered

an army and all the resources he needed to destroy them. Any defenders of Ako who did not die in battle would be executed—they would all die, one way or another. But this would be their last chance to die an honorable death, a true samurai's death—instead of the disgraceful living death they faced otherwise, as masterless ronin.

And yet if they fought, the people who had come to them for protection would die, too—and once that kind of retribution began, not even the gods knew how many innocent people would be slaughtered before it ended, simply to make an example of the rebels. Ako would be put to the torch and sword, as a lesson to any other malcontents who would deny their "higher fealty" to the Shogun . . . just as Lord Asano had feared.

And then there was Lady Mika. Even though as a woman she could not legally inherit Ako, she was the last surviving member of the Asano bloodline, and they still owed her their allegiance. She would be left with no control over her future if they allowed the castle to be taken without a fight, and only one choice—the same one her father's samurai would have—if they refused to surrender it.

Lady Mika was fully aware of the consequences, and yet she had left the final judgment to him, pragmatically acknowledging that her father would have confided in his *karou* about harsher truths and harder decisions than he could ever bring himself to share with his daughter.

Over the years Oishi had grown so skilled at the game of *shogi*—the game of generals—that even Lord Asano had claimed he would rather play dice, and leave the outcome to chance, than leave it to his "opponent's" wiliest strategist.

Only in the past month had Oishi come to realize, all too clearly, that *shogi* was a game played with wedge-shaped pieces of wood . . . not human lives.

Generals conquer, soldiers are killed. A man did not become a general by sacrificing pieces of wood.

He had not slept more than an hour or two a night, for the last week. Instead he had spent the interminable hours of darkness praying in the Asano family shrine, pleading with the gods for guidance, for inspiration that would not come.

He still had no idea what he was going to do—and at any moment, he expected a guard in one of the watchtowers to shout that the Shogun, with his newly gathered army, had just come into sight.

Which was why he was still listening to arguments over whether to bar the gates and prepare for a siege, or to throw them open and accept the inevitable.

"Promise me you will put Ako first." That had been Lord Asano's last request. And Oishi had sworn he would uphold it, even though at the time he had barely grasped the implications behind the words. He had his orders from Lord Asano; if he was true to the warrior code of *giri*, unquestsioning obedience to his *daimyo*'s orders, it should not be so hard to make this decision.

Except for one thing. Throughout this entire month, there had been a wrenching certainty in his soul that he knew exactly who, among the Shogun's favorites, would be the one to profit from Lord Asano's downfall.

It would be Lord Kira.

Somehow this was all Kira's doing, although he couldn't imagine how the man had twisted the Shogun's mind, and fate itself, into such contortions. Except that he had recalled—only after Lord Asano's death—that Kai had come to his house on the night the Shogun arrived, and tried to warn him about Kira. Kira's holdings were deep in the mountains; the idea that he might actually be in league with a *kitsune* made all too much sense, in hindsight.

But it was too late now to go back to that moment, and really listen to what the halfbreed had said . . . even though he knew many people who claimed a halfbreed and a demon were one and the same. What if Kai actually had a demon's ability to sense other demons—if he had truly seen a fox-witch, in the forest where they had killed the *kirin*, and then again in Lord Kira's entourage . . . ?

Oishi's mind refused to let him add "ignoring the impossible" to everything else he bore responsibility for, now that it was too late . . . when the danger that was approaching like a flight of arrows was already too close to avoid.

". . . What is there to think about?" Yasuno's voice rose as he tried to shout down someone who disagreed with him, dragging Oishi's mind unwillingly back into the argument going on around him. Everyone here was as close to snapping from the stress as a rotten bowstring, and Yasuno's lingering frustration over what had happened during the tournament had only made his disposition more difficult.

Hazama, Oishi's second-in-command, said again, as he had said repeatedly, "Our master accepted his sentence. So must we—"

"Our master was deceived!" Yasuno said angrily. "He would never have attacked Lord Kira without a reason!"

"The Shogun's law will demand that we give up the castle—" Horibe's indignant rasp joined with Yasuno's protest. At an age when most men sat by the fire while their grandchildren chewed their food for them, he was still as strong—and as stubborn—as a wild boar. To die in battle now would be the best thing he could look forward to . . . but that was hardly the case for most of Ako's people.

"We cannot defy him," Basho said, shaking his head. "We must think of Lord Asano's descendants—" Oishi had sometimes wondered, given Basho's irreverent sense of humor and friendship with the hotheaded Yasuno, whether he had been thrown out of the monastery where he had spent his youth. And yet at times like this, he found himself wondering whether Basho's enormous body concealed the soul of a bodhisattva.

Whenever a situation caused conflict between his moral sense and unquestioned obedience, Basho unhesitatingly chose *ninjo*, the voice of his own conscience, over *giri*. Many lords would have banished him or put him to death for such disobedience; Lord Asano had not been one of them. Oishi had never forgotten how Basho's wisdom had freed the young Mika-*hime*—and through her Lord Asano himself—from the pit of grief in which they were trapped after her mother's death.

And now only Basho, among all his commanders, seemed to fully grasp the consequences, if they defied a direct command from the Shogun: that not only would everyone in Ako suffer, but the House of Asano would disappear forever.

"His descendants will curse us if we do nothing!" Isogai said, as if it had never occurred to him that Lord Asano would have no descendants, if they were defeated in battle and Lady Mika died here. Isogai's good looks and good manners had won him the favors of numerous women; when it came to giving advice to the lovelorn he was eloquent. But when it came to comprehending the implications of a situation like this, he was too young to think beyond the point of his own sword.

Oishi looked from one concerned, anxious face to another, torn between *giri* and *ninjo.* His understanding of *Bushido,* and even his faith in the gods, had failed to guide him when he needed it most . . . failed to help him make the best choice, the wisest decision, when it came to protecting the future of Lady Mika, of his troops, and of the people of Ako. He simply did not know whether he could trust the *bakufu*'s promises, when Lord Kira could manipulate the Shogun like a puppet.

And always—always—he was haunted by the memory of his promise to Lord Asano—

Yasuno turned on him in exasperation, as he still said nothing. "Our families have served this house for generations. They taught us our duty as samurai. Honoring our master comes before anything else. We must have revenge!"

Oishi's mouth turned down, as his own choice—or lack of one—became clear to him at last. "They also taught us that to give one's life needlessly is a dog's death." He gazed steadily at Yasuno, before he looked from one face to another around the table. All at once he knew with absolute certainty what his course of action had to be, and wondered how it could have taken him so long to see something that should have been obvious. "Defying the Shogun will not set Lord Asano's soul free. Only Lord Kira's death can avenge him."

All the men around him fell silent, staring at him, their faces equally stunned. Lord Asano was dead because of Lord Kira. Every one of them knew it. And until their lord's death was avenged, his tormented soul would find no rest, on earth or in heaven.

"If we fight now, we die," Oishi said. "And not just us. Every farmer and villager in Ako will be killed." He went on meeting their eyes, searching for genuine understanding of the consequences of their actions. "Who will be left to avenge our lord then—?"

No one answered. That there had been no actual wars since the Tokugawa regime had turned the country into a military dictatorship was true. But every man around him knew that there had been occasional rebellions, flare-ups of violence—like the one they were still debating now. Whichever Shogun had been in power had made swift, brutal examples of the leaders and any supporters who were captured alive . . . and anyone else at all who had been caught up in the net of the *bakufu*'s overwhelming military force. It hadn't even mattered how many of the Shogun's troops lost their lives to achieve such a crushing victory, when the Shogunate's takeover of domains had made hungry ronin ten for a *bu*.

He had given Lord Asano his word. They had their orders—they had had them all along. "Lord Asano sacrificed himself to save Ako. His final request was that we put Ako first. . . . We must put Ako first. We *submit* and endure any shame, until they believe the danger has passed." He hesitated, feeling all their eyes fixed on his face. He looked back at them, his own gaze suddenly as merciless a hawk's. "Then we strike." The deadly promise behind the quiet words froze the men where they stood. Silent and motionless, they listened as he said, "When Kira's bloody head rests atop the grave of our lord, *that* is when we can talk of honor." He rose to his feet and left the map table abruptly, signaling for the squires standing at the entrance of the enclosure to open the closed access. Stepping out into the courtyard, he made his decision final.

As he stood looking at the samurai officers and their assembled troops deployed throughout the upper courtyard, sudden shouts of "Alert! Alert!" reached him from one watchtower and then another overlooking the road that led to the castle. The officers who had spent their last hours arguing with each other, and him, burst from the tent behind him, and headed for their command positions.

The moment he had been dreading for so long had finally arrived. He gave silent thanks to the gods that his choice had become clear to him as well . . . not a moment too soon. Glancing toward the palace, he saw Lady Mika standing on a balcony, straining for a glimpse of what the sentries had seen.

He ran to the nearest watchtower and climbed to the top. The man standing guard there handed him a spyglass and pointed wordlessly. Oishi saw, with unmistakable clarity, the vanguard of the Shogun's army descending the crest of a distant hill. Once he had identified what he was seeing, he also recognized the line of troops behind them, stretching into the distance over hilltop after hilltop along the undulating road, until they were lost in the haze.

How many troops had the Shogun brought with him? The question was as meaningless, Oishi realized, as the answer was obvious: *Too many.* He could make out the shining gold-and-black armor of the Shogun's Honor Guard at the forefront now, flags and banners emblazoned with the Tokugawa *mon.*

The Shogun had returned, as he had promised . . . and this time he had come to stay.

From Mika's outer chambers, the view of the approaching army, with its weapons and armor catching fire in the late afternoon sun, seemed like the vision of a dragon winding its way toward the castle, as unstoppable as a force of nature.

Her attendants were weeping in quiet despair all around her, but she scarcely heard them. She had moved at last beyond her own grief and fear into a place where, at least for now, there seemed to be no emotion left in her—only a perfectly rational grasp of what was inevitable, and what options remained open.

In her mind, she reviewed the events that would likely follow, and what actions she had chosen to take, depending on what Oishi's ultimate decision had been. She had trusted him to decide wisely, because she knew the respect her father had held for his judgment in matters of military strategy.

One of her attendants reluctantly touched her sleeve to draw her attention, and held out what she realized was a small sachet of poison. Mika accepted it without comment, and slipped it into a sleeve of her robes, although she had no intention of using it . . . at least not on herself.

She took her attendant's tear-wet hand in her own, squeezing it gently. *"Do not give up, just because I am gone,"* her father had told her. She would face the Shogun proudly, filled with her father's spirit, just as Oishi would today. "We have not lost Ako yet," she murmured. And then she went to the window again.

Oishi returned to the warriors positioned around the upper courtyard. There were more men assembled in the lower courtyard, as well as all along the walls and at the archer's slits in the keep.

It struck him that he had never seen all of Ako's troops assembled at the same time and place, all prepared to do battle against an enemy, real or imaginary, before. *This was not a training exercise.* All these men under his command . . . and facing the Shogun. He said another brief prayer that at the end of the day everyone in Ako Castle would still be among the living; that Lord Asano had not sacrificed his own life in vain.

His eyes searched the yard for Chikara, and found him at his post among the samurai who were charged with keeping the castle's servants and workers orderly, and getting them into the keep, if necessary. He suddenly recognized Kai, standing near his son—standing back among the other workers, but, he realized, not really standing with them. He wore a *bokken* thrust through the sash of his ragged kimono, and the look in his eyes said that he had come here to fight for Ako, again—to fight and to die, if necessary.

Oishi kept his face expressionless as he looked away from the halfbreed and started wordlessly toward the upper courtyard's closed gate. He was surprised that Kai was capable of walking, let alone fighting, even now, after the beating he had taken—and even more surprised that he had come here to fight alongside the men who had given him that beating. Had he come for Lord Asano's sake? Or because he wanted to take his own revenge against the Shogun, or Kira? Or had he simply come to die a dog's death? Whatever it was he wanted, Oishi was determined that he would not get it today. . . .

Oishi stopped before the gate, and ordered the guards to open it wide. He felt as much as heard the murmur of surprise that passed through the officers and troops as he gave the command.

Kai stared at Oishi's back, as stunned and confounded as any of the warriors around him. Along with everyone else, he watched the gate rumble open; he watched Oishi pass through it, hurrying down the winding corridor to the lower courtyard, where he shouted an order to the guards to unbar the gate in the outer wall.

After another long pause, they heard the outer gate being hauled open. The voices of the servants around him began to rise in consternation; several samurai yelled at them to be silent as Oishi finally returned through the inner gate.

Chikara glanced over his shoulder at Kai, his face as concerned as all the rest. But Kai's attention was focused beyond them, now, as he listened to what they would all be hearing in another moment.

The Shogun's army swept into the lower courtyard and his foot soldiers fanned out, creating a barrier of weapons along both sides of the pathway that Oishi had ordered cleared to the inner gate, guaranteeing the Shogun's safe passage directly to the upper level, and directly to the place where Oishi waited, forced back against the ranks of his assembled troops as more of the Shogun's guards poured into the courtyard around him.

The Shogun rode along the open corridor between his troops and into the upper yard, followed by officers of the *daimyo* whose troops augmented his own . . . and with Lord Kira riding beside him.

Oishi watched them come, with a stoic dignity that barely survived the rush of hatred he felt as he saw Kira and realized his worst fear had been justified.

Then, without saying a word to anyone, he went down on his knees and laid his swords on the ground, prostrating himself in surrender.

For a long moment no one else moved. And then, one by one, his officers did the same. The soldiers behind them hesitated, uncomprehending at first as they listened to the clatter of swords on the flagstones. Then they followed the example of their officers as if it had been a shouted command, kneeling and laying down their weapons as obediently as they would have charged into battle.

The servants and other commoners quickly dropped to their knees and prostrated themselves, too. Kai was one of the last to move . . . still unable to believe that Oishi had actually surrendered, even while all those around him were like a field mown down at harvest time.

A solitary figure emerged from the palace: Lady Mika, holding her head high, wearing the colors of House Asano with its *mon* clearly displayed on her robes. Kai watched as she crossed the courtyard to face the Shogun alone, with no one to accompany her, or even follow behind. The sight of her courage and her vulnerability made him ache inside.

She stopped at last in front of the Shogun as her own people, his commanders, and Lord Kira all looked on. She bowed deeply, but did not kneel.

"I am sorry for your father's death, Lady Asano," the Shogun said almost gently, seeing nothing before him but a lone, frail woman. "He accepted it with great dignity."

Mika looked up at him, her expression as unaffected as if he had said nothing. "Lord Shogun, as my father's only child, I ask that I may look after his lands until such time as I marry."

Surprised mutterings passed through the men around the Shogun. None of them were used to a woman—even a *daimyo*'s daughter—addressing the highest lord in the land so directly, as if she were an equal.

The Shogun raised his war fan abruptly, silencing them, before he looked down at Mika again. "I have considered this already, my lady," he said. Even as Kai wondered what exactly he meant by that, Lord Kira dismounted and walked toward Mika.

"Lady Asano," Kira said, "I don't know why your father tried to take my life, but I grieve for him and honor him." He bowed low before her.

Mika stared at him, her eyes filled with suspicion and barely concealed loathing as he raised his head, looking up into her eyes.

"If you can forgive me, I would give that life to serve you as a husband. And the people of Ako as their regent."

Watching from the crowd, Kai muttered a curse in sudden disbelief. Mika looked no less stunned, as she turned back to the Shogun to protest. "Your—"

The Shogun gestured, silencing her. "So that there is no feud between your clans, I decree that from this day they are one, sealed by the marriage bond between you."

After a long moment Mika bowed, her reluctance obvious in every rigid line of her body. But even as she seemed to acquiesce, her mind still searched for a way out of this new unexpected trap. With only the faintest trace of stubbornness beneath the respect in her voice, she said, "My Lord Shogun, tradition demands a period of mourning for my father."

The Shogun paused, and then nodded. "You are granted one year to mourn."

Mika's head rose at the small victory—

Until the Shogun said, "But you will remain a guest of Lord Kira's until you are married." If he even noticed the stark dismay that filled her eyes, he chose to ignore it.

Not a guest; a hostage. Kai's fists knotted with the knowledge that there was nothing at all he could do to stop it. He glanced at Oishi, still on his knees, head down, not objecting or even trying to intervene.

"I leave her in your care, Lord Kira," the Shogun said, looking relieved at the swift and bloodless conclusion of a potentially volatile situation, and satisfied with what he probably thought was his own wisdom. He sent a final dismissive glance toward Oishi and the other samurai. "These men will be stripped of their privileges, but none of them is to be harmed."

Lord Kira bowed. "Shogun." He looked up again and cleared his throat, as if he intended to say something more.

The Shogun glanced at him. Then, like a player who had forgotten to say his lines, he looked toward the place where Oishi was still kneeling. "Any pursuit of a vendetta in regard to Lord Asano's death is forbidden. It is my determination that Lord Kira shares no responsibility for your former master's actions. Your right under law to seek vengeance for your lord's death is abrogated, and any attempt on Lord

Kira's life will result in your being tried as common criminals. The sentence is death by hanging."

The Shogun looked away again, oblivious to Oishi's suddenly raised head, and the flush of outrage on his face. The Shogun nodded to his retinue as he swung his horse around. And then he rode back down the corridor between his troops without a glance at the army of Ako, kneeling in surrender behind them, leaving Mika, and Ako, in the hands of Lord Kira. The Shogunate troops who had come with him remained in their places, still on guard. They were here to stay, for the indeterminate future, along with Kira's retainers.

As the sound of the Shogun's departure faded, Kira stared at Mika in frank admiration, as if she was the prize possession as well as the undeniable proof of his new wealth and position. Then he turned toward the samurai of Ako and smiled with cold pleasure at the sight of his enemies still on their knees, waiting for his command merely to be allowed to stand up again.

"From this moment on," he called out, "you and your families are banished from these lands by order of the Shogun. You are ronin—masterless samurai. Those who remain will be hunted down and executed."

Kai ignored the words, which had nothing to do with him, his attention fixed on Mika.

As if she felt his gaze willing her to see him, she turned toward the crowd, searching until she found his face, and looked back at him with hopeless longing.

Lord Kira glanced at her as she turned away from him. His expression darkened as his eyes followed her yearning look into the crowd. As if he knew exactly who she was looking at, he raised his arm and pointed at Kai. "Guards—take that animal and sell him to the Dutch."

Mika's face filled with horror as Kira's men pushed into the crowd and surrounded Kai. Kai scrambled to his feet and tried to break free, but the sudden panic of the people around him blocked his escape, and then there were too many weapons. A guard seized his arm, twisting it painfully behind his back, as they forced him out of the crowd and away across the yard.

Watching with grim satisfaction, Kira saw Kai look down at Oishi with hatred and betrayal in his eyes as he was driven past the place where the *karou* still kneeled in front of his men.

Oishi glanced up as Kai was taken away; his face seemed not to change at all, as if he was completely indifferent. But Kira caught a flicker of something in his eyes, saw him lean toward the grizzled samurai on his left and whisper in his ear.

The other man nodded ever so slightly. Kira frowned, and signaled to the black-armored giant who stood waiting at his side—the same warrior who had beaten Kai in the tournament a month ago. "I don't trust Oishi," he muttered, staring at the kneeling figure across the courtyard. "He no longer has the protection of his rank. Have him thrown in the dungeon—break his will."

Mika was still gazing at Kai in anguish. She took a step toward him as he was dragged past them. Kira grabbed her by the arm, holding her in a grip like a vise. "Embarrass me, and I'll have him burnt alive." The promise in his voice froze her in place. But she went on staring at Kai as if no one else in the world existed.

As if he felt Mika's desolation, Kai somehow broke the hold the guards had on him, shaking them off just long enough to look back at her—his desperate eyes making a silent promise—before he was clubbed to the ground by a sheathed sword. Kira's guards shackled him hand and foot, and dragged him out through the courtyard gates.

Kira watched them disappear, still keeping his grip on Mika's arm. *The Dutch would find a use for that filth she thought she loved . . . one he'd never come back from. The Dutch were hardly better than barbarians when it came to their morals, but even they despised a halfbreed.*

At last he gave the order for his troops to begin collecting the weapons of the Ako soldiers—particularly the matched sets of long and short swords that only the highest ranked samurai were permitted to wear.

Technically he had no right to take their swords; while they lived, samurai blood still flowed through their veins, even if they were mere ronin now. He was simply making certain they were clear about the terms of their own survival. Their swords were their souls made visible. Men facing not only the loss of their homes and livelihoods, but also their very identities, were not likely to have the spirit or the resources to plot against him.

All of them . . . except one. One whose fate he would see to personally. "Kuranosuke Oishi?" he called out. "I require a bit of your time."

The former chief retainer of Ako Castle looked up, startled, struggling to hide the mistrust on his face as Kira approached him. Oishi was too proud to ask questions, which was just as well, Kira thought.

Because he wouldn't like the answers at all.

Oishi got to his feet reluctantly and followed at Kira's nod. Bodyguards flanked them, surrounding him immediately. Kira's men seemed to be commanded by the giant in black armor.

They walked across the courtyard, passing a number of official buildings, including the Great Hall and the palace. The concern Oishi struggled to keep hidden grew more obvious on his face as they passed beyond sight of the Ako troops. "If you wish me to show you the information about . . . your new domain, Lord Kira, the official records are—"

Kira glanced at the black-armored samurai, who made a motion as if he was swatting a fly. His gauntleted hand struck Oishi a blow to the side of the head that knocked him sprawling, and sent his helmet rattling away across the flagstones.

The giant samurai hauled him to his feet again by the back of his cuirass.

Lord Kira turned to look at him, and with an unpleasant smile said, "That won't be necessary."

The black-armored giant kept his grip on Oishi, forcing him forward again, although his head rang like temple bells, and his knees buckled with each step. He had a strobing flash of memory: *The halfbreed landing on his back in the dirt of the tournament arena, his helmet rolling to a stop twenty feet away, in front of the samurai of Ako.*

Ahead of them now lay only the castle's keep: the symbol of its strength, and its purpose—to protect the lord and the people of Ako. He remembered suddenly that the castle dungeons were beneath the keep.

He thought about Riku, and Chikara—so near, and yet suddenly so unreachable. *Would he ever see them again?* Sweat soaked his clothes under his armor; the utter totality of Ako's loss, and his own, made him want to weep. Nothing but the lifelong conditioning of a samurai kept his face immobile in front of his enemies.

He realized numbly that even his pride was nothing more than a conditioned habit; not soul-deep, as he had always believed. He was grateful for it, nonetheless, as Kira's guards forced him down the steps that led to the dungeons. Kira stayed behind, watching them descend. Midway down, Oishi's foot slipped; the giant in black let him go, and he fell the rest of the way to the bottom. Kira smiled and then disappeared, heading back to the world of the living and his new domain.

Normally it took two or three prison guards to move aside the massive iron grate that covered the pit in the depths of Ako Castle's ancient dungeon, but this time it took only one enormous shove by a giant wearing black armor.

It took four of Kira's guards to force Oishi's struggling body to the edge of the lightless hole that the lid revealed. The bottom of the isolation pit lay fifteen feet below . . . the floor of a dank stone-walled space no larger than a storage room, that the dungeon guards at Ako had always called "*jigoku*": *the Underworld . . . hell.* Rats scurried into hiding as unexpected torchlight struck their silent world from high above.

A hard blow to the back from the giant's hand knocked Oishi forward; the guards released him, and with a cry he fell into the darkness. His body hit the stone floor with a heavy thud. The shaft of light in which he lay shrank to a slit, and then disappeared; but he was no longer conscious to see the light die.

Oishi opened his eyes again in confusion, to almost utter darkness and silence, and a stench that made him want to retch—as if the pain in his head was not enough to sicken him.

Gods, what had happened to him? Was he ill . . . had he been having a nightmare?

Was something really crawling on him—?

He sat up with a curse that echoed in the silence, as something nipped his hand. Rats scrabbled off him, and away into the darkness. *Rats—?*

He swore again, as the pain of his fifteen-foot fall into the pit, and the rough handling of Kira's guards before they had thrown him into it, seemed to register in every nerve ending he possessed . . . and then the devastating totality of Kira's treachery overwhelmed him.

Yesterday he had been the chief retainer of Ako Castle, the second highest-ranking position in the domain of Ako . . . a samurai, proud of his honor and his loyalty to his lord, even in the face of the most painful choice he had ever made. He had made the sacrifice Lord Asano had required of him, and obeyed his lord's last wish.

But he had never imagined that the real choice he had been facing was an impossible one. There had been no right answer to the question of what he should do, in the face of betrayal so complete it had turned his whole world upside down, casting him down from the heights of Ako into *jigoku*.

Because he had surrendered the castle without a fight, the Shogun had ordered Kira to spare the lives of his men, and there should be no reprisals against Ako domain. But his men had all been banished, and Lady Asano had become Kira's chattel, while the people of Ako would be helpless under Kira's ruthless thumb.

And as long as Kira kept him alive, he could remain a prisoner here forever.

He pushed that thought out of his mind; it was a trapdoor to madness.

Right now only three things concerned him: What would his wife and son do? How long did Kira intend to keep him here? And could he survive, and remain sane, until he was set free . . . assuming he would be?

There was only one of those things that he had any control over at all, and that was the last one. He looked toward the slit of window high on the far wall, wide enough to allow him air to breathe, but much too narrow to squeeze through, even if he could have reached it. Outside, the world was in sunlight, and he could see the branch of a cherry tree. The limb moved fitfully as the wind blew, and a handful of petals from the last of its dying blossoms fell like snow.

I am wondering what to do
With the remaining springtime. . . .

He looked away, fighting the sudden burn of grief again as he remembered the lines from Lord Asano's death poem. There was no use grieving for what he had no control over. The Way of the Warrior taught that his reason for living was to serve his lord, unto death. His lord's death . . . or his own. If his lord died of illness or old age, it became his duty to serve and protect the lord's heir. If the lord's death was caused by treachery or betrayal, it became his duty to avenge that death.

Giri, and *ninjo:* He had not lost either of those. Lady Mika, Lord Asano's heir, was now held hostage by Lord Kira, whose greed and deceit were also to blame for her father's unjust death and his own imprisonment. Lord Kira would give him enough food and water to keep him alive, he was sure of that much, because the Shogun had forbidden Kira to kill him.

In a sudden flash of insight, he realized that Kira was a coward: the kind of man who would sooner attack someone indirectly than confront him in an honest fight. The kind of man who would rather make others destroy themselves than challenge them face to face. This was a game . . . not even of *shogi,* but of *go,* the most subtle battle of all between wits and wills.

He was not the first prisoner who had been thrown into this pit, although he couldn't recall anyone occupying it during his lifetime. How had the others survived? Had any of them survived?

If the answer was *no,* he took a silent vow to be the first. But survival would be meaningless, unless he could stay sane. Dwelling on the past, on all he had lost, would mean he had already surrendered the game to Kira. Worrying about what would become of the people he had tried to protect was equally dangerous. He had to stay focused on the future; had to keep believing there would be a future worth living for. And whatever else happened, he was still samurai, whether Kira or even the Shogun robbed him of his position and his swords.

Kira had killed Lord Asano as surely as if he'd stabbed him in the back . . . and made certain the Shogun stripped his retainers of even the right to avenge him. If Lord Asano's death went unavenged, his soul would remain trapped on the earthly plain, unable to move on—as surely as everyone he had cared about was now trapped, each in their own way. But he would be trapped forever. . . .

There were some things even the rules of an absolute human overlord had no right to deny—and one of them was justice. Oishi had been taught that even the gods suffered, when injustice unbalanced the flow of all existence. It was the gods' will that the balance must be restored—no matter how long it took, or what the cost.

Let the gods bear witness, then: He would become the instrument of their will, no matter what laws of men he had to defy, no matter how long it took, no matter the cost. *Shogi* and *go* were games of strategy, played by men as though they were the gods. The surest way to win was to plan a hundred steps ahead, even as you made your first move. He had all the time he needed, now, for that. . . .

10

The leafless branch of the cherry tree outside the window slit of Oishi's prison was covered with a rime of frost. Oishi sat huddled in a corner of his cell, his arms wrapped tightly against his body to control his shivering and keep his hands warm, because inside the cell it was nearly as cold as it was beyond the window. He had long ago abandoned his armor to the rats, because it was impossible to sleep in armor on the hard stone floor.

The rats had eagerly gnawed away all the bindings of leather and silk cord that had held together the curved plates of metal. He regretted sacrificing it now, because the armor might have kept him warmer. But by now the remains lay scattered around the cell, where he had hurled them against the walls when he still had the strength to act on the fits of anger and despair that had come over him in the early days of his imprisonment.

By now, after months of confinement and starvation rations—shared with his companions, the rats—he had so little strength left in him that to move at all was scarcely worth the effort. He had tried at first to exercise, simply to keep fit, and later to keep warm; now his body used up what energy it had with shivering.

At least the rats finally had made peace with him—they had stopped nipping him and eating holes in his clothing while he tried to sleep—and almost become his friends. But they were poor conversationalists.

By now, so was he; he had grown as still and silent as the darkness around him. At least the branch of the cherry tree, his only proof that the world outside still existed, gave him a vague sense of how long he had been here—although he was no longer sure whether that was a blessing or a curse. He was no more certain by now whether he would be able to keep his vow to live until he saw Lord Asano avenged . . . to be reunited with his family . . . or even to watch the blossoms form again on the naked limb of the cherry tree beyond the window slit.

He started violently and looked up at the sudden sounds of scraping, grating motion overhead. A crack of light appeared, as the stone slab was dragged aside. *Was it time for his daily meal already?*

He pushed himself away from the wall, crawling forward almost eagerly toward the spot where his food would be lowered down to him.

But this time the stone slab continued to open, letting in enough light to blind his eyes, which had become so used to almost none at all. He cringed like a human shadow as the full blaze of torchlight struck him, making him irrationally afraid he would disappear . . . and then simply afraid. They had not opened the stone slab all the way since they had thrown him in here.

A length of rope with a loop tied in the end of it came spiraling down to dangle in the air in front of him. He stared at it in confusion, wondering if they were offering him a chance to hang himself.

The silhouette of a guard's head and shoulders appeared in the square of light above him, and a voice so loud and harsh that it made him cover his ears shouted, "Get up, ronin!"

Slowly Oishi got to his feet, sure he must be dreaming. *Were they actually going to set him free, after all this time . . . or was this some kind of trick?*

He grabbed the rope, which felt real enough, and frantically pulled it over his head and shoulders, before it could catch him around the neck. He tightened it around his chest, with all the strength his cold-numbed hands could manage.

Someone began to pull him up; his body circled in the air, making him giddy. *Was it really possible . . . ?*

His body scraped the edge of the opening, and he was hauled up into the light, blinking and gasping. The first face he made out clearly was his son's.

Chikara's clear brown eyes shone with relief as he helped his father struggle out of the pit and up onto his feet. His son pulled the rope off of him and embraced him—as he had not done since he . . . *since* . . . Oishi couldn't remember how long it had been.

Chikara had gotten taller, Oishi thought; he had also gotten thinner, to the point where his face had lost all trace of boyishness. He no longer wore the clothing of a *karou*'s privileged son, or even a lord's retainer; his worn kimono and *hakama* looked like someone else's hand-me-downs.

Oishi glimpsed his own reflection in Chikara's eyes: filthy and haggard, dressed in rags. He was barely able to walk upright even with his son's support, as Chikara led him away from the place of his premature burial, toward the steps that led up out of the Underworld.

He was still cringing at every sound that struck his overwhelmed senses when they finally reached the castle's outer gates. The sun was hidden behind clouds that threatened snow, but still he had to shield his eyes with a raised arm against the dazzling assault of daylight.

A crowd of villagers stood just outside the gates, waiting for them. He felt Chikara hesitate, as if he was uncertain whether they were here to welcome his father back to freedom, or had been summoned to witness his humiliation and disgrace, still more of the lesson that Kira had intended to teach him . . . and all of Ako.

Oishi stopped as the villagers slowly spread out into the road, as if they meant to confront him. His fear was as painfully heightened by his long solitary confinement as his senses were. Trying to find a face he recognized, he thought he saw Riku . . . but surely that couldn't be his wife, with her hair bound up in a cloth, wearing a peasant woman's drab kimono?

His gaze slipped past her, and caught on a man standing at the edge of the crowd. Nothing really set the stranger apart from the others, and yet there was something indefinably wrong with the way the man was looking at him, so alert and yet oddly emotionless.

A spy. Kira was having him watched.

Part of his brain tried to tell him that he was imagining it: that after all this time, and punishment, even Kira couldn't still be so fearful that Lord Asano's chief retainer would attempt to seek revenge; not with his men scattered to the four winds, and his own life in ruins.

But he suddenly remembered the insight he had had about Kira at the very beginning of his imprisonment: *Kira was a coward.* And a coward never felt safe enough.

One of the guards shoved him, as he stood staring at the villagers and the world he had not seen in so long. Oishi staggered forward as Chikara lost his grip on him, and went down on his hands and knees in the slushy mud, in full view of everyone watching.

The villagers tensed, waiting for his reaction, clearly expecting him to get to his feet and show his anger.

Instead he pushed himself up until he was kneeling, and then abased himself to the guards, bowing until his forehead touched the mud. "Don't hurt me any more," he mumbled.

His humiliation doubled as he raised his head and saw Chikara's face—the anger at the guards turning to disbelief, and then to dismay, as his son stood staring at him like everyone else, speechless.

The guard turned away with a snort of contempt, and went back through the gates of the castle that had always been his home. The pass-through door slammed shut, cutting Oishi off from his former life, and his rightful place in the world, forever.

Oishi did not move from the spot where he had fallen, sitting like a beggar, his shoulders hunched, his head still bent in submission. He felt the judgment of the crowd pressing on him like the weight of the stone slab that had covered his prison cell for so long, as more and more of their faces lost all signs of hope, and their expressions turned to disgust.

A burly peasant approached him as arrogantly as if he was a *hinin,* spat on him, and then stalked away. The other villagers trailed after the man, singly and in clusters, as Oishi still did nothing but sit in the mud, trembling like a beaten dog.

But then someone else approached him and crouched down to gently wipe mud and spittle from his face with the worn sleeve of her kimono. He looked up with bewilderment in his eyes, to see Riku there beside him. It really had been Riku he saw, in the drab cotton kimono of a peasant woman, her hair wrapped in a cloth, no longer elaborately arranged with beautiful pins and combs. And yet she still carried herself with the grace and dignity of spirit that no one had been able to take from her.

He turned his face away, unable to go on looking at her, seeing the love, the heartbreak, and the compassion in her eyes.

Chikara stepped forward again and carefully helped him to his feet. As Riku tried to put her arms around him, he glanced past them and saw Kira's man still lingering in the distance, watching every move he made.

He pushed away from his son and wife, the motion filled with furious self-disgust. "Stay away. Stay away from me!" He staggered off, barely managing to keep his feet as he headed away from Ako Castle—with no idea of where he was going, except that he had to get away from here, from the past that was closed to him like the castle gate. From the nightmare he had finally lived through, but which he knew would haunt his dreams forever, like the memories of death and betrayal, the loss of everything it had been his proud duty to protect and care for. . . .

Especially away from the stranger in the distance still watching his every move.

Riku and Chikara caught up with him, at first trailing him cautiously, keeping a few steps behind his stumbling progress across the bridge, toward the village that lay just outside the boundaries of the castle proper.

Everywhere he looked as he entered the village he saw signs of change for the worse . . . the disrepair of the shops and nouses, the rubbish in the streets, the patched clothing of the people who averted their eyes as he passed. These were the people he and his men had sacrificed their lives to protect, not by dying but by condemning themselves to the shame and hardship of living on as ronin.

The reek of worse things than garbage hung like a pall over the entire village. Beyond it, the rice fields still showed nothing but stubble left from the autumn harvest, but he could spot places where the mounded earth walkways that divided the fields were eroded and uneven, as if the farmers no longer even cared for, or about, their crops, any more than they cared about their lives.

Ako had changed almost as much as he had . . . its people half-starved and sullen, the land itself lying under a curse that had infected them all. *How could it all have gotten this bad, this quickly—?*

Lord Asano had been wise enough to realize that people with enough food to eat, decent clothing, and decent homes were people who had a future worth looking forward to: strong, healthy people who would work hard, willingly, to meet their lord's needs. They had taken their duty to him seriously, because he had never taken too much away from them. The land had responded to their best efforts with its own, and all had prospered.

It was obvious that Lord Kira did not hold the same views, although that was hardly a surprise.

Oishi had hoped that seeing Ako again with the eyes of a free man would help him bring some sense of order back to his fragmented thoughts. But the reality he found here—this land of physical decay and faltering spirits, lying under a leaden sky—matched his own image of what had become of his world all too well.

As he wandered aimlessly through the streets, Riku and Chikara came up alongside him again, at last, each of them gently capturing one of his hands in their own. "Let us take you home, Father, so that you can rest and eat," Chikara said, his eyes pleading with Oishi's to show him a spark of the man he had always known.

Realizing that he had no idea even of where they lived anymore, Oishi acquiesced, allowing them to lead him down narrower streets, through alleys that reeked of communal outhouses, into the poorest part of the town.

He wondered where they were going, and why they were going this way, until they guided him down a final alley, and stopped in front of a flimsy wooden door exactly like every other door in the long row house in front of him. An identical set of row houses faced it across the narrow, muddy lane.

Chikara slid open the door, and they led him inside. *Their new home.* They didn't need to tell him that this was where they had been living while he was in prison. They removed their sandals at the edge of the wooden platform that was the single room's living and sleeping space. A small charcoal brazier, for cooking and heat, was located in the middle of the platform; an iron hook hung from a bamboo framework above it, to hold a cooking pot.

Their entire home was smaller than his study had been in their mansion on the castle grounds. But then, they had virtually no belongings left to take up any space. A small pile of neatly folded futons and blankets occupied one corner; a few pieces of clothing lay neatly in a basket in another.

It occurred to him that his wife and son should not even still be in Ako. Perhaps Kira had used the promise of his release to keep them here—to keep them from traveling to

Edo and protesting to the Shogun; although Oishi doubted the Shogun would have cared, even if they had been allowed an audience with him.

Oishi made no comment as he collapsed almost gratefully onto the platform. His legs were unable to keep holding him up, any more than his body could stop trembling from cold and shock inside the rags of his clothing. Perhaps this was still part of Kira's plan—to let him see how his dishonor had affected his family, how it would go on affecting them, for the rest of their lives.

Chikara wrapped a worn quilt around him, as Riku served up a small bowl of rice, and gave him a cup of hot tea that was so flavorless it could have been nothing but hot water. Oishi gulped the tea as if he was a drunkard downing *sake,* trying to warm himself from inside. He grabbed the food bowl like a man who hadn't eaten properly in months—which he hadn't—stuffing the plain rice into his mouth and swallowing it like a starving beggar, washing it down his parched throat with more gulps of hot tea. Riku and Chikara sat watching him in tense, pained silence; their expressions said they were staring at a stranger.

Oishi finished his rice, oblivious, and picked the last grains from his bowl with dirt-crusted fingers, which he licked off before he set the bowl down again with a sigh.

And then he glanced indifferently out the doorway that he had left half open, despite the cold and damp. He got up and moved stiffly to stand in the opening, gazing up and down the street. When he was certain none of Kira's spies still lingered anywhere near them, he slid the door closed

Moving now with something closer to his old decisive step, he turned and crossed the room to the small shrine Riku had set up. He kneeled carefully before the tiny altar, where the incense she had lit earlier to pray for his safe return still smoldered. He bowed deeply to the presence of merciful Buddha, to all the gods who had answered his prayers and protected his family as well as keeping his own guttering faith alive in the depths of *jigoku.*

And now, he prayed that they would hear him again, and help him keep the vows he had made during his time in hell, to bring about the righting of the wrongs that his duty as a samurai still demanded: vengeance against Lord Kira, which would set Lord Asano's spirit free, as well as restore the honor of the Asano family, and return Lady Mika to her rightful place as Ako's heir and regent. *Justice.*

As he repeated the vow he had made in prison, he felt the plans he had gone over and over in the darkness and silence slowly begin to seep back into his conscious mind.

The laws of men—of the Shogun—had declared that wrong was right, and his plans were treasonous. *Gods,* he prayed, *grant me the privilege of serving as the hands of a higher justice. I don't care what follows.*

He raised his head at last and got to his feet, turning back to his wife and son. When they saw his expression their faces changed, filling with startled relief. The lost look disappeared from Chikara's eyes as he found the courage and resolve in his father's gaze that he had always known and believed in.

"Where are my men?" Oishi said.

Chikara got to his feet and bowed, as if he recognized not only his father but his commanding officer standing before him once more, and realized that Oishi's spirit had not been utterly destroyed by Lord Kira—that his will had proved stronger than the enemy's. *That it had all been an act—*

In response, Oishi managed the best smile he could, knowing in his heart that by the time he was hauled up out of the pit again, the truth had come much closer to Chikara's worst fears than he could have imagined. Even now he wasn't certain how much of his behavior since he'd been released had been pretense to mislead his enemies, and how much had truly come from the place he had withdrawn into, frighteningly deep in his own soul.

But when he had been unceremoniously thrown out of the castle, and seen what had become of Chikara and Riku;

when he had realized that Kira's spies were still watching his every move for a sign that he was not completely broken . . . somehow the things meant to smother the last embers of his spirit instead had fed the guttering flame, and brought substance back to the shadow of a man he had become.

Riku was looking at him gravely, even while Chikara's smile became a joyful grin. She had known him for too long, longer than Chikara had been alive, and he saw the resignation that filled her eyes as his question confirmed her suspicions about his true intent. "They have all left Ako," she said. "I hear Hara has become a monk. Hazama a farmer."

"And Lady Asano?" he asked.

Riku looked down. "She is Lord Kira's 'guest,' a prisoner in his own domain. Her time of mourning is almost over. Lord Kira has already begun preparing for their marriage at *Shunki Korei-sai*."

The festival of the New Moon of Spring—? Hardly any time at all, Oishi realized, to find those among Lord Asano's retainers who were still willing to risk everything to bring peace to their master's soul . . . and to claim their rightful vengeance.

Oishi turned back to Chikara. "What of the halfbreed?" he asked, unable to keep the disdain out of his voice, as the memory of Chikara's loyalty to Kai pricked him like a sword's point. But still, he wasn't able to keep genuine curiosity out of the question.

Chikara looked surprised that he would even ask; his smile fell away as he said, "Kira's men took him to the Dutch Island."

Gods. They had actually done it. And he'd thought his own fate had been cruel. . . .

Oishi looked down, hiding a grimace as he wondered whether it was possible that Kai was even still alive after this long . . . and if he was, whether there was any possibility of getting him off the forbidden ground of the foreigners' island.

He realized he had no choice but to find out. Because as much as he hated to admit it, without the halfbreed's help against Kira, they would still be facing a dog's death. He looked up again, and said to Chikara, "We need horses. Three horses."

Chikara bowed, and eagerness filled his eyes along with determination as he headed for the door. He paused, glancing back at his parents with a smile; and then he let his shoulders slump, changing his expression to hopeless resignation before he went out into the street and slid the door shut behind him.

Riku stared at the doorway as their son disappeared through it. She turned back to Oishi, not quite meeting his eyes, struggling to hide her grief. After so many years of peace and happiness, and then such sudden tragedy, she had believed her prayers had brought her husband safely home to her, only to find she had already lost him again, and now her son as well, as if they were water poured through her open hands.

Oishi raised her chin with gentle fingertips until their eyes met. As he saw the sorrow she could not disguise—not from him, not after so long—he did not even try to disguise his own as he said softly, "You must make the whole world believe you've divorced me. It is the only way to protect you from what I have to do—" He broke off at the stricken look that filled her face. Pulling together the last shreds of his self-control, he murmured, "No one but you and I can know that you are, and will always be, the joy of my life."

Riku drew him into her arms, holding him close, clinging to him as if the warmth of this embrace would have to last her for a lifetime of winters. She pressed her face against his shoulder, hiding her tears, but he felt them soak through his ragged kimono to kiss his skin as he held her, as he set her long dark hair free from its cloth, caressing it with hands that had ached for so long simply to touch her. . . .

She pulled away from him at last, her breathing and her face calm again. In her eyes courage and understanding had replaced loss and grief. "I am the wife of a samurai," she said quietly. "Whatever your duties and obligations, they are mine too." She smiled at him at last, and it was not simply the smile of a dutiful wife, but of a loving, compassionate woman with the soul of a warrior.

Seeing the look in her eyes, he felt he had never loved, or appreciated her more than at this moment . . . and realized the gods were forcing him to acknowledge the true cost of giving his life to a cause greater than himself. He pulled her close again, needing her warmth now more than ever.

Chikara stood with his father in the woods near a crossroads, where he had arrived at sundown with the horses and supplies he had purchased as he wandered through town all day, keeping constantly alert for the eyes of strangers, or even acquaintances who struck him as too curious about what he was doing.

He had gone first to the place where he and his father had buried certain items before the Shogun returned to Ako: a handful of small but valuable belongings—family heirlooms, most of which he had been forced to sell during his father's imprisonment just to keep his mother and himself fed, and a roof over their heads, while they waited for his father to be freed.

His mother had refused to leave Ako as long as his father was still held prisoner here, and surprisingly, Kira's retainers had let them be. He would have done any kind of work, no matter how menial or difficult, to earn the money they needed to live on, but no one would hire him—on Lord Kira's order, he was sure.

At least there had been enough left of their ancestors' blessings to supply his father and himself for their separate journeys—and to hire a palanquin to carry his mother on the long journey to her parents' home. Her family mercifully was not from Ako; once she was reunited with them, she would be safe enough, at least . . . although from the way she had looked at him as they said their good-byes, he had wondered if she would ever smile again.

But her parting words to them both had been, "What you seek is to right a wrong that no one else will even acknowledge . . . what you are seeking is justice. Your names will never be forgotten." And the tears in her eyes had been tears of pride.

Oishi made a last silent circuit on foot through the woods around them; he stood listening, with senses still heightened from his time in solitary confinement. After a moment he sighed, satisfied at last that they were not being surreptitiously observed.

He picked up one of the two things that Chikara had been forbidden to sell—for his own safety, as well as because they were not his family's property: an ancient sword that had belonged to Lord Asano, passed down from his ancestors, which Lady Mika had given to him for safekeeping. He handed it to his son. The other item he kept: the *tanto* with which Lord Asano had taken his own life. It still had one more ritual task to fulfill, before he could lay it as an offering on the grave of his lord.

Chikara took the sword from him, gazing at the Asano family crest engraved on its hilt.

"Show them this," Oishi said, with a nod, "and tell them to meet me at the Buddha Mountain by Black Lake in . . . two weeks. Remember," he repeated for the hundredth time, "the enemy will be watching." He looked long and hard into his son's eyes, to be certain that Chikara understood just how cautious he must be, and yet how quickly he had to move, to accomplish his part in their plan.

"Yes, Father. Yes, sir." Chikara stood straighter, meeting his eyes, his own gaze unwavering and equally resolute, until at last Oishi nodded again, satisfied.

He gave Chikara a leg up onto his horse—a father's parting gesture, from the days when his son had been too small to haul himself up into a saddle on his own. Chikara smiled back at him, and held up Lord Asano's sword in a salute. The sunset that wove the day's last light through the trees illuminated the Asano *mon* on the hilt for a brief moment. And then Chikara rode away, aiming his horse like an arrow into the deepening night.

Oishi picked up the final objects remaining from their cache—a pair of matched long and short swords that had belonged to his father, with their family crest on the hilts. Kira had laid unjust claim to his own swords, the fine set that he had been given when he became *karou,* along with those of all his men at the surrender of Ako Castle.

In terms of cruelty, it had been a petty betrayal compared to what Kira had done to him afterward. But taking the swords of Ako's samurai had been a move intended to completely demoralize and humiliate them all, demonstrating that not only had he robbed them of their homes and their livelihood, but of their very identities as human beings.

It was one more act Oishi kept in his tally of things for which he owed Kira a personal share of heaven's revenge. He was more than glad now that he had been concerned enough about the future to include his father's swords along with Lord Asano's in the hidden cache.

He pushed the two swords through the belt ties of his worn but decent *hakama*. Although he had bathed and put on clean clothes, he realized that until this moment he hadn't felt fully dressed, or whole.

He climbed stiffly into his saddle, and tied the reins of the extra horse to it. He sat a moment with his head bowed in a final prayer, for his son's safe journey, and his wife's . . . and for the strength to endure the hard traveling that lay ahead of him, as well as the courage to face whatever he found when he reached his destination.

He turned his own horse in the other direction, toward the dying sunset, and began his long ride to the Dutch Island.

11

Dejima, the Dutch Island, seemed to float in the middle of Nagasaki Bay like an immense fan dropped from the heavens by a careless god. But there was no place in Japan that had less to do with the gods, or more to do with earthly temptations. The third Tokugawa Shogun, Iemitsu, had banned all Japanese contact with other nations as part of the *bakufu*'s efforts to purge foreign influences from the newly unified country, to keep them from corrupting the unique identity of its people . . . and not coincidentally, keep Japan free of new weapons or other technology that might inspire an ambitious *daimyo* to mount a rebellion against Tokugawa rule.

Only the Dutch, on their tiny island cut off even from the shore, and a small enclave of Chinese traders, were allowed to maintain any contact, and only through isolated Nagasaki. The Dutch East India Trading Company had headquarters throughout Asia, giving them access to things Japan had freely imported for centuries to the point that they had become part of Japanese life. Furthermore, the Company officials were interested only in maximizing their profit, and that made them unlikely to do anything that would upset their unique trade agreement with the *bakufu*.

Like most Japanese, Oishi had never even seen one of the foreigners—the "straw-haired men"—because even their senior representatives were allowed to leave Dejima only once a year, when they were taken directly to visit the Shogun and his advisors.

He had heard talk about them, though—their odd-colored eyes and hair, their strangely shaped faces and hairy, oversized bodies, which made them resemble beasts or demons more than human beings. Most of them had the manners of beasts and the morals of demons, as well; even their smell was offensive, because of their peculiar belief that bathing was unhealthy.

The crews of the visiting Dutch ships were completely confined to Dejima, as were the Company officials who negotiated trade agreements for the ships' captains. They lived and worked full time on the island, for years on end, their lives and homes jammed together with offices and warehouses, among a constantly shifting crowd of *gaijin*—untrustworthy strangers—from their own ships. All of that on a claustrophobic speck of land that measured barely three hundred strides from end to end at its widest point. . . . Even with docks protruding like spines into the water around it, there was little space left to lead a human life among the hoists, ramps, and passageways required to move trade items to and from warehouses and ships.

Dejima was connected to the mainland by a single narrow causeway, heavily guarded to ensure that no one entered or left without official permission. But that didn't mean the foreigners weren't curious about Japan . . . or starved for pleasure, after being cooped up on ocean voyages that had lasted months or even years. They wanted liquor, they wanted women, and they wanted entertainment—the more brutally exotic, the better. Oishi had heard more tales about what the inhabitants of the Dutch Island were like and liked to see than he had ever wanted to, after the story of the *kirin* hunt had spread through the dignitaries who had come to Ako Castle for the Shogun's visit.

And so he also knew that there were ways to make an illegal visit to the Dutch Island, just as there were ways to do anything else, with false documents and the right amount of money changing hands. . . .

The night was as bitter as the beer the Dutch preferred to drink, when Oishi at last made his way across the long bridge to the island. He staggered as the wind gusted, threatening to knock his unsteady body off balance and over the side; cold spray drenched him to the skin as waves crashed against the stone base of the causeway. Behind him the Japanese banners and flags on the mainland cracked like whips in the wind as he left his homeland behind, while up ahead the flags of the Dutch seemed to mock them with equal defiance. The moon was ringed by a faint aura of blue-white as if the sky had frozen around it, and half hidden by dark scudding clouds that made the night seem even more threatening.

He finally reached his destination, relieved to be on more solid ground . . . until he passed beneath the flags that told him he had just stepped onto foreign soil, and got his first clear look at what confronted him.

Even in the middle of the night the tiny island swarmed with bodies in active motion. Sailors and workmen—all of them far stranger-looking than he had imagined, even knowing Kai—unloaded and transported crates of supplies and trade goods.

Other men, who were not hard at work for one reason or another, gathered in clusters to drink and gamble, talking loudly in their unintelligible, guttural language. It sounded to him as though they were all arguing and cursing—and from the tone of their voices, they probably were, unless they were ogling or pawing at the half-dressed women who loitered around them. Prostitutes from the brothels in Nagasaki were ordered to the island by the local governor to keep the foreigners content in their confinement until their ships departed again.

One of the women spotted Oishi, and called out an obscene invitation in Japanese. He looked away, frowning, refusing to respond. He had never thought of himself as having led a sheltered life, even before his ordeal in Ako's dungeon. But compared to this, months spent alone in a stone-walled pit with only rats for companions suddenly seemed to him like a monk's tranquil idyll.

Everywhere he turned, the random shadow-play of lanterns swaying in the wind showed him an unreal scene, turning the foreigners and prostitutes into puppets in a haunted *Bunraku* play. The cacophony of echoing noise and voices, combined with the stink of rotting fish, unwashed bodies, urine and tobacco smoke to make him dizzy and nauseated, until for a moment he thought he was going to fall on his face, or vomit.

Through sheer discipline he forced his overtaxed body to keep moving, his weaponless hands clenched, as other women called out to him, causing heads to turn in his direction. Somewhere a shrill whistle sounded, setting off a chorus of calls and responses in the shadows around him.

He looked up, seeing the masts and rigging of the great Dutch sailing ships that loomed over the island, dwarfing buildings and people with their unimaginable size. The Shogunate forbade the construction of any ship large and seaworthy enough to risk sailing out of sight of land, to ensure that just as no foreigners were allowed to enter Japan, no Japanese were able to leave it either.

He looked down again, and abruptly found himself surrounded by a circle of thuggish *gaijin*, blocking every path of escape.

A man with a long-barreled pistol in his hand, and his skeleton on the outside of his body, pushed through the circle to confront him.

Oishi's breath stopped. He shut his eyes, turning his head away before the obscenity could suck out his soul: *They were demons. How could it be? No one had told him of—*

"*. . . an islander . . . tattooed like a skeleton!*" Abruptly the words surfaced in his memory. He opened his eyes, looking back just as the mocking, barely-subdued laughter started around him.

He forced himself to look straight at the stranger, with his eyes wide open: It was only a man, though his face was not Japanese, or European . . . *"from somewhere south of China—a* cannibal," *they said.*

Nonetheless, the islander met his gaze directly, with shrewd brown eyes that were all too human. The man was covered in tattoos so stomach-turning that Oishi was hard-pressed to keep his own eyes fixed on the man's face, which appeared to be a fleshless skull even as his mouth twisted in amusement.

Oishi had seen tattoos before; they were common on criminals in the *yakuza*. But despite the men who wore them, they were often works of art—portraits of legendary heroes, magnificent dragons, beautiful women with flowers.

No sane person would flaunt the entrails of a corpse. Anyone with such obscenities inked on his flesh would be imprisoned by the police, or killed. A dead body was unclean, haunted by spirits; even the underclass of workers who disposed of the dead were untouchable to other humans.

But this savage's face, his shaven head, his naked torso and arms all flaunted the graphically drawn bones, muscles, and sinew of a rotting corpse—worse, a corpse infested with carrion-eating vermin and hungry ghosts. Oishi wondered if he had done it to intimidate, or whether the mind of a cannibal somehow found the imagery beautiful. . . .

Oishi fixed his gaze on the man's eyes, which were not as unfathomable as his brain. They were the eyes of a shrewd, dangerous judge of human nature, one whose knowledge of the wider world far outstripped his own.

In barely understandable Japanese, the tattooed man asked, "What is your business here?" He pointed his pistol at Oishi's chest.

"I am looking for someone," Oishi replied, managing to speak clearly and with far more confidence than he felt. He rubbed his thumb against his fingers, as he had seen some of the gamblers do, a sign that seemed to mean "money."

The tattooed man gave a grunt of laughter and lifted his

pistol, letting its barrel rest on his shoulders. He beckoned for Oishi to follow him.

Having no alternative, Oishi followed him deeper into the squalid morass, and finally up a steep gangplank onto one of the looming ships in the narrow water gaps between narrower docks.

They entered the ship's interior, the islander leading him through a maze of claustrophobic passageways and dark, reeking spaces. He thought that if he had felt lost before, it was nothing compared to how lost he was now.

Just as he was about to demand that the skeleton man take him back again, the man suddenly stopped in front of a large door that opened inward. "Kapitan," he said, opening the door, and shoved Oishi through it. The door slammed shut behind him.

The cabin was small and filled with blue-gray gloom; Oishi identified the pungent odor of tobacco smoke. Smoking tobacco was one intrusive foreign habit that not even the Shogun had been able to suppress. But although—or because—the room was filled with such a haze of smoke, Oishi could not even tell at first whether there was actually anyone in it besides him.

And then the oversized bowl of a foreign tobacco pipe glowed red, as someone in the shadows drew in a breath full of smoke.

Oishi almost made out the man's face, as it shone briefly in the light—huge and distorted like a newly risen moon in the swirling haze between them—before the shadows closed in around him again.

"You look as if you've traveled far?" a heavily accented voice said. Its timbre was as deep and menacing as the shroud of darkness around them. But as Oishi's eyes began to adjust, he saw a pair of large hands pour *sake* into two flat traditional Japanese cups. "Drink." The hands pushed one of the cups forward across the surface of a waist-high table, which Oishi only became aware of as the cup moved over it.

Oishi picked up the cup and drank, with the restrained

sips of a well-mannered guest, not draining it in the single swallow that his nerves were demanding. Whoever and whatever this man was, at least he had a taste for decent liquor. He watched the Dutchman's pipe glow again, briefly illuminating the darkness. He had no idea how to begin the necessary discussion, and so he forced himself to wait, still and silent, in order to make the *gaijin* speak first.

"So," the Kapitan said finally, "why have you come here?" His Japanese was better than the savage's, although Oishi still had to listen distinctly to make out the words.

"I'm looking for someone who was sold to you," he said, taking care to speak as clearly as possible in return, so that there would be no misunderstandings.

"There are hundreds of—"

"A halfbreed," Oishi said.

The Kapitan was silent for a long span of heartbeats, and Oishi knew then that the man realized exactly who he meant. His heartbeat quickened as he realized the hesitation probably meant that at least Kai was still alive.

"The *half-bloed* is worth a lot of money to me," the Kapitan said at last.

"I will buy him back." Oishi removed a pouch from the sleeve of his kimono, and slid it across the table. His eyes were adapting more fully to the dimness of the room, which was lit only by the moon shining in through a small square of window. He still could not make out the Kapitan's expression.

The Kapitan's hands reached forward again; their size seemed monstrous to him. They were covered with tattoos and rope scars, and filthier than his own had been the day he was released from the dungeon. Oishi found it hard to believe they were even human. Small wonder that people called the foreigners demons.

The Kapitan removed the object from the pouch he had given over, and held it up. Gazing at its silhouette, Oishi felt a sudden poignant awareness of its beauty mingle with an overwhelming sense of loss. It was an exquisitely crafted, painstakingly detailed sword guard, of a kind that was no longer even made.

"This belonged to a samurai," the Kapitan said, and from his voice Oishi knew that he recognized its age, and its value as well. As the Kapitan looked up at him again, Oishi finally made out his expression. The disdain in the man's eyes said he thought Oishi was clearly no samurai—a worthless ronin at best—and that the Kapitan assumed he must have stolen, or even murdered, to get his hands on such a prize.

His jaw tightened as he kept himself from cursing the Dutchman for his arrogance. The sword guard had been in his family for generations; he had no idea exactly how old it was, or what had become of the blade it had belonged to. It had been one of a pair, all that remained of a matched set that had been some ancestor's prized possession.

Oishi had worn the matching guards on his own swords, until the Shogun's disastrous visit and pending return had made him think twice about it. He thanked the gods now for giving him that much foresight. Chikara had sold the other piece from the the set to buy their horses and supplies, and arrange for his mother's transportation back to her family. This was the last remaining fragment of their family's once-proud heritage, the last artifact of his honor. . . .

The Kapitan leaned forward slightly, his gaze searching Oishi's face. The Dutchman's pale blue eyes were like chips of ice, as cruel and soulless as a frozen sea. "The halfbreed must be a good friend for you to give it up?"

Oishi said nothing. His mouth longed to spit out the truth; it burned his throat as he forced himself to swallow it. If the gods demanded any further sacrifices of him—before the ultimate one—to answer his prayers, he would have nothing left to offer them. . . .

The Kapitan leaned further across the desk, emerging from the shadows to loom over him. Oishi suppressed an urge to draw back in disgust, or fear.

"Done," the Kapitan said, with a sudden, unpleasant grin. "We'll drink to it." He filled both *sake* cups again.

This time Oishi downed his in one swallow, eager to get this ordeal over with, and be off the island again before the guard changed on the bridge. "Now you will take me to him."

The Kapitan looked up from his drink. "Will I, now—?" he said, his smile filled with scorn. "You people and your pride." He gestured with one hand at Oishi's worn, rumpled clothing and unkempt, uncut hair. "Even in these rags, you dare to give me orders like a lord! Well, let me tell you something—we may not be allowed to set foot on Japanese soil for fear of losing our trading rights, but the blade cuts both ways. This is *Dutch* land, and I am Shogun here. I will take you to him, but on my terms . . ." His grin came back, more ominous than before. ". . . and you may find him changed."

The roar of a frenzied crowd, and the bellowing of some animal Oishi couldn't begin to identify, reached his ears well before he saw real light again as he followed the tattooed man through the ship's interior. The islander ahead of him carried only a small lantern, but there were more men behind them now, armed with pistols or swords, guarding him the same way his people would have done to them, on the mainland. The Kapitan was right—here he was the outsider, the *gaijin*.

He didn't enjoy the feeling at all . . . and he was beginning to feel worse with every step, more and more like he was being led into a trap.

The corridor angled sharply, and the crowd noise suddenly increased. In front of him was an iron-barred gate, guarded by more foreigners.

Oishi looked over his shoulder as he realized, too late, that trapped was exactly what he was. Someone behind him shoved him roughly forward; he grunted as he slammed against the bars.

Beyond the gate he made out an arena—as bright as day to his dark-adapted eyes, but nothing like the one where the duels had been fought at Ako Castle. This one was enclosed on all sides by an iron cage, taking up most of an empty cargo hold. Outside the bars, a shouting, jeering mob of foreigners had crowded onto makeshift risers or stood packed in between the cage and the wooden hull of the ship. The hard walls and enclosed space reflected sound until it rang like the inside of a temple bell.

He'd thought the stench outside was bad, but in this enclosed space the added heat of packed bodies and half a hundred lanterns made it unbearable. He clung to the bars, stupefied by the overwhelming assault on his senses as he tried make out what was happening in the arena.

The arena looked like a battlefield, littered with savagely torn and mutilated corpses. The roar he had heard sounded again, drowning out the noise of the crowd, and he saw . . . *it couldn't be . . . an* oni*—?*

An enormous *yokai* turned slowly in the center of the ring as its bulging eyes swept the space around it. Its body was a mockery of a human form, and the size of an ox, if an ox could walk on its hind legs. Sharp horns sprouted from its forehead; its scabrous, rasp-rough hide was covered with human blood. But the huge weighted chain-scythe it carried had done most of the damage Oishi could see on the mutilated bodies scattered across the arena floor.

It bellowed again, whirling the scythe overhead as it charged the lone human left alive in the cage, blocking his attempts to dodge or double back as he ran until it finally had him trapped in a corner. It towered over him as if he was a child; the human crouched down in seeming terror.

The *oni* swung the scythe in a brutal arc; instinctively Oishi shut his eyes.

He opened them again. *That man—*

He saw the *oni*'s prey launch himself away from the bars, into the air: His *katana* shone blood red as he brought it down, slashing the *oni*'s body open from shoulder to navel, cutting through heart, lungs, and entrails in one perfect strike as he dropped back to the ground.

Oishi watched the *oni* sway on its feet. Then, slowly, it toppled over onto its back, landing with a *thud* that rattled the timbers of the ship, revealing the battle's survivor to his eyes.

Another devil . . . or he could have been, with his body covered in blood until it was as red as the slain *oni,* and long filthy hair obscuring his face. But Oishi knew who he was watching, even before he could see the victor clearly. That killing stroke could only have been made by one person: *Kai.*

Or something that had once been Kai.

"You may find him changed." Now Oishi understood the full, ghastly irony behind the Kapitan's grin. All that he could see staring out at the crowd was the tortured, inhuman shell of a man who had once answered to the name "Kai." *Merciful Buddha, was there still anything like a human mind, or a human soul, left in that creature?*

The crowd of sailors and dockworkers had gone wild at Kai's victory, shouting, *"Half-bloed! Half-bloed! Half-bloed!"* Even the Dutch knew him for what he was, Oishi thought. Whether he was less than human, or something more, Kai had never been someone they considered their equal, or treated as their brother.

It struck him as incomprehensible that his own people, who hated and feared the threat of outside invaders, and foreigners who should have stayed where they belonged but instead sailed halfway around the world to barter with total strangers, would both feel the same about a halfbreed; that they would both reject a man who looked more like them than they looked like each other. *But then, maybe that wasn't incomprehensible at all. . . .*

The thought made something squirm unpleasantly inside him. He pushed it away, wondering what came next. *What was he going to do, if Kai wasn't—*

Suddenly the iron-barred gate in front of him began to

rise; he let go of it, hastily backing away. The men still standing guard behind him shoved him forward again, propelling him through into the arena. The gate clanged down again behind him.

Oishi stood where he'd staggered to a halt, dazed. All around him he saw the throng of watchers jeering and waving through the blood-splattered cage bars, or shouting out bets. He spotted the Kapitan among them, grinning down at him as he fondled two barely-clad prostitutes, holding one in each arm. The Kapitan laughed with his men about something; Oishi had no doubt that he was the butt of the joke.

Something rattled on the metal bars of the cage above his head. Oishi looked up, doubly startled as he found the tattooed islander perched on the crossbars, leering down at him like a demonic cat. The skeleton man was holding a sword; he dangled it down through the cage bars and dropped it with a nod, gesturing as it landed at Oishi's feet.

The crowd yelled its approval, waiting for Oishi to pick it up, and the islander raised his eyebrows. Oishi shook his head angrily. Instead he called out to Kai, who was slowly, warily, advancing toward him across the arena, bloody sword in hand.

"Kai!" Oishi shouted again, praying that the sound of his own name might waken Kai from his nightmare of bloodlust.

But Kai didn't even seem to hear him, let alone recognize his own name. The halfbreed had truly become a demon, in everything but form—ironically, the most human thing that remained of him seemed to be his body; and covered with blood and scars, that was terrifying enough. His hair was flung back now, so that he could get a clear view of what he was expected to kill next. Oishi saw the strange scars on his forehead, the ones he had first seen the day Lord Asano's hunting party had come upon a runaway boy, so many years ago.

"Kai—!" He tried a last time to make Kai hear him, and meet his eyes. But before he could even finish shouting the word, it was drowned out by the sound of a gong.

Kai reacted to the gong like an attack dog freed from a

leash. With a cry so inhuman it froze Oishi where he stood, Kai ran at him, sword raised.

Oishi snatched up the sword from the floorboards in front of him, just in time to parry the first of Kai's furious blows. More blows rained down on him as he struggled to find and keep his balance, desperately fending off the halfbreed's assault. It took every ounce of his strength and every bit of his training simply to keep from being cut to ribbons as he fought to get in even one counterblow.

He parried again, with a strength born of sheer desperation, and lashed out with his sword. Kai slapped the blade aside disdainfully with the back of his unprotected hand, and attacked even harder. There was no recognition in his eyes, even fighting face to face—no hunger for revenge, only a blind fury, as if what Kai really wanted was to go on killing and killing, until the entire world was knee-deep in gore.

The crowd roared even louder, almost drowning out the *clash* and *clang* as Kai's sword struck and Oishi parried, reacting as much to gleaned memories of how Kai fought as to what Kai actually did; relying more and more on pure instinct. He had been one of the best swordsmen at Ako Castle, but nothing he had ever known had prepared him for an onslaught like this, and all from one man's blade.

"Half-bloed! Half-bloed!" The fanatical crowd screamed for Kai to fight even harder, as if he hadn't really been using his full strength.

Stunned by Kai's savage reaction, Oishi realized that for the first time in his life, he was truly fighting for his life. But his refusal to go down only maddened Kai, who used not just his sword but knees and elbows and fists as well, seeming as insensible to pain as he was to his opponent's humanity, or his own. With a sudden twist-turn and strike that would have dislocated another man's arm, he stripped Oishi of his sword; a blow from his fist smashed his enemy to the ground.

As Kai raised his sword for the killing blow, Oishi flung up his arm, and shouted, "Mika!"

Kai's sword froze in mid-downswing; he stared at Oishi with what looked like disbelief . . . then incredulity . . . and finally, recognition.

Around them the crowd was screaming for blood— Above them the islander shouted unintelligible threats down at Kai for Kai to deliver the death stroke that would split his opponent like a ripe melon. Instead, Kai slowly turned his blade aside, and the final blow did not fall.

But then anger began to smolder again in the halfbreed's feverish eyes, like a firestorm rekindled from blown sparks. Abruptly he raised the sword again and brought it down—narrowly missing Oishi, who rolled clear, hardly believing his luck as he caught up his own weapon and scrambled to his feet.

Kai attacked him again, hard enough to force him backwards toward the gate where he had been thrown into the cage, finally pinning him against the bars. With a raw cry of triumph Kai lunged and slashed—and his sword whipped past Oishi with the kiss of a burning wind, to kill the guard standing just outside.

Oishi gaped in disbelief, but without conscious thought his own body responded, turning in place to cut down another guard who was aiming an arquebus at Kai. Oishi caught the man's arquebus before it hit the deck, and pulled it between the bars, lit fuse cord and all. He took aim into the crowd, flicking aside the safety lid on the priming chamber. He pulled the trigger.

Near the front of the screaming crowd, a blood rose blossomed on the Kapitan's livid face just above his eyes, and he toppled forward.

Pandemonium broke out in the stands, as Kai made short work of the other guards, who had unwisely been pulling open the gate to get at them. The two men ducked under it and ran.

Oishi followed Kai until they were through the ship's labyrinth of passageways, relieved that one of them could find the way out, whether it was from experience or sheer instinct.

As they emerged onto the deck he abruptly got his bearings, and ran for the gangplank.

Kai ran after him, as the islander burst out of the darkness behind them. The tattooed savage raised his pistol, taking aim at Kai because the gun held only one shot. Kai dodged through the maze of crates, keeping the islander distracted until Oishi reached the gangplank and headed down it, half running, half sliding.

Oishi heard a gunshot and skidded to a stop, looking back just as Kai either leaped or fell over the ship's rail onto the gangplank below him. Kai tumbled through a forward roll and onto his feet before Oishi could reach him; he was running before Oishi could gasp out a word.

Side by side they burst from the dock into the hive of activity that was Dejima's night. Their sudden appearance, blood-soaked and brandishing weapons, created a fresh disruption, but the reaction of the guards positioned everywhere to keep order was swift and overwhelming.

Oishi and Kai fought their way through the crowd toward the bridge, but the wake of injuries and screaming behind them only drew more men toward them. Oishi didn't need to look back to hear the tattooed man shouting, and to know he was still pursuing them. Guards armed with pistols and swords appeared seemingly from nowhere to join him. The pistols were hopelessly inaccurate from any distance at all, but the men carrying them were gaining, with the islander in the lead, even as Oishi glimpsed the flags that marked the bridge up ahead. *They weren't going to make it—*

They passed a barrel of whale oil used for lanterns, sitting outside a warehouse; Kai kicked it over, barely breaking stride. As the oil spilled across the path of their pursuers, he grabbed a lantern hanging from a support and hurled it. The liquid fuel went up in a roar of flame, blocking their pursuit with a wall of fire.

Oishi could still hear shots being fired behind them, shouts and furious curses, but every step they took left the danger of being hit further behind them as they ran out across the bridge toward safety.

12

Mika gazed silently at the view of jagged peaks covered in snow—all she could see through the open doorway of the room that looked out across the lower courtyard of Kirayama Castle. That scene, or one too much like it, was all she could see from anywhere in the castle that was Lord Kira's mountain stronghold. She would have found the view breathtaking, under other circumstances . . . any other circumstances than the ones in which she found herself: a "guest" held hostage by Kira, unable even to return to Ako until her year of mourning was up, and she had been forced to become his wife.

Kira had not lingered long in his promised fief after the Shogun departed. He had stayed only long enough to betray and imprison Oishi Yoshio, her father's chief retainer and trusted friend, who had always watched over her like an older brother . . . the only person who might have had enough influence among her father's troops or the citizens of Ako to strike back at the man who had stolen their lord's life, his lands . . . and his daughter.

Even though the Shogun had forbidden a vendetta; even after her father's retainers had all become ronin and Kira's borrowed army had made sure they were driven from the domain, taking nothing with them but the knowledge that if they ever set foot in Ako again they would be killed on sight . . . still Kira had been so fearful of his own safety that he had thrown Oishi into the castle dungeon. *And Kai—*

No. Not now . . . not yet. Her hands clenched in a silent vow, hidden by the folds of her sleeves as she imagined taking his hand in hers. The only chance she would possibly have of helping either one of them would come after she returned to Ako.

Soon . . . soon, she promised herself, struggling to keep the frozen mask of her expression in place. It would not be too late . . . *if she could only endure just a little longer.*

She had fully understood why Kira had coveted Ako for so long only after she arrived here. It was everything he had never had: its rich fertile land, its beauty and warmth . . . even the noble heritage of the Asano name that she symbolized as its last surviving heir. Even though he had taken all those things, he would never possess their honor, not even when he stole her name as well, to become the new Lord Asano, controlling Ako as well as her life.

Lord Kira was a ruthless, manipulative coward, who had used his glib charm and handsome face—and probably witchcraft—to curry favor and maneuver his way into power—and then used the power of others to get him what he wanted, so that he never had to fear the direct cost of failure.

Even his concubine, Mitsuke—the uncanny, strikingly beautiful woman with a fox's shadow and a witch's power—seemed under his thrall, somehow. Mika had heard stories of *kitsune* falling in love with humans . . . but how could this one not see that she had fallen in love with a man as hollow as a suit of armor, and so deceitful that he was more deadly than any wild beast?

Perhaps even *yokai* had their limits, when it came to understanding love. Mika knew the witch watched her with feral jealousy—with a gaze that would have struck her dead, if the *kitsune* hadn't feared destroying Kira's love as well. Mika wished she could make the fox-witch believe she had nothing to fear from someone who would never feel anything but hatred toward Kira.

At least the witch kept Kira occupied in his own bedroom often enough that he had not tried to force himself on Mika, although she suspected he was even afraid of that . . . afraid that if he violated her honor she would kill him, or if she failed, kill herself. Either way, she could guarantee that he would never become the true Lord Asano, no matter whose lands he ruled. She took every possible opportunity to subtly remind him of that fact.

Her hands had grown numb with cold from the chill draft that entered through the wide open door; she pushed them into the sleeves of the kimono buried beneath layers of robes and her quilted silk cloak, and glanced at Kira across the low table that had a charcoal brazier beneath it. A quilt covered the table, trapping enough heat to warm their legs; a tray with a pot of hot tea and two cups sat waiting for them. Kira had insisted they take meals together, and spend other time together, whether she wished to or not.

She had acquiesced, because if she refused too often, the true ugliness of his spirit showed itself all too quickly—and he had learned to take out his cruelty on the helpless people around her while she watched, because he knew that it pained her more than if he had slashed her with a knife.

Lord Kira cleared his throat and Mika looked back at him, reminded again that she was not sitting here alone; that she had been sitting here in brooding silence much longer than she had realized.

Because there was a pretense of spring in the air today, Kira had decided they should engage in a pretense of having tea outdoors—in this room where all the seasons existed at once, but only in two dimensions. The wall screens had been painted with poignantly beautiful landscapes of springtime's blossoming plum and cherry trees, summer's camellias and hydrangeas. Birds soared in blue skies, carp and dragonflies shimmered against blue water where cranes and egrets waded. The green of grass and trees shaded gradually into the flaming reds of autumn maple leaves, the rich multicolors of chrysanthemums—all the languorous beauty of Ako's seasons, which were squeezed into a hand span of weeks here in the mountains, but were missing the rest of the year, as the colors of the land and sky were reduced to black and white and shades of gray.

The real world that she shared with Kira, bleached to the deathly shades of winter, was visible through the wide-open doorway that let in the chill mountain air, and completed the *Kabuki* theater unreality of their surroundings. Sitting on the floor beside them, a scrawny boy in a threadbare peasant's tunic and leg wrappings played a *samisen* with remarkable skill—although it had only seemed to win him a slave's place at their side, and not even warm clothing.

How fitting, Mika thought, that the unreality of the murals surrounding them imitated life so well—like a play within a play—because she felt now as if she was always an actor in a play.

"Perhaps if you took some tea, my lady, you would not feel the cold," Kira said, with the seeming kindness that always masked some other emotion. He sat across from her wearing no cloak or even a quilted jacket over his richly woven kimono in shades of blue-gray. He seemed as comfortable as if it really did feel like a spring day to him.

Mika stared at the artistry of the *raku* cups into which Kira poured their tea. The random pattern of iridescence on the subtle deep green glaze contrasted perfectly with the smoke-black smudges, also random, produced by the special firing process of *raku*-ware. The tea set had been made by someone who had a genuine sense of *wabi-sabi*—who worked in harmony with nature's unpredictable artistry, embracing the joy of creation, the frustration of failure, the sorrow of forever parting with his most cherished work . . . the solace of new creation.

The set must have been very expensive. She wondered how many of Kira's people had suffered through the long winter without sufficient food or clothing so that their lord could continually impress his hostage with gifts of fine clothing, or a tea set like this.

She removed her hands from her sleeves and looked up at Kira, meeting his politely solicitous gaze without expression. "Please do not concern yourself with me. I am the daughter of a samurai."

The anger that always smoldered beneath the surface calm of Kira's manner rose suddenly into his eyes. She saw how close he came to the limits of his self-control just to refrain from lashing out at her, and realized that after they were married, he would not have to hold back. . . .

She looked away to avoid pushing him further, too aware of the helpless boy sitting beside them. She had reacted with resentment to the suggestion that she was weak; but his overreaction to her words told her too much about the dragon smoldering in the depths of his volatile soul.

She had only spoken the words in self-defense, not as an attack on his own heritage. But that was how he had taken it. His brittle arrogance was just one more mirror-image of his insecurity, another disguise for the profound sense of inferiority that fed the dragon coiled around his heart.

Even becoming the new Lord Asano would not lay that monster to rest, because each act of betrayal or malice Kira committed only made it more impossible for him to face himself honestly, less able to acknowledge his own humanity, or lack of it. He was far beyond hearing the truth from her—especially her—or anyone else.

She found herself staring at the boy playing the *samisen,* as if she had been listening to his music. He was shivering visibly. "The child is cold," she said quietly.

Kira bent his head at her, as if he was looking for what, if any, insult she might be implying by focusing on the boy instead of him. He turned on the cushion where he sat, legs warmed beneath the quilt, and asked, "Are you cold, boy?"

As usual, there was nothing wrong with the innocuous question. And yet as always, just below its surface lay terrifying depths. . . .

The boy glanced up, down again, shaking his head. He went on playing, flawlessly, as if his life depended on it.

Kira looked back at Mika with a smile. "You see," he said. "He comes from country stock, like me. We accept things as they are." He glanced reassuringly at the boy as he listened to him play.

Loathing rose like bile into Mika's throat, as her worst fear filled her mind: the fear that by the time they returned to Ako, there would be no one left who could act to stop this monster from consuming her home the way he had consumed his own poor land, sucking the life out of its people; no one left to avenge her father, and set his spirit free . . . *no one except her.*

She slipped her hand into her kimono sleeve and touched the small sachet of poison she had kept with her all this time. Kira's fear of betrayal rarely left him, even within the walls of his own castle . . . and she knew that if she killed him, she would never see Ako again. But what would returning mean, if there was nothing to return to? All that she needed was just one moment—

Kira's gaze had wandered out across the lower courtyard, where a group of his soldiers were performing martial arts drills under the critical eye of an instructor.

She removed the small sachet of poison from her sleeve, and put out her hand, giving the sachet a hard pinch that ruptured its fragile cloth. The fine, odorless powder spilled into Kira's tea and dissolved instantly.

Mika slipped the remains of the sachet into her sleeve, just as Kira turned back to her again. "Soon we will return to Ako, my lady, and you will not find the winters so bitter. . . ."

She picked up her cup of tea, and sipped from it, for once meeting his eyes as he spoke.

". . . and I should like to see the spring there for myself." Kira's smiled widened with anticipation as he picked up his own cup, raising it to his lips.

Mika went on gazing at him, trying to keep her expression natural as she waited for him to take the first sip; concentrating so intently on him that she barely remembered to breathe.

Kira hesitated, as he noticed her unusual attentiveness. She glanced down, trying to pass off her response as if it had been the thought of returning to Ako that made her look at him so hopefully. He smiled gently. "Perhaps I was mistaken. The child does look cold." He lowered his cup again, and held it out to the boy instead. "Here, warm yourself."

The boy looked up, startled by the gesture. After a moment, he laid aside his instrument and took the cup in his hands, comforted by its heat.

Mika watched him, frozen with horror, aware that Kira's eyes were fixed on her now. The boy raised the cup to his lips—

"No—!" Mika leaned out and slapped the cup from his hands with a cry. The exquisite *raku*-ware smashed on floor, spraying the *tatami* with poisoned tea. She looked up at Kira, hatred and outrage plain on her face.

He stared back at her with an expression of reproachful disappointment, and then abruptly he reached out and grabbed her wrist. His hand closed around it so tightly that tears of pain burned her eyes. Desperately struggling to hide her sudden fear, Mika broke his gaze as movement caught the corner of her vision. Someone was watching them from the doorway behind him. *The witch.*

Oblivious to Mitsuke's presence, Kira twisted Mika's wrist, forcing her to look back at him. His words were as soft as ever, even though his hand trembled with fury. "How many men have died," he murmured, "and how many more must die, so that a woman like you can have hands like these?"

His hand tightened even harder around her wrist. She saw the desire and the frustration in his eyes as he forced her to lock fingers with him. "My ancestors were farmers once, not noblemen like yours. They worked the land here. The poorest in Japan. But they were clever, and patient, and in time they learned that not even the ice could stand in their way." His cold hand squeezed hers, cutting off the circulation, until she felt as if his coldness was crawling up her arm, freezing her flesh; making her a prisoner of the ice forever. "We are used to waiting for what we want. First you will be my wife, then you will grow to love me."

She wanted to scream at him that she had never wanted to live a meaningless, pampered life at the expense of others. That whatever money he had spent on this tea set to impress a spoiled *daimyo*'s daughter had been wasted. That if he thought he possessed the equal of his own ancestors' courage and endurance, or a fraction of the strength it took the people he ruled now simply to endure the burdens heaped on them by him, as well as by nature—he was a madman. That the fact he had exploited these people all this time, and was now about to abandon them without a thought made him more of a demon than his *kitsune* lover—

Her father had been an honorable, compassionate man, whose ancestors had paid with their own blood, for generations, to finally reach a place where her father and the people whose lives were his responsibility could live in peace. Even if laws and traditions set in stone meant they would never all be equal, still her father's understanding of his duty as lord had ensured that at least everyone in Ako had enough so that they could live their lives like human beings.

But then Kira and the witch had murdered him, and nothing would ever be the same again.

She would never love a man like Kira—even if he pursued her through all eternity. She would never feel anything for him but hatred and contempt.

She longed to throw the truth in his face like scalding tea: *She loved Kai, and no matter what happened she would always love him, only him, forever—*

"Sell that animal to the Dutch." She could hear Kira's final order, as clearly as she remembered his threat to her: *"Embarrass me and I'll have him burnt alive."*

Kai. . . . She swallowed her furious words as if they were poison, with agonizing difficulty, dropping her gaze as she let her arm go limp in Kira's grip. She glanced away . . . and saw the fox-witch, still in the doorway, staring back at them both in silent, murderous envy.

It had been sometime in the middle of the night when Kai and Oishi had made their escape across the Dejima bridge. The Dutch had not dared to follow them, but Kai could still hear their shouted threats, their screams and curses. . . .

Oishi had blurted something Kai didn't understand to the guards standing watch at the mainland checkpoint when they had tried to block his way. The guards backed up to let them pass, and turned so that their spears and arquebuses pointed toward the island instead, just in case any of the foreigners were really insane enough to pursue them.

Oishi had two horses waiting. Kai pulled himself into the saddle and gave his horse its head, knowing it would follow Oishi's as they rode away. His mind, his identity, everything beyond his instinct for survival, seemed to be gone, left behind somewhere in the nightmare of cages and mazes where he had been held for . . . he had no idea how long. At first even the feel of the wind against his face and the sight of the starry night sky seemed like a hallucination. *Was he free—?* Or would he only wake up to find he had been beaten senseless again . . . or worse, feeling a sword slit his throat, or an *oni* tearing out his liver . . .

Who was that man up ahead of him? Some still-sane fragment of his mind, almost buried alive, had recognized Oishi's voice as the stranger shouted Mika's name. But from what he'd seen of the man, Oishi had somehow changed nearly as much as he had.

Oishi did not speak to him as they rode, and for a long time there was nothing in his own mind that resembled a question, or even a coherent thought. The night sky flowed like molten glass, moving and changing patterns as the road they were on turned and folded with the land.

He watched the sky, trying to make sense of it, until at last the random motion of the stars no longer reminded him of ships' lanterns glimpsed on the sea. Slowly they began to resolve into constellations, whose outlines and stories he remembered, from another life, one where he had also been told that they were guides—and guardians—for life's night passages.

And then suddenly he saw the moon, rising above the hills to light the way ahead . . . like the glowing lantern of a celestial maiden, who had come to him when he was lost, long ago, to guide and watch over him. . . .

Mika*hime*. . . . *Mika*-hime . . . *Mika*. . . . The name filled his mind like his own heartbeat in his chest; his mind caressed the word with a tenderness he had forgotten even the meaning of. Her name, her face, became the focus for his scattered memories, reawakening his humanity, reviving his awareness . . . illuminating the way back to his humanity like the moonlight on the road ahead. Fragmented images of his former life and the language he had once spoken—until the Dutch had threatened to cut his tongue out—began to coalesce again into actual patterns of thought, like stars scattered across the night slowly reforming into constellations. Bit by bit his memories of Mika's loving kindness stitched together the past, and reattached it to his present, with a thread of gossamer silk.

By the time dawn broke on a new day, he had remembered that his name was *Kai,* not "*Half-bloed.*" He remembered who he should have been, where he truly belonged, and how he had come to be where, and what, he was when someone had thrown Oishi into the iron cage with him like a piece of fresh meat.

Oishi was a better fighter than he had expected . . . at least when the only alternative was death. *But then, so were most men. . . .* Kai glanced at the man riding ahead of him, seeing him clearly at last as the day brightened. He was sure the man was Oishi—but he still looked so different that even if Kai had been perfectly sane when he first laid eyes on him, Oishi would have been unrecognizable—until he'd cried out Mika's name in a last desperate attempt to save his own life.

But then, maybe the fact that he had been unrecognizable was all that had saved his life, until then. Kai had been at the end of his strength by the time he had finally killed the *oni*; and then they had thrown one more enemy at him. *He had been so tired of killing.* But if he had known instantly that it was Oishi—the man who had surrendered Ako Castle without a fight to the Shogun and Kira—Oishi never would have had a prayer.

But what was Oishi doing there? He had obviously come prepared to make an escape, so he hadn't been sent to the Dutch Island by Kira, as punishment. It seemed as if the only possible reason Oishi could have for taking such a risk was to rescue him. But weighed against what he now remembered about the past, that made no sense at all.

The sunrise gleamed off the surface of water, and he realized that the road they were on had been following the path cut by a wide stream. Before him a waterfall spilled down a rocky cliff face, forming a pool in a hollowed-out basin.

"Stop," he called to Oishi, as he pulled his horse to a halt; his own voice speaking Japanese sounded unrecognizable.

Up ahead Oishi reined in his mount and looked back. "What?" he said sharply. His face turned both querulous and concerned as Kai slid to the ground. "What—?" he said again.

"Water," Kai muttered, heading down the bank to the stream, irresistibly drawn to it. He reeked of death, he was covered in blood . . . and until those things were no longer true, his body would not begin to feel alive again.

He waded into the pool at the bottom of the cliff. It was ice cold, but the feel of icy water had been a part of his existence for so long he didn't even pause. He stood directly under the falls, letting its fluid purity pour down on his face and hair, sluicing over his rags of clothing as he scrubbed himself with his hands. Up on the hillside, he could hear Oishi shouting at him, as if there was something so important it couldn't wait long enough to let him wash away at least the outward signs of the living death that Oishi had saved him from.

Standing under the waterfall, he couldn't even make out what Oishi was saying. He turned his mind inward: *Inhale . . . focus . . . remember. Exhale . . . cleanse . . . forget. . . .*

He could not bear to think of how Mika would look at him if she saw him now; couldn't even begin the search for her, until he had erased as much of the filth and defilement as he could, the obscene reminders of what he had become in order to survive. Whether the core of his spirit was intact or whether it was corrupted beyond all hope of redemption, he could at least search for her, do whatever was necessary to save her and get his revenge on Kira. Beyond that, the future was empty of all meaning. He seemed to remember that it always had been.

He stood beneath the waterfall for a long time, with his hands pressed together in prayer—though time had no real meaning for him, yet—until his trembling body's instinct for self-preservation would no longer let him focus on his soul, and he grew so cold that he realized the water's chill had progressed beyond numbing the pain of his unhealed wounds into the bone-deep ache of hypothermia.

He waded out of the pool again, and stumbled back up the stream bank before his brain shut down entirely.

The air was much warmer now than the water had been, even though the wind still made him shiver. He was surprised to see how high the sun had climbed in the sky. The stream's course was lined with trees and shrubs; he was even more surprised to see new green leaves and blossoming flowers—to realize that it was already spring. Nagasaki, where Dejima lay, was on Japan's southernmost large island, but spring in Ako would not be far behind it. . . .

The wet rags of the foreigners' cast-off jacket and pants he wore clung to him uncomfortably as the breeze plastered them against his body. Shreds and strings of raveled cloth flopped against his skin as he walked, as if he was covered in some loathsome fungus. But he had no other choice except to strip naked—and either way, if Oishi showed the slightest hint of disdain at his appearance, Kai was not sure he had enough self-control left to keep from killing the man right here. He rubbed his arms, hoping Oishi had at least started a fire and cooked some food while he waited.

Oishi lay stretched out in the grass beside the horses, fast asleep. Kai felt like kicking him. But instead he gazed down at the other man, able to stare all he wanted without offense, observing the ways in which Oishi had changed physically from the man he remembered.

His samurai's topknot, always neatly tied in the back, trimmed off straight, and held in place on the shaven top of his skull with spearmint oil, was now a carelessly tied mass pulled back simply to keep it out of his eyes. The once neatly shaven patch on the top of his head had not even been cut, probably in all the time that Kai had been gone. Oishi's once-fine samurai clothing, made of brocades and heavy silks, was gone, too. Now he wore only a plain kimono with loose *hakama* tied over it, made from cotton or even hemp, and it was hard to tell what color they had originally been. There was no clan *mon* anywhere in evidence on them: *Oishi had become a ronin.*

And yet, there were *ronin,* and there were *ronin.* Kai had not expected Oishi to give up his former pride and dignity along with his lord's castle. He was the last man Kai would have expected to lose heart so completely. No matter what else he thought of Oishi, he'd at least believed Oishi possessed that much backbone. Had the shock of all that had gone wrong changed him so much?

Or was there some other reason . . . ?

Oishi had lost weight—a lot of it. His skin, where it didn't bear fresh sunburn from his ride to Nagasaki, was as pale as the skin of a man who had been sick for a long time. There were deep shadows like bruises under his eyes. And to find him sleeping in such a vulnerable pose, not even stirring as Kai approached . . . it was as if last night had used up the last of his endurance, and he had keeled over from exhaustion where he sat.

Now Kai was even more surprised that Oishi had actually survived their fight in the arena. He saw bloodstains on Oishi's clothing, but no sign of any serious wound. Some kind of strength must still remain inside him, a remnant of the man Kai remembered—some urge that still burned so fiercely that, even as weak as he seemed now, Kai had not been able to cut him down in one blow.

Kai leaned over, reaching out to shake Oishi, to see if he was really just sleeping, or had passed out. As his hand closed around Oishi's arm, cold water dripped from his long hair and sodden clothes.

Oishi's eyes opened and he leaped to his feet, reaching for his sword; then he staggered, as if his sleep-addled brain hadn't caught up with his reflexes.

Kai stood staring at him, expressionless, hands down at his sides.

Oishi stared back, frowning. He wiped the water from his face, looking for a moment as if he thought he'd been spat on. Kai watched him trying to guess whether he was still facing a feral killer, or whether Kai had actually regained whatever wits Oishi gave him credit for.

The *katana* and knife Kai had kept with him from their escape lay in the grass where he'd dropped them; he made no move toward them, no movement at all, simply waiting.

The wariness drained from Oishi's face and posture. Finally he turned away, as if he had made up his mind, and moved to the nearest horse's saddlebags. He pulled out what appeared to be a bundle of clean clothing. Turning back he held it out. "Put these on."

It wasn't an offer. It wasn't a request. It was an order—as if nothing at all had changed, at least between them.

Kai folded his arms. He met Oishi's stare directly, for once making no secret of his resentment, or his refusal to obey. "Why did you come for me?" he asked. "You've hated me since we were children."

Oishi tossed out the armload of clothing; it landed at Kai's feet. For a moment something flickered in his eyes as his thoughts flashed back to the memory of their first encounter—resentment, at the idea that Kai had thought of him as nothing more than just another child, for all these years. But his expression showed Kai only the same quiet disdain he had always shown. "I told you. Lady Asano is to be married at *Shunki Korei-sai*."

The New Moon of Spring—? Kai started. He remembered Oishi saying nothing of the kind. Perhaps that was what he had been shouting about, ignoring the fact that a man standing under a waterfall was functionally deaf.

"What do you care?" Kai said bitterly, as the full implication of what he had just heard registered in his mind. His stare was like the edge of a sword, honed by memories of betrayal and futile rage. "When Kira took her away, you were on your knees."

Oishi reacted as if he'd been struck in the face; his eyes shone with anger. "We would all have been killed," he said flatly. "You too. What use are you to her dead?"

Kai grimaced. "What use am I to you?"

Oishi simply looked at him, refusing to dignify the question with an answer—as if he still expected Kai to follow his every order without an explanation. As if, even looking the way he did now, he believed his samurai blood was as obvious as a halfbreed's mixed blood, and demanded strict obedience from his inferiors. "Either follow me, or go back to what you were." He turned to his horse, yanked the reins loose from the bush where it was tied, and started to climb into the saddle.

Kai moved at last from the spot where he had been standing—to grab Oishi by the arm, jerking him down and around again. "Don't you turn your back on me, ronin!"

Oishi's sword was out of its sheath, and poised to take off Kai's head.

Kai looked at the sword, and back at Oishi's face, without even blinking. His stare was as cold as Death's. But then, slowly, his expression changed into a stubbornly human refusal to be ignored. "Follow you *for what*?"

Oishi held his gaze for a long moment without speaking,

as if right now he would sooner choke to death on the words than explain himself to the man he had risked his life to rescue, only last night.

Kai wondered if Oishi would ever see him as a human being, even after all he'd done to save him . . . even after all that Lord Asano's former *karou* must have been through himself, in the past year. Did he really believe that just because he had stolen a halfbreed from the Dutch, the halfbreed now belonged to him, to be used as he saw fit—?

Kai waited, equally silent and unyielding, refusing to back down, or to accept anything less than Oishi's acknowledgement of him as a complete equal . . . or else death. After all he had suffered at the hands of the Dutch, even death meant nothing to him, compared to his right to be treated as a human being.

At last it was Oishi's gaze that broke. He sheathed his sword, in tacit acknowledgment of the truth: *The year that had passed had changed everything.*

Kira's treachery and pitiless whim had rendered their former relationship meaningless. He had stripped them both of everything that had ever mattered to them, and racked their sanity to the breaking point. They had both been transformed irrevocably into lost men . . . sea-changed men, strangers even to themselves.

Oishi swallowed painfully, as if he was literally swallowing his pride, before he spoke again. "Kira has a thousand men under his command. He is also protected by witchcraft."

Kai stiffened, as the word ripped away the fragile membrane that covered an unhealed memory. "When I told you that, you sent me away—"

"I was wrong." Oishi forced the words out, barely more than a whisper, still staring at the ground. "I failed my lord." He raised his head again, and for the first time Kai saw something he knew, something he could actually relate to, in the other man's eyes: *Remorse, and shame.*

For the first time Kai began to grasp the real reason for everything Oishi hadn't told him, and the reason why explaining it had cost him so much . . . how unfathomable the depths of humiliation, grief, and betrayal Oishi was feeling must seem, to a man who had never learned how to swim.

"I don't know who or what you are," Oishi went on, "but I need your help." There was nothing apologetic about the words, but they were the truth, as transparent as the water flowing behind them.

It was Kai's turn to hesitate, as something close to desperation filled Oishi's expression. Kai wondered more than ever where Oishi had been, while he had been fighting to stay alive on the Dutch Island—what had left the deep lines that had prematurely aged Oishi's face and put the look of endurance strained to its limits in his bloodshot eyes. He looked as if he had been an outcast ronin for half his life, instead of less than a year. . . .

Kai looked away, frowning. Wherever Oishi had been, what in Enma's hell did he really think the two of them could do to avenge Lord Asano's death, and save Mika from Lord Kira?

Kira had a thousand men at his command. Did Oishi expect him to kill them all, on his own? There was an old superstition that a man who slew a thousand other men became a demon . . . *if he hadn't been a demon to begin with.* Did Oishi believe human life had come to mean nothing to him, after his year on Dejima? Or that he could battle Kira's *kitsune* lover on her own sorcerous ground?

Even if they could gather some of Lord Asano's scattered retainers, there would never be enough of them to make a difference. It would be suicide. But perhaps that no longer mattered to Oishi. Maybe he had decided after all that it was better for a samurai to die like a dog, battling hopeless odds, than to die of shame.

But Kai was no samurai. He hated Kira for what Kira had done to him, as well as for Lord Asano's sake . . . but did he hate him enough to die seeking revenge? He was free now, and grateful for that. But Oishi hadn't done it for him; he owed no debts to Oishi. Was this even still his fight—?

But then he remembered Mika. *Mika* . . . her name, her eyes, her smile. The simple fact that they still existed in the same world.

That knowledge was all that had pulled him back to sanity. He loved her; he had always loved her, so much that he would gladly have done anything for her . . . except ruin her life.

If he did nothing to help Oishi, could he live with himself, knowing that the man who had ruined all their lives and gotten away with it now controlled not only Ako, but every breath Mika took?

Even if it was his own destiny never to lie beside her, to be a husband to her, or a lover, what would knowing they still shared the same world with each other mean—what would anything mean, if she was forced to share the bed of the man who'd killed her father?

Maybe the only way he would ever be able show Mika how much she had meant to him all his life . . . how much he'd wanted to give his life to her . . . was to give it up for her.

Kai turned back at last to Oishi, testing the depths of his eyes for the depths of his resolve. "If you ever kneel before Kira again," he said, "I'll take your head."

He gathered together the pile of clothing Oishi had thrown in front of him, straightened up again in time to see the shock on Oishi's face at hearing a halfbreed threaten him with a samurai's revenge. But the disbelief dissolved into something far more like relief, as he realized that it meant Kai had just agreed to join his vendetta. He sighed, as Kai headed off to change.

"Where did you learn to fight like that?" Oishi called out suddenly.

Kai looked back over his shoulder, and irony turned his half smile into a smirk. "From demons."

13

By the time they reached the Buddha Mountain where Oishi had told Chikara to meet him, it was sunset on his fifth day of traveling with Kai.

He had spoken little during their journey, and Kai had said almost nothing, only asking him an occasional monosyllabic question: *Where had he been all this time? Where were they bound? Who would be there? And what then—?*

He had answered as best he could, finding that it got easier to give explanations the longer they rode together. He was still relieved that Kai felt less compulsion to make conversation than he would have expected if they had been two strangers accidentally traveling the same road, headed toward the same destination . . . the same destiny. *All wanderers were not necessarily lost.*

He had asked Kai only one question. He had seen—and experienced—more than enough in his few hours on the Dutch Island to give him all the other answers he needed. But as they rode, Kai would sometimes mumble something inaudible, always staring straight ahead, or down at the ground. When his behavior had irritated Oishi to the point of speech, he had finally asked Kai what he was doing.

Kai had looked over at him as if he'd forgotten someone else was even beside him. "Praying," he murmured. He looked away again, as if it was nothing.

After that Oishi was sure one of them had gone mad, but he was no longer so certain he knew which one it was.

Although Oishi doubted that Kai had ever ridden a horse before, the halfbreed handled his mount with the same unconscious ease he had shown in taming the castle hounds as a kennel boy . . . as though he communicated with animals on a level no ordinary human ever could. But then, he was able to see demons, which no ordinary human could, either. . . .

Oishi felt less certain about what the halfbreed really was than he ever had. And yet, the more often he glanced over at Kai riding on horseback beside him—with his long hair tied back, clad in a kimono and *hakama,* wearing a sword thrust through his belt ties—the more easily Oishi could have mistaken him for an anonymous ronin. *Another anonymous ronin,* he corrected himself, as reality jabbed him.

At last they caught sight of lit torches and a small cluster of campfires in the gathering darkness on Buddha Mountain, Oishi's silent doubt about how his comrades would react to his bringing the halfbreed with him faded, as the thought of being reunited with longtime friends filled him with fresh optimism.

As they closed in on the firelight, he counted the silhouetted figures of twenty men standing in front of the ancient ruined temple that gave the mountain its name. Some of them shouted and waved, but he could tell they were watching him now with mixed anticipation and curiosity, as they realized that he was not traveling alone.

He dismounted, and the men gathered around him, calling his name and their own, reaching out to him like a longlost brother. Surrounded by the warmth of their welcome he smiled, for what seemed like the first time in a year—and probably was—as he greeted them, joking with some, embracing others, his smile widening as he found Chikara, and praised him for the good work he had done in such a short space of time.

He only realized that Kai had not joined him when one of the men asked who the stranger was. When he answered, all their heads turned in Kai's direction, their surprise turning to disbelief, and then contempt, as they realized the man they had taken for another samurai was only the halfbreed, passing for human.

Kai stared back at them; his eyes were dark wells of memory as he met the gazes of the men who had beaten him so mercilessly the last time they had stood this close together. He still held the reins of the two horses tightly, as if he was ready to bolt if the men made any move toward him.

Only Chikara came forward, grinning with relief as he reached out to take the reins of his father's horse from Kai; Oishi saw him give a brief but visible bow to his former *sensei,* and a smile of welcome so genuine it was as if he was personally trying to make up for all the suspicion and hostility on the faces of the men still gathered around Oishi.

Oishi experienced an odd moment of disorientation as only his son, out of everyone there, greeted the halfbreed in the same way that his men had greeted him; he felt as if he was standing outside of himself, watching a scene in a play without understanding what was happening.

He sighed, looking around again, as Kai went with Chikara to help him tend to the horses, and the rest of the men turned their attention back to him.

Oishi spent what energy he had left listening to Chikara's report, and then to the individual stories and information brought in by the ronin Chikara had tracked down—the ones who had been willing to join him. They managed to contribute a gratifying amount to his basic knowledge of the situation.

By the time he had heard all their separate reports and repeated his own story, it was well into the night. He had sent them all off to get some sleep, and would have fallen asleep where he was sitting, on a camp stool by the fire, if Chikara had not forced him to lie down, and covered them both with his cloak against the cold.

Oishi's last thought, as he closed his eyes, was that he had not seen Kai since they arrived. He wondered whether the halfbreed had listened to the conversations from somewhere just beyond the light of the campfires . . . whether he had preferred to sleep with the horses rather than sleep with samurai who had lost everything but their belief in their own superiority . . . whether he would still be here, in the morning. . . .

Morning came all too soon, as the sun's blinding rays pried open his eyelids with the insistence of a mother forcing her laggard son to get up. When he was finally conscious enough to remember where he was, he finished waking with a jolt of anticipation that startled his whole body into alertness.

Most of the other men were already stirring, bringing the banked fires back to life to fix tea and a meal, as eager as he was to see the puzzle pieces they had gathered fit together into the plan he had promised them. They were filled with the hope of something more meaningful than a lifetime spent laboring at menial jobs that were beneath them, or even legally forbidden to them as samurai . . . or a life where they fit in nowhere at all.

Together they stood gazing at the panoramic view that had been hidden from Oishi when he arrived last night: the reason why this place was called the Buddha Mountain. Once, eons ago, it had been a much larger mountain, a volcano that had exploded with a violence that must have hurled cinders into the eye of Amaterasu herself. What remained, after countless centuries of nature's healing, was a vast, steep-sided bowl covered in a layer of rich volcanic soil, now cloaked in golden-green by a new season's emerging plant life.

Equally steep approaches on all sides led to the jagged rim of the bowl. At the highest point along the rim sat the remains of a Buddhist temple, ancient now in its own right and long since abandoned. It still gleamed in the sunlight with traces of the gold leaf that once had decorated its roofline and entryway; the men faced it in a group and bowed their heads in silent prayer.

Oishi had first come here when he was a boy, accompanying his father and a much younger Lord Asano on a pilgrimage after the death of their lord's wife. Oishi remembered the surprise he had felt when he found the temple in ruins. The area's frequent earthquakes had opened fractures in the bedrock beneath it, and a landslide had taken half the ground on which it had stood . . . and half of the temple too.

Oishi had not understood why Lord Asano would choose this lonely, abandoned spot as the place where he came to pray and seek solace. Only his lord's fearlessness—his father's unquestioning trust, or obedience—had convinced Oishi to accompany them into the ruin: Broken spines of wood protruded into empty space where once the image of Amida Buddha had gazed with infinite compassion upon those who came here seeking comfort.

But once inside the creaking, sighing temple, Oishi had been amazed to find that the gaping hole where the statue had been now opened on a world of green hills and blue sunlit sky, a view as idyllic and beautiful as any he had ever seen—a new world framed in the ruins of the past.

He had felt as if he was being shown a glimpse of what lay beyond today and tomorrow: a vision of the place where the soul rested between one human lifetime and the next during its ongoing process of transformation, until at last enlightenment was achieved, and with it, eternal rest on that exalted plane. Only then had he truly understood why the priest who accompanied them had said the meaning of life was not to seek happiness, but to become wise. . . .

A lone figure emerged from the shadows of the temple's timeworn entrance, carrying his sandals. He stopped on the stone steps outside to put them on, and then began to make his way down the hill toward the spot where they were camped. *A ronin, who had unsuspectingly taken shelter there during the night—?*

No, he realized, startled again by the unexpected revelations of this place. *It was Kai.* The halfbreed walked with his head down, not looking toward them or acknowledging that he wasn't alone, but still coming toward the place where they were gathered.

Had he simply chosen to sleep there, overnight? Or had he gone there to pray, to continue the cleansing of his spirit, after all he had been forced to do, and all that had been done to him, since the day of the tournament in the Shogun's honor nearly a year ago? Had the halfbreed really been reciting prayers during their ride . . . did he actually understand what prayer was, or the significance of holy ground? Oishi shook his head, as something Basho had told him once about Kai brushed the edge of his consciousness and vanished again before he could capture the thought.

He turned back to face his men, whose heads were still bowed in prayer, without saying anything to draw their attention, aware that they might take Kai's inexplicable behavior for intentional desecration of holy ground.

"I ask your forgiveness," he said at last, and their faces rose, focusing on his; their expressions showed curiosity and incomprehension.

His handful of officers . . . of lordless ronin . . . of still-loyal retainers listened in expectant silence, as he said, "I told you nothing before now because the enemy was watching, and I had to be sure. But now the time has come. Kira's spies think we have become beggars and thieves and are no longer a threat."

The men glanced at one another, their curiosity turning to surprise and darker emotions, although they were still uncertain of what they were hearing.

"What I propose ends in death," he said bluntly. "Even if we succeed, we will be hanged as criminals for defying the

Shogun's orders." Because the Shogun had specifically forbidden them from taking revenge on Kira, they would not even be able to regain their honor through *seppuku.*

Oishi went on speaking, expressing the thoughts that had occupied his mind all during the long hard ride to Dejima and back, trying to make clear to everyone there the larger picture of what they were up against.

He had no proof of whether the Shogun believed Kira was innocent of wrongdoing or not, but in his own mind, he suspected that the Shogun had intended all along to seize Ako and award it to Kira, one of his most favored counselors. He had seized the fiefs of outsider *daimyo* like Lord Asano often enough in the past, for offenses that ranged from petty to absurd—following the pattern of his predecessors for the past hundred years.

However, under the *bakufu*'s laws, all parties involved in an act of violence were ordinarily put to death, no matter who was the instigator. It was extremely rare for one man to be spared when the other had been condemned, particularly if the Shogun was nearby, because it implied a threat to his life as well.

For the Shogun to spare Kira, and then prohibit a vendetta against him, was more than unusual . . . it was an outrage against the code of the samurai whose ultimate lord he claimed to be. The Shogun himself was untouchable, because his position made him the one to whom even *daimyo* owed their fealty.

But not Kira. Whether it was the blindness of *Inu-Kubou* himself, the insidious political maneuvering of Kira, or witchcraft that had made the Shogun deny Lord Asano's former retainers the right to bring peace to the soul of their lord, that no longer mattered.

As ronin, they were free to walk any path, because they had nothing left to lose. They were even free to defy the law of the land—but not free of retribution. That kind of freedom was a terrifying thing, which was why few men chose it willingly.

Oishi wanted any man who followed him to understand from the start that what they were facing was suicide without honor. This was not simply *giri*—their final duty to their lord—or a commitment any man should make who felt the slightest conflict between *giri* and *ninjo*. Both their loyalty to Lord Asano and their personal belief in a higher justice that must be served had to be absolute.

Perhaps they would die in battle, attempting to avenge Lord Asano. But any men who survived to place Lord Kira's head on Lord Asano's grave, so that his suffering spirit would know it had been freed at last from this world, must then follow him by their own choice into the next—or they would be hunted down and executed like common murderers. Either way, they would have broken the *bakufu's* laws, and not only their peers, but their servants . . . even the lowest beggars and outcasts . . . would spit on their corpses.

And yet if they succeeded the gods above would know they had acted honorably, to right a wrong. Laws were made by men, and men made mistakes. Their vendetta would correct the imbalance human injustice had created—and even more importantly, it would have been done for the sake of Lord Asano's soul. Their true purpose would be remembered—and hopefully in the eyes of their families, if not the world, the stain would be erased from their names.

At last he took a deep breath, and said, "I take a vow before you that I will not rest until justice is done. Will not sleep until our master lies in peace. And will not pray unless it is to ask the heavens' forgiveness for sending Kira to hell!"

A stunned silence met his words, but the expressions on his men's faces—some of them close to tears—moved him more deeply than any tribute he could ever remember. And then one voice, and more and more, rose in a cheer as the ronin shouted their defiance to fate, or raised their arms into the air to grasp the tail of destiny. He saw the courage in their eyes—the eyes of men who were willing to fight for what they believed in, to the death; who were born to the belief that what they dared might be doomed to failure, but those who never dared had never truly been alive to begin with.

Kai sat by the fire, eyes closed, listening to Oishi's speech without seeming to do so as he waited for the morning meal to finish cooking. Beside him Chikara stirred a pot of rice, his eyes shining as he listened to his father's speech.

Kai glanced up as he heard the ronin cheering. The Way of the Warrior was the way of death, some men claimed . . . and claimed it with pride. These days, most men who claimed that were fools who had never been in a real battle, or even believed in anything they would actually defend to the death.

But there were some things, some people, and some truths that were worth risking even death to defend . . . and in the time when battle had been the true calling of the samurai, he would have been one with these other men, no matter who or what or where he had been born; because when chaos had ruled over order, how well you fought for whatever you believed in had counted more than the meaningless facts of a forgotten childhood.

And right at this moment, it struck him that whether they knew it or not, the ronin who stood cheering their leader, and cheering the meaning he had given back to their lives, were closer to being what he really was than they had ever dreamed.

Kai sighed and took out his knife. He pulled his long hair forward and raised his knife to it . . . And then he hesitated. He put the knife back in its sheath, and pulled his hair up into a ronin's unkempt topknot again—his own personal gesture of defiance in the face of all the laws of men, even the men with whom he would soon be facing death.

Chikara smiled as the other ronin cheered his father and shouted their own vows of resolve to bring justice to the lord they all still served in their hearts, standing before the shrine of the Compassionate Buddha, and in the full view of their ancestress, the sun. Then he looked back at Kai, watching him finish tying up his hair with a look that was equal parts satisfaction and heartfelt understanding.

The other ronin gathered around Oishi as he signaled Horibe to unfold the map of Kira's fortress and the surrounding mountains he had brought with him. The men murmured in surprise.

Hazama, Oishi's former second-in-command, said in disbelief, "How did you get the plans to the fortress?" He looked up at Horibe.

Oishi nodded with a smile toward the man who was old enough to be his grandfather. "Young Horibe seduced the architect's daughter," he said, unable to keep his smile from widening into a grin, as Horibe shrugged modestly.

The others—all of them at least young enough to be Horibe's sons—looked at him with an amazement that made Oishi burst out laughing. The others laughed with him, shaking their heads or slapping the old man on the back, as companionship and a sense of belonging filled their hearts again, after far too long, with something warmer than the morning sun; something they had all been missing for as long as Oishi had missed the sunlight itself.

Oishi reached down, pointing at the layout of Kira's fortress, regretting that they could not afford to hold onto this sunlit moment any longer. But a goal without a plan was nothing more than a wish. "Unfortunately, there are only two ways in. The main gate, here, and these cliffs beneath the west wall, both of which are heavily guarded. Our best chance is to strike when Kira leaves the safety of his fortress." He glanced toward Horibe again.

Horibe took over speaking, pointing to another location on the map. "The day before his wedding he will travel to his ancestors' shrine to offer prayers. We don't know yet which route he'll take, or how many guards he'll have."

Oishi looked over at Isogai, whose young, handsome face

still looked mildly peeved that Horibe, out of all of them, had stolen his spot as the envy of every man there. "Isogai, you'll ride ahead to his temple town and see what you can find out. Remember, even near holy sites there are brothels and plenty of loose-tongued officials who visit them."

Isogai turned red-faced as the men laughed again; but their laughter was good-natured, and so was the smile he gave them in return. He nodded confidently to Oishi, getting to his feet as the others leaned over the map once more, studying the imposing, mountainous terrain.

Kai leaned back against the rocky outcrop by the cook fire, stretching out the stiffness that plagued his legs and spine after the long ride. There was nothing much he could do right now about the pain of the injuries he had brought with him from his long nightmare on Dejima, except try to be patient. He wondered if he would ever be entirely free of the pain, or whether his nerve-endings, and his mind, had been violated beyond any hope of recovery. *Time healed all wounds,* he had been told, long ago. *One way or another.*

Chikara had stopped dishing up bowls of rice, and was looking at him; he saw the boy's eyes go to the sores on his wrists, still raw and inflamed, where the shackles he had worn on Dejima had eaten into his flesh. Kai knew he would wear the scars for as long as he lived, even if he lived long enough to rid himself of the memory of the heavy iron and chains that had made his struggles to escape worse than useless.

He glanced at Chikara again, at the painful empathy on the young ronin's face, the fear in his eyes that asked too many of the questions the boy couldn't ask out loud. He remembered what Oishi had been through, and that Chikara knew about it.

There was no need for Chikara to bear his scars or his memories as well: The boy's father was asking enough of him as it was. Kai managed a reassuring smile and reached without comment for a bowl of rice.

Chikara set the warm bowl into his hands, relieved enough to smile back at him as he went on dishing out food.

Kai got to his feet, digging rice from the bowl with his fingers and pushing it into his mouth as he crossed the short but infinitely wide distance between the place where he had been sitting and the spot where the others were gathered around the map.

Hazama was studying the map now, his expression growing more dubious as he glanced up again at Oishi. "Even if we know the route, we will need more men for an ambush."

"Then we'll get them," Oishi said. "You, Chuzaemon, and Okuda will gather as many of our former samurai as you can, and meet us . . . here." He pointed to another spot on the map. "At a farm house Horibe has found for us."

Basho grinned. "Did he seduce the farmer's daughter too?"

There was more laughter at that, but Hazama still looked unconvinced. "Forgive me, sir," he said to Oishi, "but we are ronin. Who will sell us weapons?" The *bakufu* kept strict track of who bought weapons—especially in large numbers—for no discernible or approved reason. "I am ready to give my life, but how can we succeed without good swords?"

Oishi hesitated, and his gaze flickered with something that looked oddly like pain. Then, pulling his own sword free, he held it out to Hazama.

"Take mine," Oishi said. "When we meet again, I'll have more waiting for you."

Hazama stared at him in disbelief for a moment, as if Oishi had just offered him his soul . . . which, under the code they lived by, he had. Hazama took the sword from his hands, and bowed. His look as he straightened up was filled with humility and awe. He bowed again, more deeply.

Kai saw Oishi's family *mon* on the sword's hilt, and realized that the blade he had given Hazama was not some scavenged piece of steel. It just might be the last thing Oishi actually owned that bore his family crest, the only remaining proof of who and what he had once been. *He'd just torn his soul out by the roots and handed it to Hazama. No wonder there'd been pain in his eyes.*

To Kai's surprise, he felt respect for Oishi's wisdom, as well as for his selflessness and resolve as a leader. He strolled over to where Oishi stood and stopped beside him, still holding the bowl of rice as he glanced at Hazama, and then from face to face around the circle of ronin.

Yasuno glared back at him, as if his very presence on the same patch of dirt with them was a profound insult. Kai dug another handful of rice from the bowl and put it into his mouth, looking back expressionlessly at Yasuno.

"The rest of us will go to Uetsu," Oishi said, seemingly undisturbed by Kai's presence, or the fact that everyone else's attention was suddenly fixed on him. "The finest sword makers in the land work there—"

"Why is the halfbreed here?" Yasuno demanded, unable to control his mouth even after a year without the immunity bestowed on a *daimyo*'s retainer. His hand moved to his *katana*. The tension among the others around him was suddenly so thick that he could have sliced it with his sword.

Kai went on gazing at him, chewing rice.

As Oishi glanced at Kai, a phrase from Musashi's *Book of Five Rings* flashed into his mind: "*Do not let the enemy see your spirit.*" His expression froze as he remembered how the halfbreed had looked at him, during their confrontation after the escape from Dejima. Oishi realized suddenly that the seeming lack of emotion on Kai's face was something far more dangerous.

Before Yasuno could get himself killed, Oishi fixed him with a stare of mild rebuke, and said, "I asked him to come."

"We can't take him with us!" Yasuno said angrily. "He's not a samurai—"

"None of us are samurai anymore!" Oishi shouted, lashing out at them all with the truth that the halfbreed had forced him to acknowledge.

Yasuno bristled like an angry dog. But the smoldering

disgust in his commander's eyes finally silenced him. His hand dropped away from his sword. The others around him looked down, or away, equally chastened.

Kai glanced at Oishi, his expression as unreadable as his reaction—as impenetrable as the tangle of emotions he was still struggling to separate, or even identify in his mind. He looked away again, and went on eating.

14

Mika kneeled in front of the low tables that had been placed before her, staring at her dinner, a meal truly fit for a *daimyo*'s daughter. Surrounding the traditional heart of the meal—rice, in an elegant, lacquered bowl—were dishes of salted vegetables and pickled plums, and smaller bowls of condiments—*wasabi,* soy sauce, and others particular to the area, the names of which she had never bothered to ask. *Sashimi* prepared from fish freshly caught in mountain streams, and thinly sliced roast venison were laid out in graceful arcs on dishes to one side; on the other was the *raku*-ware teapot, and a cup already filled with steaming tea.

She stared at the food, with her hands in her lap, making no move to touch anything. The beautifully prepared meal made her mouth water, but her stomach clenched like a fist at the thought of eating in front of her dinner companion.

It was not Lord Kira; she had not seen him all day. She supposed he must have more important things on his mind for once than one more silent pretense of a cordial meal with her . . . probably preparations for their wedding. She looked down at her hands. There had been a time when she thought the very prospect of seeing him again would make her too ill to eat, although she knew she must eat to stay strong, in the hope that one day, somehow, her chance would come. . . .

But her chance would never come while she was trapped here, deep in the mountains that Kira knew so well. She had vowed to herself that she would live to see Ako again. And then, one day, she would take it back—

"Eat, my lady."

Mika looked up, frowning at her companion for the evening—the shape-changing witch who was Kira's consort. Kira had made certain that she would never be lonely . . . or alone . . . at a meal, even when he was away on long visits to the Shogun's court.

The witch kneeled across from her, dressed as always in the finest, most elegant silks and brocades—as always in the variegated woodland shades that suited her so well. The colors and imagery of her clothing seemed to change subtly, constantly, even when she sat perfectly still as if, like the leaves of the deep woods, their patterns were touched constantly by an invisible breeze.

As Mika made no move to eat, the witch smiled, as amused as if she was watching a stubborn child. A lock of the *kitsune*'s black hair slithered free of the combs and flowered pins that decorated her elaborately arranged hairdo, and drifted like a snake in water through the air above the table surface.

With her hands resting on her knees and a faint smile still on her lips, the witch watched the strand of hair move with a life of its own to pick up Mika's chopsticks, and select a piece of fish. She held it in front of Mika, invitingly.

Mika looked back at her with a gaze like steel, moving neither to accept the bite of fish nor to avoid it. She would not give the *kitsune* the satisfaction of betraying any fear or revulsion—anything at all that would give the witch a sense of control over her. When Mika was first brought here, the witch had tried everything in her power that she dared to frighten and demoralize her rival—everything that Kira would permit.

Mika had quickly realized that the *kitsune* wouldn't actually harm her; no matter what she was capable of, she was in Kira's thrall as much as he was in hers. It was not simply that their goals were the same—although they were, fortunately, because for now those goals included keeping their hostage alive and well.

As Mika continued to gaze back at her in cold defiance, the witch moved the piece of fish back and forth sinuously, like a lure, in front of her. "You think I care if you starve?" Her smile turned mocking. "Soon my lord shall have what he wants, and you can take your life like your father—"

Mika's mask of control suddenly shattered, as the words struck her like a fist. "*You* killed my father!"

"Did I—?" The witch raised her eyebrows in innocent surprise. "Weren't you the one who broke his heart? He took in the halfbreed out of pity and you betrayed him with your lust. You wanted the one thing that was forbidden to you." The words dripped venom. Another lock of hair snaked free, caught up another bite of raw fish, and crushed it between chopsticks. It writhed in a travesty of anguish, as if it was alive, and still struggling to break free. "Your love brought down Ako, my lady. . . ."

Mika stared at the other woman, her eyes blurring with pain, her defenses crushed in a vise of grief and shame. As she did, the *kitsune*'s face dissolved, transforming, until its features became her own face, gazing back at her in a travesty of desire—her eyes brighter, her lips redder, tremulous with the kind of longing that Mika instinctively knew must have lit her own face every time she gazed at Kai.

"Are we so different . . . ?" the witch whispered softly, and the mirror-image of Mika's lower lip suddenly quivered; her longing eyes filled with the terrible fear of losing her only love.

Mika's mouth opened, but no sound came out.

The shape-shifter suddenly broke into peals of laughter, as her own face slid back into place, banishing the stolen image of Mika's. The sinuous black strands holding the chopsticks dropped them, fish and all, onto the table and whipped back into her upswept hairdo. She rose to her feet abruptly and left the room, still laughing.

After she was gone, the laughter seemed to haunt the room. Mika covered her ears with her hands and shut her eyes, as tears slid out from under her closed lids. But it was not the laughter she couldn't block out; it was the way the laughter rang hollow . . . and the devastating, all-too-human fear of loss she had seen in the witch's eyes as she'd asked if they were so different, in their yearning for a forbidden love.

Because Mika realized now that only the fear had been real. . . .

The ronin arrived on the bluff above Uetsu at midday, under a sky that was gray with lowering clouds, with a chill wind at their backs. They stood on the rim, looking down at the road that led into the town, searching the scene below for signs of trouble.

They had already dismounted, leaving their horses among the trees at Oishi's order so their arrival would create less disturbance, because he had no idea what kind of response it would get.

Uetsu had been part of Lord Asano's domain; its expert metalworkers supplied most of the weapons his warriors had carried, as well as tools for farmers, carpenters, and other craftsmen throughout the area. The people of Uetsu had taken great pride in their work, and also in the fact that Lord Asano rewarded them well for it. If anyone in Ako was still willing to help their former lord's retainers to avenge his death, the people of Uetsu should be first among them.

But it had been nearly a year since Lord Asano's death. While the feelings of the inhabitants of Uetsu were unlikely to have changed, Kira's appointed *karou* and his retainers, and the Shogun's stand-in troops, had been in charge of the domain and its inhabitants for all that time. It was impossible to predict what might have changed since their lord's demise.

Oishi led the men down the sloping trail from the top of the bluff and past the first houses at the edge of town, taking care to walk softly, because most of them were walking unarmed into whatever reception awaited them.

Kai trailed behind, head down, not following closely on anyone's heels, still too aware that his presence among them was only tolerated, not accepted.

But knowing his place served more than one purpose. Away from the others, his senses could read the signs they couldn't, without them being aware of it . . . and following separately, he was free to move unseen in any direction.

He was certain there was no one behind them . . . but the town they were entering disturbed him already. This place was far too quiet to be an enclave of metalworkers, and as he looked around, it seemed more and more like it had been abandoned. The street and shops around them were empty, even though he could hear vague echoes of human speech from somewhere ahead. He smelled smoke from fires, which he would have expected, but there was none of the accompanying clangor of metal being worked and shaped. He heard no hiss of steam as a heated blade was plunged into water to cool it, no clearly audible voices shouting and calling to each other over the racket. But Oishi and the others kept moving, and so he followed, saying nothing, waiting.

Suddenly Oishi held up his hand as if he too realized what Kai had already observed—that the shops and houses at the edge of town were all empty. He gestured for the others to keep silent as they started on, going deeper into the town's heart, where they could all hear the sounds now that Kai had registered as they entered.

By now he could tell that the sounds were all wrong—sounds that could only mean trouble. He hoped it wasn't more trouble than a handful of ill-equipped men could take on. The ronin ahead of him closed ranks, and he closed the gap between himself and them, stopping beside Chikara, the one person he trusted not to object suddenly and loudly.

They turned another corner among the winding streets and alleys—and suddenly found themselves face to face with a handful of Kira's soldiers, loading an oxcart with whatever valuables they had discovered in the abandoned houses. In the distance Kai saw the smoke he'd smelled—not coming from forges, but from buildings at the far end of town, which had already been looted and set on fire.

Kai began to edge forward, as the soldier who seemed to be in charge of looting confronted them suddenly, his sword drawn.

"Who are you?" he asked Oishi, his eyes narrowing as he saw the men who were with him. As his own men gathered around him, drawing their swords, he added, "You must be lost." His mouth turned up in a smile that was not even slightly amused.

Oishi bowed, as humbly as any peasant. "We are farmers from Shimobe, sir. We have come to buy tools." Shimobe lay just over the border, in another lord's domain, implying that they not only had permission to make this journey, but that they might actually be ignorant of what was going on. His face was the picture of innocent confusion, but Kai could see his eyes, and the look in them was far too wary to make his expression believable.

Kai took an inventory of his own as Kira's soldiers spread out around the group—noting their positions, calculating the time it would take him to reach any one of them. *There were only four. That was lucky.* But they were well-armed, and suspicious. He watched how they took in the appearance of the men around him, scanning the group of supposedly humble farmers, observing the half-grown-out hair of ronin, and clothing that, despite its shabbiness, was unusually sophisticated for a cluster of peasants.

"This is Lord Kira's village now," the lead soldier said, as he stopped by Chikara. He looked him up and down—and suddenly grabbed his arm, revealing the sword Chikara had been trying to keep out of sight. His face hardened, as he raised his own sword.

Kai leaped forward, stripping the sword from his hand with a wrist-snapping twist, and ran him through with it. Before they had even realized what was happening, he cut down soldiers two and three. The ronin around him stood gaping as if they had just seen three men struck by lightning.

But the fourth of Kira's men, standing on the other side of the gathered ronin, wasn't as slow to grasp the situation.

Before Kai could get to him, he was gone, running for his horse. He swung into the saddle and booted his mount hard, heading down an alley between two buildings before anyone could stop him.

"He's getting away!" Chikara shouted, pointing.

Kai snatched up the bow and arrows from one of the dead soldiers, and ran to the alley mouth. The rider was still in his line of sight; he took aim and fired. The man pitched from his horse and lay still, as the horse ran on.

With a sigh of relief Kai headed back toward the others. No unwelcome news would reach Kira, or his minions, about who had attacked his men . . . at least, not today. He watched the ronin relax as they saw his own relief, and instinctively reacted to it. Ignoring their stares as he rejoined the group, he kneeled down by the nearest corpse and began to strip it of armor, piling the dead man's weapons together with the bow and quiver of arrows.

Finally he glanced up, as the other men did nothing but stand and stare at him, their faces reflecting a range of conflicted emotions. They remained motionless, like *Kabuki* actors frozen in a tableau, even when he went so far as to hold up a sword for someone to take.

"What is he doing?" Yasuno said to Oishi, his voice filled with indignation.

"We need armor," Kai said, ignoring Yasuno's question as he continued to gather pieces.

Oishi glanced at him, and nodded. "He's right. Help him."

Across the street Chikara emerged from a sword-maker's shop, grimacing. "There's nothing here," he said. The first drop of rain from the leaden sky landed by his foot, pocking the dust of the street.

The rain began to fall in earnest after that, and the ronin brought their horses down from the bluff, finding shelter for the animals and themselves in the abandoned shops and houses. As Oishi had hoped, the pouring rain doused the fires started by Kira's troops—saving the whole town from burning to the ground. The people who had lived here might actually have something to come back to someday, if they were ever allowed to return.

Not that it meant anything had really changed, for him or his men. After the worst of the storm passed they had searched every weapon-maker's shop in town, but he could count on one hand the number of usable blades for swords or spears they had found, most of which lacked hilts or hafts.

Oishi sat on the veranda of the cottage where he had planned to sleep, if only his mind would stop leaping from one useless idea to another like a squirrel in a cage. He stared blankly at the map they had brought with them from the Buddha Mountain, as if the solutions to his problems lay somehow hidden between the lines of the drawing, or written in disappearing ink that he didn't know how to make visible.

Kai stepped up onto the porch, shaking water from his hair like a dog. Oishi wondered what he had been doing, that he was still so wet. *Standing under another waterfall—?* Oishi didn't flinch, aware that even if he'd had the energy to protest, he owed the halfbreed that much forbearance, for saving Chikara—and probably several other men—from being killed this afternoon . . . for protecting them all, by keeping someone from getting word of their existence to Kira.

And for making them face the truth, again.

Kai looked down at him, at the map spread out beside him.

"We can go to Hida," Oishi said. He pointed to its location. "They will give us weapons."

"Hida will have nothing," Kai said flatly. "Kira's men will have swept through this entire region."

Oishi didn't answer, having expected exactly what he heard, because he had already realized that was the most likely scenario. He waited, sensing that the halfbreed had come here with something more on his mind than simply pointing out flaws of logic that Oishi could see for himself.

Kai stood, staring into the darkness, as if for some reason he was having a hard time bringing up what he had really come to talk about. "There is another way," he said at last.

Oishi glanced up.

"You will find swords in the Sea of Trees. The Tengu Forest." Kai went on staring out at the night and rain.

"That's just a myth." Oishi shook his head, disappointed in spite of himself.

But the halfbreed looked down at him with the unnerving gaze that so rarely let anything out, and never let anyone in. "They're real," he said softly. "I've seen them."

Oishi's expression changed from annoyance to something else entirely, as a ripple of emotion disturbed Kai's face at last . . . as the haunted look of a man who had literally been bedeviled all his life rose into his dark eyes, filling them until it seemed to be all Kai had ever known.

All his life people had accused the halfbreed of being a demon, and he had always denied it. But now . . . what was he trying to say? Oishi got to his feet. "Come inside," he said.

Kai followed him into the warm interior of a stranger's abandoned home, glancing around in curiosity. Commoners who worked as craftsmen ranked below farmers socially, because what they produced was not as vital to life. But metalsmiths, especially those who made fine swords, had always been in demand, and the people in this village had begun to acquire a few possessions which were beautiful, not simply necessary . . . as the looters they'd caught here had realized.

Oishi kneeled on the *tatami* by the glowing brazier at the center of the room, and gestured for Kai to join him.

"How do you know about the Tengu Forest?" he asked, as Kai settled across from him.

"I was raised there," Kai said, looking away, "before I fled to Ako." He looked up again, into Oishi's incredulous stare.

"Those scars on your head—" Oishi gestured at the few not completely hidden by the halfbreed's hair, remembering the strange inscription etched into his shaven scalp when he had first arrived at the castle. "Are they the ones who marked you?"

"Yes." Kai's fingers rose to his face, touching the scars above his eyes as gingerly as if they were still fresh wounds, but he said nothing more.

Oishi tried to recall what he knew about *tengu* . . . demons who were rumored to be everything from flying pranksters not much better than crows, to shape-shifters who were savage fighters and used their demonic powers to forge their own swords. "And they taught you to fight—?"

"Yes," Kai said again. He looked at Oishi wearily as he replied, as if he didn't expect him to believe the truth when he finally heard it.

But the halfbreed's story was not the first Oishi had heard about a man learning martial arts from the *tengu*. Legend said that *tengu* had trained the general Minamoto no Yoshitsune as a boy during the Genpei War, five hundred years ago—and the same thing was claimed about a commander in Hideyoshi's army, less than a century and a half ago.

Although there were also tales that Miyamoto Musashi had defeated a *nue* . . . but there was nothing in his *Book of Five Rings* about slaying *yokai*. . . .

And yet seeing Kai's haunted eyes and the strange inscription above them, Oishi suddenly found the old tales about *tengu* entirely believable.

Kai looked down at his hands, which were covered with old scars as well as the half-healed wounds from his time on the Dutch Island. "They wanted to show me that this life has nothing to offer but death. They wanted me to be like them, and renounce the world. But I believed my place was among other men." He raised his head again and held Oishi's stare a moment longer before his vision drifted beyond him, and Oishi glimpsed the lifetime of sorrow, disillusionment, and aching loneliness that had come of Kai's decision—the same decision Oishi knew he would have made, if he had ever been in such a position, the only human being living in a world of demons.

He forced his mind to refocus on the present, where he knew the halfbreed preferred their conversation to remain. "And you think these *tengu* will give us weapons?"

"We will have to earn them." The bleakness in Kai's voice told him that it would not be an easy task.

"How?" he asked.

"They will test our will." The look in the halfbreed's eyes now warned him the outcome of the test would be life or death: Failure was not an option.

Oishi considered the words, weighing them against all that he and Kai, and his men, had already been through, their lack of viable options . . . and their goal. At last he nodded, looking up again with eyes that held only certainty.

15

The loud *crack* of colliding *bokken* rang across the upper courtyard of Kirayama Castle as Lord Kira fought two men at the same time, moving with a speed and agility he had never shown before. He struck one man down with a vicious blow to the head, and in the same move disarmed a second opponent.

The man started forward to pick up his wooden sword. Kira's *bokken* came down on his hand with brutal force; the man cried out and fell back, cradling his broken fingers. Kira stepped away, smiling.

Mitsuke looked on from the doorway of her chambers, observing the results of her latest spell-casting with a private smile of her own. She had given Kira the strength and skill of a true warrior, as part of her attempt to give him the confidence and abilities he would need to rule Ako, once he was truly its master.

Kira was a creature of the Edo court, with a preternatural skill that was all his own when it came to battles fought with words, or invisible blades of rumor and innuendo sunk into the backs of his rivals. But if he was to be a true *daimyo,* with rich lands that others desired . . . if he was to succeed in his greater ambition of ruling more than just Ako . . . he would need the physical presence and courage that he lacked, to directly command the respect he craved.

Now she had given him at least the seeds of it, hoping they would take root and grow . . . even though he was still obsessed with the cold, unattainable heart of Lady Mika. She could have given him Lady Mika's loving devotion far more easily than she could create in him the strength and skill to face any kind of battle and win it.

But he was hers. She truly loved him—his beauty and his ruthlessness, his passion and his fears—without needing any form of enchantment to blind her to who and what he really was. She understood him; they were alike, in so many ways.

And she knew that he truly loved her too, despite his human flaws. His lust for a woman who was nothing but a pawn, a symbol of all that would be his when this game of *shogi* was over, would turn to boredom quickly enough, when he found that bedding a woman who loathed him was as stimulating as sex with a wooden game piece.

She would tolerate her rival until Kira was secure in his role as the new Lord Asano, ruler of Ako. And then—if Lady Mika had not ended their marriage and her humiliation of her own free will; or if Kira continued his obsession, even when she was completely his—there were ways to solve the problem of a rival that Kira would never even suspect.

Kira stood catching his breath while his unfortunate opponents were helped from the practice area. His attention turned suddenly toward the figure approaching him from the gateway of the upper courtyard—the head of his personal intelligence network, which rivaled the Shogun's in its thoroughness when it came to his personal enemies. He crossed the courtyard to meet the man, concerned as always by his unpredictable arrivals.

The man dropped to his knees, bowing. Raising his head, he said, "My lord, forgive me. The halfbreed has escaped from the Dutch Island." He paused, his discomfort showing. "They say a samurai helped him."

Kira's frown of surprise changed to an expression that held more concern, and a trace of alarm. "What news of Oishi?" he demanded.

The spy shook his head. "He left for the pleasure houses in Kyoto after his wife divorced him—but he hasn't been seen since."

Like a lantern in daylight . . . Kira thought, frowning. He sensed more bad news coming, as the man glanced down again.

"One of your border posts was attacked yesterday. Five men were killed."

Kira swore under his breath. He ordered the man to rise, and dismissed him. As his intelligence officer hurriedly departed, Kira turned toward Mitsuke, who had come out into the yard to watch and listen. "Find them," he snapped at her, giving her orders as if she meant no more to him than the pathetic wretches still waiting their turn for a beating at his hands.

She looked back at him, her own gaze matching his coldness. "What empty promises will you make me this time—?" she said, stung, letting him see her displeasure at his arrogance.

Kira's frown suddenly turned ugly. "I took you in and protected you, witch! Disobey me and I will have you turned loose and hunted down with the rest of your kind!"

She held his stare, but her anger was suddenly mingled with hurt and a trace of fear. She bowed, deeply and gracefully, more to hide her misgivings than to express her obedience.

He turned away, anger and fear sharpening his every movement, and signaled two more unfortunate soldiers to step forward and oppose him. He was more than ready to take his anger out on them, two at a time, until he had gotten it out of his system.

Mitsuke moved slowly back toward her chambers, her thoughts troubled as she listened to the clash of *bokken* begin again. She had hoped that increasing his physical skills might improve his temper, along with his self-confidence . . . but what she had seen so far suggested that more power would only lead to more corruption in his soul. *Well, what had been done could always be undone, if he betrayed her.* She had always made certain of that. She had not survived for so long that her fur had turned white by behaving like a foolish kit in first heat.

The ronin paused their horses at the edge of the vast forest called the Sea of Trees . . . or more often, the Tengu Forest, apparently not without reason. They sat staring mutely at the shadowland of the primeval woods, as even Kai made no move to start forward again.

"My grandmother used to tell me stories about this place, when she wanted to scare me," Basho said at last, breaking the silence that had fallen over them all. "It always worked," he added. He looked over at Yasuno, who was struggling as usual to control a horse afflicted by his own restlessness. Basho gestured courteously. "After you," he said, and grinned.

Yasuno glared at him, and urged his horse forward.

The halfbreed followed Yasuno, his expression more resigned than resentful.

Oishi followed too, leading the rest of the men into the forest, and daylight faded swiftly behind them.

As they rode deeper into the trees it became impossible—for anyone but Kai, at least—to tell one direction from another, let alone how to retrace their path back to open ground. Even Yasuno had quickly dropped back to let Kai take the lead, as Kai rode past him and immediately altered the direction in which they had been heading.

There was no sign of a track, not even a faint animal trail through the underbrush. If the land hadn't continued to rise, they might have been riding in circles as they traveled, always having to keep their horses at a walk because of the unpredictable course they were following. But even the rising land was no guarantee that they were on a path that would ever lead them to *tengu.* At long last, Oishi understood why Lord Asano had valued the instincts of his head tracker so highly.

The morning mist that had hung over the Tengu Forest as they approached it did not burn away as the sun rose higher. Instead, it seemed to grow ever thicker, as if it was a manifestation of the place itself, the exhalation of the ancient trees, which had grown so tall and densely branched that they completely blocked the sky. Their gigantic trunks were layered with moss and fungi, and there was always a sound of condensation slowly dripping from leaves and needles.

The men had heard virtually nothing else, only the occasional *clack* as a horse's hoof struck a stone. Whatever ordinary creatures dwelled here seemed to regard their trespassing on the forest's peace as unnatural; they waited, hushed and hidden, until the strangers had passed. The ronin looked around constantly, and back over their shoulders, with a growing sense of unease. Human sight was no match for the impenetrable maze where something unseen seemed to be waiting, watching, just beyond the limits of their vision.

A soft moan sounded, in the fog ahead of them, and then another and another, as if the land itself had begun a choir of lamentation at their intrusion.

"What's that noise?" Hara asked, finally breaking the spell that seemed to have paralyzed their own throats.

"Ghosts—" the halfbreed said, barely looking back over his shoulder. He sounded as if he was reluctant to answer, even though no one's expression held anything but a desperate need for an explanation. "The cries of the old and infirm who are left here to die." He looked away again, and murmured, "Unwanted infants, too."

Oishi glanced over at him, hearing something more than mere reticence in those final words. He knew that peasants who were too poor to support their families were forced by need to abandon elderly parents or unwanted infants, leaving them to die in a forest or on a mountainside. *One of his duties as Lord Asano's* karou *had been to ensure that no one in Ako domain was ever forced to make such a choice. . . .*

Kai's gaze dropped to the forest floor that lay hidden in the fog swirling around their horses' legs.

Barely controlling a shudder, Oishi looked ahead again, and saw flickering blue lights like uncanny fireflies forming and fading in the mist.

"What about those flames?" Basho asked, pointing. He seemed to be the only one among them still willing to ask questions.

"Their souls," the halfbreed muttered, "trapped, like their bones are under your feet." His shoulders tightened, as if some invisible pressure was closing its hand around him, trying to crush him out of existence.

In the blue-green light, the halfbreed's face was as pale as a ghost's, almost translucent; as if, at any moment, he might become a spirit himself and vanish, leaving them all stranded here. Kai's name meant "the sea"; but Oishi suddenly remembered that when written with a different *kanji*, it meant "ghost." Kai went on gazing down into the fog, at nothingness . . . or perhaps it wasn't *nothing* that he saw. . . .

Basho glanced at him in concern and then looked down too, his brow furrowing with concern, or something closer to consternation.

When Chikara saw Basho's expression, he shook his head and smiled with the oblivious amusement of the young. He failed to notice that as his father went on watching Kai, the look on Oishi's face had become more like Basho's.

The halfbreed's aura of unease was palpable now. He stopped his horse and stood in his stirrups, looking from side to side, searching as if there might be something to see. There was nothing anywhere but the same labyrinth of trees twined with eerie fog, the blue lights shimmering and fading wherever they looked, as far as Oishi could tell . . . and all around them the sound of dripping water, and the moaning, mourning voices of the abandoned dead.

But maybe Kai was seeing, hearing . . . sensing something to which the rest of them were blind . . . third-eye blind.

Kai dropped back into his saddle, raising a hand to his head with a grimace of sudden pain. He pressed his palm against the scars on his forehead, as if they had begun to throb.

"Are we lost?" Oishi asked, trying to keep the anxiety out of his voice.

"No," Kai muttered, "it's this way." He turned his horse to the right, and started forward again.

Within a few paces the fog cleared in front of them as if a brisk wind had blown it away, although there was no breeze at all. Oishi sucked in a gasp of surprise, hearing exclamations and sounds of disbelief among the riders behind him.

They were face to face with a *tengu*—a *tengu* twice the size of a man, and more terrifying than Oishi had ever imagined, with a sharp hawklike ripping beak in the middle of a strangely human face, its skin shriveled like a reptile's, formidable talons on its hands and feet . . . and wings, for pursuing and sweeping down on its victims.

The halfbreed dismounted and stood in front of it, looking up. His face was filled with resignation and resolve, but not a trace of fear. "We'll leave the horses here," he said.

Oishi realized with sudden disbelief that what they were seeing was only an image carved from stone, guarding the entrance in an ancient wall, not a living creature at all. He took a deep breath and let it out, wondering as he swung down from the saddle how he could actually have believed the stone carving was alive, only a moment before. He heard other murmurs and sighs of relief as the men behind him began to dismount.

The halfbreed waited until all the horses had been tethered, and then he turned without a word of explanation and started walking, passing through the entrance in the wall of stone as if the giant *tengu* had ceased to exist. Something about the way he carried himself as he entered the place where he had been raised kept anyone else from calling out to him. No one followed him closely, but they followed him, just the same.

Beyond the stone wall the haunted forest suddenly became a grove of bamboo. Oishi was surprised again, because they had not seen bamboo growing anywhere until now. It was almost as if it had been planted here . . . although that must have happened centuries ago, judging from the size of the largest trunks and the vast expanse of the grove.

Kai walked with his head down, his shoulders still tight with tension. No expression at all showed on his face when he occasionally glanced up, or from side to side—but Oishi could see that he was still as pale as a ghost. Oishi wondered why the halfbreed had been willing to return to a place that clearly caused him such pain, both physical and mental. He wondered even more that Kai had willingly suggested it to him, in order to get the ronin the weapons they needed for their plans to have any chance of success.

He had no idea what motive had been strong enough to drive Kai to this. Did he hate Kira so much that he was willing to go through this to repay him for what had happened on Dejima? Or did he truly love Mika so much—enough to die for her? Was it actually possible that, by the inscrutable will of the gods, the body of a halfbreed outcast had been the receptacle for a samurai's reborn soul, making him as honor-bound to avenge Lord Asano's death as any man here . . . ?

Kira had been born a samurai . . . but not a man of honor. Even the Shogun was not—Oishi forced himself to stay focused on where he was, and why. He wondered if the test of wills had already begun. His hands tightened at his sides, as something new became visible through the tendriling mist.

This time, to his astonishment, it was the gigantic image of a reclining Buddha, emerging from the face of a cliff. The outcrop of rock that had provided long-dead artisans with a place to express their vision was far larger than the pillar of stone that had been transformed into a *tengu*. Oishi stopped, and shook his head. Out of all the things he had been expecting to come upon, an image of Buddha was the last. But suddenly, finding a bamboo grove here made sense to him: This had been the site of a temple, once. Major temples and shrines were almost always surrounded by bamboo, as a sacred barrier against evil.

He glanced at Kai again, to be sure they were seeing the same thing. The halfbreed had slowed down, looking up as if he too saw the figure. Then he looked down at its base, at the shadow below its neck. He raised his hand to his forehead again, pressing hard against his scars; his jaw clenched as if he was reliving the pain of the moment when they had been inscribed. But he kept walking toward the cliff, and so Oishi and the others followed, all of them trying to walk as softly as if they didn't exist.

Kai reached the base of the carved Buddha, which even reclining was as tall as four men. He stopped at last before the shadowy cleft below its neck—the joining place of body and mind—and then he put his hands together, bowing his head. He began to murmur the words of what sounded like a prayer, although Oishi could not make them out clearly.

Oishi glanced at his men, who had stopped when he had, keeping their distance from the cliff face. The ronin watched the halfbreed nervously, their tension only growing as he finished the prayer and turned back to them.

The relief that showed on his face vanished as he looked at them, seeing their obvious fear. His eyes went to Yasuno's hand hovering over his sword, before he finally looked at Oishi. "Only you," he said, pointing at Oishi. "The others must stay behind."

Oishi frowned at the prospect, like all the rest of his men. He looked back at Kai uncertainly.

"Leave your weapon," Kai said, as if he hadn't noticed Oishi's reluctance, and was ignoring the hostility of the other men. He pulled his own sword from the belt ties of his *hakama* and laid it on the ground. Then, with a final expectant glance at Oishi, he turned away again and disappeared into the darkness of the tunnel that lay hidden beneath the sleeping Buddha.

Oishi watched the halfbreed melt into the shadows and vanish as if he had never existed—and suddenly he couldn't move. Some oddly detached part of his mind looked on in disbelief, as his body stood frozen with superstitious fear. *He had never imagined anything like this.*

He was torn between his terror of the unknown and their only hope of avenging their lord . . . whose soul would remain caught forever between worlds, a tormented ghost like the moaning spirits in the forest behind them, if his *karou*'s cowardice kept him from following a halfbreed *hinin* into the dark.

"Sir," Horibe said, "let me come with you—"

"No." Oishi shook his head, the word making up his mind for him. There was no turning back now. Even to have hesitated, after he had given Kai his promise, was shameful. Cursing himself under his breath, he began to pull loose the sword he had gotten in Uetsu. But he hesitated and pushed it back into place, even as he told the others, "Do as he says." *Stay here.* His glance raked his men, coming to rest on Chikara.

His son watched, hands tightening at his sides, as Oishi walked toward the hidden entrance beneath the gigantic Buddha and disappeared into the darkness, just as Kai had done. Yasuno took a step as if to follow him anyway, but Basho blocked his way with an outstretched arm, shaking his head.

Kai kept moving deeper into the darkness, even though he heard no footsteps behind him. Now that he had come this far, and been granted entrance, there was no way back for him. What the others chose to do now scarcely mattered. The past closed around him like a caul until his senses were suffocated by memory, as if he was making his way through a tunnel in time, not space . . . returning of his own free will to the womb.

He became aware of his shuffling footsteps, his shallow breathing, blood rushing in his ears . . . the feel of unnaturally matted growth, the roots and fungi that covered the tunnel wall he traced with outstretched fingertips as the darkness became complete, forcing him to reach out with his other senses. The smell of dampness and decaying plant life, the sense of becoming a part of the earth itself as he passed beneath the massive stone ceiling, the essence of Buddha and the earth conjoined . . . the source of strength for all those who truly became one with the power of the mountain places. *He remembered all of it, as if he had escaped from here only yesterday, not twenty years ago. Because, just as the Old One had prophesied . . .*

The sound of footsteps behind him, stumbling as they hurried to catch up, broke the spell of time and memory that held him captive. Oishi collided with him, and grunted in surprise. Kai turned, catching hold of the other man with an unsteady laugh. Oishi said nothing, but his hand rested lightly on Kai's shoulder in reassurance and apology before they went on, side by side.

Kai realized he could hear chanting up ahead now, the same eerie chanting from his memories, the sutras and mantras repeated endlessly by voices that reverberated with disturbing overtones before they were absorbed into the root-and-fungus-encrusted walls of the chamber up ahead. He remembered from his youth the scene they would come upon, that was about to challenge Oishi's perceptions of reality far more profoundly than Kai's first encounter with human beings had confused and terrified him. He at least had seen books and scrolls, and had the chance to spy on occasional groups of humans, when he was a boy . . . but he doubted that any other living human had seen what Oishi was about to see.

He put up a hand, halting Oishi beside him as the brightening of the tunnel and the clarity of the chanting told him they were about to reach its end. As he turned toward Oishi and at last saw the other man clearly, he realized with a pang of disbelief that Oishi was still wearing his sword. But then, until a moment ago he'd thought Lord Asano's former *karou* had lost his nerve completely. He swallowed his frustration, trying to feel relieved that the man had only balked at entering a demon stronghold unarmed.

In any case, whatever they encountered from here on was already beyond their control. The only thing they possessed that was still meaningful was their strength of spirit—their resolve to achieve their goal no matter what they were forced to endure. The ultimate outcome, as he had tried to warn Oishi back in Uetsu village, was something no amount of blind courage or physical strength, but only willpower and self-control could determine.

He held Oishi's gaze as he said, "Whatever happens in there—whatever you see—*don't draw your sword,*" willing Oishi to believe what lay in his eyes, to hear the urgency of his warning, and—*gods, just this once*—obey him unquestioningly.

Oishi nodded, his expression determined, but with anxiety shadowing his face as he glanced down at the *katana*.

Silently amazed . . . *still, after all these years* . . . by the narrow boundaries within which most human beings defined their existence, and what did or didn't belong in it, Kai started on toward the chanting and the light, with Oishi unconsciously following behind him, glancing over his shoulder at the way back to the world outside.

Still waiting in the world outside, in the oppressive heart of the Sea of Trees, the other ronin paced restlessly or shifted from foot to foot, unable to stay still as the seconds seemed to trickle down and drip like condensation from the fog. Around them in the eternally shifting grayness, the haunted moans and cries of the equally restless spirits peeled their nerves like a knife blade.

"How do we know the halfbreed hasn't led him into a trap?" Yasuno demanded suddenly.

Basho looked over at him, equally uneasy, but somehow no longer able to believe that whatever happened would be the result of the halfbreed's treachery. "Oishi trusts him," he pointed out, hoping that would ease Yasuno's concern.

But Yasuno only looked back at him in disgust. "He has no choice. We need weapons. If he doesn't come back soon, I'm going after him." He looked toward the entrance, his hand tightening over his sword hilt again like a pledge.

Basho looked past him at the benign visage of Buddha, lying in repose, with eyes closed and a gentle smile of contentment on his face. Praying that Buddha truly was wiser than any of them could ever hope to be, he still couldn't help thinking that only an image carved from stone could look so utterly peaceful in a place like this.

Oishi stopped, staring in wonder, as they entered a natural cavern where men with heads shaved like Kai's had once sat chanting in the sanctuary of a Buddhist shrine. *Monks . . . in an abandoned temple in the Tengu Forest—?*

The monks, dressed in robes of rough, undyed cloth, sat in the lotus position, meditating and praying in the torchlight in orderly, curving rows that reminded him of waves on the ocean sweeping toward land. Before them, at the far side of the cavern, was a statue cast of metal and layered with gold leaf. It sat as they sat, but on a base of stone, and rather than raising its arms with fingers forming graceful mudras, it held a sword in one hand and a length of rope in the other. Its expression was not the serene gaze of Buddha, but a wrathful, suspicious glare; fangs protruded from its snarling mouth.

Fudou Myo-o. Oishi bit off a sudden exclamation as he recognized the image of the Immovable Protector—the Buddhist deity who burned away all impediments, to aid the living in their quest for enlightenment.

He realized then that this must have been, perhaps still was, a hidden shrine of the *yamabushi*—ascetic monks who combined worship of Buddha's divine spirit with Japan's native Shinto tradition, and for whom the unyielding figure of Fudou Myo-o held special significance.

But this image of Fudou was like none other he had ever seen. Instead of the usual aura of flames surrounding its body . . . it had wings. They had not been part of the original casting; they had been spun like spider-silk from some material he couldn't imagine, and woven into patterns that gave them the diaphanous quality of a dragonfly's wing, although their form was more like a bird's.

He could make out their tracery so clearly because they glowed, eerily illuminated by countless red lights. He couldn't really be sure if he was seeing hundreds of tiny candles in translucent bowls, or if an unknown species of glowworm had settled permanently on the wings. Either way, the effect was as magical as if they had truly been touched by Fudou's purifying flame.

Perhaps these were simply *yamabushi* who sat chanting here now, not demons. *Yamabushi* roamed alone or in small groups all through the mountains, which they believed contained the most powerful *chi* on earth. Leading rigidly disciplined lives that combined prayer and extreme martial arts training, they were said to have the ability to perform feats of incredible strength, as well as miraculous healing.

It was even said that long ago they had converted the savage *tengu* to their beliefs, and the *tengu* had been transformed, body and soul, until now they had become the protectors of abandoned temples . . . *like this one.*

He looked back at the monks again, where they continued to sit and chant, seemingly oblivious to his presence or even Kai's. He saw them more clearly as his eyes adjusted . . . beginning to realize that what had looked deceptively like men were actually something stranger, as strange as an image of Fudou with wings.

They could almost have passed for a gathering of *yama-*

bushi, their forms were so deceptively like humans whose bodies were the end result of years of prayer and fasting—emaciated almost beyond belief, and yet still somehow powerful-looking, as if there was nothing but muscle and bone beneath their wizened skin. But . . .

Oishi moved forward slightly, to get a better look at the monks' faces, and suddenly their resemblance to humans vanished. Their faces, withered to masks by the same self-mortification that had transformed their bodies, were far more like the faces of birds of prey. *These were* tengu. *Tengu monks.*

Before each meditating figure a gleaming *katana* stood on its tip in midair, perfectly balanced.

The *yokai* of stories and legends, who had trained heroes to fight like demons, were real . . . and the same creatures who had trained Kai, just as he had claimed.

That they had learned the ways of Buddhism from *yamabushi,* and evolved through their communion with the same spiritual energy sought by humans, must be true as well. They had become the devout warrior monks of the *yokai* realm, guarding and worshiping in temples that had been abandoned to the elements.

The halfbreed had not moved from beside him, still watching the monks at prayer, but there was no trace of awe on his face. In his eyes, Oishi saw only the pooled memories of his own early years, not fragments of myth and legend.

"Wait here," Kai said.

"Where are you going?" Oishi asked, startled.

"To pay my respects to my former lord." Kai looked away from Oishi toward the back of the cave, where more shadows waited beyond the statue of Winged Fudou.

As Oishi followed the halfbreed's glance, his own eyes settled on the monks again—on the gleaming swords impossibly suspended in front of each one of them. *Kai had been telling the truth about everything.*

"Don't be tempted," Kai said sharply, seeing where his gaze had gone. And whatever happens—*don't draw your sword.*" He looked at Oishi for another long moment, with the promise in his own eyes that any trace of weakness or failure of will would be punished with instant death . . . if they were lucky

Oishi nodded, suddenly finding it hard to meet the gaze of a man he had always thought of as his inferior, as he realized now how much weakness that man had found in him. He swore to himself that he would not fail, as he would have sworn it to Kai, if he thought the halfbreed would have believed him.

Before he could ask any details about where Kai was going, or what he actually intended to do, Kai was walking away from him toward the Winged Fudou. The halfbreed passed the rows of chanting monks and disappeared into the shadows behind the statue, leaving Oishi standing all alone in a cavern filled with well-armed demons.

16

Kai followed another tunnel, equally familiar to his mind's eye, that led to the inner sanctuary of the temple, where Sojobo, the lord and high priest of the *tengu* monks—and once his own lord and foster-father—spent much of his time in solitary meditation.

Kai stopped, just inside the entrance of the inner sanctuary. The sword of his former master stood balanced on its tip at the absolute limit of the ledge that formed the meditation space, precariously balanced on the rim of the abyss that lay beyond it. The sword's edge, he knew, was sharp enough to cut through stone, and so finely honed that it could slice a hair in half lengthwise. The wave-patterned steel was polished to such mirrorlike brightness that it seemed to absorb all the light from the space around it.

The solid ground of the inner sanctuary was only a few strides across. Beyond it an even larger cavern opened out—one that his imagination had never been able to encompass, because its heights and depths and distant walls were lost in darkness. The sound of rushing water made him glance to the side, where an underground river plunged over a ledge above the one on which he stood, and fell away into the blackness. Its closeness to the place where he stood, and its seemingly endless fall into the depths below revived a long-forgotten combination of awe and terror inside him;

its muted thunder echoed in the hollow space beneath his feet.

Kai looked back at the sword, feeling the unexpected ache of a much more familiar emotion, the desire to hold a blade like that in his hand again, to feel its perfect balance and the way it moved, like a sentient extension of his own body, as he blocked or turned aside any blow that came at him, defeating all challengers with his skill, even among the *tengu*. All but one—

"So the terrified boy returns as a man . . ." said the one, from the shadows behind him.

Kai's breath caught; sheer instinct almost made him leap forward and grab the sword to defend himself. He froze before his body could make a move, remembering his own warning to Oishi just in time . . . remembering how different the rules here were from those in the world outside: here, where nothing was as it seemed, including the speaker whose voice he had just heard.

He turned to face the *tengu* lord, who stood before him looking just as he had expected, deceptively as old as time, dressed in robes cut like those of a priest but made of fabric that would have suited the Shogun when he held court. *The Old One had always had an unbecoming streak of vanity.*

But above the robes that proclaimed him the one whose physical and spiritual prowess made him the lord of his kind, Kai saw the face that he remembered far better than the affected manner of dress.

The *tengu* lord's raptor-like features were less disturbingly otherworldly than those of his disciples in the main chamber. But the baleful golden eyes with pupils as long and sharp as sword blades had not changed—eyes that were devoid of mercy. Kai met them and couldn't hold their gaze; the same fear and helpless anger those eyes had always evoked in him reduced him again to a child.

Don't—Kai slammed a lid on his fear. His one-time foster father could sense everything that whispered through a human brain; anything he thought or even felt would be used against him. Kai buried his human emotions beneath the strength of his will as if he controlled the power of the earth over his head—the way he had finally learned to do, so long ago, in order to escape the complete destruction of his humanity. In order to escape . . .

Fear is not the enemy . . . it is your edge. To fight your fear instead of your enemy only leaves you open to attack. He took a deep cleansing breath and bowed, with the respect due to a lord. "We are in need of swords. I've come to you for help," he said, speaking the words with perfect evenness.

The *tengu* lord smiled, whether at the words or the fact that he still remembered his lessons so well, Kai had no idea. His former *sensei* gestured at the gleaming blade. "No, Kai. You have come to finish your training."

Kai's eyes narrowed as he saw the gleam of a challenge come into his lord's golden stare. *The one who had controlled his life from the first moment he could remember would never forgive him for his personal betrayal, and for abandoning his people. . . .*

"I am *not* one of you." It was more difficult to keep his voice even this time, but his determination only grew stronger. He looked toward the sword again, his hand closing over empty air beside him, as Sojobo stepped into the light, staring down the tunnel that led back to the main cavern.

"Nor are you one of *them*," Sojobo said, gazing at Oishi. He looked back at Kai, and his voice took on the edge of his sword's blade as he said, "You risk your life coming here, for men who will never accept you."

Kai met the baleful eyes, the scorn in the *tengu* lord's voice, and said with utter conviction, "They are good men. Their cause is just."

"So you say . . ." Sojobo turned away, looking toward Oishi again. "The test then. You told him not to touch his sword. If he does—" Kai's foster father turned back, the harsh voice grated, "he and all his men will die."

Kai glared at him. These well not his people, but this was his territory—demon territory—now, and no amount of samurai arrogance would stop Oishi's samurai blood from spilling like any other man's if he lost his own battle with fear.

There was nothing he could do for Oishi now but endure his separate testing, and end it as quickly as possible.

Out in the main chamber, Oishi took a tentative step, and then another down the open row that divided the two sections of chanting monks. He wondered if they could possibly be as unaware of his presence as they seemed to be. His glance wandered left and right, as the tantalizing gleam of their swords caught at his eyes. He forced himself to focus on the statue of Fudou, straight ahead of him, praying silently for the Immovable Protector who gave strength to the yamabushi to strengthen his own will.

But as he approached the statue a strange vibration began to fill the air, almost but not quite an audible sound, as if the cavern around him was humming with energy. The longer he stared into the face of Fudou, the more he felt as if he was becoming one with its outrage and fury: Fudou, the violent, wrathful one, whose fire burned away all impediments, who would not be turned from his path. . . .

Kai shifted uncomfortably, glancing toward the outer cavern as Oishi moved beyond his sight.

"Was it worth it?" Sojobo asked, forcing him to look back and meet his foster father's pitiless stare. "What you found in the outside world? The love of a woman you can never have?"

Kai blinked, caught by surprise by the unexpected direction of the attack. But he kept his own gaze steady, meeting the impenetrable golden eyes, remembering Mika's eyes as he said, simply, "Yes."

An amused smile distorted the mouth below the cold inhuman stare. The *tengu* lord made a sound of contempt. "Let me tell you of love. The love of one night that brought you into this world. An English sailor and a peasant girl sold to a brothel. . . ." He paused, watching Kai, measuring his reaction. "And not long after, your loving mother abandoned you to die in these woods . . . her monster halfbreed child."

Kai's eyes widened; his focus dissipated like mist, leaving him defenseless, as his former master struck at the core of his entire being . . . his lifelong need to know who he was, or had once been meant to be.

"Yet we found you," Sojobo went on, his voice as close to consoling as Kai had ever heard it. "Accepted you. Trained you. We taught you many things. . . ." His eyes, and his voice, were suddenly pitiless again, "But you fled and you turned your back on those gifts."

"Gifts of death," Kai said with disgust. His hands knotted at his sides. Whatever motives the *tengu* had had for taking him in, they had not been moved by any emotion he had ever longed to see in someone else's eyes. Sojobo had lied to him before, about humans; how could he be certain this wasn't another lie—? Had he trapped himself, already, in a snare of his own making?

In the main cavern, Oishi turned back from gazing at the face of Fudou, startled out of his trance by the sound of his men entering the cavern behind him.

"What are you doing here?" He glared at them, suddenly furious, as he started back toward the entrance. He had told them—*ordered* them—to remain outside. But they had disobeyed him, every one of them, even Chikara. *Curse that boy, wouldn't he ever learn to obey orders, even if he had no respect for his father's concern about him—?*

"We should go!" Yasuno said angrily, gesturing at him as if he was the one disregarding orders, and not the lot of them.

"Don't—" Oishi raised his hands, trying to keep them silent and stop them from coming further in.

But it was as if they didn't even see him now: They were all staring past him at . . . something, in speechless dread.

Oishi realized that the chanting had stopped behind him. He turned back, and saw that all the monks had raised their emaciated heads, and were glaring over their shoulders at the intruders with the fierce eyes of hawks gazing at an invasion of rodents.

For a long moment, tense silence held between the two groups . . . and then the *tengu* began to quiver, all of them together, their bodies vibrating with the incredible energy that Oishi had sensed as he'd moved among them.

He looked back at his men in frantic concern—and saw Yasuno reaching for his sword. "*No—!*"

But it was already too late. Yasuno drew his blade.

The *tengus*' bodies burst open where they sat, as their shape-shifting spirit-forms rose from the shells of the praying monks. Hissing in fury, the demons flew at the cluster of stunned ronin, grasping their swords in claw-fingered hands.

Oishi watched in despair as his men—all the ones who had weapons—drew their blades or raised their spears to fight back, taking the lead as the others swung at the demons with heavy sticks, or their bare fists.

To his amazement, they fought well, better than he could have imagined, as they beat back the onslaught—disarming or disabling their *tengu* attackers. But they were hopelessly outnumbered, and the battle was spreading out, drawing the men further away from the tunnel that was their only hope of escape.

He shouted at them to close ranks and retreat, to get back to the exit and get out— But it was as if he had been struck dumb, or disappeared: Driven by their own pent-up hunger for battle, his men waded deeper into the sea of demons. Swords lost by the *tengu* continued to drift in the air, some of them drifting toward him, as if they were pleading to be seized by another hand—*his hand*—and used to help his men.

"Don't be tempted." Kai's deadly serious warning echoed in his head, and he could still see the doubt, the mistrust, that lay in the halfbreed's eyes. *He was being tested . . . but was this really just demon trickery, a hallucination?* It looked and sounded as real as his own existence He glanced down at his sword, still sheathed at his side. If the test meant he had to let all his men be slain by demons—

Someone screamed, a human scream, and he saw blood spray in a bright red arc. His fists tightened as he heard someone else cry out. *His men were dying— How long could he stand here and watch his men die, and do nothing?*

"Kai!" he shouted desperately, but still Kai didn't return, as more of his men began to fall. . . .

Kai swallowed the knot of pain in his throat that kept him from speaking, almost from breathing. "I don't believe you," he said to the *tengu* lord. "You know nothing about humans. Or love—"

"Don't I?" Sojobo's too-knowing smile filled with secret knowledge. "Your father *loved* your mother for a night." He echoed the words, and again Kai was snared by the elusive, tantalizing voice that belied the tragic unfolding of his life story. "When she found she was pregnant, she fled from the brothel, back to her village, because she *loved* the child growing within her. But her parents, who had *loved* her before they were forced to sell her, threw her out of their house when they saw that her bastard child was a halfbreed."

The sound of rushing water seemed to fill Kai's head, as if the mixed blood in his veins was at war with his senses; he felt dazed with grief and anger, but he had no idea where to place the blame. There had been a few Englishmen among the ships' crews on Dejima. He had hated them as much as he had hated the Dutch. But more of them had red hair, or light brown, than the straw-haired Dutch; and he had remembered something half-heard among the soldiers on the day he'd been captured by Lord Asano's men: "English, maybe . . ."

He remembered one English sailor, in particular—how, when one of the Dutch men had remarked that the *half-bloed* claimed to be half English, the sailor had flattened the man with one punch. And then he had unlocked the door to the cell where Kai huddled, chained to the wall.

Images burned his eyes like acid as the Old One went on relentlessly telling him the story he had always longed to know—his mother's story—to its hopeless, bitter end: "Everywhere she went people turned her away, cursed her because of her demon son. In the end, she came to this forest to take her life. That's how we found you."

Kai turned away from the merciless eyes, filled with hatred not only for the *tengu* lord, but for the weakness and cruelty of the human race, and for himself most of all, for the grief his very existence had caused not just him, but everyone he had cared about, when all he had ever wanted was—

Somewhere a familiar voice, a human voice, shouted his name desperately.

He turned back, suddenly remembering that he had left someone in the prayer hall . . . *Oishi.* Had Oishi just shouted his name?

He faced the *tengu* lord again with fresh anger and grief burning in his eyes . . . burning his sight clear. There in front of him was the demon who had dared to tell him he was more like a demon than like his own kind. *Who meant to prove it to him, once and for all. . . .*

This was still a test—and he hadn't failed it yet.

"Now that you know what you are, do you still choose love over hate?" The *tengu* lord smiled, and this time the mockery and spite that combined to distort his inhuman face were as clear to Kai as his obsession.

Mika's face formed like a vision inside Kai's thoughts. He held on to her memory, letting her love enfold his spirit like an aura.

Looking past the *tengu* lord's shoulder, he suddenly saw

Mika—*no, that was impossible; Mika couldn't be here*—entering the chamber. She walked toward him, smiling, as insubstantial as the fog but looking exactly as he remembered her.

He was being mocked again. But even the illusion was all he needed to remind him that the way humans lived was not unchangeable; nothing about them was absolute . . . not even their lives. *Tengu* were not immortal, they could be killed—but he had no idea how ancient the demon lord was who had trained him to fight without conscience or mercy, and taught him that life was nothing more than Death's messenger. No wonder life held no meaning for beings whose very existence resembled a living death.

But he had known true kindness in the human world as well as hatred and cruelty, and he had loved another human being. He kept gazing at Mika's phantom standing before him, her face filled with love that reflected his own.

A flicker of genuine anger sparked in the *tengu* lord's eyes as he saw Kai's longing. "I have seen a thousand versions of the future in which you try to save Mika—" he rasped, gesturing at the phantom, "and each one ends in your death. Knowing this, do you still choose love?"

"I would for her." Kai raised his head.

The phantom Mika reached out to him, and then vanished as suddenly as she had appeared.

"No matter what you do," the Old One said, "Mika will never be yours in this life."

Kai absorbed the pain of the words with quiet resignation, numbed by the awareness that they were nothing more than the truth he had always known. "Then I will go to my death," he said, "and pray I find her in the next."

The *tengu* lord's eyes blackened as the slits of his pupils opened, revealing the emptiness that lay in his soul. Kai saw pitted against him the Old One's utter determination to crush his will, once and for all.

He remembered that his former lord's name meant "High Priest of Buddha," but suddenly realized that anyone could call himself *priest*—or call himself *samurai* and it said no more about who he truly was inside than *demon,* or *half-breed. . . .*

Kai glanced at the waiting sword, and dared to feel hope.

In the main chamber, the demons had lured the ronin away from the entrance and separated them from one another. Now, finally, they were free to unleash the full power of their more-than-human swords and inhuman abilities, attacking the men in packs and cutting them down.

Hara lunged at one of the *tengu*—but instead of running it through, his sword passed through it as if it had no body at all. The demon wrapped itself around him like wind-blown fog, and, suddenly solid again, it slashed him open with its own blade. Yasuno and Basho fought back to back, with the courage of twin dragons, trying to defeat the impossible, or forestall the inevitable, while Horibe swung his *katana* at another *tengu,* only to have its blade cut in two by demon metal as more *tengu* swarmed in on him.

Oishi stood paralyzed by anguish like he had never known, watching as his men were cut down one after another. *Tengu* swords drifted everywhere around him, like mosquitoes on a summer night. He dodged them helplessly, knowing that he needed to take only one—*just one*—

He looked down at his own sword again, his hands trembling as he made certain it was still firmly in its sheath. Somehow Kai's haunted gaze stayed with him, along with the words of warning, and he did not allow himself to touch its hilt, or so much as let a demon sword brush his sleeve.

The battle was moving still further away from him; not one of his men had looked back or even called out to him, as if he truly was invisible, forgotten by everyone involved, men and monsters.

But then he suddenly realized that he could still be involved—all he had to do was not draw his sword and use it against the *tengu.* He broke into a run, following the pursuers and their victims, determined to help his men even if he had only his body and his bare hands as weapons.

He collided with a mass of *tengu*—solid enough when they chose to be—grabbing arms and elbowing faces, kicking and tripping and head-butting them in his frantic need to break through their ranks and reach his own people.

He saw Yasuno stagger as a sword gashed his leg; saw Basho try to shield his friend with his own huge body, only to be set on by a mass of other *tengu,* whose slashing swords hacked him down where he stood.

Seeing them both fall, Oishi fought more like a demon than he had ever imagined possible, ducking and weaving his way past the *tengu* and their blades. His body used every low trick he had ever seen or even heard described, including moves Kai had used against him back on the Dutch Island, without bothering to get his mind's permission.

The more headway he made, and the closer he got to reaching his men, the more viciously the *tengu* began to fight back against him. He flung up his arm, trying to protect his head, and a slashing blow from a sword laid it open. He dodged aside, barely managing to escape a worse wound, but pain seared him and blood soaked his clothing as his whole arm suddenly became useless. More blades cut his flesh, sharp edges flaying him but not killing him, as if the *tengu* meant to destroy him for his human arrogance by slicing him to pieces. *This was real. By the gods, it was no dream, it was real—*

The *tengu* lord smiled in triumph at Kai. "You admit it, then. Running away was meaningless."

Kai stared at his former master, uncomprehending. "What?"

"The 'human life' you longed for was a dream. Your existence in their world never had any real purpose."

"No—" And then Kai realized the truth he had just acknowledged: What he'd believed was a selfless vow of undying love was nothing but the devastating confession that, in trying to make a place for himself in the human world, all he had gained was a life filled with suffering.

All the things that he had believed defined a human being were illusions. He had suffered because he could not let go of them, and in the end there would be nothing left for him but a death as meaningless as his life had always been, just as Sojobo had predicted.

Kai stood perfectly still for a long moment, looking down at his scarred, battered body, taking inventory, as he tried to be certain he had truly lost to his own argument . . . and not to the *tengu* lord's twisted logic.

And then his glance went from the empty ties of his *hakama* to the gleaming *tengu* blade that still called to him from the edge of the abyss. *If you meet a swordsman, draw your sword. Do not quote poetry to one who is not a poet.*

He looked up again, into his former lord's expectant gaze. "No more talk," he said. "Will you give me what I ask?" He looked toward the sword shining like hope in the darkness, and back.

Sojobo shrugged. If he had any reaction to Kai's abrupt refusal to argue further, it was completely hidden. "Take the blade, Kai . . ." he said. But something changed deep in his blackened pupils that Kai recognized instantly, even after so long, as he added, ". . . *if you can reach it before me.*"

Oishi barely dodged between two more slashing demon swords, and suddenly saw Chikara. His son was retreating in panic from one of the *tengu,* his *katana* gone and the *tengu*'s sword reflecting light from a red sheen of blood as it tried to reach him, hungry for more.

Oishi forced his way through the mass of supernatural enemies raining blows on him, heedless to the damage they did, and ran toward his son. He hurled himself at the *tongu*, trying to drag it down before it could cut either of them. But Chikara's attacker turned intangible as he struck it, and then sent him sprawling with a heavy blow to his back.

Oishi landed hard, scrambled up again and spun around, feeling no pain now but only desperation as the *tengu* closed in on his son, raising its sword. Another demon caught Chikara from behind, holding him helpless as the first one brought its sword up for the killing strike.

Oishi searched frantically for something he could use to stop the *tengu* before his son died.

His hands dropped to his sword, his right hand closing over its hilt. But there was nothing; nothing but—

Kai took a deep breath and closed his eyes, deliberately leaving himself defenseless against attack. His mind fell away from the present, into his past with the *tengu*, into duels fought with moves no human being had even dreamed of . . . moves on the hidden Path of the *yokai*, which he had deliberately closed his mind to when he fled to the superstitious human world and became nothing more than it allowed him to be—

His eyes snapped open as Sojobo entered the Path in a flash of golden aura. Kai phased at the same instant into the spirit realm, onto the Path between the interstices of space and time. Human reality vanished like the illusion that it was. Sojobo's spirit suddenly became visible to him again, flowing like ice transformed to water, as the distance separating the *tengu* from his glowing sword vanished too, and he reached for its hilt.

But this time Kai was faster, because he had to be.

Anticipating the *tengu* lord's move, he dropped onto his back, aiming his foot at the tip of the blade as he slid toward the spot where it had seemed to balance precariously at the edge of the precipice. He kicked it, hard.

The sword flew free, slipping through the fingers of the

tengu lord as it arced upward, becoming a ray of light as it spun and shone in its passage through the intangible space between worlds . . .

. . . into Kai's outstretched hand, as he reappeared where he had been standing and snatched it from the air. His fist closed over its hilt and he swung around, thrusting it out—as his former *sensei* materialized in front of him, only to find its tip precisely pressing his throat.

In the temple chamber, Oishi saw the *tengu*'s blade slash through the air toward Chikara's head; his left hand pushed his sword loose in the sheath, freeing the blade; his right hand closed on the hilt and drew—

Suddenly both Chikara and the *tengu* vanished in front of his eyes, as if they had never existed.

Oishi's hand opened in a spasm, releasing the hilt of his half-drawn sword. He looked from side to side, searching the space around him for some trace of Chikara or the demons . . . for a trace of any of his men, dead or alive. There were no other human beings anywhere in the cavern. The *tengu* monks still sat in their places, chanting, unperturbed, as if they had seen nothing, heard nothing, done nothing at all but sit and pray.

Oishi looked down at himself. The crippling wound on his arm, as well as the countless bloody gashes, had vanished. He felt no pain anywhere, as if the blows and bruises he had given and received—everything he had just experienced—truly had been nothing but a phantasm. He thrust his half-drawn sword firmly back into its sheath, heard the satisfying *clack* as it locked in place again. And yet as he started back across the cavern his hands began to shake, and then his whole body trembled uncontrollably; the shallow gasps of his breathing sounded almost like sobs.

Sojobo glanced down at the sight of his own sword pressing his throat. Then he looked along its length to Kai's hand, and up at his face. At last their eyes met, and for once Kai saw no anger or disgust, or even nothing-at-all in his foster father's gaze. Instead, only the flicker of respect he had waited so long to see.

He was unsure what showed on his own face, only certain that whatever the *tengu* lord's expression had been, he would have been able to face it unflinchingly. His eyes asked his former lord again for the answer to his question.

Sojobo nodded slightly in response, and Kai lowered the sword—his sword, now.

"Kai . . ." His former lord seemed almost to sigh as he spoke the name, moving his head from side to side. "If you leave here again, you will meet your doom." There was nothing resembling a lie, or even a threat, behind the words.

Kai looked into the strange golden eyes that had once seemed so familiar, and found only resignation there, no trace of self-interest or deceit. His own gaze didn't waver. "I'm willing to face it."

Only as he began to turn away, leaving his ex-master forever, did he murmur, "My choice was made the moment I saw her."

As Kai made his way back through the passage to the prayer hall, a fragmented whisper followed, in the air or inside his mind, carrying the regret-filled words that his former lord believed he spoke only to himself, "I know. . . ."

Oishi stood staring at his empty hands, with his mind just as empty, for what seemed like a long time before he became aware of footsteps coming toward him.

He looked up—and saw the halfbreed emerge from the shadows near the statue of Fudou, carrying the most beautiful sword he had ever seen. But Kai moved as though he had been the loser, not the winner, in his struggle with his former lord; the blade he carried seemed to weigh more than stone.

Oishi stared at Kai the way he had stared at his own hands, his vision still overlain by the red nightmare of what he had just lived through . . . *thought he had just lived through. . . .*

Kai stopped in front of him, taking in his expression, and the fact that every breath he took still made his body spasm. Kai's face seemed almost to mirror his own as the halfbreed asked, "What did they show you?"

Oishi glanced away, swallowing hard, before he was able to force an answer out of his mouth. "My men."

Kai looked at his reddened eyes again; looked into them for a long moment. He nodded slightly, and Oishi saw a faint trace of respect, and the beginning of trust, in the half-breed's gaze for the first time.

And then Kai looked away, gesturing with the magnificent *katana* he carried. "You have your swords."

Oishi followed his glance. On the battleground where he thought he'd seen his men being slain, a shining pile of *tengu* swords lay waiting, as promised.

He realized then that there was one more blade, lying in front of him, gleaming gently in the torchlight. Kai picked it up and placed its hilt in his hand.

17

The ronin made their way back through the bamboo forest to the place where they had left their horses, each of them wearing a *katana* sheathed at his side . . . knowing they now carried swords that were without equal in a land known for making the finest sword a man could possess: *Demon steel.*

Oishi walked beside Chikara, whose relief at seeing him return from the *tengu*'s temple in one piece, with a blade that shone like fire in the afternoon light, was nothing compared to his own at finding his son alive and whole, and waiting for him . . . having strictly obeyed the orders that had saved his life.

Now as they walked side by side, he felt Chikara stealing glances at his face. "What happened in there, sir?" Chikara asked at last, as his brooding silence went on longer than his son could stand.

Oishi looked over at him, with a sudden overwhelming sense of pride and protectiveness. The urge to hug his son, to tell him how much he loved him, filled Oishi as it had not done since his son was too small to find it humiliating.

It was far too late to do that now, especially not here, and so Oishi only shook his head, giving Chikara a fond, reassuring smile. "I don't remember," he said.

Chikara looked surprised, but also reassured, as they walked on together.

Kai led the ronin back through the forest of bamboo as he had led them in—walking well ahead of them, not by choice, but because the others still kept their distance. He did not look back, or even slow his pace, as if he expected someone might make an effort to walk beside him if he did.

Oishi realized, as the reaction to his own test of will faded, that the halfbreed had not been wearing his usual impassive expression when he had first returned from wherever he had gone. The shaken, heartsick look Oishi had seen had not been his own reflected in a mirror . . . it had been a mark of Kai's separate ordeal. There were no physical wounds on him, either . . . but Oishi was sure they were there on his soul. He doubted his own soul would ever be the same.

Oishi had been too concerned about Chikara to think past the fact that his son was alive and unharmed—and then too busy brushing aside congratulations and unanswerable questions—to reflect on it before, but now he realized that none of his men had said or done a thing to express their gratitude to the halfbreed. Only he—and perhaps Kai—knew that if Kai had not won his duel with the *tengu* lord when he did, his own weakness would have doomed them all. It was as if the terrible perfection of the swords Kai had promised them, and then won for them, had done nothing but prove to the others that all their worst fears and deepest prejudices were true.

He realized suddenly that even he had said nothing to Kai. He had been too traumatized by his own ordeal to ask Kai whether he was all right, or what he had faced—although he doubted the halfbreed would have answered him, any more than he had told the truth to his son. And afterwards. . . .

His sense of honor told him his behavior was unconscionable, that he should thank Kai immediately on behalf of them all. But now that he was safely back in his own world, among his own kind, the urge to humble himself to the halfbreed warred with his ingrained pride of place, which said that Kai was with them by his own choice, for his own reasons. The same implacable inner voice insisted that their respect, or even their gratitude, would mean no more to Kai now than it would have when they had only called him a demon out of spite, never realizing how close they were to the truth. . . .

Kai kept his mind on the way ahead, keeping his eyes on the angle of the sunlight splintering down through the towering thicket of bamboo, eager to reach the stone guardian of the demon gate that would mark the last he ever saw of the *tengu*. He felt only relief at the prospect, and a sense of closure. After twenty years he had finally proved, in a way his former lord could understand, that he had the right to make his own choices about his life, and had not merely run away out of weakness.

He tried not to think about Mika's phantom, or hear his foster father's voice, knowing that although Sojobo was capable of lying at least as well as any human, he had realized that simply telling his adopted son the truth would inflict far deeper wounds. Even the unexpected conflict in the Old One's mind as he had walked away had only been more painful for being true.

And his former lord's pronouncement had proven as prophetic as ever: *"They will never accept you."*

Winning swords for the ronin had not closed any gaps of misunderstanding, or earned him their trust, let alone their respect. The men for whom he had risked everything, to whom he'd offered his life, with whom he had shared his deepest secret, trailed farther behind him now than they had before.

But he hadn't done it for them, he reminded himself angrily. They had hated him forever; why should he expect anything to change that now? He was doing this for Mika . . . for himself. For the proof that he was human enough to love, and to be loved, even if it all came to nothing in the end. He would save her from Kira, give her back her life, even if it could never be spent with him because he was and always would be a halfbreed, caught between worlds, fitting in nowhere.

"Halfbreed—!"

Kai jerked, startled out of his thoughts by someone shouting the epithet that might as well be his name, because it had belonged to him from the moment he was born.

He heard heavy footsteps rustling the leaves behind him and looked back to see Basho coming forward, his long strides closing the space between them. Kai looked ahead again, not slowing down, wary but saying nothing.

The huge man with the face of a boy who had never quite grown up . . . and probably never would . . . slowed his pace as he reached Kai's side. Basho was one of the few men Kai had met that he had to look up at, standing face-to-face, although he didn't bother to look at him at all now.

Basho unsheathed his new sword, and Kai glanced sidelong at him, seeing nothing more threatening than curiosity on Basho's face. "What's so special about these swords?" Basho asked. "What do they do?"

Kai suppressed his urge to answer with the obvious, or not answer at all. Despite the abruptness of Basho's arrival and question, he realized suddenly that the ronin hadn't joined him just to harass him . . . that Basho was making an actual effort to communicate. More than a little surprised, Kai nodded at the sword and said, "It depends on who uses them."

"No riddles," Basho said. Kai had heard that he'd been a monk in his youth. He wondered if it was a dislike for Zen *koan* that had caused Basho to leave the monastery or, given his personality, whether he'd been asked to find some other occupation.

Kai shrugged, and kept on walking. "If a coward holds it, it feels heavy in his hand. He won't be able to lift it."

Basho's eyebrows rose. He went on trudging alongside Kai, looking down at the sword in fascination.

"For the reckless man, it's too light. He'll swing but never find his mark."

Basho glanced over his shoulder, as if the comment put him in mind of his friend Yasuno. But he only looked back again, and grinned. "What about a tall, strong, fearless man like me?"

Kai drew his own sword, and held it up. "It cuts." He swung at a stand of bamboo with four-inch-thick trunks.

Basho watched in amazement as the blade cut a swath through the bamboo as easily as if it was slashing silk.

Still grinning, Basho swung his own sword with the confidence of a skilled martial artist, and laughed in elation as he cut through several more with the same ease that Kai had shown.

Kai laughed with him, unexpectedly, in relief and release: relieved to see that he hadn't risked everything to win these men swords they couldn't use, and because, at least for one of them, it had made a difference in how he used the word "halfbreed"—as if it was no more than a nickname that Kai had earned, just as Basho had gotten his own. He remembered again what he had realized, when he had confronted the *tengu* lord—that names and titles were only meaningless noise, because they could never describe what truly lay inside someone.

And he had earned it, he thought, remembering the crowds on the Dutch Island shouting *"Half-bloed! Half-bloed!"* . . . the looks on the faces of the ronin when he had taken down all of Kira's men single-handedly at Uetsu village . . . even the crowd at Ako Castle as he had fought Kira's champion, disguised by armor emblazoned with the Asano *mon.*

He would always be different, *gaijin,* an outsider, no matter where he went: There was no escaping that truth. He had been born with the very blood in his veins at war with itself; he had been raised by *tengu*—he fought like a demon, not an ordinary man. . . .

But he was a born warrior, as surely as any of the men around him who carried the blood of samurai in their veins.

Because he was a halfbreed. In all darkness, it was said, there was a seed of light; in all light, a seed of darkness . . . In that way, the universe constantly restored its balance when the nature of existence became unsettled.

Halfbreed. He smiled at Basho as he sheathed his sword, as the big ronin continued to walk beside him, actually carrying on a conversation. Kai glanced back only once at Yasuno, seeing the perplexed look on his face as he watched Basho talking and joking with the man he now despised more than ever.

Isogai propped himself on one elbow on the scarred table in the brothel that doubled as a cheap inn, pretending that the *sake* he was drinking had gone to his head much faster than it had. The cheap inn's cheap *sake* was terrible; he had no difficulty drinking it in very small sips. The fact that he was actually here on his leader's orders was as hard to believe right now as the fact that he had to be here alone: When he went out to have a good time, he preferred to go with friends, and all his friends were a long ride away right now.

But Oishi was right—they needed information about Kira's plans, and this was the best kind of place to get it, the worst sort of place in town. It was filled with overfed merchants and petty *bakufu* officials disobeying their own edicts against samurai patronizing places of moral turpitude.

The audience around him guffawed at the outrageously bawdy play being performed by a group of wandering performers, as they drank themselves into enough of a stupor to find the women who refilled their cups beddable—since most of the women were about as attractive as the villain of the play, an actor wearing a grotesque *oni* mask. Isogai had never expected to be so glad that his orders hadn't forbidden him from sleeping alone.

He sighed loudly, remembering to play his own part in this farce of an evening, in which he was posing as a morose husband. He leaned toward the drunken official sharing his table. "My wife won't stop nagging me," he said, having to raise his voice just to make himself heard. "She wants me to find her the best view of Lord Kira's procession."

The official looked over at him in bleary surprise. "What procession?" he asked. "He'll leave his fortress at sunset, say his prayers at the shrine, then hurry back." He shrugged, as if Kira's obsession with his own safety was a given to the people who lived in this domain.

The official grinned lopsidedly and turned away again, reaching out to catch a passing woman and pull her down into his lap. Isogai drained the rest of his sake in one swallow, then sat staring into space, not even needing to feign his dismay. *Gods, what were they going to do now?* It was unlikely anyone here knew what road, or even what night, Kira would actually choose when he paid his visit to the shrine; he was far too cautious for that. And the whole group of ronin could hardly gather nearby and remain unnoticed for days. Kira's spy network was very thorough.

A prostitute was kneeling beside him, he realized finally, waiting in polite silence for him to give her permission to refill his cup. He was mildly surprised by her manners, since most of them did not wait for permission, being too concerned with their own business of getting a man drunk and bedded in order to earn their keep.

He glanced over at her, and was startled by how young and lovely she was, with an aura of purity about her that was somehow untouched by the sordidness of her occupation. It was as if she had been here scarcely longer than he had. . . . He nodded, giving her permission to refill his cup, and studied the sensuous curve of her neck, the delicacy and grace of her movements as she poured the *sake*.

He wondered if she was the daughter of some samurai who had fallen on hard times; he knew that it was not just peasants who were forced to sell their children into indentured servitude, usually in brothels. Gazing at her fragile face, her modestly downcast eyes, he wondered how any father, no matter how desperate, could have parted with her.

But desperate men did desperate things: Anyone who knew what he and his fellow ronin were plotting now would probably call them all insane.

In spite of himself, where he was and why, he couldn't help asking, "What is your name?"

"Yuki," the girl answered, still keeping her eyes modestly downcast. The name meant *snow*: a fitting name for any child born in this mountainous domain . . . and for a girl with such an aura of purity about her. As he thought it, she looked up at last into his eyes, and he had to hide his surprise. She must be partly blind—one of her eyes was pale blue. But in spite of that, the sight of her face gazing back at him took his breath away. He found her completely bewitching.

After that somehow the *sake* that he drank tasted like new-fallen snow and cherry blossoms in spring, as Yuki sat at his side refilling his cup. Soon he was offering her *sake,* and smiling blissfully as they drank from the same cup. *Live drunk and die dreaming.*

Before long, without quite remembering how it had happened, he found himself lying in her bed in a small candlelit room, completely drunk, not just on *sake* but on the intoxicating sensation of her slim, supple body pressed against his. She rested on one arm, stroking his face, her touch tender and yet sublimely sensual, her long black hair caressing his skin.

"You're much kinder than the men who usually come here," she said softly. "More noble."

Isogai smiled, his eyes closed, his senses completely entranced by the delicate touch of her fingers. He knew he hardly looked like the lord's retainer he had once been, but still. . . . "Perhaps I am," he murmured, enjoying the thought.

At least he still possessed one thing of which he was justifiably proud: *Bushido.* He had always applied its code of virtuous behavior to anyone, no matter how humble—as

Buddha willed. He treated all women, even a prostitute, as courteously as he would a highborn lady . . . while most men of his class treated all women, even their lady wives, with no more regard than they gave to a prostitute. That was the true secret behind his reputation as a ladies' man—and the one thing that even his best friends had never seemed able to grasp.

"My prince in disguise." Yuki smiled shyly back at him.

"Not quite a prince." His own smile widened.

"A warrior then . . ." she whispered, leaning forward.

His answer was a moan of pleasure as she kissed him, long and deeply, draping her silken hair across his neck.

"I want you to tell me all about yourself, my beautiful samurai. . . ." Her voice caressed him, as languorous as her kisses.

But as he slowly opened his eyes to look up at her face, the hair she had draped around his neck so lovingly, like a caress, suddenly began to thicken and move as if it had a life of its own. Like a snake, it slithered all the way around his throat, and began to tighten.

Isogai gasped for breath, struggling in panic-stricken disbelief. He raised his hands, clawing at the hair, trying to pull it free; but the coils only tightened even more, impossibly strong, impossible to fight—*impossible*. . . .

His hands loosened and fell away, as he stopped struggling at last. His body lay motionless, his eyes open wide with horror but beyond seeing anything at all.

18

The ronin were on the move again, pushing their mounts as hard as they dared as they traveled toward Kira's lands. Now they were forced to travel mainly overland, across increasingly rough terrain, because not only the guards at the Shogun's checkpoints, but also Kira's spies, would be watching any main roads.

They followed meandering footpaths made by woodcutters and peasants, as Kai searched for barely detectable byways that were sometimes not much more than animal trails. Often they rode single file, picking their way up or down winding paths along the ledges of cliffs; sometimes they were forced to backtrack because a decaying ancient footbridge would never withstand the weight of their horses.

The weather grew increasingly cold as the land rose, until the year itself seemed to have slid backwards behind them, taking the last signs of spring with it. Freezing nights, freezing rain, and finally snow made them lose more time as they stopped to cut dry grass, stuffing it into their sandals to protect their feet from frostbite, and then to harvest rushes and vines in an icy marsh to make head coverings and capes that would give them protection against the weather.

As the weather worsened, Oishi developed a chronic wracking cough that made his chest ache as if he'd cracked a rib; it woke him constantly during the night until he fell asleep in his saddle as he rode.

He realized he had not taken time to rest between his ordeal in Ako's dank dungeon and his hard ride to Dejima to get the halfbreed back from the Dutch, even before they had started on this journey. But he cursed his lack of discipline, telling himself that the weakness lay in his will, not his body . . . that for a samurai, will alone should be enough. He saw the worried looks in the eyes of some of his men, but he refused to acknowledge it, leaving even Chikara helpless to express concern.

So, predictably, it was the halfbreed who finally confronted him, in the middle of one night when he woke, coughing, and forced himself to get up and check on the sentries he had posted rather than disturb the others' sleep again.

As Oishi approached the spot where Kai was standing guard, the halfbreed tilted the black-lantern he held so that its shielded candle shone directly into his eyes. "Why are you up?" Kai demanded.

Squinting, Oishi saw the tip of Kai's sword extended toward him, although he had no sense at all that Kai had been caught by surprise. "I was checking the sentries," he said, in a thick voice, and promptly doubled over, coughing.

"Fool!" Kai pulled him out of the wind, into the lee of the rocks where he had been keeping watch. "If you want to kill yourself, ronin, just slit your belly. Don't waste everyone's time coughing your guts up."

"You dare . . . speak to me like that?" Oishi mumbled. "You're not—"

"What?" the halfbreed said sourly. "Your lord? Your leader? Your equal—?" He stared down Oishi's furious indignation. "I'm nothing to you. You're nothing to me. But these men here are counting on you! When the time comes to deal with Kira, they're expecting you to lead them. They won't have you, if you keep treating your body like a piece of wood."

Taking a step back, he nodded in the direction of the sentry post Oishi had just left. "If you believe in your men, don't treat them like incompetents. If you value their lives at all, then start valuing your own more. Get some rest!" He turned and stalked away into the night before Oishi could react.

Oishi stood where he was, propped against the freezing surface of the stones, his whole body shaking with what he thought was rage . . . until suddenly his knees gave out, and he wound up on all fours, coughing until he retched.

Eventually Maseki, the sentry he had spoken to before he encountered Kai, came to check on him and helped him back to the fire.

The halfbreed sat waiting there, holding a cup of hot tea in his hands while the others slept around him—as if he had nothing better to do in the middle of the night. He forced the cup of tea on Oishi, who with one sip realized that it was Basho's medicinal tea for treating illness in the throat and chest, combined with other herbs he couldn't identify. He drank it down while Maseki stood by, watching him with a worried frown. He thanked Maseki, and ordered him back to his post.

Before he could look at Kai again, the halfbreed was gone, back to his own sentry post. Oishi lay down by the fire, sullenly wrapping himself in his cloak of rushes.

The next thing he remembered was waking in the morning, with his memory of the previous night like a bad dream—except that Basho was there, insisting he drink more medicinal tea, and giving him a salve to rub on his throat and chest. Chikara began watching him while he ate, making certain that he did. After that he began to sleep through the entire night, and woke feeling gradually stronger and more alert with each new morning. His cough, and finally his resentment, faded, but not until well after both common sense and utter exhaustion had forced him to accept the wisdom of the halfbreed's remorseless solicitude.

Meanwhile, he grudgingly acknowledged that Kai—with his demon-honed instincts and tracking skills—could guide them safely on his own and keep them on course to the destination he had begun to think they would never reach: the abandoned farmhouse where they would rendezvous with Hazama, and whatever retainers of Lord Asano he and the other scouts had managed to enlist.

In giving Kai permission to take the lead without consulting him constantly, he also knew that he had willingly surrendered more responsibility to a halfbreed raised by demons than he had ever granted any normal man, no matter how highly ranked.

But Kai was a tracker—and a survivor—and those were the qualities his men needed most in a leader, at least until they reached the abandoned farm. And after the visit to the *tengu* cave, Oishi realized that in his soul he trusted Kai to be as loyal to their cause as any samurai—no matter what his personal motives were.

Oishi had lost track of the days they had traveled—although Chikara swore to him that they were still in time—when they spotted the abandoned farmhouse at last. It lay in the middle of a wide open space, where the late-morning sun gleamed off a thin rime of snow covering fallow fields.

Hazama, Chuzaemon, and Okuda had all reached the rendezvous point ahead of them, bringing a welcome crowd of recruits with them, and relief doubled the enthusiasm of their jubilant reunion, as old friends, fathers, sons, and brothers who had not seen each other for a long, hard year—and feared they would never see each other again—shouted, called out greetings, and hugged one another, trading tales of what they had been doing and where they had been.

Kai moved through the room like a shadow, once more alone in the crowd, searching for a space where he could be alone by himself. He had been through so much with Oishi and his original group by now that they actually tolerated him, if only for his usefulness. Chikara and Basho willingly conversed with him, and Oishi himself had quietly informed everyone that Kai was the only man among them who could get them safely to this rendezvous. Kai had grown used to the change, all too easily. . . .

Stupidly, he realized now. Because now that time was over, and he was surrounded again by Ako retainers who saw him only as an outcast or a demon. It was worse than being among strangers; being reminded of the truth was like being struck with the flat of a sword.

At least the newcomers were too preoccupied with their reunions for now to harass him simply for being there. But with so many men present, there was nowhere inside the dilapidated house where he could find solitude or even a place to rest. He headed back toward the entrance, seeking the cold peace of the farmyard.

Outside on the veranda, he saw Oishi heading across the yard toward the sagging barn, where Hazama waited to inventory the supplies and weapons the others had brought back along with enough volunteers to more than triple the number of men now prepared to carry out vengeance against Kira. Kai leaned against a support post, waiting for them to disappear.

Oishi had begun to think that his face had frozen into a perpetual grimace during their long, freezing ride through terrain where even spring was reluctant to set foot. But the sight of Hazama warmed him with relief and the pleasure of seeing his longtime comrade safe and smiling. He smiled back, and returned Hazama's bow.

"Your sword—" Hazama reached for the sword he carried—the one Oishi had given to him just before they'd parted—to return it to its rightful owner.

"Keep it." Oishi's smile widened into a grin. "I told you we'd bring others." Hazama stared at him in near disbelief, and then bowed more deeply at the honor he had been given. Oishi rested a hand on his shoulder as they reached the barn door.

As they went inside, Hazama said, "We have bows, armor, even gunpowder." He gestured at the equipment neatly organized against the back wall of the barn, in which most of their horses were also stabled. He had led the men that he and the others had reunited on a successful raid against one of the border outposts at the edge of Kira's lands, taking them completely by surprise, and gaining a victory that had given the ronin not only confidence in their ability as warriors, but also a gratifyingly large cache of weapons and other much-needed supplies.

Oishi nodded in approval, feeling his own enthusiasm begin to return. Things were coming together, at last. Now all they needed was the key piece of information about when and how Kira would be venturing out of his stronghold to visit his family's shrine. "What news from Isogai?"

Hazama paused, his smile disappearing as he glanced away. "Nothing. He hasn't shown up."

Oishi stopped moving to stare at Hazama in surprise and concern.

Still watching the two men from the veranda of the house, Kai saw their bodies register the signs of trouble, although he couldn't hear their conversation. He frowned, wondering what had gone wrong. But he stayed where he was, not willing to approach Oishi when Hazama was with him. Whatever was wrong, he'd know about it soon enough.

He stepped down off the weather-beaten porch and wandered out into the farmyard, making a long, slow circuit around the house, looking at the lopsided outbuildings, some of which now held their own horses . . . and taking note of where the guards had been stationed who kept a lookout for unwelcome visitors.

This had been no common peasant's property; it must have belonged to someone like Oishi, a chief retainer of some *daimyo,* before the Shogunate had begun enacting laws that replaced land with a stipend as a retainer's reward for loyal service, stripping away from the samurai class one more respectable alternative to being a warrior, in a land without wars.

In their own way, Kai thought, the Tokugawa lords were as perverse as the *tengu* lord. They had consolidated their rule by eliminating the options of their most loyal supporters until the word "samurai" was becoming as hollow as an abandoned helmet.

A country always at war was a vision of hell—out of balance in a way that destroyed not just lives but the spirit of the land itself. But so was the opposite extreme, when peace was maintained by binding the country hand and foot, and putting a gag in its mouth.

"The essence of life is suffering." Sojobo claimed those were Buddha's own words . . . and he was not the only one who claimed that. But by now Kai had heard so many things attributed to the Enlightened One—so many of which were contradictory—that since his final encounter with Sojobo, he no longer had any idea what was true.

Even if it was all true, did that prove Buddha had become enlightened to the true nature of the world in a way no ordinary man could ever hope to be . . . or did it just prove that he had become a babbling madman—that life had driven him insane?

Kai rubbed the scars on his forehead, feeling as if he had suddenly fallen into an abandoned well where the depths held not water but despair . . . not even knowing why. *He was tired . . . he was so tired, maybe that was all.*

He hadn't dared show any weakness in front of Oishi, afraid of triggering his self-destructive samurai pride again. But when the others left the barn, he ached to head for it, to lie down in the hay and sleep until his thoughts had regained something like clarity, and his emotions were no longer lying like a raw wound on the surface of his mind. But if his count of the days that had passed was right. . . .

Mika, he thought. He repeated her name like a silent mantra, picturing her in his mind. He had come here for her sake, as well as for the memory of her father's kindness and his need to ensure that Lord Asano's soul would truly be at peace after death.

Mika was still alive, and even if she could never belong to him, it didn't matter—because that wasn't what love was.

Love was. That was all he was still certain about. And he would prove his loyalty to her father in as meaningful a way by setting her free as Oishi would by taking Kira's head.

He heard the voices of Oishi and Hazama, returning from the barn to the house. He glanced with longing at the barn . . . but if he helped the ronin achieve their goal, there would be all the time in the world for him to rest, when he was dead. He finished his circuit of the farmhouse, making sure the others had gone back inside before he slid the door open just enough to enter, unnoticed—ready to find out what was wrong.

As he closed the door behind him, Kai saw that the map of Kirayama Castle and the surrounding area had been spread out on the floor; Oishi's officers were all gathered around it, his captains kneeling and his lieutenants standing as they tried to get a better look.

"Kira could take any one of these roads," Yasuno said, pointing. "And have an army with him!" He waved a hand in frustration.

Oishi stared at the map, frowning in concern; his expression was reflected on every face around him in one form or another. Without Isogai's information, it would be impossible to attack Kira outside of his castle, where he would be vulnerable to their small group . . . and they were rapidly running out of time.

"Isogai may still show up. We should give him more time—" Hara said.

"He won't come!" Hazama snapped, his temper flaring unexpectedly with tension. "He's fled, like the coward he is—!"

"Hazama!" Oishi said, his voice filled with warning. He took a deep breath as the room fell silent. Then he said, with calm authority, "Isogai has come with us this far. We must not doubt him now."

Hazama bowed apologetically, and turned his eyes back to the map, keeping his head down.

So that was the problem. Leaning against the wall by the door, Kai knew he was wondering the same thing as everyone else: *Were they really going to be blocked by fate now, when they had already come so far, and risked so much—?* He glanced away from the others as he heard faint sounds outside . . . the hoofbeats of a horse on frozen ground, rapidly approaching the yard. "Oishi—" he said.

Oishi looked up at him, and then the others looked up too, as they all heard the clatter of hooves, and the voices of the sentries calling out challenges or questions. Kai pulled open the door as the men started toward it, carrying their sheathed swords in their hands.

As the ronin scattered in the yard, overwhelming relief wiped every other emotion off their faces. Watching from the doorway, Kai saw Isogai, sitting like a lord on a stunning white horse as the men gathered around him. He dismounted, making his way through the others directly toward Oishi. He bowed, saying, "Forgive me for being late, sir. Lord Kira leaves for his ancestors' shrine tonight. I know the route."

Kai had never seen Oishi look happier than he did in that moment, as he threw an arm around Isogai's shoulders in congratulation. "Come, Isogai," he said, heading toward the barn where their weapons and supplies were stored. "Gather the men!" he shouted to the officers in charge of various units during the raid.

Kai glanced at the white horse again, wondering how Isogai had managed to get hold of a horse like that at the same time he had been gathering information about Kira. Maybe he had won it gambling, from some passing samurai. But there was something about the animal that disturbed his eyes, something he couldn't put a name to. . . .

He realized his hand was pressing his forehead. He forced it down to his side; forced himself to stop obsessively looking for signs of witchcraft, simply because their fortunes had suddenly taken a turn for the better. Isogai had arrived in time; perhaps the gods would smile on them after all.

And yet as his eyes followed Isogai, he still felt the same twinge of disorienting wrongness that he had come to trust far more than he wanted to. From what he could tell looking at the crowd of ronin, that was the Isogai he knew, but he hadn't been able to take a good look at him up close, and he doubted he'd get another chance soon.

But Oishi had made him a part of the group that would directly attack Kira, while other units eliminated any troops or outlying guards. He would have another chance to look Isogai in the eyes then, if only for a moment. . . .

Hazama and the others had done their job well. From the confident way Oishi moved, he guessed that Kira must be bringing minimal support with him on his surreptitious visit to the shrine.

As Kai started toward the barn, he saw Chikara approach his father and say, "Sir, I want to go with you."

Kai felt surprise that Oishi had forbidden his son to participate in the raid, after allowing him to come this far with them.

Oishi didn't slow down or even glance at his son, for once. "Horibe, stay with him," he said, with a peremptory nod to the old ronin.

Horibe looked taken aback, but only slightly. He had contributed more to this mission than most of the ronin had already, and no one there was likely to forget it.

But Kai saw the crestfallen expression on Chikara's face, the disappointment and frustration that stung worse than a slap, as his commander and his father, in one voice, declared him unfit to fight as an equal alongside his fellow ronin.

Kai glanced at Oishi, wondering why in the name of all the gods he had done that to his son—until he saw what lay in Oishi's eyes. It was the same look he'd glimpsed when he had asked Oishi what he'd seen in the *tengu* sanctuary, and Oishi had said, "My men." *His men dying . . . and him unable to do a thing to save them. His son, dying—*

Kai looked down, filled with unexpected compassion for both father and son, wishing there was some way he could make it up to them. But he realized that once any of them had chosen this course, the way their individual destinies played out was beyond anyone else's control.

There was not enough time in the world to go back and change the past; now there was only enough time for him to prepare himself, like Oishi, to face battle once again.

19

In the upper courtyard of Kirayama Castle, Lord Kira stood waiting by his horse while his escort of warriors finished the last of their preparations for his journey to his family's shrine.

But they were not all he was waiting for, with his usual deceptive expression of patience. Finally his eyes found the one thing he had needed to see before he departed: Mika, accompanied by her attendants, was being led past his heavily armed guard troops by her own assigned group of guards, until at last she halted in front of him.

Mika's attendants knelt and bowed at his feet; the guards who accompanied her bowed before him. But Mika herself did not even lower her eyes, staring back at him with the same look of defiant pride that she had shown him throughout the past year.

He gazed back at her in quiet admiration. "I ride to my ancestors' shrine to offer thanks for our wedding," he said, and then asked, with exquisite courtesy, "Is there anything you wish me to pray for?"

Mika's eyes left his face for a moment, glancing at the enormous samurai in black armor who accompanied him everywhere, his bodyguard as well as chief retainer. She looked back at Kira again. "My lord will not like my answer," she said, her voice perfectly even, and equally polite.

Kira gave her a tender smile. "Then I will answer for you. In two days we shall be married, and I will rule Ako by your side." Mika's gaze turned as icy as the wind, but he held it, unflinching. "You may look down on me, my lady, like your father—but our children, and their children, will be of one blood." He turned away from her and put his foot into the stirrup, swinging up into his saddle.

The ronin reached the location where Kira's family shrine lay just as twilight was deepening to night, giving them barely enough time to leave their horses well hidden among the trees, and cautiously move closer on foot.

There was no moon to shine down like an unwelcome lantern on their surreptitious movements. The myriad stars gave the ronin just enough light to let them see their surroundings; but like candles burning unreachably far away, they offered no comfort at all as the last of the day's warmth bled away into the open sky.

The silhouette of Kira's family shrine looked more like the outline of a shed than a temple. The isolated structure faced a muddy track through fields where spring planting was still weeks away. The shrine held only a small wooden statue of Buddha and a place for offerings, with barely enough sheltered space for three or four people to kneel and pray at one time. Kai wondered if Kira had left it unchanged as a tribute to the humble origins of his ancestors . . . or, more likely, he suspected, it symbolized Kira's desire to disassociate himself from them.

Large haystacks formed an alley through the stubble, pointing directly to the shrine from the place where Isogai had led the others out of the woods. It provided them with a clear view as well as cover that they could use to approach it.

But the longer Kai studied the scene before him, the more the conical forms of the haystacks silhouetted against the sky seemed to shroud something far more eerie. He felt as if he was seeing the spectral tombs of long-dead kings, lining a processional route to something that should have been far more imposing than the humble wooden shelter that protected a simple shrine.

He pressed his hand to his forehead, trying to blind himself to the perverse image filling his mind's eye with an aura of unnatural power . . . a power that seemed to emanate from the shrine itself.

He forced his senses back under control. Since they had reached the farmhouse, he had been much too tired and far too uneasy for his own good, or the good of the others. He realized again how much the hostile stares of too many men who hadn't grown used to his presence had heightened his feelings of unease.

But even setting out on their mission hadn't improved his mood. He told himself it was only a case of pre-battle nerves: *They had all been waiting so long for this.* He wasn't facing a *kirin,* and he wasn't facing the *tengu* lord. And this time he wasn't facing the enemy alone.

Fear is your edge. . . . He absorbed his restlessness, accepted his unease, telling himself that it was only the night wind that made him shiver; that if he saw an aura around the shrine, perhaps something more had been there once . . . but now it was only a humble roadside shrine like the ones he saw everywhere, never with an aura like that. Even if it was the shrine of Kira's ancestors, haystacks were only haystacks, and they were nothing but convenient cover that would allow the ones who had come here on a mission to achieve it, and fulfill their sacred duty. He could see a figure already at the shrine, limned by the flickering glow of a single candle, kneeling in prayer, as Isogai had predicted: Kira himself, Kai was sure, from the familiar outline of a *daimyo*'s robes.

Oishi stood near him at the edge of the trees, also studying the approach. In a low voice he began giving orders to the men around him, dispersing them to search for outlying guards or troops waiting in ambush. Despite Isogai's claim that Kira was bringing only a handful of guards for security, counting on secrecy and the darkness to protect him, Oishi had obviously studied Sun Tzu's *Art of War.* He was going on the assumption that even what the local *bakufu* had been told was not necessarily the whole truth. *To be adaptable was the best tactic.*

With the handful of men he had chosen for the direct attack on Kira gathered around him, he told the last of the ronin, "Stay back and keep lookout for Kira's men." Taking Kira's life, and his head, were not enough; someone had to survive to make the journey back to Lord Asano's grave.

Then he signaled to the core group of his best fighters, and Kai followed him into the field.

Isogai led the way with Oishi, as Kai and the others spread out across the frozen ground behind them. The stirring night wind rustled the stubble in the field, helping to hide any sound made by their armor or their swords as they moved like windblown shadows from one looming patch of deeper darkness to the next along the corridor.

The men dropped to their hands and knees as they drew closer to the shrine, and then onto their bellies. Kira's figure was clear to all of them now, his attention completely on his prayers, doubtless asking the gods that all he had plotted and betrayed and destroyed lives for would come to pass in two more days.

And it would. . . .

Unless someone stopped him tonight.

As the ronin closed in, they could see a pair of guards—but only a pair—standing near Kira. The men waited at a respectful distance, holding the reins of his horse and their own.

Kai raised his head slightly as the wind picked up, whispering through the field like spirit voices, its cold breath raising gooseflesh wherever his skin was unprotected. All his senses grew hyper-alert again. He still could not banish the sense of a nameless energy stirring—power that had no place here. His inner vision saw the dark figures of Kira and the two guards as clearly as if there was a full moon, even though the last trace of the waning moon was not even visible; he could see the faint gleam of the *tengu* swords that Basho and Yasuno held ready in their hands. He saw Hazama clutching the sword that had been Oishi's own, and saw Oishi draw Lord Asano's *tanto,* as he prepared at last to take his revenge.

Nothing was wrong. Everything was going perfectly according to plan. Kira was theirs, no matter what happened.

Then why did he feel like disaster was so close he could grab it by the throat, if he only knew which way to turn—?

Oishi and Isogai, still in the lead, split off in opposite directions. Circling around the outsides of the last haystacks in the row, they crept up on the guards and pulled them down into the darkness. Both guards were dead before they could make a sound. Oishi and Isogai stood up silently and started toward Kira, who still kneeled before the shrine.

Kai got to his feet with the others; the death of the guards was their sign to move in. But as he started forward, the dim aura surrounding the shrine blazed up like fire, as if the power he'd thought lay buried under eons of time had suddenly erupted into their present.

The praying voice changed too, from an indistinguishable murmur to a distinct, high-pitched woman's voice, reciting an incantation that made his flesh crawl.

The wind hissed through the dead stubble on the field and rattled the haystacks as Isogai stumbled to a halt, and his eyes turned a blind, milky white.

"Isogai!" Oishi started toward him.

Kai flung himself at Oishi, catching his arm. "It's a trap! Run!"

Angrily Oishi jerked free, heading toward Isogai again.

Isogai turned his clouded gaze on Oishi, and a voice that might or might not ever have belonged to him said, "Sorry." Flames burst from his mouth.

Oishi skidded to a stop, flinging up his arm, the sudden horror on his face reflecting in the light of the flames.

The figure that had never been Kira rose to its feet and spun around, revealing a woman's form:

The *kitsune*.

Her voice rose, wild with the ecstasy of spirit energy flowing through her, as she began to recite the final part of her incantation.

Isogai burst into flames.

Foxfire— Kai had never seen it before; he had only heard of it from the *tengu*. He had never imagined that it had such terrible power. He backed away along with Oishi, shielding his face from the inferno.

As they stumbled back from the ghastly vision of their comrade's death, the flames that had completely engulfed Isogai's body suddenly arced outward, splitting in two. The lines of fire struck each haystack like a dragon's lightning-breath, and ignited the stubble between them—trapping the men who had been set to attack the witch inside a ring of flames.

As the fire blazed up in front of him, Kai cursed himself for not trusting his instincts . . . for trying to be only human, when the most human thing about him had always been his denial of reality.

Desperately he turned his focus to finding them a way out, before the flames became inescapable. The light of the fires blinded him from every direction; black smoke from the burning haystacks made it even harder to see a place where the flames might not have them completely cut off. He heard the panic stricken voices of the others shouting, "Get out!" "This way—" "Over here—!" as they ran frantically through the field. The wind was lifting clumps of burning hay from the stacks now, dropping it inside the circle of their trap, starting more fires everywhere in the dry stubble.

Searching for Oishi, Kai caught a glimpse of the witch through the wall of flames—and a line of Kira's archers suddenly forming around her, rising from hiding places in the field behind the shrine. At her side was the gigantic samurai in black armor—the one who had defeated him in Lord Asano's tournament, what seemed like a lifetime ago.

As Kai saw the witch, she saw him, and shrieked with laughter as she lowered her hand: Kira's archers drew their bows and fired at the men trapped inside the flames. The shouting around him was punctuated with sudden screams of pain. One of the guards' horses that had been trapped inside the ring of fire bolted across the field, more panic-stricken than the men it knocked aside as it tried to find its way out.

Kai looked toward the far end of the field as Oishi came up beside him. It was the point furthest from the archers, and he realized suddenly that the haystacks there had been set the farthest apart, to funnel them into the trap. He pointed, and Oishi nodded. As they began to run, Oishi shouted orders at anyone they saw to follow him until his voice was a harsh croak. Kai added his own voice, hoping someone would listen, as the next volley of arrows fell like deadly rain. Beyond the burning ring he could hear the sounds of battle, and realized that other ronin had been caught in ambushes of their own.

Basho ran up alongside them, with Yasuno following behind, just as the terrified horse re-entered their line of sight. It ran straight at them, maddened by its instinctive fear of flames. They dodged desperately, but it swerved and struck Yasuno as it galloped by. Just as Yasuno fell, Kai glimpsed the end of the haystack corridor they had been running toward. He could make out the forms of trees beyond it; there was still a chance they might make it through.

He turned back, shouting and gesturing, pointing toward the narrowing gaps in the wall of flames. But as he looked back, he suddenly realized that Yasuno had not gotten up again; the horse had knocked him unconscious. Basho realized it at the same instant. Without hesitating, he turned back through the burning field, through the rain of arrows toward his friend.

Kai watched Basho's progress from where he stood urging

the others who struggled toward him to keep moving, pointing out the spot where the flames were the lowest, pushing them toward it. Meanwhile Basho made his way through another volley of arrows; Kai saw him stumble as he was hit time and again.

But Basho didn't slow down until he reached Yasuno's unconscious body and picked it up in his arms, sheltering Yasuno with his own body as he carried him back, staggering now as more arrows hit him from behind, catching in his armor until it looked like he was covered with spines.

But his armor didn't cover him like it did most men; there had been nothing they'd found or captured that was large enough to fit him properly. Kai wondered grimly how many of those arrows were actually finding their mark.

He glanced away over his shoulder, seeing a few men still making their escape through the flames. As he did, he realized that Oishi and Hara were still inside with him, helping the others through—neither one willing to leave, any more than he was, until they had saved as many lives as they could.

As he looked toward Basho again, Kai realized he could no longer see the witch at all, where she stood beyond the solid wall of fire. He hoped that she couldn't see the men who were escaping, either. A group of ronin were gathered outside the ring of fire now, helping the others who broke through it extinguish their burning clothes.

Basho had almost reached the place where Kai waited with Oishi and Hara. They ran forward to help support him as he carried Yasuno, and then all together they turned back to face the wall of flames. Hara plunged into it first, and the men waiting there swiftly wrapped him in a blanket to put out the flames.

Kai glanced at Oishi; the two of them caught Basho's arms, supporting him as they ran forward, eyes shut, and flung themselves into the fire.

And then they were on the other side, free of the ring of death, falling to the ground while the others moved in to cover them with more blankets stripped from bedrolls on their horses.

Oishi staggered to his feet, looking back through the flames to see whether there was anyone still alive and trapped inside. "Hazama!" he shouted suddenly, waving his arms, as he saw his second-in-command stumbling toward them through the burning field.

But suddenly the samurai in black armor emerged from the flames just behind Hazama like a *shinigami*, a spirit of death come to claim his soul. Hazama turned back to try and defend himself—but at the sight of Hazama's sword the giant lunged at him, bringing down his enormous blade just as the fire in flared up—blocking their view, and the last hope of escape for anyone left alive.

Oishi gave a cry of fury, and started back toward the flames as if he'd lost either his vision or his mind.

"No—!" Kai caught him from behind, not letting go this time as he dragged the other man away from the brink of immolation, fighting Oishi's insane urge to stop the unstoppable, or even avenge what was impossible to avenge, now.

"Oishi, he's dead. . . ." Kai kept his hands firmly on Oishi's shoulders, even as his voice dropped from desperation to gentleness.

Slowly Oishi's compulsion released him, leaving him with the empty gaze of a lost child.

"We have to go," Kai said.

Oishi nodded, and Kai released him as he felt the other man's conscious mind take control of his body again. They turned back, Oishi pulling himself together at the sight of the men waiting for orders. "The others?" he asked, his voice raw from the smoke he had inhaled.

"Some are still fighting out there—" One of the men glanced off across the dark fields, where they could still hear sounds of battle above the roar and snapping of the flames.

"Signal a retreat," Oishi said hoarsely. A man with a bow took out a signal arrow and fired it, and then another; the sound of their shrill whistles trailed after them deep into the night. Hara was already standing, plucking out the broken shafts of arrows lodged in his armor, as Yasuno struggled to sit up, rubbing his head. Hara helped him get to his feet, steadying him. Kai reached down to help Basho.

"Come on—" Kai said, with a half frown of concern, as Basho looked up at him but didn't even lift a hand.

Basho went on looking at him, blinking but still not trying to get up. With an odd expression on his face, he said, "I can't move."

Kai looked back at the others, as all their expressions became one, sickened by the same apprehension.

Together the four men raised Basho's head and body carefully up off the ground; it took all the strength they had left to drag him away into the woods, with his feet still trailing behind.

The witch waited with inhuman patience until the fire she had started had run its course. She moved cautiously through the remains of the field, among the flickering cores of the nearly burnt-out haystacks, and the charred remains of bodies. In the distance the stubble of the field still smoldered, as the heart of the fire crept away to die . . . *like a mortally wounded warrior.* She smiled to herself, and went back to searching the ground for clues to the identities of the dead men around her.

Puffs of ash rose around her feet; a dark cloud of soot and ruin followed behind her trailing robes. The wind, which was now smothering the stars behind clouds of equal darkness, whirled tendrils of smoke into her eyes, but no tears rose to wash them clear. She waved away the smoke impatiently, searching among the remains for some sign of proof that her plan had succeeded—a sign that even Kira could understand.

The black-armored giant—her creature, not Kira's, no matter what Kira liked to think—followed silently behind her. He claimed that he'd killed Oishi, the former *karou* of

Ako Castle, after recognizing him by the family crest on his sword. She had no reason to doubt him. But Kira would need to see the proof that sword would provide—and so she needed to see it as well.

At last she spotted the gleam of one more blade gripped in a charred hand, still catching the light in spots beneath its coating of ash. Her servant stooped down and picked it up, wiping the ashes and soot from the hilt before he offered it to her. A fine sword . . . made all the more beautiful by the *mon* of the Oishi clan imprinted on its hilt.

Kira was waiting in his chambers when Mitsuke finally returned to the castle. He had never really left it, because after transforming herself into his likeness, she had made his show of filial piety and bravery for him—announcing that she was leaving the fortress to pray at the family shrine simply for Lady Mika to witness. Kira had made whatever prayers he was moved to make at the shrine that lay within the castle's walls, while her samurai commander and the men who had appeared to be guarding their lord followed her lead instead, and carried out the ambush against the traitorous ronin.

Her lord had been content, as usual, to keep his hands unstained, and let others do his bloodletting for him. *He was a true genius at delegating,* Mitsuke thought, without irony. She knew it was a vital talent in a leader, as well as she knew how easily it could turn from a strength into a weakness.

She entered Kira's chambers, bowing low before him, showing him the respect and humility that Lady Mika would never deign to give him, and attempting to remind him of her grace and devotion. *She had not failed him.* Surely what she had wrought tonight, and the proof of it that she carried with her, would rekindle the spark between them. . . .

She held out the sword. "It belonged to Oishi, my lord," she said, in her softest, most beguiling voice.

Kira stared at the blade, recognizing the crest just as she had. His tense, expectant face eased for the first time in a year; true relief shone in his eyes. He took the sword from her, and she thought that now, at last, he would return to being the man she had known and loved.

She put her arms around him, pressing her face against his shoulder, willing him to put down the sword and come lie beside her.

But he shrugged her off, moving away, the sword still clutched in his fist. He smiled as he raised the sword and brought it down in a ruthless slash, as if he was imagining striking his enemy's head off. Then he drove the sword into the floor of his bedchamber with all his strength; he left it there, a quivering symbol of his enemies' defeat.

As he turned back to her, she saw hunger in his eyes—but not for what she would offer him now; not for what she was aching for . . . not for anything she really recognized.

He looked at her, distracted, as if he wondered why she was still standing in front of him, arms outstretched. Then suddenly he smiled, and took her hands in his. "You've done well. Everything is perfect now." He pressed her hands to his lips. But there was no warmth in his touch as he gently lowered them to her sides again, and released them.

"I have things I need to do," he murmured, already beginning to turn away. "You must be weary. Why don't you go to your rooms, and sleep?"

As stunned as if he had struck her, Mitsuke could do nothing but bow and obey. She backed from the room and his presence, closing the door quietly behind her. But as she turned and started away down the silent hall, foxfire burned in her eyes, and what pulled back her lips no more resembled a human emotion than the look in Kira's eyes had resembled love.

20

Chikara and Horibe emerged from the farmhouse, their swords drawn, as they heard the sound of riders approaching.

Their expressions turned from worried to relieved, and then appalled, as the men who had ridden out to what had seemed like a certain victory returned as victims—half frozen, covered with ash and blood, weighed down by loss and despair. They carried their wounded with them—far too many of them, slumped in their saddles, or on makeshift stretchers. The old man and the boy ran out into the yard to help get them inside.

There were too many who needed wounds treated, or simply a place to collapse and sleep, for the decaying farmhouse to shelter them all. The barn became a makeshift field hospital where the worst of the wounded could be treated, lying on pallets of hay and straw and protected from the night's cold with whatever clothing and blankets the others could spare.

Oishi oversaw the treatment of the men who were less badly injured, leaving Kai to tend to Basho's wounds. Basho had always been the one who had seen to injuries that occurred when the men had been away from Ako Castle . . .

back when there had been an Ako Castle, with experienced doctors, for them to return to. Basho had brought what medicines and supplies he still possessed on this final journey, but no one had expected him to be the one who would be most in need of them—especially not Kai. But no one else had the skill to use them, or to cope with the wounds Basho had received, except Kai.

Yasuno hovered close by his friend like a guard dog, at first trying to keep Kai from even touching him. But Basho himself had instructed Yasuno, painfully, to let Kai help him.

"He knows what he's doing," Basho had murmured, and Kai's memory flashed back to Basho treating his own wounds, as he lay helpless after the beating the Ako samurai had given him. Only a year ago. . . . It seemed to him now as if it had occurred in a previous incarnation.

Yasuno had bowed his head, acquiescing to his friend's request. He had helped Kai remove more arrows from Basho's armor, and carefully take the armor from his body.

But too many arrows had found their mark; aside from his burns, Basho had lost too much blood—far too much. . . . Kai could see the pallor of his skin as he gently cleaned the areas around each wound.

He knew that what Basho had told him was true: after the fight with Kira's champion, and what had followed it, he would have died, left all alone. He had been too helpless to help himself, if someone had not cared for his wounds then.

But now he found himself in a position to repay his life-debt to the man who had become his unlikely, unexpected friend . . . and he realized, despairing, that he couldn't do it. Basho was dying, and even the *tengu* had no secrets for healing beyond what they had taught to him.

All that he knew, all that he could do, was to keep applying salve that would ease the pain of Basho's burns and wounds, to help him pass whatever time he had left as comfortably as possible. Kai had no idea how long that would be. He only knew that he had never realized before what it was like to lose a friend.

He glanced at Yasuno, who crouched on Basho's other side, barely able to contain his grief. It was the first time Kai had ever seen an emotion as profound as sorrow on Yasuno's face; it only deepened his surprise to realize that for once he knew exactly how the other man felt.

Chikara came and set down another bowl of clean water at Kai's side, picking up the one that had turned the sickly shade of blood dissolved with ash. Kai nodded briefly; he looked back as Basho whispered, "Halfbreed?"

He met Basho's swollen eyes with as much of a smile as he could manage, as Basho forced them open wide enough to look at him. He could never resent hearing that name from Basho's lips, ever since they had had their first real conversation after leaving the *tengu* cave. He no longer resented it so much from anyone, thanks to the insight he had gained, along with Basho's gesture of friendship—and he owed Basho for that, too.

"I have a confession to make," Basho said, and Kai's eyes widened slightly. Even now, Basho managed a grin, somehow, although Kai heard apology in the words. "When I was a boy . . . I used to wait in the woods outside your hut . . . and when you came out I'd throw stones and cow dung at you, then hide."

Kai went on carefully applying salve to his wounds, his own smile growing a little wider at the memory. He had never been hit once; he had always been too quick. "I have a confession to make, too. I knew it was you. I could see your belly sticking out from behind the trees."

Basho tried to laugh, but all that came out was a painful, viscous cough. Kai tried to keep the smile on his own face, although he knew too well what the sound meant. He tried to tell himself that it only meant Basho would not have much longer to suffer. . . .

Kai glanced back as Chikara suddenly turned where he had been standing and walked away; Kai realized that the boy's eyes were full of tears.

Just then Oishi came back into the barn from checking on the men who were being cared for in the house. Chikara lowered his head, ashamed, as he saw his father looking at him from the doorway.

But there was no disapproval on Oishi's face, only compassion. He had not come here to pass judgment. He stood aside until Chikara had gone past him and out, then shut the door against the cold draft from outside.

Oishi's eyes went to Basho, then from one man to another among the ronin who lay around him, most of them quietly enduring, a few unconscious or moaning with the pain of wounds and burns. The look on his face turned from compassion to grief, and then to the most profound guilt that Kai had ever seen—as if he, and not Kira, was to blame for every wound they had suffered, for every death that had occurred.

Kai looked down again, feeling his own control falter: He focused on applying more salve to Basho's blistered skin, concentrating on keeping his movements as light and soothing as he could, wishing that he could absorb even a little of the pain into himself, to ease Basho's suffering, to distract himself from his own helplessness.

He had wished his entire life for even one true friend, someone who accepted him as an equal and willingly returned his trust, his loyalty, his gestures of friendship. Only now, when it was too late, did he realize that in friendship, like everything else that defined being human—that defined life itself—the light had its darkness, and the darkness had its light.

Never having had someone he could call a friend meant never having to lose something as rare and irreplaceable as a friendship, any time the great wheel of life turned and threw individual lives out of balance once more. . . .

Basho's hand reached out and caught his. Kai looked up,

eyes filled with apology, afraid his attempts to ease Basho's pain had only hurt him more. But Basho's hand went on gripping his own, the way a man would cling to a lifeline at the edge of the world, and Kai realized Basho had not meant to stop him . . . but instead that what he needed even more was something—someone—to hold onto. To feel the warmth of human contact . . . to prove to himself that at a time like this he was not alone.

Kai held onto Basho's hand, raised his other hand to cover it, reaffirming the contact, reassuring the man whose hand clung to his like a child's that he mattered more to someone at this moment than anything else in existence.

From the corner of his eye, Kai saw Yasuno rise up onto his knees from where he had been resting, silently watching over his friend, unable to do more. He stared at Basho's hand, at Kai's hands clasping it—with an expression of utter surprise, but without envy or resentment. Relief, and completely unselfish gratitude, filled his face, as if all that mattered to him was that someone was there who could answer his friend's need.

"You know what I want more than anything in this life?" Basho whispered, suddenly opening his eyes. Kai looked back at him, not answering, only waiting, while Basho's face turned thoughtful and his eyes distant. And then a grin turned up the corners of his mouth for the last time. "Some air."

The light went out of his eyes as if someone had put out a flame, and they were both left staring at nothing at all. Finally, reluctantly, Kai reached out and closed his eyelids, because there were no longer any secrets left that either of them could share.

Kai raised his head at last to look at Yasuno, to confirm that Basho's suffering was over. But Yasuno was already gazing down at Basho, not needing to be told. The stoic expression of a samurai had vanished from his face, and only the grief of a heartbroken friend remained.

Kai looked down again, releasing Basho's hand as gently as he had held it at the last. He got up slowly and walked away, granting Yasuno privacy to say his final prayers of farewell for his old friend.

As he left Basho's side, Kai saw Oishi still standing by the door, watching them all with a depth of sadness that had transformed his face until it was almost unrecognizable. He turned his face away as Kai stopped moving and stood looking at him. Then he opened the door just enough to slip outside, closing it again silently behind him.

Oishi kneeled in the withered grass of an empty field, listening to the moan of the wind as it wrapped its arms around him with the deathly embrace of winter. He took Lord Asano's *tanto* out of its sheath and held it in his hands, staring down at it, his mind too full and too empty all at once.

The starlit sky of earlier tonight was almost hidden now behind windblown clouds; the first flakes of a fresh snowfall whirled past him like the ashes of a burned-out fire . . . like the petals of fallen cherry blossoms swept away in the spring wind.

"The way of the samurai was the way of death." He had heard that said all his life, and yet he had never actually understood. . . .

He had always believed that if he lived and died with honor one day he would be reborn into the world, as surely as the cherry blossoms returned in the spring, and that thought had always comforted him. But if the purpose of reincarnation was to learn the lessons each new lifetime had to teach, until eventually the soul became enlightened, set free from all earthly limitations . . . how did dying before life's lessons could be learned fit into that vision?

He had read, and even written, poems that compared samurai to cherry blossoms, at their peak of glory in the springtime of life, when their world was young—living for a brief beautiful time, and then falling, too soon. *A beautiful death,* they called it. He realized now that he had never had any understanding of the reality hidden behind those words . . . he had never had any experience genuine enough to weigh against them, until he had taken part in Lord Asano's *seppuku.*

Words were only a veil of fine silk used to disguise an ugly scar, he thought, like the heavy scent of incense as prayers were murmured for the dead, disguising the memory of bodies left to rot on a battlefield.

To compare death to the falling snow was far closer to the truth—though even that remorseless promise of oblivion held far too much purity, compared to the bloody memory of his lord's death, or what he had witnessed tonight.

His ancestors had been true warriors. He was nothing but a sword-carrying bureaucrat who played too many war games—just like all the self-proclaimed "experts" who had not even been born when the Age of Wars had ended, but whose books about *Bushido* he had always revered. . . .

He glanced up from the dagger in his hands at the sound of footsteps behind him, and looked back to see Kai crossing the field toward him.

Of course. His mouth thinned. *If he had a mind to, Lord Asano's head tracker would find him even if he threw himself into the sea. . . .*

Oishi looked down again at the dagger he held, wondering what the halfbreed was doing here but refusing to acknowledge him.

Kai stopped beside him, saying nothing, as if he was wondering the same thing about Oishi. He glanced at the blade in Oishi's hands with more than casual curiosity. At last he crouched down on the frozen earth, as if he was trying to will Oishi to meet his eyes.

Oishi kept his head down, as he said, finally, "I should have acted the day Lord Asano died. Our anger should have been sudden and swift, then even if we'd failed it would have been with honor."

Kai's silent presence was filled with sorrow and empathy that Oishi could feel in every fiber of his being. But still he could not bring himself to look up, as he murmured, "Now my men have died for nothing."

For a long moment the halfbreed remained as silent as the snow that fell softly on them both, clinging to their skin, covering their wounds and their bloodstained, ragged garments with lies; hiding the traces of their defeat, even as it covered the bleakness and neglect around them, the remains of some long-ago surrender. At last Kai said simply, without reproach, "You are a samurai."

Oishi looked up at last, startled by the words, and more than surprised by the emotion they stirred inside him. *A samurai should be prepared for death at any time; that was part of his duty as a warrior. But certain defeat was not.* How would dying in a rash, mindless attack have been more honorable than carefully planned vengeance, which would have succeeded, if not for witchcraft? That made no sense. *When had he begun to believe that—?*

Kai met his gaze with quiet determination. "We still have swords, and the advantage of surprise." He hesitated, glancing at Lord Asano's dagger, and then something gleamed darkly in his eyes as he added, "Kira also thinks you've failed."

Oishi stared at him.

"Your men will have died for nothing if you stop now," Kai said. He held Oishi's gaze for another long moment, before he pushed to his feet again and began to slowly walk back toward the barn.

Watching him go, Oishi realized that the halfbreed was still wearing his piecemeal armor; he had not even paused to remove it before focusing on Basho's wounds. *There was no way at all to tell that he was not a samurai.*

Oishi looked away, up into the sky, as his mind considered the things Kai had said to him. The snow continued to fall, and yet somehow the world around him gradually began to brighten, as if each flake shone with captive light, like feathers drifting down from a *tenyo*'s magical cloak.

All at once he remembered the words of Confucius, whose teachings infused so much of *Bushido*: *"It does not matter how slowly you go, so long as you do not stop."*

He climbed stiffly to his feet, no longer feeling the cold as he reflected on the words, and on the possibilities for new plans of attack that their presumed death offered them . . . on the fact that no matter how long this mountain winter, or this endless night, continued, a new day would dawn, and spring would come again, whether he was here to see it or not.

He put Lord Asano's *tanto* back into its sheath. *Ako and his lord were waiting for his return.*

Mika woke with a start from a nightmare filled with flames and screams of pain. She sat up in bed, her heart pounding—and gasped as sudden fright shocked her fully alert.

Crouched at the bottom of the futon was Kira's witch. Although she was in her human form, she was poised not like a human, but like an animal about to attack; a dagger was clutched in her hand.

"I promised my lord I would not harm a hair on your head." Her voice was filled with something more baleful than envy, more pernicious than hatred. "But what you do to yourself is not my concern. . . ." A slight, and slightly inhuman smile touched her lips.

She moved along the side of Mika's bed with a slithering motion that was not even foxlike, but completely alien, her robes trailing on the floor as if she was boneless, although she still held the dagger tightly in her hand.

"I bring you sad tidings, my lady," she said, still wearing the fey, inhuman smile. "Your halfbreed is dead."

Mika stared back at her in disbelief, but her body began to tremble helplessly as she looked into the *kitsune*'s mismatched eyes, and saw utter conviction. She felt the power of the witch's certainty banish all hope as if Mitsuke had snuffed out the sun; the evergreen place that her belief had defended so fiercely all this time began to wither and die within her, as Kira's icebound world closed in around her at last.

Watching Mika's denial break down, the witch's smile widened, turning more feral. "So are dozens of your father's men. . . . All killed trying to save you."

Mika shook her head, trying to shake loose the images of burning death that seemed to have come straight out of her dream, as if she had wakened from one nightmare into another. Her eyes felt as if they were on fire as the images refused to vanish, no matter what she did, as she realized that the real nightmare had begun a year ago, and that now it would never end.

The witch raised the dagger high, her arm trembling with the desire for death. "Perhaps now you understand the price of your love—" Her hand fell from the air like a bird of prey and buried the dagger in the floor, a handspan from Mika's side.

Her smile widened again with savage satisfaction. She turned and slithered away, her kimono trailing behind her as she vanished out the doorway.

Mika lay on her side, her knees drawn up, her teeth clenched on the bedding she had pressed to her mouth to keep from crying out, from making any sound at all that would betray the agony filling her now.

All her most precious memories, and even the hope, however futile, that had allowed her to hold on to her dignity, her strength, and her sanity had been torn from her in a moment . . . locked away in Kira's eternal prison of ice, where she could never touch them, or let them warm and comfort her again.

All her prayers had been answered . . . but the answers had all been *No.*

She stared at the *tanto* reflecting the glow of the lantern at her bedside, and thought of her father. The reservoir of tears she had held back through the interminable year since his death suddenly spilled down her face, soaking the mattress beneath her cheek. She reached out, stroking the *tanto*'s cold sinuous steel, running her hand along its finely honed edge, until suddenly it opened a deep gash in her palm that burned like the fire in her nightmare. Her hand ran red with blood like bodies of the dead soaking the futon along with her tears.

She was samurai, and when all hope of victory or honor was gone, a true samurai, man or woman, would choose death on her own terms rather than the terms of her enemies.

She tightened her hand around the knife's hilt, struggling to pull it out of the floor. But the blood on her palm made it slippery, and she couldn't get a solid grip. She pushed herself up with a noise of frustration, reaching out with both hands.

Slippery . . . deceitful, treacherous; as cruel as her master and as pitiless as any predator—

Mika's breath caught. That was Mitsuke—*the witch, the shape-changer, the betrayer, who had destroyed everyone she'd ever loved.*

And had left her with a dagger.

What you do with it is your concern. . . . Mika glanced toward the closed door of her room. *Why had the witch come here now, tonight, to tell her what had happened—before the wedding, not after it?* She remembered the strange emotion filling the *kitsune*'s eyes when she first looked at her.

Who was it Mitsuke's vengeance really wanted to destroy, so deep inside her own twisted heart that even she had not realized it . . . ?

With a determined wrench, Mika pulled the *tanto* out of the floor. She got to her feet, finding a scarf to wrap around her bloody hand. She wiped off her arm, and then the dagger. Because she would need it, one way or another, before the new moon was old. . . .

The blood red sun rose over the snow white fields of the abandoned farm, painting a glaring crimson path toward the way ahead for the ronin, who were already up and stirring, tending the wounded and gathering their equipment from the barn.

If any of the men were inclined to see morbid symbolism in the break of day, they didn't show it, least of all Oishi. He moved briskly from house to barn and back again, supervising the progress and checking on the condition of his men, a leader again after his moment of agonizing doubt and self-recrimination.

Kai watched him with a feeling of profound relief from the field where they had spoken last night. His own few belongings, such as they were, were already packed on his saddled horse, and he had already done all he could to help the men who were tending the wounded. Although he'd felt them watching him all the while, no one had refused to let him assist them, which had been even more unnerving.

Still too unsure of his place in their world to do anything else but stay out of their way, he had wandered the fields when he was finished, just so that he could breathe again.

He moved on as his feet began to get numb, making a seemingly casual circuit of the farmhouse and the outbuildings where the sentries watched the brightening land with anxious eyes. He saw Chikara, crouched by himself at the edge of a field, peering through a spyglass at the fiery dawn.

Kai walked toward him, wondering how the boy was doing after last night—and what he was doing: Whether he was really trying to blind himself by peering through a spyglass at the sun, or if there was something on the horizon to see.

Chikara glanced up at the sound of his approach, his tense expression turning to relief as he saw that it was Kai—and not, Kai suspected, his father.

"What are you looking at?" Kai asked.

He had tried to make the question a casual one, but after yesterday Chikara seemed to find double meanings in everything. The young ronin forced a smile as he looked up. "I can see gold on the sunrise. It must be a good omen." He offered the spyglass to Kai.

Kai smiled back at him, and then raised the spyglass to look at the sun. He was surprised to see that there actually was an unusual streak of gold on the horizon. He lowered the glass, peering at the same spot with a frown of curiosity that verged on concern, and then raised the spyglass to his eye again. Fixing all his attention on the line of gold, this time he could make out the distant silhouettes of figures carrying banners . . . but not men in armor, as he had feared. The strange procession of ghostly figures, banners glinting in the sunlight, was something else entirely. His smile returned, edged with amusement and sudden inspiration.

He handed the spyglass back to Chikara with a nod of thanks, and went to find Oishi.

A few hours later, Kai had a much closer view of the procession he had seen on the horizon, while he waited hidden among the trees with Oishi and a group of other ronin—all the ones who had been fit to go on—as the troupe of traveling players approached their hiding place. He was startled to realize that he recognized their leader: the man named Kawatake, whose actors and musicians they had all seen perform at Ako Castle, on the fateful day of the tournament.

He nudged Oishi, who was crouched at his side. Oishi nodded, with a smile that could have been on the face of any god who happened to be watching them now, amused by the improvisational *Kabuki* of human existence.

As far as Kai was concerned, gods had nothing to do with it; this play belonged strictly to the *tengu*. When he had seen the troupe through the spyglass just after dawn, a story he had heard from the *tengu* had come back to him . . . history from a time before they had taken to religion. Once, when their kind had simply been malevolent, violent tricksters, a group of them had invaded a castle, having disguised themselves as traveling players. Why they had wanted to, or what their intentions were, he had never heard; their pride seemed to be in the achievement itself—although in the end they had been discovered, and forced to vanish.

He looked toward the approaching troupe of entertainers again. If the ronin could win the players' cooperation, this time the story would have a very different ending . . . one way or another.

With Kawatake in the lead, the performers—most of them dressed in pieces of colorful costume, some of them carrying banners woven with bright metallic threads—filled the space around them with a sensory feast. Singers chanted fragments of legendary tales, musicians played flutes that wove melodies through the rhythmic beat of small drums, actors rehearsed bits of a mock-duel or formal dance movement as they went along.

Kai watched in fascination as the troupe combined rehearsal and advertisement of their skills even as they traveled, entertaining any other travelers or the people of towns they passed through, at the same time distracting themselves from the boredom of their endless journeying. He knew the social position of actors was no better than his own, and that among themselves their vanity and competitive envy was as legendary as that of the samurai. But still the sight of them made him wish that in some other life he would be reborn as an actor, if only for the few precious moments like this. . . .

Which the ronin were about to bring to an end. It was Oishi's turn to nudge him, as the ronin rose from their hiding places among the bushes, and stepped into the roadway, blocking it.

Kawatake stopped in his tracks, staring at them. His expression of stunned alarm bore no hint of theatrical pretense as he took in the band of ragged, disheveled, well-armed men who stared back at him with an equally genuine determination to keep his group from passing.

Oishi stepped forward and bowed respectfully, as Kai drew his sword.

Before long, the performers were sitting in a long row in a glen where the ronin had left their supplies and horses. The players' reactions to their situation ran the gamut from extreme nervousness to a peculiar fascination, as they watched the men they clearly had taken for a gang of bandits going about their business. The ronin served them a meal of tea and rice accompanied by any bits of smoked fish or wild game they had left from their own journey, doing their best to treat their hostages as honored guests.

At last Kawatake, as the troupe's leader, dared to speak up, apparently emboldened by the meal, and the fact that the "bandits" were treating them with more consideration than most lords.

Oishi and his commanders stood in a semicircle around the actor—their arms folded, their faces not quite as impassive as they would have liked—while Kawatake flayed their ears with an outrage that must have been backed up by all his skill as an actor, considering the position he was in.

"You will hang for this!" Kawatake said, and the men listening glanced at each other with faint smiles of irony. "We are not some village troupe to be held up by bandits! Lord Kira himself has hired us to perform at his wedding! I have the letters and passes to prove it—!"

"There is no need," Oishi said mildly, holding up his hand at last to silence the man. "We saw you perform in Ako."

Kawatake's mouth snapped shut in surprise; he stared at Oishi for a long moment, with eyes used to seeing a man's face behind the disguise of a mask or stage makeup. "You are Lord Asano's men?" he said finally, and it was not really a question. He glanced at the others around Oishi, and his face furrowed with understanding as he realized at last that the men he had taken for bandits were the same men he had last seen wearing the fine clothing and bright armor of Lord Asano's most highly ranked retainers—that they had been reduced to this, following the condemnation and death of their lord.

Oishi stared back at him, seeing understanding, and then actual sympathy, in the eyes of an intelligent man who knew as much about the politics of power as about the vagaries of fate. Hoping that what he read in Kawatake's eyes meant what he thought it did, Oishi said, "We need your help."

The sun was falling toward the western horizon before the long afternoon of argument and emotional debate, tension and sheer fatigue drew to its close. To the intense relief of the ronin, it ended with an agreement between two groups who might as well have come from the opposite ends of the earth, only to find in the final accounting that when it came to the things they truly valued above all else, there was really nothing to disagree about.

Now the troupe of actors sat silently looking on, witnessing a ritual that might have come directly from a scene in an ancient *Noh* drama they had performed.

But none of them had ever witnessed a genuine moment remotely like this one, coming as it did from inside a world as far removed from their personal experience as the legendary heroes and gods whose stories they reenacted with pantomime, song, and dance . . . a tradition which had begun nearly a millennium ago, and half a millennium before the *Noh* theater itself . . . the heritage of the samurai.

The ronin kneeled in rows before Oishi, who knelt beside a low table that held Lord Asano's helmet and the *tanto* with which he had committed *seppuku,* along with a scroll of paper. His hand rested on the piece of paper, which held their pledge to avenge their lord's unjust death, as if he was protecting it from the whim of a passing breeze. He had signed it already, in his own blood.

Kai kneeled to one side, keeping his head bowed. He had no right to take part in this ceremony, yet he was unable to separate himself from the others now, even if the law forbade him from ever being a part of their tradition, and tradition forbade him from officially joining them in their vow. He saw the others lower their heads for a moment as well, out of respect for the courage of their fallen lord and the men who were unable to be with them here.

Then Oishi looked up again, gazing out at the somber eyes of the remaining ronin as he said, "None of us knows how long he shall live. Or when his time will come. But soon all that will be left of our brief lives is the pride our children feel when they speak our names."

His men looked back at him, their faces pensive, but their eyes alive once more with the pride of identity that had been passed down to them through centuries. Their heritage could not be stripped from them so easily, either by the laws of the *bakufu* or the personal decree of the lord they were told to hold above all other lords—the Shogun himself. The laws of the land were made by politicians . . . and politicians were not gods. Even the Shogun was only a man. "The law" and "justice" were not interchangeable.

The men who kneeled here were not gods either, any more than the "Tokugawa Peace" was truly peace. But they were warriors whose ancestors had established a code of conduct, with roots that predated even the rank of Shogun, in an attempt to preserve the difference between a man who fought for a cause, and a man who fought because he had lost his humanity.

At the core of *Bushido,* the Way of the Warrior, were seven moral values on which a samurai was expected to base his life's conduct: *justice, courage, compassion, respect, honesty, loyalty, and honor.* The fact that those values had existed for so long, unwritten for most of that time yet basically unchanged, only proved their wisdom. The fact that so few men who called themselves samurai could actually live up to their own standards only proved how necessary it was for such a code to exist.

Oishi nodded at the table beside him, and the symbolic objects lying on it. "When a crime goes unpunished the world is unbalanced. When a wrong is unavenged, the heavens look down on us in shame. We too must die for this circle of vengeance to be closed—there is no other way—so I leave the choice to you."

Kai watched the men before Oishi considering his words and their full implications, through a moment when time seemed suspended like a hawk's back on the wind. He knew what Oishi had said was the truth. If the ronin succeeded, they would restore their lord's honor, and Mika's birthright would be restored to her, if there was any true justice at all left in the *bakufu*'s legal system.

But if the ronin outlived their vendetta, they would have violated a direct order from the Shogun. If they did not acknowledge the laws of their society as well as the higher justice they sought, the world would remain unbalanced. A circle of vengeance must be closed before it spiraled out of control. One life, or ten, or a hundred, were a small thing, weighed against the great cycle of Life itself, which must be allowed to move on.

And yet, to each of those individuals, one life was his entire world. . . .

Horibe rose from the spot where he was kneeling, and walked to the table. He kneeled down again before Lord Asano's helmet, and bowed. And then he pricked his finger with Lord Asano's dagger, and signed his name on the sheet of paper, swearing in blood his vow to avenge his lord. Hara rose next and came forward. The other ronin followed, one by one, pledging their life's blood to their lord, as they had been born to do.

Oishi watched them sign, one by one, and move on, until suddenly he looked up in surprise, to find his son kneeling down before him.

Chikara reached for Lord Asano's *tanto,* and his father's hand reached out to stop him. As Oishi gazed at his son, Kai saw the same haunted look that had been on his face when they left the *tengu* cave.

"A father should not live to see his son die before him." Oishi shook his head, his hand still immobilizing Chikara's.

"You are not my father, sir," Chikara said, looking straight into his eyes. "You are my leader. A father should not die without seeing his son become a man."

Oishi blinked as if he'd been struck by a *shakabuku,* a moment of stunning revelation, lying hidden within the words of his own son. His face filled with both admiration and reluctance, neither emotion able to completely dislodge the other even as he nodded at last, freeing Chikara's hand, and allowed him to sign the oath.

Kai watched more men follow Chikara until only a few remained, waiting to sign. As Yasuno approached the table, Horibe's glance counted the men still in line, and said, "We are forty-six."

"No—" Yasuno said, as he finished signing. He turned to look at Kai, who was kneeling just out of reach of the table. "Halfbreed?"

Kai stiffened, his hands tightening into fists as his sudden surprise curdled into humiliation and anger. He glared back at Yasuno, unable to penetrate his expression, unable to comprehend *why, now—?*

But Yasuno went on looking directly at him, as he said clearly enough for everyone to hear, "Forgive me for not thanking you for defeating the *kirin,* and saving my life." He took a deep breath. "A samurai does not take credit for the victories of others." And then he leaned forward in a deep bow.

Heads turned on every side, as the ronin stared at them both in disbelief; the silence around them was complete, and eloquent.

No one's disbelief could have been greater than Kai's. He sat back on his heels, feeling as if his mind had suddenly dropped through a trapdoor.

Yasuno raised his head again, and then carefully withdrew a *wakizashi* from his belt ties. He held the side sword out to Kai in his open hands. "This belonged to Basho."

Kai stared at him, down at the *wakizashi* in his hands. He shook his head, looking at Yasuno in confusion.

"A samurai wears two swords," Yasuno said quietly, still holding the sword out to him. For the first time Kai saw everything that lay open in his mind: *The shame and remorse, the longing for forgiveness . . . the pain of a man who had lost his best friend, only to realize that his friend had not left him alone, if he just had the wisdom to acknowledge his insecurity and behave with honor.*

Slowly Kai reached out, accepting the sword with hands that almost trembled.

Still uncertain, still holding the *wakizashi* at arms' length, he raised his head and looked toward the rest of the gathered ronin.

Not just Chikara, but all of them were looking back at him now with eyes that actually saw *him*—someone who had earned their trust and respect, a man they welcomed as a companion and a peer.

For almost a thousand years it had been their right to honor a man by bestowing on him the rank of samurai, when they felt it had been justly earned. The law that had proscribed that tradition had been in existence for barely a century.

These same men were now signing, in blood, an oath that said they no longer were willing to accept *giri,* strict obedience to duty, when it violated *ninjo,* their own conscience; that some things were worth fighting—and dying—for; and that they were willing to give their very lives to claim the higher justice *Bushido* demanded of them.

That tradition also said that to acknowledge a man's proven worth and courage was only right, and just.

Kai looked at Oishi last of all. He saw in Oishi's eyes

complete approval, welcome, and—as Oishi's glance moved from his own face to Yasuno's and back again—something that looked oddly like relief.

Still holding Oishi's gaze, Kai moved forward to the table, kneeled, and pricked his finger. He signed the oath.

"Now," Oishi said, "we are forty-seven."

21

It was the eve of the First New Moon of Spring. Sunset tonight would mark the start of the wedding day of Lord Kira and Lady Mika. Although any stirring of life still lay hidden beneath the snow and frozen ground, guests would soon be arriving, and Kira would greet them in his courtyard . . . a courtyard laboriously cleared of any snow . . . for the final time. The festivities would extend through tomorrow, and their official wedding ceremony; after their wedding night, the new Lord Asano and his Lady would travel to Ako.

There the cherry trees were already on the verge of blossoming, and spring would be waiting to greet them as he took full possession of his new future as well as his new wife, in a world that was fully alive.

And yet, still Kira had needed to consult the signs, to be certain that nothing had been left to chance that could possibly stand in his way.

The deer bones of Mitsuke's divination spell glowed and pulsed in the brazier that sat between the two of them; he watched her pluck a bone from the coals without flinching. *What a remarkable creature she was. . . .*

Even though tomorrow he would take a wife who was truly worthy of his position, still he must be certain that she also stayed with him, even if her jealousy had become like a grindstone, wearing away at their intimacy. He knew she still shared his ambition to be more than simply what fate's design decreed—and only she could ensure that his future did not end with becoming Lord of Ako.

His desire for Mika would mean that Mitsuke could never again keep him utterly in her thrall. The thought of losing the intoxicating intimacy they had shared for so long, when they had been only two—lost spirits bound by their mutual hungers—saddened him, but not so much that gaining the life he had always deserved would not make up for it.

Mitsuke still loved him as she always had, he was certain. He must be careful not to neglect her. He would always need her, and so he must always keep her at his side. If all else failed, he had seen the fear in her eyes when he had threatened her. The further away she was from her true home in the mountain forests, the more dire those threats would be, and the more genuine. . . .

He looked up again, finally, making certain that no hint of his thoughts was visible on his face, or even on the surface of his mind, as he watched her running her fingernails over the gleaming cracks in the bone she had chosen. "What do you see?" he asked, leaning forward.

Mitsuke hesitated a moment, staring at the fiery cracks, something she had never done before, because there had been no need to hide the sorrow in her eyes at what she had seen. "The omens are good," she murmured, still gazing down. And then, choosing her words with infinite care, she looked up at Kira and said, "Soon you will travel far. In every town and village people shall bow before you. . . . Even the Shogun will look upon your face in awe. . . ."

Kira still leaned forward, his eagerness for her words illuminating his eyes, making his beloved face shine in the way that had always made her smile, and until now had always fed the passionate desire inside her. For the first time, she had to struggle to keep any smile at all in place.

Kira did not seem to notice, which relieved her, until he asked, “And Mika?”

She lowered her eyes again, hiding the tears that suddenly filled them . . . *true too-human tears* . . . as her fingernails traced the gleaming cracks once more.

In her chambers, Mika kneeled in the formal wedding robes chosen for her by Kira, while her attendants carefully applied her makeup. The kimono and outer robes were made of the softest quilted silks and most beautiful satin brocades, trimmed in fur to keep her warm. Every piece and layer was exquisitely designed and embroidered . . . and all in white. *Of course,* she thought. For a wedding in this snowbound land, Kira had chosen to dress his bride in a *siromuku.* Its name was its description: “pure white.” So fitting to the domain that Kira himself hated nearly as much as she did, but which had made him the man he was.

But she realized that the *siromuko*’s traditional symbolism had been meant to convey a message to her, personally, as well: Its whiteness presented the bride as a blank canvas, ready to learn the habits and expectations of her husband, and dutifully obey them.

And there was one more reason for her to wear white . . . which had struck her instantly, as both unspeakably appropriate and so unbearably cruel that she was not sure even Kira could have thought of it, at least consciously: *White was the color of death.* Her father had committed *seppuku* dressed in white; he had been cremated dressed in white. The mourners at his funeral had worn white.

She thought of her mother’s *uchikake,* the bright traditional over-kimono that had been handed down from her great-grandmother. She had always expected to wear that when she married. She remembered taking it out, as a young girl, wrapping it around herself like her mother’s arms and daydreaming. Its background and lining had been bright red, the color of Ako, of life . . . and its brocade and embroidery were shot through with gold and silver threads, making the colorful images of pines, chrysanthemums, birds, and flowing water all sparkle.

And after Kai had come into her life, in her prayers she had pleaded that the gods would someday grant her beloved *tennin* the chance to prove his courage to her father through such an impressive feat of bravery that her father would adopt him. And they would be betrothed. . . .

Mika gasped out loud and jerked away from her attendants, as her patient resignation was betrayed by an invisible dart poisoned with grief.

Her hands clenched into fists inside the long sleeves of her outer robe, her nails biting into her palms and her arms trembling as she fought to bring herself back under control. She realized that her attendants had all bowed until their heads touched the floor, begging her forgiveness—that they thought their ministrations were what had hurt her. She wiped the telltale wetness from her eyes, smearing chalky face powder, while some part of her mind managed to find the words to tell them to get up, that the powder had made her eyes sting, that it was no fault of theirs.

They rose, gratefully, and went back to their endless fussing with her clothing and face, as well as their murmured *ooh*s and *aah*s, praising her beauty with an enthusiasm they had not shown about anything she could remember before now.

She went on kneeling as the formal makeup of a highborn lady turned her face as white as her dress, artificially reddening her lips and cheeks until in her mind she resembled Yukihime, the cold, passionless goddess of winter. She meditated on the image of her self-will as something turned to ice by Yukihime: hard, cold, and remorseless. . . .

By dusk Kirayama Castle was alive with color in the glow from hundreds of lanterns. The lights illuminated the festive decorations and artful flower-printed *tobari* that disguised the bleakness of the walls, the countless *origami* blossoms that mimicked plum and cherry blossoms, cleverly fashioned out of paper and tied to the branches of trees which had not yet begun to bud. To the startled eyes of the newly arriving guests, it seemed as if the actual flowers of spring had opened in celebration, while high above them the indigo-printed banners of Kira's clan fluttered side by side with the scarlet of Ako.

Latecomers were still arriving, having struggled miserably on their way up to the castle, despite the help of the workers and guards stationed all along the steep, slippery track that led to it.

Among the slowly moving crowd that had reached the final bridge, which arced across a last deep chasm to the fortress's nearly impregnable gate, was the colorfully dressed troupe of actors Kira had remembered from the Shogun's visit to Ako Castle. He had wanted them here for this occasion as well; they had put on an excellent performance, one fit for a Shogun.

Kawatake, their leader, presented his pass to one of the guards, who waved him on with his troupe. Oishi, dressed in a gaudy costume, followed Kawatake, keeping his head down as if he was too exhausted by the climb even to look forward to their destination.

The rest of the performers moved past, in clusters as dense as the narrow span of the bridge allowed, as if they were more than ready to reach journey's end. The guard posted at its entrance watched them pass with more than his usual interest, although it was simply the sight of any performers, in their rainbow of bright clothing, that made him stare. The fact that there might be former retainers from Ako Castle among them never entered his mind, as Horibe and a handful of the other ronin passed by unnoticed, a few in costume, the rest serving as porters.

At the rear of the group, an unusually tall porter, bent under a load of stage decorations and extra costumes, followed the rest, apparently slowed by his burden.

The heavy burden attracted the guard's attention more

than the man carrying it. He stepped in front of the porter, lowering his spear to block the access to the bridge. "What have you got there?" he demanded.

Another guard came up alongside him, waving him off. "I've checked it," the second guard said.

As Kai hesitantly started forward again, Hara—passing as a guard in armor stolen from Kira's own border post—gave him a nod that hid a smile, and waved him on with what appeared to be mere impatience. Chikara, who had turned back when he saw the guard block Kai's way, glanced toward heaven in relief.

The troupe of performers—professional and amateur—filed across the bridge, which spanned a cleft so deep that by now there was only darkness below them, and entered the lower courtyard of Kira's fortress. Kai looked from side to side; he felt as fascinated as the guard had been at the sight of the players. If Kira was attempting to capture the atmosphere of Ako Castle's preparations for the Shogun's visit, he had come close to succeeding, even here in this dismal, nearly inaccessible spot.

But the style and apparent richness of the decorations only reminded Kai that Kira had always preferred to spend his time in Edo, as close as possible to the Shogun's side, rather than here in this remote corner of the realm. He wondered where Kira saw himself residing in the future . . . if they failed to see him in hell tonight.

Up ahead plain undyed *tobari* marked off the stage area, with spaces for the actors, stagehands, and props set up and waiting. The disguised ronin split up, the men with the actor's troupe following Kawatake toward the stage, while the ones who were passing as porters laid their burdens down as directed, and then made their way around behind the audience seating to take up their watch positions.

Kai settled himself where he had a clear view of the stage and the one guard tower situated too close by for them to take out its sentry unobtrusively. From where he stood he was also set to relay Oishi's signal to Chikara, who was hidden out of sight, armed with a bow. The attack would not begin until after the play had started, and he had nothing to do until then but remain unnoticed, easy enough when he stayed in the shadows. He began to search the audience that was already gathering, trying anxiously to catch a glimpse of Mika.

Oishi, among the actors, peered out through a slit in the *tobari* at the back of the makeshift stage; his hand tightened with impatience on the hilt of Lord Asano's *tanto* as he waited with equal intentness for his first sight of Kira. . . .

Mika walked down the palace corridor, flanked by attendants, as radiant as a goddess in her wedding robes—a goddess of winter, with a soul of ice. She saw Kira waiting at the corridor's end to escort her outside for the inspection of the waiting crowd. The look of admiration in his eyes came as close to awe as anything she could have imagined. Seeing that look in anyone else's eyes—anyone's at all—might have stirred some warmth inside her. But the sight of his face only honed the edge on her loathing.

The servants she passed along the way bowed deeply. At the end of the row she was surprised to see the witch waiting alongside them, rather than beside Kira. Mitsuke was dressed in her usual elegant, sensuous layers of forest green; but today she bowed, as though she had been instructed to treat Lady Mika as if she were already Lord Kira's wife, someone whom she must serve. . . .

Mika caught the barest glimpse of the witch's expression before her graceful bow hid her face—saw the *kitsune*'s fury as the witch realized all chance of driving Mika to take her own life before the wedding was gone.

Mika felt her spirits rise as she saw her enemy's disappointment, and realized that she had been right. She had not surrendered to an act of treachery or her own despair. Even if everyone she had loved was dead, she still lived . . . and she would not rest until she had set free the souls of every one of them.

When she reached Kira's side he bowed to her as well, murmuring praise she ignored. She did nothing in return, as usual, but there was nothing she could do to prevent him from clasping her hand in an iron grip. They passed through the doorway to the outside and crossed the lower courtyard to the place where the guests were waiting expectantly.

They passed along the edge of the seated crowd to murmurs of congratulations, envy, and praise, and took their places in the first row, directly in front of the stage. Only then did Mika realize that the witch and Kira's monstrous bodyguard were positioned directly behind them.

On the rear wall of the fortress's upper courtyard, a lone guard restlessly paced back and forth, stopping frequently to warm himself by the stand that held a charcoal brazier. He cursed his fortune triply—for being born in this miserable land; for being born into the service of a lord like Kira; and tonight, most of all, for having been ordered to stand watch here, where he could scarcely even see the lights of the distant wedding celebration and his only view was of the castle's vertiginous wall and the cliffs below it, still shrouded in snow. The pinnacle of rock on which the fortress was located was so steep, and the space for construction so limited, that there was not even a lower courtyard on this side of the keep, since the cliffs had always been defense enough.

He pressed his hands against his frozen face until all the warmth was gone from them, and then held them out toward the brazier's stand again, staring at the snow-covered cliffs below him. And then he blinked suddenly and rubbed his eyes, wondering if a man could be dreaming wide-awake: The pristine sheets of snow that covered the slopes below seemed to be . . . moving. Upward. Toward him.

He left the brazier, taking his spear with him as he headed for the small footbridge that gave access to the castle's shrine, which sat precariously on its own separate spire of rock. The bridge would give him a clearer view; he had to be sure. If he was right, this would change his life forever. But if he was wrong, and he sounded an alarm now, he would find out personally whether the legends about this wall were true: that no one who had been pitched over it as punishment had even hit bottom yet.

In the lower courtyard, Kai restlessly paced back and forth in the shadows, straining for a clearer view of Mika. He had glimpsed her being guided to her place in the front row, along with Kira . . . but once they were settled and she was kneeling on a cushion, he could barely see anything but the top of her elaborate white headdress.

Looking out through the *tobari,* Oishi could now see both Kira and Mika perfectly, sitting directly in front of the stage. On stage, the musicians took their places. Okuda, the ronin who bore the closest physical resemblance to Kawatake, came forward to Oishi's side, looking ill, as if even facing a *kirin* would be preferable to facing a crowd of strangers while pretending he was someone else, and remembering to say words that were not his own. At least Kawatake's stage makeup covered the pallor of his skin. "Act like your life depends on it," Oishi whispered. "*All* our lives," he added, and gave Okuda a gentle shove.

He wondered how the musicians and chorus members felt—they were actual performers, since none of his men were familiar enough with *Noh* to take their places. Kawatake had chosen a warrior play taken from *The Tales of the Heike,* an episodic account of the Genpei War. Most of the ronin had seen the play, or at least read the stories it was based on. The drama, which most of the audience would recall at least vaguely, required little in the way of poetic speeches, and almost no dancing. And Oishi intended to bring it to an early end, as soon as all his men had had time to accomplish their assigned tasks.

Okuda walked out onto the stage with the bearing of a samurai, and Oishi saw with relief that only face-to-face was it actually obvious that the man was close to fainting. Clasping his shaking hands in front of him, Okuda bowed deeply to Lord Kira and the audience, and straightened up again. His eyes lingered on Lady Mika for a moment, as if the sight of her was like a beacon seen from a ship on stormy seas. Then, looking respectfully back at Kira, he said, "Lord Kira, we are proud to present to you our performance as a gift for your wedding."

And the play began.

The guard who thought he had seen the rocks—or at least the snow—move reached the spot on the wall where the bridge to the shrine joined it. He moved out onto the bridge, looking down at the face of the cliffs until he could get a clear view of the spot where he had seen the snow shifting.

Peering downward, he never saw the shadow that detached itself from the deeper darkness behind him before a hand covered his mouth and a knife cut his throat. The shadow pushed the man's body over the wall of the bridge, into the abyss below. The guard never knew when he finally hit the bottom.

The shadow materialized into the form of Yasuno, who stood on the bridge and waved his arms toward the snow-covered cliff.

For a moment there was no movement on the pristine white surface. And then the sheets of snow rippled and came alive, flying away into the wind like startled ghosts, as thirty men threw off their camouflage and at his signal began to climb the castle wall, forming a human pyramid as they found hand- and footholds in the chinks between the rough-cut blocks of stone that rose from the base of solid rock below.

As they reached the top of the wall and climbed over it, Yasuno gave them silent directions, and they moved away with equal silence, choosing targets among the guards stationed along the walls or positioned throughout the upper courtyard.

In the lower courtyard, the play was proceeding as everyone expected, so far—since it was based on a semi-legend that most educated people knew, as Kawatake had predicted.

The villain of the ancient tale was played by the ronin Fuwa, who was a natural in the part, Oishi thought, having a personality better suited to a battlefield than most. Fuwa emerged suddenly from between the *tobari* wearing period armor, including a general's helmet with a face guard painted red to symbolize rage. He forced the false Kawatake and the other actors to their knees.

Kira sat watching the play, so mesmerized by the unfolding story—and the unusually genuine emotion the performers conveyed within the stylized conventions of *Noh*—that he had even forgotten to look down constantly and fondly at Mika, who was kneeling beside him.

Mika seemed only vaguely aware of her surroundings, or even that for once he was paying no attention to her. Her eyes barely registered the action on the stage; her mind seemed to be wandering through worlds of its own, questioning, considering, rejecting choices as she played out possible scenarios within the unfolding drama of her own future. . . .

Oishi stopped watching her and Kira, when Horibe—dressed in the traditional all-black clothing of a stagehand—nudged him, holding out a helmet. Oishi tugged a last time at the elaborate, surprisingly solid armor of his own costume, before he exchanged an ironic glance and a grim nod with the old warrior. Then he settled the helmet with its protective half mask over his head, to become a Hero out of Legend, as well as to effectively disguise his face. Taking a traditionally flimsy prop sword from Horibe, he pushed through the curtains and strode out onto the stage.

As he made his appearance, Okuda/Kawatake—serving as narrator as well as an extra—rose to his feet in slightly hammy relief, and began to recount the singsong legend of the hero's mysterious birth. Oishi thanked the gods that it was a story everyone only knew vaguely.

Kawatake had rehearsed the ronin's parts with them on the way here, and reassured them that if they forgot a line they could be creative. The genuine actors rehearsed any role they played strictly on their own; they had only rehearsed this play once as a group. It was better done that way, Kawatake explained—it kept the actors' emotions fresh and the story alive if each performance was *wabi-sabi,* always subtly changing. Considering the troupe's reputation, Oishi assumed he must know what he was talking about.

But tonight's performance would be unique in a way no other would ever be, if the gods were smiling. . . .

Oishi confronted the enemy general, brandishing the fan they were all expected to use, and the prop sword that was hardly more substantial. But his real concentration was fixed on the true villain of the piece now, sitting barely twenty paces away from him in the audience.

Kai saw Oishi appear onstage, and saw where his real attention was fixed, on Kira. He moved out of the shadows into the lantern-light, where he would be visible to Chikara, and edged his way forward. He could see Kira's demon-masked samurai in the second row, with the witch at his side. Mika was kneeling in front of her, beside Kira . . . but even from here, Kai could barely see the profile of Mika's face. Wearing the white face powder and red-rouged lips of a lady at a formal occasion, she looked like a character from the play who had wandered into the audience, her expression as fixed as the mask of a *Noh* maiden.

He looked back at Oishi up on the stage, slowly maneuvering his way closer to the place where Kira sat, as he improvised a mock battle with Fuwa. *It was almost time.* He glanced up at the guard tower, and toward the area where he knew Chikara was waiting.

Mika's head moved slightly, her eyes wandering as if she was not even watching the stage—where she might at least have recognized Oishi's eyes, having known him all her life, and realized something unexpected was about to happen.

Kai began to move along the narrow space next to the audience, his back pressed against the *tobari* as he tried to reach a position closer to the spot where she was kneeling. *If her attention wandered enough, she might even look his way.* She was in danger where she sat, not just because Kira was beside her, but because the witch and the black-armored samurai were right behind her. *If he could let her know—*

On stage, Oishi struck a pose, gesturing like a magician with his fan. At his prearranged signal, lights were extinguished all around the courtyard, creating a moment of stunning supernatural effect onstage. The audience gasped in awe and appreciation, their attention—Kira's most of all—riveted on the actors.

No one glanced back, as Kai did, to see the guards disappear inside the two other watchtowers that were within his view.

It was all was going as planned. The darkness would give Yasuno and his men more freedom to approach the front of the upper courtyard, taking out more guards, laying charges in the armory, and spiking shut the doors to the barracks of the low-ranking samurai who made up the majority of the castle's defense.

Meanwhile, all around the lower courtyard, ronin dressed in the black clothing of stagehands were taking weapons out of hiding under the cover of the darkness.

On stage, Fuwa feigned an injury in the mock sword fight. Backstage Horibe and his fellow stagehands eliminated the guards who were keeping watch there, and unpacked the sharpened bamboo stakes Kai had shown them how to make.

The bamboo stakes were as effective as iron for digging into unmortared stone; ronin scattered, using them like claws to scale the wall of the upper courtyard.

As they reached the top they spread out, killing more guards with silent efficiency, and putting on armor to take their places.

Meanwhile, in the play within a play, Oishi neared the front of the stage, where the unsuspecting Kira gazed up at him in awe, so taken by the authenticity of the sword duel that he saw only a legend unfolding before his eyes, never imagining that the avenging hero's hate-filled eyes were focused on him—the true enemy still waiting to be slain.

Mika looked away again from the blur of motion in front of her, as her mind finally grasped the fact that Kira was so caught up in whatever was taking place in the play that she dared to shift her position, soothing her eyes by gazing at the shadows outside the glare of lanterns' lights onstage.

Kai saw her turn her head at last toward the place where he stood. He stepped forward just far enough for the light from the stage to illuminate his face, willing her to see—

Mika's eyes caught the motion as he suddenly appeared . . . found his eyes looking back at her, just as they always had, through so many years. But this time her gaze filled with disbelief and terror, instead of longing—as if she was seeing a ghost. Her hand went to her mouth.

But she went on staring at him, as certainty finally replaced the shock in her eyes, and her face filled with relief and joy. As he looked back at her, everything else ceased to exist . . . time itself stopped, capturing them inside a moment.

Kira glanced down at Mika. Seeing her staring off into space, he lowered his hand and took her lightly by the chin, turning her face back toward the stage as if she were a child.

Kai swore under his breath as Kira reached casually into their timeless moment, and stole her from him again. He stepped back into the shadows, struggling to make himself remember where he was, and why—knowing that even as her eyes had left him they had still been full of joy because she knew that he was here.

But that wasn't enough to make her realize the danger she was in. At least if she was looking up at the stage now she might recognize Oishi, and guess what was about to happen.

Kira's attention was fully on the stage again. At least Mika's wandering gaze had not aroused his curiosity. Kai kept his own eyes fixed on her face, hoping to see recognition there as she watched Oishi . . . hoping that she might even dare to glance his way again.

Watching Mika so intently, he did not even bother to glance at the demon-masked samurai, or the witch.

But Mika's transformed face had drawn the witch's attention. Wondering what could have changed her mood so suddenly and completely, Mitsuke glanced toward the spot she had been focused on. *Kitsune* eyes penetrated the shadows, to pin a face and then a name on the figure who stood just out of view, hidden in the darkness from everyone but her.

Her breath caught; her hand reached out, digging fingers like claws into the metal-plated leather gauntlet of the giant beside her. *The halfbreed with the demon sight was still alive.*

22

As the black-armored samurai beside her looked down at the witch's hand digging into his gauntlet, she leaned toward him and hissed a warning into his ear, nodding toward the place where Kai stood. Then, with a sudden premonition, she looked back at the stage again and used her skill at unmasking to search the faces of the players.

The demon samurai rose to his feet. His eyes scanned the castle walls, the watchtowers, and he realized that the guards he had put in place were no longer there. He drew his sword. The seated guests around them murmured in startled distress as he turned toward the place where Kai stood watching.

Chikara, hidden too far to the side to view the stage clearly, saw the samurai rise to his feet, turning toward the place where Kai should have been, drawing his sword. Chikara looked back, and saw Kai suddenly freeze, as if he had just seen the same thing.

Chikara ran back along the base of the upper courtyard wall, carrying his bow into plain sight, risking exposure for a position where he could see the stage, and his father, for himself. He saw his father, already near the front of the stage, toss away his helmet and his prop sword as Horibe appeared to hand him his *tengu* blade.

Frantically Chikara drew his bow, taking aim at the last

watchtower, the one with the direct view of the stage—and the guard he had been ordered to take out before the guard's arrow could stop his father.

Oishi started toward the edge of the stage, raising his sword. Chikara released his arrow, watching it arc upward toward the guard—

And saw it miss.

Before he could nock another arrow on his bowstring, or his father could reach Kira, the guard in the watchtower fired.

The guard's arrow struck Oishi's sword arm; his raised *katana* fell from the air, his right hand still clinging to the hilt but suddenly unable to lift it, as his other hand went to the wound and he staggered. The sword's point scraped the floor of the stage as Kira's gigantic bodyguard threw himself forward, blocking Kira like a human shield.

Oishi jerked the arrow from his arm as more guards leaped onto the stage, attacking him; Kai ran forward, drawing his own sword, as chaos broke out in the crowd and the other players on the stage ran for their weapons, or their lives.

People in the audience rose to their feet in panic, pushing, cursing, and screaming as they tried to escape the fight that had suddenly become all too real, as legend spilled over into reality.

The samurai in black and a cordon of a dozen guards surrounded Kira and Mika, hurrying them toward the upper courtyard and the safety of the palace, with the witch following in their wake. Horibe and his archers, positioned now along the upper courtyard wall, held their fire for fear of wounding Lady Mika if they tried for a shot at Kira, or even the guards around them whose positions were constantly shifting. They watched in frustration as the group guarding Kira and Mika disappeared into the zigzag security corridor that led to the upper level.

Behind them and beneath their feet, Horibe heard more shouts, along with pounding and splintering wood, as the troops who had been sealed into their barracks heard the commotion and began trying to hack or smash their way out to join the fighting.

In the lower courtyard, Kai and Oishi had shoved their way through the panic-stricken crowd, only to come up against a fresh line of guards as they fought their way to the walled corridor. Horibe and his men began firing on the guards who were coming toward them or still in their way, clearing a path to the upper courtyard entrance.

Looking back over his shoulder, Horibe saw Yasuno's ronin run forward to meet the men who were beginning to pour out of the barracks. Standing on the wall, Horibe shouted down to Yasuno, "Light it!"

Yasuno finished off the spearman he had been fighting, and headed toward the armory, followed by a handful of his men who made certain no one stopped him.

Kira arrived at the entrance to the upper courtyard with Mika and the witch, as the samurai in black ordered their shield of guardsmen back down the narrow corridor to halt anyone who tried to follow them. Kira stared in disbelief at the fighting that had already broken out on the upper level. Suddenly he spotted one of the ronin crouched by the door of the armory. He saw a spark of light.

"Stop him!" he shouted, pointing. The demon-masked samurai ran toward the armory, plowing his way through the battling warriors.

Oishi and Kai started up the narrow, twisting passage that led to the inner courtyard, only to be met by Kira's guards coming to confront them. Oishi cut down the first of the guards as Kai gutted the next one, but not before the third one rounding the corner raised his *katana* for a deadly overhand strike.

The blow never fell, as the sword stopped in midair, and the guard fell out from under it. He lay dead on the stones, with an arrow between his eyes.

Oishi looked back, stunned, to see Chikara at the foot of the ramp, lowering his bow. Their eyes met in the fleeting acknowledgement of a grateful warrior to his comrade as Chikara joined him and they followed Kai on up the passageway.

They fought their way into the upper courtyard just in time to see the samurai in black reach the armory. And then the sky turned blinding red and an earsplitting explosion staggered them, as the armory blew itself and the barracks around it to pieces, along with anyone still inside.

Cursing and holding their ears the three men ran for cover, along with everyone still fighting in the yard, as rubble and burning wreckage rained down on them. Kira's bodyguard had been standing in the armory's doorway; there was no doorway or armory to be seen now, only a smoking hole in the wall.

And no trace of a samurai in black, wearing a demon-faced mask. . . . Chikara laughed out loud in triumph. Oishi smiled a smile that held no elation, but enough satisfaction to make up for it. Only Kai's face wore no expression at all, as Oishi glanced back at him.

Behind them, part of the wall in the passageway collapsed into a smoking heap of stones, blocking the access from the lower courtyard against any other guards who had been trying to come up.

Oishi looked away again as the sounds of battle picked up in the yard, and saw his men fighting for their lives against too many of Kira's troops, who had escaped the barracks before the explosion.

"Kira—" Kai touched his arm, pointed, and headed toward the palace.

Oishi saw Kira still standing at the entrance with the witch, holding Mika's wrist in what was nearly a closed fist while he gaped at the results of the explosion . . . until suddenly he saw Kai, with Oishi standing behind him. His face paled visibly; he turned and disappeared into the palace, dragging Mika with him, the witch following. Oishi glanced at Chikara, who nodded and ran to join the others holding off Kira's troops, as Oishi followed Kai into the palace.

In the entry hall, Kai and Oishi came face to face with half a dozen more guards. As the guards surrounded them, they instinctively turned back to back, fighting with unspoken teamwork and an unflinching instinct for survival that Oishi had never realized he possessed before today. The two men fought Kira's six as if they were surrounded by wolves, and the *tengu* blades repaid every minor wound they took tenfold.

As they slashed their way through the barrier of guards, they saw Kira and Mika still on the other side of the hall, where Kira had stopped to watch them fight for their lives with the same breathless anticipation he had shown while watching the play.

But this time Mika's attention was fixed entirely on him. As Kai and Oishi cut through the last of the samurai, she pulled a dagger from her obi, and drove it into Kira's arm. With a curse he let her go, clutching his bloody sleeve. Mika turned and ran, disappearing down a side corridor. Looking back at Oishi and Kai, Kira pulled open a door behind him and abruptly vanished through it.

Kai and Oishi exchanged looks, neither one having to ask what the other's ultimate goal had always been.

"Go to Mika—" Oishi said, and started across the entry hall after Kira.

Kai ran toward the corridor Mika had taken. He shook the blood off his sword as he entered the hallway and saw more guards gathering ahead of him—as if they really thought they had a chance of stopping him now. . . .

Oishi pushed open the sliding panel and entered the palace, stepping through into a scene of more eye-stunning chaos. Terrified servants who had already seen their lord rush past, bleeding, stared at him as if Bishamon, the armor-clad god of vengeance, was invading the very heart of their castle, his sword dripping red and his eyes filled with an unsated hunger for retribution.

Oishi passed through their midst as if they didn't exist, barely slowing as he cut down another guard who tried to block his way.

He pulled open the next sliding panel he reached, and saw Kira at the end of the corridor beyond it, staring back at him in open alarm. As Oishi started toward him, Kira pushed aside another screen, and disappeared through the doorway.

By the time Oishi reached it, the room beyond was empty. Moving into the chamber, Oishi opened the next sliding panel he found, but again there was no sign of Kira beyond it—only a room with a dozen sliding screens located all around its walls. He realized he had entered a maze of interconnected chambers—that even within Kira's palace there were elaborate security measures designed to confound his enemies. *But this time nothing would be enough. . . .* Muttering a curse, he slid open a random door.

Mika ran out into a secluded section of the upper courtyard, a small open space enclosed by palace buildings and a high gated wall. It was a place she had never seen before, with a wide processional path down its center between two columns of towering stone lanterns nearly twice her height. She guessed this place must be meant for some religious ritual Kira did not observe, even though the palace servants kept the oil lamps within the gigantic pillars burning even now.

Even this closed-off area had been cleared of snow; but more snow had begun to fall, and already a thin layer was covering the flagstones, turning the space around her blue-white and golden in the light from the lanterns. She moved slowly out into the silent, pristine space, grateful for a moment's respite and time to think as she looked around her and saw that she was truly alone—

But only for a moment. She heard someone else enter the courtyard behind her and turned around, certain in her heart who it would be.

Kai— Her eyes filled with relief and then with joy as he stopped, gazing back at her. And then she ran to him and he took her into his arms, holding her as if he would never let go of her again.

"I knew you'd come," she murmured, looking up at him.

His eyes shone with the love that she had always seen there no matter how he'd tried to hide it, from himself as well as from her. Tenderly he touched her cheek. "Mika. . . ."

And then his arms pulled her to him and he kissed her hard on the lips, his eyes burning with a fierce, uninhibited passion she didn't recognize—like the hunger of a wild animal, nothing like the man she had always known.

And yet his lips were ice-cold. . . . Something inside her rebelled; she pushed him away, wiping her mouth, her reaction closer to fear than revulsion. *This was wrong, this wasn't*—

As she looked at him in stunned confusion, he pulled her close and smothered her mouth with another kiss. This time something in the contact seemed to paralyze her, as if the kiss was intended to steal her very soul. She struggled to break its hold, to free her will for just long enough to free her hands—

And then, suddenly, Kai recoiled. He stared at her, incredulous, before he looked down to see the *tanto* driven into his chest . . . the *tanto* she had used to wound Kira; the same one the witch had left her.

He looked up at her again, clutching the dagger with his hands, still with the same disbelief in his eyes.

Mika went on gazing at him, her own eyes filled with a molten fury that seemed to dissolve the mask of his deception until his features began to distort and shrivel like burning silk, revealing the face of the *kitsune*.

Before Mika's eyes the shape-shifter transformed back into a human woman, still struggling to pull the dagger out of her chest.

With all her strength Mika threw her body against Mitsuke's, driving the blade in up to the hilt, taking her vengeance at last against her cruelest and most insidious enemy: the one who had really been responsible for her father's death; who had almost stolen Kai's life from her, and her own life as well.

"Perhaps now you understand the price of my love." Her breath turned the air to frost as she released the dagger's hilt; her words were as remorseless as a blade of ice.

With an animal howl of agony and despair, Mitsuke collapsed on the paving stones. The seemingly solid form of her human body sublimed like melting snow, until there was nothing left except a dagger lying on the stones.

Mika looked down the bloodstained purity of her white robes to the spot where not even a tuft of white fur remained on the flagstones at her feet. Looking up again, she saw the footprints of a running fox appear in the snow, as the vixen fled back into the invisible world where she belonged, the moonshadow world of the *yokai.*

Mika's gasp of relief hung in the cold air as she turned toward the palace entrance again, and saw Kai . . . the genuine Kai . . . leaning against the doorway, as if his own relief had left him strengthless. He looked back at her, his sword running red with blood, his clothing covered with it, but his gaze filled with an emotion that she had seen, and understood, from the first moment she laid eyes on him.

Almost hesitantly, he began to move out into the courtyard. A crooked smile spread across his face; his eyes were filled with pride, respect, and love, telling her that he had witnessed her vengeance against the *kitsune,* and was glad. She started toward him; his pace quickened as he saw the certainty in her eyes—

But then suddenly his gaze leaped from her face to something in the air above her. His expression changed as he ran forward, his free arm sweeping her aside as he brought up his sword.

Mika turned, stumbling against a lantern's base as she looked back. An enormous white snake hovered overhead as if it had materialized out of the falling snow and darkness. The demon snake dove toward her, then veered suddenly from its path to attack Kai as he came between them. It's mouth opened wide, revealing long glistening fangs as it spat venom at him. Forced to dodge aside as he swung his blade, he only managed to shear off some of the demon's tangled mane. As the long black-and-silver strands fell free they transformed into strands of rainbow, like brightly dyed silk from a kimono. The strands ignited in the flame of a lantern, and vanished like tendrils of smoke.

"Down—!" Kai shouted, as the snake whipped back around in midair. It dove toward her again as if it only had eyes for her; she gasped as she realized that one of its eyes was blue, and the other one was brown.

She fell to her knees, covering her head as the demon swept past. Its burning breath seared her hands; she cried out as its heavy tail struck her side and knocked her flat. Toppling the stone lantern behind her, it whiplalshed again in midair to confront Kai's next attack.

Kai pushed off from the base of another lantern, leaping higher than she would have believed possible as the snake lunged at him. He twisted as lithely as the demon itself as it tried to sink its fangs into his body, or crush him against the lantern's stone and flames; his blade slashed downward, striking the snake's blue eye. The snake shrieked in pain and fury as it crashed into the lantern, breaking it in two. Kai tumbled to the ground, and falling debris from the lantern's shattered column rained down on top of him.

But the lantern's topmost piece, which sheltered the burning oil lamp, struck the snake's head and sprayed its body with flaming oil. The snake's mane ignited, and then red and gold flames spread along its entire length, flinging off rainbow sparks.

Shrilling with rage and half blind, the demon crashed into more lanterns; its writhing body knocked them over, scattering flaming debris across the courtyard. But still it hurled itself headlong toward Mika, as if it was determined to immolate her along with itself. Still dazed from its first blow, Mika struggled in her heavy garments to drag herself out of reach as the flaming apparition plunged toward her like a meteor, its savage mouth gaping wide, toppling more lanterns as it came. She covered her head against the hail of debris, and shut her eyes at the sight of death descending to clim her.

And then lightning seemed to strike itself, in a blinding flash and whirlwind that took place inside her mind more than in midair.

She cried out, and the sense-twisting, invisible blow forced her eyes open in spite of her fear just in time to see the snake vanish as impossibly as the witch had. But this time there was not even a trace of an invisible spirit fleeing, only a last wisp of smoke that transformed into mist, and was lost in the falling snow. Mika's eyes searched the yard in stunned confusion. Kai had vanished, too, from the place where he had fallen after blinding the snake's blue eye.

A sound behind her made her look over her shoulder in sudden alarm. Her breath caught as she found Kai beside her, down on one knee and leaning heavily on his sword, still breathing hard as he glared up at the sky. Strangely viscous blood covered his sword's blade from its tip to its hilt—and what looked to her dazzled mind like the echo of a burning demon still deep in his eyes.

"Kai . . . ?" she whispered. Even that one word almost failed her, as she found him kneeling so close to her that she could touch him—but on the opposite side from the place where she had seen him attack the snake in midair. She shook her head, blinking. *How—?* She pushed herself up, trying to get him to meet her eyes.

Kai looked away instead as he shook the demon's blood from his sword and thrust it back into its sheath. Then, hesitantly, he turned back, reached out to push aside her hood. "Mika, I—" He broke off, glancing down. "I mean, my lady . . ." he murmured, withdrawing his hand, and instead kneeled and made a formal bow before her, as if they were strangers. The echo of demon-fire was gone as he glanced up again, but not the hesitation, and in his eyes the soul-deep concern seemed to border on fear. "Are you . . . unhurt?"

"I'm fine . . . now." She smiled back at him in tender reassurance. Raising a hand she caressed his face, and gently raised his chin with her fingertips until he no longer bowed even slightly before her. His concern changed to relief as her eyes met his without hesitation. "Oh, Kai, I thought . . . they told me you were dead!" Her voice trembled with reaction as she remembered her first glimpse of him during the play, when she'd thought she'd seen a ghost. The smile on her lips spread to her eyes.

Kai took a deep breath of relief and smiled at last, tentatively, as she smiled at him with all her heart. Mika let go of the question that it was impossible to ask now, or even find words for. *She must have been dazed, or too terrified to remember clearly how he had come to be standing beside her.* "How . . . how did you kill it?" She raised her hand, gesturing at the air above the boulder field of broken lanterns.

Kai glanced down at his *katana*, and his smile widened. "It's a good blade," he said, as if the sword deserved all the credit. She only then fully grasped that he wore two swords at his side—and his hair tied back like a ronin's. Suddenly the memories of the slain *kirin*, and the way he had fought in the arena at Ako Castle, filled her head and left her mind even more dazzled. For the first time in her adult life, she dared to wonder how Kai could possibly have learned to slay demons like a legendary hero . . . *like a* tennin.

She looked away, and up, as she asked, "Was that . . . Mitsuke? I thought that I—killed her." She dropped her gaze toward the spot where she had seen the footprints of an invisible fox disappearing in the night.

"You did kill her." Kai followed her gaze. "As far as this

world is concerned. . . . You destroyed her avatar; our plane of existence is closed to her. She was very powerful, very old . . . but she'll never ruin another human life." He glanced away at the dagger still lying on the flagstones, slowly disappearing under a layer of fresh snow.

"Then what was *that*—" She pointed at the empty air above the tumbled stone lanterns, "if it wasn't her?"

A look oddly like sorrow touched his face. "That was something . . . different." He shook his head. "Most *yokai* want nothing to do with humans. When shape-shifters put on a human form it's usually trickery to gain something that they really want. *Yokai* don't possess *yokai*. But there are some demons that feed on human emotions, and they do possess humans." He glanced away. "The one you saw feeds on jealousy; it was possessing Mitsuke."

"It had her eyes . . ." Mika whispered. But then she leaned forward, catching hold of his jacket. "But how could anything have grown that monstrous feeding on Mitsuke's *human* jealousy? She wasn't human!"

"That's why it was so terrible . . . so powerful, I mean." He grimaced, and something in his voice caused her to wonder again how he knew so much about *yokai* and their ways. The same thought kept her silent, although she was sure he could read it in her face.

Kai only said quietly, "Mitsuke would never have become fully human—but she was in love with Kira. It's said if a human truly falls in love with a *kitsune*—if he unselfishly gives her his whole heart—the witch may become human enough to return his love . . . a human love." He looked toward the barred gate at the end of the courtyard. "Kira must have loved her that deeply, once."

"I . . ." Mika bit her lip. "I thought that when a human 'freely gave his heart,' it meant a living, beating heart, torn from his chest." She shuddered, and pressed her hand against her own heart, finding cold comfort in the proof that it was still beating. She remembered the false Kai's kiss: *It had felt as though the* kitsune *was trying to suck the breath, the very heart, out of her—to steal her soul.* "But why would any kind of demon ever want to feel what a human feels?"

Kai only shrugged and climbed wearily to his feet, still avoiding her gaze. "Who knows?"

She said nothing, remembering how deeply her soul had been blighted by the same corruption that had destroyed the rarest love imaginable, the love that had once existed between her captors. *Kira had even destroyed that, with his poisoned touch.*

And then she remembered the many times when she had looked at Kai, and seen her own yearning reflected in the eyes of the man everyone around her called a demon. . . .

He turned back at last and she looked up at him. Without hesitation she accepted the hands he held out to help her rise.

23

Oishi circled the empty room, pulling open one screen and then another. Each sliding panel opened on another chamber filled with sliding walls; the labyrinth had multiplied his choices until he had no way of making a rational decision, or even a likely guess about which one Kira had chosen to escape through. He realized he might never find his own way out of here . . . and that Kira's guards were likely to find him before he ever laid eyes on Kira.

His hand tightened around his sword hilt in frustration until pain shot up his arm. He glanced down, and saw that the blood covering his hand and running down the *katana*'s blade now was all his own. His mind had been so focused on pursuing Kira and fighting off his samurai that he had not even registered the pain from his arrow wound until now. He was still wearing his costume armor from the play; pulling loose a sash, he wrapped it tightly around the bloody gash, knotting off the end.

He wiped his sword clean and sheathed it, looking down at the stain his blood had left on the matting. *At least he would be able to track his own blood back to the entrance. . . .*

And all at once he realized that there was a way to track Kira. *Lady Mika had marked Kira as prey, when she had wounded him with the dagger.* It didn't matter how serious the wound was—it had been enough to leave a trail of blood.

Carefully Oishi retraced his own path back to the first doorway. Crouching down, he searched the spotless matting around the door where Kira had entered the first room. . . . *There.* Not so spotless after all: A small red stain, not from his own bleeding arm, showed on the *tatami* by the entrance. He touched it with a finger; it was wet.

His eyes scanned the floor in widening circles from that point until he found another, and then another—leading him directly to the screen he needed to pass through. He moved on, into the next room, following the faint trail of Kira's blood to another closed screen.

He opened it, finding another chamber beyond. Still tracking Kira's blood-trail, he entered yet another mazelike room.

But this one held no clues at all, as if Kira had realized that his blood was leaving a trail, or as if he had felt secure enough to stop and cover the wound with a bandage of some sort. Safe enough to stop running . . . but not to stop hiding, in his attempt to save his worthless life from the retribution it had earned.

If that was the case, Oishi knew he would find Kira somewhere in this room. He drew his sword again, and moved along the walls as quietly as possible, listening for any sounds, easing open any panel that would slide with his free hand.

He had gone nearly halfway around, and had just begun to push open another screen, when Kira's sword shot out through the opening and drove deep into his shoulder.

As Kai helped Mika to her feet, a shadow fell across them.

He glanced up, startled, just as a giant's fist in steel-plated leather came at him out of nowhere and knocked him sprawling.

Kira's demon-masked warrior strode past Mika as if she didn't exist, toward the place where Kai lay. As he walked, he drew the blue-black *odachi,* ready to finish the battle they had begun in the arena at Ako Castle a year ago, when their duel before the Shogun had thrown their entire existence out of balance, and sent them all spinning into the abyss.

Kai staggered upright, his feet slipping in the new-fallen snow, stunned as much by what he saw confronting him now as by the blow—and yet somehow not surprised at all. He waved Mika back out of harm's way as he drew his sword, knowing he would need every bit of his concentration just to save his own life.

The demon warrior had escaped unscathed from the exploding armory. And it was a demon. If he had ever had any doubts, they were gone now. Nothing human-made could kill a demon protected by sorcery. And even though the witch was gone, the warrior's armor still scintillated with the protection of her spell-weavings, and the demon-face of its mask still writhed and shifted in his sight until he was forced to look away.

Whoever—whatever—inhabited that armor still lived, and no one else was controlling its actions. Mitsuke had not summoned it, yet the demon had come for him anyway, on unfinished business; it had a memory and a will of its own. Kai was certain it had enough intelligence to take full advantage of everything it knew. If it killed him, where would it go then . . . and what would it do, when all it knew was killing and destruction?

And who would there be who could stop it?

Oda Nobunaga, the first of the Three Unifiers who had ended the Age of Wars, had taken almost complete control of Japan; but he had been such a monster that his own generals had turned on him and killed him. He had been called "the Demon King" by some, who had claimed he truly was a demon, and would someday return to take his revenge. Like the thing confronting him now, Oda had been the perfect tyrant, combining a demonic will with a soul as hollow as the soul of whatever was facing him now.

Japan would probably survive a Shogun the people called "*Inu-Kubou.*" But what would happen if they faced one called *"Oni-Kubou"* . . . who might just rule forever?

Even on the Dutch Island, fighting day after day after day to survive until he had lost all memory of time, of the deaths on his conscience, of his own identity . . . even then Kai had never come to crave swords for their cutting edge, or killing for the sake of death. While he still possessed a mind capable of thought, all he had dreamed of, all he had prayed for, was to be returned to the world of things that a sword had only been meant to protect, to defend.

His prayers had been answered . . . and this was his karmic debt. In his hands he held a *tengu* sword, a true death-dealing blade . . . and the chance to make it a life-giving one. A demon blade, against a demon warrior.

But still, his own body was only human—

"What is learned in the cradle is carried to the grave," the *tengu* lord had told him, when he was young. He had learned to fight like a demon, and his year in the hell of Dejima had honed his rusty skills until they were in every way the equal of the sword he held. This time he would not fail, because the alternative was unthinkable.

A rush of purifying energy cleared his head like a freshening wind as he raised his *katana* to meet the attack of the approaching warrior. As they began to circle, as intent as two carnivores, he heard the distant sounds of the battle still being fought between the other ronin and Kira's men, and remembered his concern about Oishi finding Kira. But everything, even Mika's presence, faded as the world around him shrank until it contained only the orbit of two bodies in motion.

Kai let go, falling into the silence at his center, becoming hyper-aware not just of his opponent's slightest movements, but also his own. He heard their feet shifting cautiously on the rubble-strewn flagstones, where more snow was collecting, hiding icy pavement. He estimated how much of his energy he had used up in his battle just to reach this point, and in entering the *yokai* Path to kill the demon snake; how much lost blood every smarting cut on his body signified . . . things not to be afraid of, but simply considered. They were limits—there were always limits, and limits could be overcome, but not forever.

He remembered his enemy's fighting style, and how to defend himself against the demon's superior strength and reach; but he had no idea what his opponent's limits were, or even if the explosion had affected them at all. He would find that out soon enough—

Their cautious circling ended in an explosion of movement, as the warrior attacked him almost faster than his eyes could follow. His sword collided with the demon's as he blocked the angled downswing and skidded under the giant's arm, hearing the blade hit the pavement behind him.

He swung back around, using his momentum on the ice to bring his own sword into position faster and harder, only to see sparks fly as the demon's blade ran up it, jumped the hilt, and almost took his head off. Kira's champion hadn't forgotten how *he* moved, either.

Kai let his eyes slip out of focus, for a split-second, until the *odachi* and the huge figure in front of him were a moving whole amid the forest of lanterns, the piles of broken stone. He surrendered his tight focus on the demon's sword, letting go of all conscious thought—releasing his entire body to react with moves so deeply conditioned that they were almost instinct, gaining him one step ahead in time.

He struck and parried, leaped and kicked, slid and dodged, using the hazards all around them for distraction and defense. His mind was aware only of a blur of motion that seemed to merge their two bodies and blades into a single entity, a vision of the whirling heart of chaos. The showering sparks, the deafening clang of metal on metal, the jarring impact of deflected blows as their swords collided went on until he began to feel as if his bones would crack and split, although neither of them had yet managed to land a solid blow on the other.

Gasping for breath, his lungs burning for air and his muscles burning from exertion, Kai used the rebound from another strike to slide out of range. He could read no emotion in the sulfur-yellow eyes behind the demon warrior's mask; the hideous writhing shapes on the metal might as well be the demon's true face, because nothing truly human could possibly ever have existed inside it.

The enemy came after him, not giving him time for more than two or three deep breaths before he had to leap backwards again to keep the blue-black length of steel from cutting him in half. He skidded to a stop by an intact lantern; pushed off from the stone pillar, giving him the speed to duck under his opponent's reach, bringing his *katana* up in a sideward slash—

The blow fell short of a serious wound, but Kai shouted in elation: The *tengu* blade hadn't shattered—it had sliced through the coruscating black armor as if the demon was wearing bamboo, and drawn blood, or something like it.

The demon samurai glanced down, more startled than concerned; then looked up at Kai's sword. Kai saw a reaction show at last in the eyes behind the mask; like distant lightning that warned of a storm, it somehow conveyed both surprise and consternation, as well as something far more terrifying. . . .

The demon started toward him again, sword high, without hesitation.

Oishi's half curse, half cry of pain as Kira jerked the sword out of his flesh disappeared into the noise of his own sword slashing apart the screen as he attempted to cut Kira down. But the blade struck only thin air. He plunged through the ruined screen into the next room.

The next room was another maze of sliding walls, and Kira was nowhere to be seen. Oishi sheathed his sword and pressed his hand against his bleeding shoulder; the blood spilled through his fingers like water through a broken dam as he stood in the doorway of the new room . . . or was it one he had seen before? He had paid so little attention to the imagery on the walls that he could be chasing Kira in circles, for all he knew.

He forced himself to control his breathing, which was still ragged with pain, and tore a sleeve off his costume. He wedged the wad of cloth under his armor's padding and straps, grimacing as he put pressure on the wound. It wasn't near anything vital; he would be all right as long as he didn't let the shock make him dizzy. Standing perfectly still, he let focus and concentration take root again in his mind as he listened for the slightest sound. His breath caught as he heard the creak of wood, somewhere.

He looked around the room from screen to painted screen, this time deliberately ignoring the distraction of their too-similar paintings of flowers and birds, trying instead to use the fact that they were only translucent paper, which would reveal light and shadow. He searched each one carefully, focusing on the area where he thought he had heard a sound. Behind one of the screens, he made out a faint shadow.

He lowered his hand from his shoulder, wiping it clean of blood, and unsheathed his *katana* again as he began to walk toward the shadowed screen, and then intentionally walked on past. At the sound of a faint creak behind him, he lashed outward with his sword in a reverse strike.

As if the *tengu* blade had a sixth sense as ironic as it was deadly, it tore through the paper panel and slashed Kira's shoulder, almost exactly as Kira had done to him. Kira fell back with a cry, and Oishi turned in his tracks, ripping his way into the next room, to finally stand face-to-face with the man he had come to hate more than he loved his own life.

Kira was on his feet, bleeding too, but with both his *katana* and his *wakizashi* drawn. His whole manner had changed like the eyes of a cat: His stance was expert, as if he had suddenly remembered—now that his own life was truly in danger, and his opponent's ability to fight was doubly impaired—that he was an able swordsman.

Oishi moved in on Kira heedlessly, as memories drove into his brain like a *tanto*'s blade: *humiliation, loss and cruelty; heartbreak, physical pain and excruciating death*—every outrage, every act of betrayal, from the petty to the unspeakable, that had driven him to this moment. His soul filled with a need to see the man before him lying dead, a need that stripped away all skin-deep pretense of honor or fair play. There might be only two of them on this field, but outside his men were engaged in a battle for their lives. This was war—the worst of times in a human life—and there was nothing further from the noble sentiments of *Bushido* than what he was feeling now. This was the territory of demons, and now he knew at last that all men were demons, under their skin.

Kira suddenly lunged at him, with a deadly feint-and-thrust. But the most skillful move Kira knew was no match for Oishi's fury. Oishi blocked him with the *tengu* blade, and sent the *wakizashi* spinning out of his hand. Beating back Kira's *katana* with a brutal flurry of blows, Oishi drove him instantly onto the defensive and barely able to maintain that.

Oishi forced the other man back across the chamber, the way Kai had once driven him backwards across the arena on Dejima and beaten him down in a frenzy of madness that no sane mind could defend against.

Knocking the sword from Kira's hand with a final blow, Oishi dropped his own sword and grabbed Kira by the front of his robes, hurling him to the floor. Using his bare fists, he beat Kira's struggling, clawing, kicking body into submission.

Oishi pulled back at last, the worst of his rage spent, and hauled Kira, battered and bleeding, up onto his knees. He stood over him, drawing Lord Asano's *tanto* from its sheath on his belt. Pulling together the last shreds of his own sense of honor, he held the knife out, hilt-first, in front of Kira's eyes.

The giant in black armor started toward Kai again, now stalking him deliberately, as if the demon's awareness of the unusual sword its foe carried had only heightened its sense of his human weakness—the toll that exhaustion and blood loss would take on even the strongest man. As long as the enemy was sure Kai himself was only human, despite the sword he held, it could be equally certain that he was swiftly reaching the end of his endurance.

Kai backed away, suddenly too aware of the icy ground beneath his feet, the scattered rubble from broken lanterns that could betray him at any slight misstep; too aware in his own mind that the strain of the battle was beginning to affect his coordination and speed. It was only luck and instinct that had let him score that last blow, the one that had cut through the demon's armor. . . .

But he had cut through the demon's armor. The image of Yasuno's fine steel *katana* shattering like glass the last time they had fought had haunted him ever since. *But this sword was different.* His opponent's witch-crafted armor offered no unnatural protection against him now. This time it would be blade on blade, even if both blades had been forged by demonspell.

The demon samurai struck at him with vicious suddenness, and Kai parried with the flat of his sword, the blades *screel*ing as they collided and slid apart. Kai dodged away from the interrupted strike, scrambling out of the demon's reach.

But this time his foot slipped on a hidden patch of ice, and his body couldn't recover. The demon reversed its blade; the cutting edge caught Kai from behind, laying open his back from the shoulder down.

Kai cried out as pain lashed down his spine like a whip strike and his back burned with his own blood. He skidded and then stumbled, falling—

He hit the flagstones and slid across the snow-covered pavement in a smear of blood, hanging onto his sword as if it truly was his soul, until he slammed to a stop against the pile of shattered stone at the base of a broken lantern.

He lay on the freezing ground, unable to get up or even to

lift his hand; barely able to draw a breath, through an agonizing moment when he thought the demon's sword had crushed his spine. Only able to move his eyes, he saw the look on Mika's face, saw her start toward him—

No, run, get away—! Lacking even the voice to warn her, Kai threw all his will against the paralysis that seemed to have seized him from head to foot. His hands twitched, and he gasped in desperate relief as he began to drag his sword in toward his body. He forced more air into his lungs, realizing as he did that he'd only been stunned by the blow, not paralyzed. He struggled upright until he got his feet under him again, and dragged himself up the pillar's broken column until he was leaning against it, his sword in his hand. He waved Mika away, needing desperately to prove to her, to his attacker . . . to himself, that the wound hadn't crippled him.

And it hadn't—but it was bleeding badly, and he had no time to do anything about that. The numbness he felt spreading through his body wasn't simply from the cold . . . more sword fights ended when someone bled to death than from a direct killing strike. He needed to finish this, soon. *A single, killing strike.* And he knew exactly how to do it . . . as surely as he knew that he didn't have enough strength left in him to enter the *yokai* Path again.

He held the *tengu* sword more tightly in his hands. Samurai believed a sword was an extension of a man's soul. It was even said that some swords had a soul of their own, good or evil depending on how much blood they had taken, and whether it came from enemies or from victims—that the soul of such a sword could come to possess its owner. . . .

Would the blade of an ageless demon lord grant a willing human a demon's strength, spellbind him for long enough to make one perfect strike, without claiming his soul forever?

Kai focused on the sword in his hands, and felt a throbbing ache begin behind the scars on his forehead. He ignored it, as he ignored everything else now but the faint aura he saw beginning to shine around his blade. Whether it would grant him one boon, or curse him forever, he had no other choice—he opened his mind to the flow of *chi* in the sword's shining aura.

Yes! he thought, to the unspeakable question, and felt something uncoil inside his brain, a savage, seductive corruption that made everything he knew meaningless, except for the understanding of exactly how easy it was to destroy anything he desired: love, hope, self-respect . . . even a demon.

He could see the shimmering aura of *yokai* power radiating from his enemy; see the spot where his sword had slashed through the spell-infused black armor crackling like flames—breaking up the fluid perfection of the magic that protected its wearer. He wondered what the demon warrior saw now, from where it stood watching him.

Again something showed in the eyes behind the demon mask; something as disturbed as it was disturbing, this time. The sulphur-yellow irises began to glow, reddening around the edges as if they were heating in a forge: *A demon knew a demon, when it saw one.* Kai started forward, raising his sword, no longer permitting himself to be prey without hunting in return. . . .

Oishi stood looking down at Kira's battered face, into his terrified eyes. Disgust filled his own expression as he continued to offer Kira Lord Asano's dagger, hilt first. "Know now the depth of Lord Asano's courage—"

He waited, holding the dagger out in hands that dripped with blood . . . waiting to see if Kira had the strength of will to take responsibility for his own life, let alone to acknowledge the evil he had done to others.

Lord Asano had done nothing to deserve death, at his own hands or anyone else's. He had been betrayed by Kira. But with selfless courage and honor, he had sacrificed his life for the sake of others—taken on the burden of protecting his family and the people around him, hoping that with his actions he might be able to save the House of Asano, and Ako, from what he had already known was their likely fate.

Kira shrank back from the dagger, the blood, and all it implied, as if even now he believed there was no blood on his own hands, simply because he had always used others—humans, and even *yokai*—as cat's-paws. "Your master tried to murder me in my sleep!" he shouted. "He broke the laws of the land—"

"And you broke the laws of nature." Oishi stood over Kira, gazing down at him with the merciless eyes of Bishamon, the samurai's god of judgment. When Kira still made no move to take the dagger, Oishi dropped to his knees again, turning the *tanto* in his hands. He drove the blade into Kira's belly, jerking it across and up, the way Lord Asano had done, as against his will he had watched every nightmarish second of his own noble lord's suffering; as he had waited, praying for the sign to act—to end his lord's agony the only way he could, by murdering the man he honored, respected, and believed in above all others. . . .

Kira made an indescribable noise of horror and disbelief. He looked down in bewilderment as his own blood and entrails spilled over his hands, covering his elegant, richly-woven wedding garments in lurid red and purple.

Leaving the knife where it was, Oishi pushed to his feet. Tears burned his face, for the first time since that terrible day a year ago, as he moved back across the room to pick up his *tengu* blade.

Standing over Lord Kira again, Oishi held the sword above his head. "In the name of Lord Asano of Ako . . ." he murmured.

Kira's agonized eyes widened in fear, and then he bared his neck in acceptance of the mercy blow that would end his suffering, and his life.

Just as he had for Lord Asano, Oishi raised his blade, and brought it cleanly down.

Fountaining blood, Kira's body collapsed on itself and toppled over at Oishi's feet.

One man—so much blood. . . .

Oishi stood looking down for what seemed like an eternity after the final moment . . . staring not at the lifeless corpse, or even the expression frozen on the face of Kira's disembodied head . . . but at his own reflection, shimmering in the lake of Kira's blood.

The two demon warriors circled, locked in mutual obsession as the snow went on falling, shrouding the world that lay now beyond Kai's reach. Grays faded out of existence, narrowing everything to absolutes until only black and white remained . . . *life and death . . . but which was which . . . ?*

Kai stayed well beyond the reach of the demon's sword; he saw that the demon made no effort to close the gap between them, as if it was now equally cautious. The movements of the two swordsmen slowed until finally possessor and possessed both stood motionless with swords poised, as if the icy paralysis of spell and counterspell had frozen them in place. Deliberately Kai closed his eyes.

And the black-armored warrior attacked.

The space between their two separate figures vanished in a streak of blinding gold, as they transfigured into one entity that smashed its own defenses like waves in a violent crosscurrent, exploding into a spray of crimson.

Kai fell to his knees as reality re-formed beneath his feet, and the demon slid past him. The armored giant circled back, moving through an arc without seeming to move at all on the frozen surface of the courtyard. Kai struggled to his feet, leaning on his sword, staggering as he turned to face his enemy. With an effort he raised his head, waiting, watching with fathomless eyes as the demon warrior readied the *odachi* for another strike. . . .

And then, at last, he saw what he had been waiting to see, as a sudden line of red split open the front of the demon's black armor.

The tengu *blade had found its mark.*

The inside of Kai's vision turned white-hot again as the armor's spell broke and spirit-energy zigzagged like lightning down the split. Blood as red as any human's spewed from the wound, turning the snow scarlet. Kai heard Mika's cry of awe and horror from somewhere far away. He didn't even glance toward her, only went on relentlessly watching his enemy die.

The masked warrior's breathing came in strangled heaves as the demonic face looked down at the wound in disbelief. The sword fell from its gauntleted hands as whatever had worn a samurai's armor and walked like a man collapsed onto its knees. Its hands clutched the front of the armor as if somehow it could seal the black metal plates together again over the gap where its life was spilling out.

And then it collapsed facedown, motionless.

Kai stared at the body until he was certain it would never move again, and then for a moment longer. There was no emotion inside him at all that he could name—no pride, no satisfaction, not even a trace of reluctant gratitude to the demons who had made him into a demon-killer. *Relief.* Maybe that. Maybe there was that much human feeling left in his soul. The sword dropped out of his grasp and clattered on the stones.

At last, with a painful effort, he turned back to face Mika, and saw her staring at him, as motionless and expressionless as Yukihime, the goddess of winter. *No . . . not expressionless . . .* stunned, confused, terrified . . . *afraid even to move.*

Mika—His lips formed the word, like a talisman, a prayer, a plea; but he had no voice. He looked at her, helpless, and all at once he remembered longing, grief, desperation—

"Kai . . . ?" Her voice trembled as she called out to him. And then suddenly her eyes filled with the joy of prayers answered, and he realized that the only fear she had felt had been for his sake—for his safety, for his very life—and now at last she was certain that he was the one who had survived. Her face turned luminous as she smiled in the way that she had only ever smiled at him, with all her love—as if nothing he could do, even demon sorcery, would shake her belief in who he truly was.

Love . . . pride, satisfaction, gratitude; he felt them all, overwhelmingly, as he looked back at her. He turned away from the demon of death and the demon-slaying sword as he started toward her, his body filled with the strange sensation that he was walking on clouds. Some part of him realized that he was getting light-headed, but whether he was halfway to collapsing, or halfway to heaven, he had no idea. Mika met him halfway, burying her face against his chest as if the only thing she needed to know was that his heart was still beating. He thought he heard her murmur, "Oh, my *tennin*. . . ." But that made no sense.

All he knew was that he was holding her in his arms at last, and there was, for that moment, nothing in his mind but perfect peace.

Yasuno and his remaining men, along with Chikara, Horibe, and the last of the ronin who had escaped from the lower courtyard, were fighting with their backs against the wall, literally now. The sheer numbers of Kira's warriors had forced them to retreat until they were pinned against the wall of the palace itself, with nowhere left to turn. Only the unmatchable *tengu* swords had kept them alive and still fighting back for this long; but even so, they were reaching their own inescapable human limits of strength and endurance at last.

The ronin huddled closer together in the bloodstained snow as Kira's samurai closed in on them, about to overwhelm their defense from all sides—

And then suddenly Kira's men stopped pressing forward. They lowered their weapons and began to back away, as disbelief and terror filled their faces.

The ronin glanced at one another in confusion, too dazed

for a moment to realize that Kira's men weren't staring at them, but at something behind them. . . .

Oishi.

Oishi emerged from the palace entrance and halted at the top of the steps. In one hand he held Kira's severed head by its hair, and in the other, the bloody *tanto.* He stood staring out at the mob of enemy soldiers.

Stillness descended on the courtyard like falling snow. All that Oishi could hear was the muted sound of banners flapping in the wind. He stood above his beleaguered men, facing Kira's samurai, holding their lord's head aloft for all of them to see. He stayed that way, motionless, expectant; waiting for the arrows, the spears, the swords that would close the circle of vengeance, so that the greater circle of time itself could move forward.

But no arrow struck him, no spear, no sword. Not one of the enemy made a move toward any of his men. They simply stared at him as he stood before them in the armor of their warrior ancestors, holding aloft their *daimyo*'s severed head. His expression showed no fear, no doubt, only the righteous anger of Bishamon's divine justice. . . .

The shock and disbelief on their faces began to transform into something more. One by one, they dropped their weapons and fell to their knees in the snow, bowing in surrender.

Kai and Mika emerged from the palace, Kai leaning heavily on Mika's shoulder, their own faces filled with uncertainty at the sudden silence that had replaced the sounds of battle. They stood together in the entrance, registering the same astonishment as they gazed at the victorious ronin, gathered now around Oishi in front of the palace entrance—and Kira's head, still held high in Oishi's grasp, as Kira's samurai bowed before them in surrender.

"For Lord Asano!" Oishi shouted, and Lord Asano's ronin cheered.

24

Dawn broke over the mountains, and sunrise brightened the stark monochromes of Kira's fortress, painting the walls and keep briefly with the vivid reds and golds of Ako's surviving banners, as the ronin and Lady Asano prepared their horses and themselves for the long journey back to their home.

The indigo and gray of the defeated Kira colors hid in the shadows as all the men who were able to work packed supplies and assembled litters to carry home the men who were not. Kira's former samurai helped fetch and carry, under Oishi's watchful eye. With his right arm bandaged and in a sling from the wound Kira had given him, he wasn't up to anything more physically challenging himself.

His mind was still too numb to be anything but glad for the help, right now. It astonished him that all of his own men had actually survived the night. No one had survived uninjured, and some of them were so badly wounded that they had to be transported on the litters. But they would all live to see Ako again; somehow he was certain of that.

They had all been willing to die last night . . . some might even have preferred it. But the justice they had sworn their life's blood to claim would not truly be complete until they had returned to Ako Castle, to Lord Asano's grave, and presented his spirit with the proof that the wrong committed against him had been avenged. It was as though Bishamon truly had been with them last night, and had granted them all the opportunity to fulfill their vow completely, before they paid their own debt to the law.

Once Kira's men had laid down their weapons and surrendered, their cooperation had not even seemed grudging. Oishi remembered how they had stared at him yesterday—as though they were seeing a vision of Bishamon as well. But today he wondered whether they were simply relieved that the ronin from Ako were departing without further retaliation—or whether they were actually glad to find themselves suddenly masterless, after living in the shadow of Kira, a witch, and a demon.

Whatever their reasons, he was grateful for any assistance. The guests had fled as soon as the fighting had broken out, and he knew word of the attack would reach the Shogun well before the ronin were back in Ako. The sooner he got his men and Lady Asano out of here, the better.

He looked around as Yasuno approached, and bowed.

"Everything is ready, sir," he said. "We should have everything we need for the journey back." He nodded toward the horses, where men were beginning to mount up already. Oishi saw Chikara helping Lady Asano up into her saddle, although something in her smile suggested that she was only tolerating his help; for years her father had allowed her to ride horseback whenever she chose.

Yesterday, when Oishi had first laid eyes on her, Mika-*hime* had looked like a *tennyo,* a vision of heavenly beauty; today she was dressed like a ronin, her face scrubbed clean of powder and her long hair tied back like the men's.

A faint smile turned up the corners of his mouth, and he shook his head. "It's nothing," he said to Yasuno, who looked like he was about to ask. "How is Kai? Can he ride?"

"He says he can." Yasuno's expression said he wouldn't have believed anyone else who told him that.

Oishi had seen what the black-armored demon had done to Kai's back; silently, he agreed.

"I can give him a hand." Yasuno smiled. "If he needs it."

Oishi nodded, and they started toward their waiting horses.

"Oishi-*sama*!" a familiar voice called out.

"Kawatake?" Oishi stopped, looking around in surprise as he saw the troupe of *Noh* performers being escorted across the yard by a handful of ronin.

"We've arrived, and to prove it, we are here." Kawatake bowed before them.

Oishi nodded, smiling wryly. "Like a buddha met with in hell. You are all unhurt—?"

"Yes, thank the gods." Kawatake glanced back at his people, and then away toward the place where the stage had stood last night. "And Lord Kira is dead. 'The spit aimed at the sky comes back to one,' they say. . . ." He shook his head, looking at Oishi again. "In any case, we couldn't possibly leave without congratulating you on your remarkable performance. The odds of biting one's own navel are better than the odds of successfully capturing a castle with only forty-seven men."

Yasuno raised an eyebrow. "Then why did you agree to help us?"

Kawatake chuckled. "Well, my philosophy is, 'we're fools whether we dance or not, so we might as well dance.' " He shrugged. "And I believe we should live by helping each other in this world."

"We would never have gotten across the river without the loan of your oars." Oishi bowed in acknowledgment. "We are forever in your debt."

"Oh, no need to feel that way." Kawatake waved his hands. "All you have to do is pay us. Double or nothing, I believe, was the agreement? Plus damages."

Yasuno burst out laughing. Oishi's smile became a grin. "That was the agreement." He nodded toward the handful of Kira's men who stood by, looking on with unreadable expressions. "Your former lord has an outstanding debt. Find me someone with access to his storehouse. I'm sure he would wish us to fulfill his final obligation."

He looked back at Yasuno. "Go with them. Make sure the performers are paid what they're due, plus proper compensation." Glancing up, he saw Lady Mika start her horse in their direction.

"Divide up whatever is left in Kira's coffers, and bring half the money back here." Lady Mika reined in her horse alongside them, and looked down at their startled faces.

Yasuno stared at her in disbelief; Oishi put his hand on Yasuno's shoulder as he saw the light in Mika-*hime*'s eyes.

"It will be distributed to the local villagers on our way out of here, Sir Yasuno," she said, with a smile that held both reassurance and deep satisfaction. "It should be returned to the people it was stolen from . . . before it ends up in the *bakufu*'s treasury." She glanced away at the dubious gazes of Kira's former retainers. "And have the half that's left distributed among the inhabitants of this castle; they've earned it."

"Yes, my lady!" Yasuno bowed deeply. Oishi's smile spread to the faces of the Kira ronin, whose bows to the former captive of their former lord were even deeper than Yasuno's.

Standing beside Lady Mika, he watched Yasuno and Kawatake scramble to catch up, as Kira's men ran ahead in search of someone with a set of keys. He doubted that dividing Kira's fortune would delay their departure long

---

To the surprise of the ronin, the players did not leave as soon as they had received their payment. Kawatake seemed to have been serious when he claimed to believe people should live by helping each other. Since the performers had few possessions left that had survived the night, they gave themselves over to helping transport the wounded down the slippery, treacherous route from the mountain fortress.

The players continued to travel with them through the remote back country of Kira's domain, assisting in whatever ways they could. "No road is too long in the company of merry companions," Kawatake insisted, as if now that the actual danger had passed, the players could not resist the lure of traveling in dangerous company.

Oishi hoped Kawatake was referring to the performers when he used the word "merry." That was the last word that occurred to him when he looked at his battered, exhausted men. But their condition forced him to admit that any assistance at all was welcome at this point, and the presence of the traveling players actually seemed to raise spirits among them, especially the worst-wounded, taking their minds off their fatigue and pain.

Once they were clear of the heights where Kira's castle lay, they left the last of winter behind as well. As the first faint signs of spring returned to the land, they distributed parcels of Kira's gold and silver to the headmen of the villages they passed through, just when the desperate, desperately grateful people most needed it to buy seed for spring planting. If the traveling players seemed to enjoy playacting the role of chivalrous brigands far more than the ronin did, Oishi supposed it was simply their nature. He was more than glad to let them provide a magnet for the farmers' awe and curiosity, which the ronin neither needed nor wanted.

Like everything else under the sun and moon, however, even the willing assistance of Kawatake and his "merry companions" did not come entirely without its karmic debt. The performers themselves began to ask endless questions about the attack on the castle and the motivation of the men who had planned it, about Lady Asano, about witches and demons and details of the lives of samurai. Oishi supposed that was simply part of their nature, too.

Lady Mika was as gracious as she was grateful for the help, but she rode all day beside Kai, protecting him like Kannon, the hundred-armed goddess of mercy, as Kai somehow managed to guide them despite his injury.

Yasuno muttered that the players were worse than children at a festival, or a dog that would not stop fetching sticks—and at Oishi's suggestion, he took on the task of keeping questioners away from both Lady Mika and Kai.

Oishi said as little as it was possible to say, and was relieved that Chikara's numerous superficial wounds were not enough to keep him from talking sufficiently for both of them. Like some of the other men who were able to endure interrogation, Chikara almost seemed to enjoy it, particularly once Kawatake told them he knew playwrights in Edo who would give anything to tell the story of the ronin's vengeance . . . because they all know he meant that literally. It was sometimes said "the tongue was more to be feared than the sword," and that fact had not escaped the *bakufu*'s notice.

Oishi was not overeager to have their story spread through all of Edo any sooner than necessary, but he made no protest. It occurred to him that a plague of tales about the ronin's vengeance would infuriate *Inu-Kubou* and his censors—and that defiant reminder of their deed was all the satisfaction they were ever likely to get against the Shogun who had wreaked havoc with such indifference in the lives of Lord Asano and Lady Mika, and in their own lives.

Eventually they reached the boundary of Kira's domain, and the inevitable end of the ronin's star-crossed travels with the troupe of players. Kawatake and his performers were headed toward Edo, well to the northeast; they were free to travel the main roads, and by now were pressed for time to get there. Ako lay west and south, and the ronin could not take any road where they would be stopped at checkpoints.

All those who met were destined to part . . . but by the time the ronin said farewell to the players, it was with a surprising amount of regret.

Once the company of players had departed, the ronin were faced with more work of every kind simply to ensure their survival—especially the survival of the wounded—as they traveled on alone. But Oishi was grateful to the performers in a way he had never expected to be, as he realized that his men were also better able to cope with what needed to be done because of the help they had received.

It also surprised him to find that a growing sense of peace seemed to descend on their group as they continued homeward through the newly awakening countryside.

The first signs of spring that had greeted them after they left Kirayama Castle had become a profusion of budding trees and early wildflowers. New grass and newly planted fields turned the earth a shade of tender green that Oishi never saw at any other time of year as they rode steadily southward and toward the ocean. The warmth and fresh color were healing in their own way, after everything the ronin had endured to reach Kira's fortress.

Without the need for stealth that had haunted them on the way to attack Kira, and with the wounded to consider, Kai found them an easier route home, along rarely traveled back roads. Occasional isolated villages of farmers or artisans gave them places where they could stop for any supplies they ran short on. Lady Mika had kept aside a handful of Kira's silver and coppers, enough to pay for food and medicine; as a result the astonished villagers who watched them ride in with something close to terror watched them ride out again with shouted prayers, as well as relieved expressions.

Oishi had been concerned about how Kai would withstand acting as their guide for the entire journey home. His own wounds pained him enough, even traveling at a pace that the seriously injured could survive, and exhaustion still plagued him. But with the witch-slayer Lady Mika riding at his side, as confident and uncomplaining as the legendary Tomoe Gozen riding with her beloved Yoshinaka, Kai seldom betrayed a trace of his discomfort.

The two of them seemed to be in a world of their own . . . one where fatigue and pain had no more meaning than class differences, as long as they were free to look into each other's eyes, and occasionally exchange a few words, reassuring themselves that they were truly together.

Oishi realized that the sight of them no longer angered him at all. Like so many things he had once been certain about, the true nature of love was no longer a meaningless abstraction to him. Seeing the two of them merely made him think of Riku, with sorrow and longing.

He began to ride beside Chikara as much as possible, talking with him about things they had never discussed before, getting to know his son in a way he'd never had a chance to do, when he had spent virtually all the time they'd been together teaching his son the duties of a *karou.*

Several others among the ronin were fathers and sons, or brothers; most had family somewhere. They spent their time as he and Chikara did, talking of home and the past—of how proud they were of each other, and how they prayed their families would remember them with pride. They did not dwell on the future, beyond the moment when they would stand together at Lord Asano's graveside.

Like Kai and Lady Mika, everyone among them seemed to recognize that this brief time between their act of vengeance and the moment when they finally reached Ako Castle was a gift not to be wasted, *wabi-sabi,* unexpected beauty in the purest sense: Each day was filled with *awaré*, the poignant sorrow inextricably bound to all moments when the soul seemed poised in perfect balance, because all such moments must end too soon: the last sip of fine *sake,* fireworks illuminating the sea on a summer's night . . . or simply the flawless blue of a spring sky.

And yet, because of that or in spite of it, on nights when his wounds, or the sounds of other men whose sleep was disturbed by pain kept him awake, Oishi was left with a great deal of thinking to do: questions that needed to be resolved, peace that he needed to make with himself, about *giri* and *ninjo* . . . if it was actually possible to reassess his entire life in the time that he had left.

On one of those nights, when the ronin slept in a peaceful clearing among the trees, he lay wrapped in a blanket from Kirayama's keep, gazing up through the branches at the waning moon. The breeze carried the scent of new grass and ancient pines, and for once his body felt almost comfortable. But still he could not sleep . . . or he thought not, until he rolled onto his side, looking over at the spot beside him where Mika-*hime* always slept.

She wasn't there.

He sat up too suddenly, and gasped out loud from the pain. Across the glen movement caught his eye, telling him someone had turned to look back at the sound. *Someone—*

Wrapped in a silk-covered quilt, Lady Mika seemed to glow with reflected moonlight as if she carried a lantern. She stood by the isolated spot where Kai lay, watching over him like the goddess Kannon even now. Kai slept, as always, well away from the others, either out of habit or because he knew all too well where the woman he loved was sleeping.

How long had she been standing there, silently gazing at Kai as he slept? Had she done this before, often? Kai seemed to be sound asleep, although Oishi doubted anyone could surprise Kai in his sleep, no matter how exhausted he was.

Yet neither he nor Mika made a move to act on the desire that was so obvious between them, in their every waking moment and even now. Love had bound their souls for a lifetime, despite their living in a world that denied them even the right to talk freely to each other or spend idle time together—that forbid them on pain of death from marrying, or ever experiencing the sensual intimacy that was love's ultimate physical expression.

Oishi had always accepted and lived by the social codes

that kept Kai and Lady Mika separated—just as Lord Asano himself had, up to the very end, despite his unshakeable belief in Kai's character. And yet here, now, in this space beyond the limits of the world they had always known, Oishi saw only two people in love, two people for whom past and future were meaningless. And yet, still they did not act on their freedom, when they could. . . .

Why? he thought, and did not even wonder that he thought such a thing. He remembered the joy of his body joined with his wife's in the act of love; thought of their son, born of their passion. Physical love had never been meant to be separate from emotion; it was as natural, and as necessary to life, as breathing. . . .

Mika was still looking in his direction, frozen in place as if she didn't know what to do. Quietly Oishi lay down again, and rolled onto his side, facing away from her, as if he had simply been disturbed by his pain.

My lady, he thought, *life is only a butterfly's dream. Dream well. . . .*

As he closed his eyes, he remembered that he had used those lines once before, in a poem he had written for his wife as she lay sleeping, at dawn on the morning after their third night of marriage. At first the memory caused him pain as deep as any wound and as profound as the loss of love, almost unendurable. But he repeated it like a silent mantra until the pain faded, and his memories slowly dissolved. . . .

And to his surprise, he slept very well.

It was barely dawn when he was wakened by someone's tentative prodding, and opened his eyes to find his son staring back at him.

"Wha'?" he mumbled, groping for his sword. "Trouble?"

"No. No, sir—" Chikara whispered, shaking his head. His hand pinned down Oishi's arm, and his sword with it. "But . . . Mika-*hime* . . ." It was still too dark for Oishi to see Chikara's expression clearly as the boy glanced at the place where Lady Mika should have been sleeping, but was not.

"Mm . . ." Oishi lay back with a smile of contentment, and closed his eyes.

"Father!" Chikara shook him again, his hushed voice caught somewhere between panic and disbelief. "Sir . . . Father. . . . She's with Kai please sir don't kill Kai—" He leaned on Oishi's injured sword arm so hard that Oishi choked off a curse of pain and cuffed him on the head.

"I have no intention of killing anyone . . ." Oishi muttered, as Chikara fell back, looking dumbfounded. "Or telling anyone, either."

"But I was afraid, if the others—"

"Keep your voice down, or they will. Why are you awake?"

"I had to take a piss."

Oishi sighed. "Stay a moment," he said, pushing himself up as his son crouched beside him. He rubbed his eyes, trying to order his thoughts. "Chikara . . ." He took a deep breath. "Have you ever heard it said that 'the Past is like another country; they do things differently there'?"

Chikara nodded, looking puzzled but intent. "Although it seemed to me it was only said in order to defend the present."

"Wise beyond your years. . . ." Oishi smiled wryly. "The Land of the Past is where everyone here vowed to spend the rest of his days, when we defied the Shogun to claim rightful vengeance for our lord. And in the Land of the Past—where a man could still earn the title of "samurai" by his own actions—marriages were not just an exchange of pawns made to strengthen political alliances. A couple who wished to be wed only needed to sleep together, for three nights. . . ."

Chikara's eyes widened, and Oishi could see his expression quite clearly this time. His son leaned forward, and unexpectedly bowed to him. "Forgive me, Father," Chikara murmured, "I shall never be as wise as you."

Oishi smiled again, but this time it hid a pang of sorrow. "It was you who first opened my eyes to the truth." He glanced away into the trees, toward the place where Mika and Kai lay sleeping, holding each other in a heart-to-heart embrace. "Now," he looked back at his son fondly, "will you please let me rest . . . at least until the sun has fully risen?"

Chikara got to his feet, bowing once more before he went back to his own sleeping place. Oishi lay watching until he had settled beneath his blanket, and was once more peacefully asleep.

Oishi rolled onto his back again and covered his face with his hand, not to block out the growing light of day, but instead to hold back the sudden surge of emotion that overwhelmed him, body and soul, filling his eyes to the brim of overflowing.

As the band of ronin began to stir and make preparations for a new day, Oishi woke to find Mika-*hime* lying in her place at his side, as though she had never left it. He wondered for a moment if his memories of the night just past had all been a dream, until she stirred and opened her eyes. As she gazed back at him, her glowing eyes and shy smile offered him a bouquet of irises: *her gratitude, faith, and a bond of trust that would last through all eternity.*

He acknowledged her gift with the briefest of smiles in return, before he occupied himself getting his aching, weary body to sit up and finally stand, in preparation for a new day. He took no visible notice of her unself-conscious stretching and sighs before she pushed away her quilt and got lithely to her feet. He thought he heard her singing softly as she walked barefoot through the dew-wet grass to the place where Kai still slept as soundly as any ordinary man who had been awake for half the night.

Nonetheless, Oishi noticed, as he watched them without seeming to, she did not even have to speak to Kai to wake him. He raised his head to look at her before she even put her hands on her hips and seemed to start chiding him for his laziness. But a smile spread across his face at her words, and then he laughed, a sound so unexpected that Oishi shook his head in disbelief.

Kai bowed his head to her as if in apology for his behavior, and pulled himself to his feet, using the trunk of the tree beneath which he had been sleeping to help him stand. He made no attempt even to touch Mika, who maintained a respectable distance between them and did nothing to aid him beyond folding up his blanket. She passed it to him as if it was a beloved treasure she could scarcely bear to part with, but Oishi doubted even Chikara was paying enough attention to notice her expression.

Mika came back to the place where Oishi was now rolling up his own blanket. Kai followed her with his eyes until his gaze encountered Oishi, watching him. He bowed, an ordinary gesture of greeting between equals. But Oishi could not remember Kai ever having bowed willingly to him before, and what showed on Kai's face then was the most extraordinary emotion Oishi had ever seen.

Kai turned away at last and headed toward the place where the other ronin were gathering, waiting while their morning rice cooked; he didn't look back again. Mika gathered up her quilt and began to fold it, as if this was simply another morning for her as well, and she was a ronin like any other.

The dwindling days of their journey back to Ako continued much as they had, with the ronin taking pleasure in dreary days of rain just as they did in sunlit days when the sky admired its reflection in an infinity of newly-flooded rice paddies. Every sight under heaven, even the most commonplace, became new and wondrous to eyes that could not know whether today would be the last time they would ever see it.

Kai and Mika still rode contentedly beside each other, speaking only a little more, perhaps smiling more often, but otherwise behaving as if nothing had changed between them. But each night Mika slipped away to Kai's bed, as the nights dwindled like the days; although by sunrise she was always back in her spot at Oishi's side. The night kept their secret well; and if any of the ronin besides Oishi and Chikara even suspected something, no one dared to mention it.

As the ronin finally crossed the border into Ako domain, the cherry trees were in full bloom . . . and the report of their vengeance had preceded them, as they had known it would—but in a way they had never expected. News of the deed seemed to have spread through the entire country like the change of seasons. They had already heard that Kyoto and Edo were alive with the talk of it. But equally surprising to them, in remote Ako itself the people of every village, and every field where farmers prepared the paddies for rice planting, knew exactly who they were, and stopped to bow or wave and call out blessings as they passed.

When they finally reached the village below Ako Castle, such a crowd had gathered along the main street that all the ronin who could dismount did so, leading their horses, for fear that someone would be trampled.

Oishi insisted that Mika remain on her horse for her own dignity and safety in the mob, even as she led the column—still Lady Asano, the heir to all of Ako, whether the justice of the gods could move the Shogun to restore her to her rightful place or not.

Beside her Kai dismounted without a word, but with a grimace that held more, and deeper pain than he had ever allowed himself to show until now. Still silently, he began to lead his horse back into the company of ronin, nodding for Oishi to take his position at Mika's side—an unspoken acknowledgement that the journey back, and the too-brief freedom it had granted them all, was over.

Mika watched just as silently, keeping her head high as Kai walked away; but her eyes were dim with sorrow as Oishi brought his horse forward to join her, holding his own silence. He glanced up at their offering to Lord Asano, tied in a sack, displayed prominently at the tip of a spear fastened to his horse's saddle.

As they began to make their way forward through the crowd, Oishi was surprised in a new and disconcerting way by the reactions of the townspeople. There were almost none of the proud, admiring looks they had been encountering more and more along the way. Instead he saw troubled faces and downcast eyes, people who prostrated themselves as if they were expecting the Shogun's wrath. He knew the response was not because Lady Asano and her retainers were passing—since they were no longer what they had been, or even looked the part—and yet still the people behaved as if they felt the need to abase themselves.

A large burly farmer stepped directly into the street in front of Oishi and kneeled down, pressing his forehead to the dirt. "Oishi-*sama,*" the man mumbled, "I beg your forgiveness. If my life is all that can repay you, then. . . ."

Oishi stared down at the man, incredulous, until the peasant finally raised his head, and something about their positions triggered his memory at last. *Their positions had been reversed.* It was the man who had spat on him, the day Kira's guards had finally released him from the dungeon and thrown him out of the castle.

A tremor of emotion ran through him as he remembered that day—not years ago, but somehow only weeks, although it seemed as if it had been years. . . . He realized that if he had not been desperately playing a broken man to put Kira's spies off their guard, he would have killed the wretch—a mere peasant—on the spot for such an insult.

Obsessively planning the details of how he would claim

vengeance against Kira, for Lord Asano, for himself—for everyone—was all that had kept him sane enough to survive those months of hardship and utter isolation. But in all that time he had learned nothing about himself except how far down into the depths of his soul the fire of his hatred could burn.

But now . . . Oishi looked down at the man kneeling before him and saw only a man, not a monster . . . or a subhuman creature it was his right to kill on a whim, simply because he had been born a samurai and the other man had not.

The man was only a peasant . . . and yet he had a sense of honor so strong that a petty act of spite, against someone he had considered a coward and a traitor, had filled him with such remorse that he had just offered to die of shame.

"You are forgiven," Oishi said quietly. He reached down for the man's arm, urging him to his feet. "Your life is a gift from the gods. As are all our lives. From now on use it in a way that is worthy."

The man backed up out of their path, his eyes filled with disbelief, mumbling in barely audible gratitude.

Oishi felt a hand touch his shoulder, and glanced up. Lady Mika smiled at him. "*Kuranosuke* Oishi," she murmured, calling him by his former title as her father's chief retainer and most trusted advisor. "I thought my father could not have been prouder of you than he was, for obeying his wishes to the last—or for how you have served him since. But I was wrong. *Now* he could not be prouder of you."

Oishi's face reddened and he looked down, shaking his head, though not in denial as he walked on at her side.

He looked up once more as he sensed something changing around them—the sounds of the crowd, the atmosphere itself. He watched the expressions on faces begin to turn like the tide, from morose and ashamed to amazed, and then relieved, finally filling with celebration. Their voices began to rise, until people were once again cheering the return of Lady Asano, and the courage of her faithful retainers.

Someone else pushed forward in the crowd ahead of them, not quite into the street but just enough so that he would notice her: *Riku.*

His face filled with astonishment and joy as he saw tears of happiness and welcome, of pride and longing, shimmering in her eyes. She smiled back at the look in his eyes, her lower lip trembling. But she did not rush out to embrace him, allowing him his dignity while preserving her own, like a proper samurai—yet still and always his loving wife.

Her eyes, and her smile, found Lady Asano next. Beside him, Mika smiled back at Riku, as if she had finally been given the proof she needed that she was truly home.

But as they passed, Riku was already glancing away again, searching the troop of ronin who followed them up the street until she found Chikara.

"Chikara—!" she called out. He looked up, and his face broke into a grin, his eyes filling with amazement. Kai, who was beside him, nudged him toward the edge of the column. This time, samurai or not, his mother didn't spare his dignity but ran out into the street to take him in her arms, holding him close; she glanced toward Oishi with unspoken gratitude for bringing their son back alive and whole.

Chikara did not look self-consciously toward his father, or even at the other men around him, as she held him in her arms. He took her hand in his own, keeping her by his side as the ronin continued their winding progress upward toward the castle; his expression was no less a man's, but now it was proud, completely content.

More villagers began to step forward, offering all of them food, or water, or their prayers. The prayers were accepted with nods of gratitude, the food and water waved aside with smiles of thanks. The thoughts of every man, and of Lady Mika, were now fixed on the way ahead. They would let nothing more delay them until they had reached their pilgrimage's end.

They crossed over the river that marked the perimeter of Ako Castle at last, uncertain about what kind of reception awaited them—only certain that now not even the Shogun's samurai could stand in their way. The villagers had told them *bakufu* troops had arrived before they had, and ousted Kira's retainers. But the Shogun's men had not departed; the castle gates had been closed, and guards posted—and that was how it had remained, until today.

But the graveyard lay outside the castle's walls, watched over by the willows and cherry trees along the riverbank. The Shinto traditions of their ancestors—the will of the very gods who had raised the islands of Japan from the sea at the beginning of time—forbade the remains of the dead from occupying the same ground as the homes of the living. Those gods now graciously shared heaven and earth with the divine essence of Buddha, and Buddhist priests presided over funerals . . . but in the most basic matters of life and death, their ancient rules still held.

The party of ronin, trailed at a respectful distance by people from the village, turned off the road to the castle gate, instead heading out across the open field beyond the castle walls. Keeping their horses at a sedate walk, they followed the line of blooming cherry trees along the river toward the burial ground.

The men standing guard at the gate, wearing the Shogun's black armor with its gold *mon,* watched them from the distance. Other Tokugawa samurai began to gather on the battlements, looking out at the procession. None of them made a move to leave the castle, even though they had to know perfectly well who the group of battle-weary ronin were. They also surely knew why the ronin had come—and were content to leave them in peace to perform their sacred ritual at Lord Asano's grave.

Kai joined the rest of the men as they formed a semicircle ringing Mika and Oishi, and bowed his head with the others. For the first time he saw the actual gravestone, its rectangular base with the pillar bearing his lord's name beneath which the urn holding Lord Asano's remains lay at home in the earth of Ako.

Although he could not see it, he knew the restless soul that had once belonged to his lord was still chained to this place as well, unable to depart for a more peaceful realm, let alone begin a new existence. As the thought filled Kai's mind, a sudden breeze whispered through the grass that had already grown long around the grave. There were none of the wooden prayer boards usually set in place by mourners and family members beside the headstone, and no offerings had been left in front of it—no flowers or incense, no other signs of remembrance, not even a solitary rock. Mika looked down, blinking too much as she took in the cruel disrespect of Kira's men, and the fear they had instilled in the people whose lives they had controlled in her absence.

Kai's hands tightened, as the longing to hold her in his arms again, just for a moment, filled him. He stayed where he was, telling himself that her mere presence here would comfort her far more in the end, and comfort her father's spirit as well.

And what they carried with them today would make up for the time Lord Asano's spirit had spent lost in the wind—the year they had all spent, lost—plus so much more.

Mika glanced back as Yasuno unfastened the spear with its well-wrapped bundle from Oishi's saddle, and passed the cloth bag to him. Oishi carefully accepted it with his free hand, his wounded arm still nearly useless. Kneeling awkwardly before the grave, he placed the bundle on the flat stone surface at its foot, then drew the *tanto* from its sheath at his side—the *tanto* that had taken the lives of both his lord and Kira—and placed it on the gravestone as well.

"Rest now, my lord," he murmured. "You are avenged." He bowed, lowering his head to the ground in final tribute, and got to his feet again.

Mika kneeled in turn before her father's grave and

bowed, before she laid an offering of spring flowers given to her by a village woman beside Oishi's gifts. She closed her eyes, whispering a prayer that only her father could hear.

As if in answer, the wind sighed through the cherry trees along the river, and a flurry of cherry blossom petals drifted gently down on them all, like a gesture of farewell.

Mika rose to her feet, her face serene as she turned to the men waiting around her—as if her prayer, whatever it had been, had been answered.

"Looking up, we are not ashamed in the presence of heaven," she recited, gazing into their eyes, "nor bowing down are we ashamed in the presence of earth." She bowed to Oishi, and then bowed to the ronin behind him. As she looked once more at Kai, he thought he saw a glimmer of her father's spirit gazing out at him, at all of them, with the gratitude of all his ancestors behind it.

One by one, the ronin began to kneel and bow their heads, those who could move freely aiding those who could not. Yasuno came forward to offer Kai his arm; he had been helping him on and off his horse throughout the long ride home, whenever Kai's back had been too stiff or he had been too exhausted to manage on his own. After the long walk to the castle, Kai gladly accepted the help, as he sank down onto his knees.

As Yasuno kneeled beside him, Kai's prayer of gratitude to Lord Asano for the gift of his life expanded to include the comradeship of the men around him, as well as Mika's unfaltering love. He finished his silent prayer with a plea that his gratitude would be accepted, and his love for her forgiven.

When all had been said that remained to be said in their prayers, the weary men settled down to rest in the shade along the riverbank. The people who had followed them from the village, and stood by somberly watching the ceremony, were at last free to bring food and drink to Lady Asano and the ronin, welcoming them home.

But Mika left Kai's side after a time, to rejoin Oishi. Kai watched them mount their horses and ride toward the outer gate of Ako Castle, unable to truly rest until they had seen what had become of their former home.

The guards stationed at the gate watched them come with more curiosity than wariness. When the two riders drew close enough that their faces could be seen clearly, the Shogun's men bowed in respect, as if they already knew the identities of the dusty, sunburned woman wearing a man's clothes and the battered ronin with one arm in a sling.

Mika identified herself and Oishi to them anyway. Then, respectfully and with far more confidence than she would have felt without her ancestors watching over her, she requested permission to enter Ako Castle.

To her surprise, the captain of the troops stationed there came to the gate himself, and ordered the pass-through opened to let them enter. He returned their polite bows as if he was honored by their presence, and not face-to-face with felons—a runaway bride and the wanted criminal who had killed her intended husband. Mika and Oishi exchanged uncertain glances as he sent them on with one of his lieutenants to the inner gates, through which they were allowed to pass as well, entering the grounds of the upper courtyard at last.

Mika entered the inner courtyard hesitantly, not because they were being observed by the Shogun's samurai, or even because they had been forced to come like beggars to the gates that by right should have stood open to welcome them . . . but because in the last year so much had changed, in her life, in her mind and heart, that nothing about the place she had always thought of as her home seemed familiar to her anymore.

She saw the same disorientation in Oishi's eyes, before a bleakness that matched the view replaced it, as they stared at the deserted palace where Lord Asano had once ruled. Oishi looked off into the distance, and she knew he was looking toward what had once been his own home, a mansion befitting the *karou* of a castle, which he had shared with the woman who had once been his wife, and the sixteen-year-old ronin who had once been his son and heir . . . until Lord Kira had come into their lives.

She looked toward her father's garden, seeing only withered or overgrown bushes choked by weeds, all that survived of the beauty he had tended with so much care and pleasure, as neglected now as his grave had been.

Yet even here the cherry trees were covered of their own accord with a profusion of blooms—tangible proof of a transcendent existence that continued without human permission, beyond human control, oblivious to the fleeting sorrows, fragile moments of happiness, or futile longings that made up the sum total of a mortal life.

Wabi-sabi . . . She found herself thinking of her father's *koi* pond, wondering with sorrow whether there were any fish still alive in it, or whether they had all flung themselves out onto the stones, committing their own strange form of *junshi,* following their lord in death. With a hesitant bow, the lieutenant inquired whether she would like to enter the palace. She shook her head, suddenly unable even to imagine setting foot inside it, let alone seeing her father's rooms, or her own, after they had belonged to the enemy for a year.

The breeze stirred, raising a veil of dust and a flurry of petals to complete their vision of desolation. She looked back at Oishi at last. "What will become of us now?" she murmured.

He met her eyes, seeing all that lay behind them . . . all that was gone. "Ako's honor will be restored, my lady," he said, his voice as bravely confident as if somehow he still believed the justice of the gods would save Ako from the greed of men.

But as she held his gaze, he glanced away.

She nodded toward the inner gate, seeing faint surprise on the lieutenant's face as she told him they had seen enough.

As they crossed the lower courtyard toward the outer gate, the guard commander approached them again. "Lady Asano," he said, "the Lord Shogun will arrive today. He expects to see you, and . . ." He cleared his throat and looked down uncomfortably. "Well. You should not have long to wait."

She nodded in acknowledgment, hiding the sudden coldness that filled her at what the man had said, and what he had not said. "We will wait by my father's grave, then." She nodded toward the gate, as if she was certain he would let them pass through it.

He bowed once more, and signaled the gatekeepers to open the pass-through. "It has been an honor," he said, looking at them both as he said it, leaving her more confused and conflicted than before as she started back down the corridor that led to the outside gate.

"What did he mean by 'It was an honor'?" she said softly to Oishi, as they walked side by side toward their waiting horses.

Oishi shrugged, with a slight smile. "I suppose the honor of meeting you, Lady Asano."

They took the reins of their horses from the guards and swung up into their saddles; she smiled wryly back at him. "Perhaps I should roll in the dirt and wear men's clothes more often. . . . I wonder whether the Shogun's adjutant will actually find that I'm visible, today." Her smile turned utterly humorless.

Oishi's smile became a rueful grimace as they rode back across the field toward the others. "You will always be a very difficult person to ignore, Mika-*hime*. It is in your blood."

But then his expression turned somber again, as he looked away at the bridge; his gaze searched the still-empty approach to the castle. "The Shogun's spies are more efficient than I thought," he muttered.

"They would have had to be blind and deaf, not to know

where we were by the time we reached Ako. Everyone knew about us." Mika shook her head, in amazement as much as despair, remembering the people who had gathered to watch them pass along obscure back roads, or called to them from fields.

All at once the deference that the Shogun's own samurai had shown them made unexpected, yet perfect, sense to her. She looked over at Oishi, and her sudden smile surprised him even more because her eyes were filled with pride. "Everyone. . . ."

25

The Shogun did not give Lady Asano and the exhausted men resting in the shade long to anticipate his arrival, for which they were both sorry and relieved. The distant sound of riders and marching feet made everyone look up, as a column of troops in black and gold armor topped the rise of a distant hill.

The ronin, and the villagers who lingered among them, watched with a shared sense of déjà vu as the Shogun's procession approached Ako Castle again, the way it had on that fateful day the previous spring. But this time the column was neither as resplendent nor as long, and their arrival was not a cause for celebration on anyone's part.

One by one, helping each other to their feet, the ronin slowly made their way back to their lord's grave. Mika was there already, as she had been since she had returned from the castle, kneeling in prayer.

The Shogun's Honor Guard turned off the road into the open field as they saw the ronin gathered by Lord Asano's burial site. Mika rose to her feet and went to stand near Oishi, stepping out in front of the others as if she could protect them from the approaching troops with her own body.

The Shogun and his entourage drew to a halt in front of her and sat on their horses, looking down. Mika bowed, but did not kneel. Having grown used to treating Kira with disrespect, she found it impossible to show a man so easily manipulated by Kira any more honor than he deserved—even if that man was the Shogun.

The ronin around her seemed to share the same opinion. They kneeled respectfully, but did not prostrate themselves in a formal obeisance, or even lower their heads.

The Shogun stared at all of them from where he sat among his honor guard, registering their small gesture of respect combined with unmistakable defiance. He urged his horse forward, ahead of his samurai, and dismounted in front of Oishi, who continued to kneel gazing straight ahead.

"*Kuranosuke* Oishi?" the Shogun said.

Oishi looked up finally, as much in surprise at hearing the Shogun address him by his former title as in willing obedience.

"I gave you a command forbidding you to take revenge," the Shogun said coldly, as Oishi met his eyes. "You disobeyed me."

Oishi's unyielding stare turned slightly harder. He raised his hand, pointing toward Lord Asano's gravestone, and the bundled offering sitting before it. "What lies atop that grave is justice."

A murmur of surprised indignation passed through the Shogun's attendants, at the arrogance of a ronin who dared address the lord of lords as bluntly as if he were an equal.

But the Shogun only raised his hand for silence. "What law is that?" he asked, with an edge in his voice.

"A man may not live under the same heaven as the murderer of his lord, nor tread the same earth." Oishi recited by heart the centuries-old oath of vengeance—aware that the Shogun already knew it as well as he did.

But the Shogun's mouth turned down in dismissal. "The laws of heaven have no place here. Only the rules of men."

Oishi nodded, still holding his gaze. "I know that, my lord, and know also that to restore order to the world we too must pay with our lives. My men and I followed the old ways of *Bushido,* to honor our master and avenge Lord Kira's treachery. We acted knowing the penalty was death. We are samurai. This is our fate." As he finished speaking, he held out the scroll the ronin had signed in blood—the declaration of their intent to seek vengeance against Lord Kira.

The crowd of villagers who had lingered to see the outcome of this meeting murmured in surprise and admiration.

The Shogun was silent for a long moment. He had not expected such a straightforward acknowledgement, or acceptance . . . or the crowd of villagers who were bearing witness to their confrontation. He considered the fact that even here in Ako, the people who had despised Lord Asano's men as cowards the last time the cherry trees were in bloom now considered them to be heroes.

By now the story of the attack on Kira's fortress had spread to the far ends of the country. He would have to imprison half the people in Edo itself to silence all the treasonous praise about the "valiant forty-seven ronin" that had been reported to him. Someone had actually written a play based on them already; people had flocked to see it until he ordered his censors to shut it down.

He understood that the people needed heroes—and the samurai class had always given them their heroes, until now. But without constant warfare and endless battles to be fought, too many potential heroes had become sword-wearing bureaucrats, troublemakers, or beggars.

In the eyes of the people these ronin were already heroes. Even his own understanding of *Bushido* filled him with an unwilling admiration for what they had accomplished.

He must handle this with all possible caution—or he would turn the forty-seven men who kneeled in front of him, condemned to die like criminals, into something far more dangerous to his position than simply heroes.

They had disobeyed a direct command from him. They could not be pardoned; it would undermine his authority too greatly. *Nonetheless* . . .

They had brought Lord Asano's heir back to Ako. Perhaps they hoped that restoring their lord's honor might cause him to restore Ako Domain to her. *And perhaps . . .*

"You are proud of your men?" he asked Oishi.

Oishi raised his head again, meeting the Shogun's eyes directly as he said, "They are the bravest I have ever known, my lord."

The Shogun nodded, and smiled faintly, as the narrow path guiding him between a cliff and a precipice began to widen. "I grant you a samurai death. To die as your lord, and be buried at his side. With honor."

Oishi's face filled with surprise and relief. That he and his men would have their good names restored, along with Lord Asano, was a thing he had not even dared to pray for—and far more than he had expected of *bakufu* justice. But then he hesitated, and said, cautiously, "All of us, sir?"

The Shogun glanced past him, scanning the faces of the other ronin. With a start, he saw the reason for Oishi's hesitation: Kneeling near the place where Lady Asano now stood was the halfbreed who had fought for Ako in the tournament last spring—the misbegotten outcast that the samurai of Ako had beaten with *bokken,* at his order. But now the halfbreed wore his hair in a topknot, and two swords thrust through his belt: *He was one of the forty-seven.*

The Shogun stared, in spite of himself. *But it didn't matter. . . .* However the halfbreed had come to be accepted as an equal by these men, it made no difference now. Still gazing directly at Kai, the Shogun said, "I see only samurai before me."

The halfbreed looked up in disbelief, his eyes filled with amazement and then gratitude, as if simply being recognized as a human being meant as much to him as being recognized as a samurai.

Lady Asano kneeled finally—but only to kneel at the halfbreed's side and take his hand in both of hers. As she looked into his eyes her smile was radiant, even as her mouth trembled with some barely controlled emotion.

"Thank you, Lord Shogun," Oishi said humbly. He bowed, at last.

The men behind him bowed, as well: Fate-tossed "wave men" who had finally found their way back from the sea, or warriors who had fought against impossible odds, and at last returned home victorious, they paid their due respect to their lord of lords with the dignity of the true samurai that they were, and had always been.

Solemnly he bowed in return.

When everyone else had been settled within the walls of Ako Castle, Kai walked alone back to Lord Asano's grave. Mika was having an audience with the Shogun even now to work out the details for the transfer of Asano holdings. He had given his word that Ako would be returned to her, as everyone among the ronin had hoped.

But the Shogun did not intend to stay away from Edo any longer than necessary. Kai had realized this would be his only chance to spend a few quiet moments with the man who had been more like a father to him than anyone, human or not, that he had ever known.

Kai looked down at Lord Asano's gravestone. Mika had already begun to heal the signs of neglect, pulling out weeds and dead grass around the pillar's base. Someone else had already pushed two prayer boards into the earth behind it.

Moving slowly and carefully, Kai got down onto his knees and placed the stick of incense he had brought with him into its holder before the grave. He lit it and bowed his head, thanking Merciful Buddha for the compassion that Lord Asano had shown him, and for everything that had come to pass in his life because of it. He thanked the gods as well, not only for allowing him to have a part in the events that had freed Lord Asano's spirit, but also for ensuring Mika would have her rightful heritage restored to her.

And then he let his mind empty, allowing memories and emotions to pool quietly in its depths, as he reached out to the part of Lord Asano's sprit that remained within the land he had loved. He felt its presence resonate in his soul . . . as it would for all those who had been touched by it so deeply that its essence had become a part of who they were.

He heard a noise behind him and glanced up, startled yet not really surprised as he saw Oishi approaching. Apparently Oishi had had the same urge to spend a few final moments alone with their lord and his memories, as well as his prayers; to take an accounting of his life while he still had a chance, before it was time for his own journey into the unknown.

Kai began to get up, struggling to keep the pain of the abrupt movement off his face.

But Oishi gestured for him to stay where he was—acknowledging his own intrusion, and also that there was enough room for both of them in the presence of Lord Asano's soul, as there had always been in his life.

Kai settled back again, watching as Oishi set down a small bottle of *sake* and two cups that he had brought, to share with his master a traditional farewell drink. He poured the *sake* into the cups, one for himself and one for his lord. He drank from one cup, leaving the other among the offerings, and then bowed his head in prayer.

At last he looked up again, looking at the gravestone. "Tell me," he said, as he turned to face Kai, "when my master found you in the forest and you held that knife to my throat—would you have killed me?"

Kai stared at him, surprised by how far away in time Oishi's thoughts had wandered. He considered the question for a moment. "Would you have killed me?"

Oishi glanced away, considering his own answer.

"Yes—"

"—Yes."

The words collided in midair, as if here and now their thoughts were united by something more than simply shared memories.

They smiled together, and then laughed, sharing the irony

and the appreciation of a mutual respect that had been far too long in coming.

Oishi looked back at Lord Asano's grave. "I told him you were a demon and he should leave you to die. . . . " The humor on his face turned to chagrin as he remembered his lord's wisdom, and his own rash judgment. "He said you were just a frightened boy." He glanced down. "Like me."

Kai met his gaze, seeing Oishi's regret-filled acceptance of the limitations he had been too arrogant to see, then and for so long.

But no longer. Oishi poured another cup of *sake* and held it out. Kai accepted it with a bow, and drank. When he lowered the cup again, Oishi was looking at him with a sympathy that surprised as much as confused him.

"Lady Asano is like her father," Oishi said. "She will make Ako great again."

Kai realized that it was not a random remark, but an attempt at consolation, as well as a further sign of how close they had grown without realizing it. Oishi understood not simply all that he had gained, and learned—the things that had prepared him to move on from this stage of existence to the next—but also what he was being forced to sacrifice, the one thing he treasured most, that had sustained him through so much of his life when he had had nothing else: his love for Mika, and her love for him.

But Mika was again her father's daughter, the heir of House Asano and formal Regent of Ako. She still had unfinished duties and vows to fulfill, before her time here was through.

"I know," Kai said, with a trace of a smile.

" 'Those who are born must die. Those who meet must part. . . .' " Oishi murmured the familiar lines. "But what we share in this life can never be taken away." He smiled as well, as their eyes met in a moment of shared *awaré.*

Kai set down his cup, his smile widening; he bowed a last time before Lord Asano's grave, murmuring his final farewell. As he got to his feet again, his body unexpectedly allowed him to rise and stand with dignity.

Surprised, he took a slow experimental breath, and exhaled without regretting it, for the first time since they had left Kira's fortress. Sometime during his prayers a part of the crippling pain inside him had disappeared, pain that he suddenly realized had not all been caused by his wounded back.

Kai glanced a last time at the gravestone, remembering the Tengu Forest—the haunted cries of the abandoned dead, the shimmering phantoms of their forsaken souls, his own mother's among them.

The lost boy from the Sea of Trees that Lord Asano had taken in so long ago had been a ghost as well, chained to his physical body by *tengu* magic, and nothing more. All his life he had been afraid to trust any insight that he gained, or any lesson that he learned, when it had applied to him. He had even been afraid, he realized, to fully accept the gift the ronin of Ako had freely given him—the oath signed in their own blood that swore he was their equal, as surely as they were all his brothers.

And yet, as he rose from Lord Asano's graveside just now and looked back at Oishi, all at once he felt as light as though his chains had somehow vanished, along with the pain. But he had not been cut loose from his mortal body; he was more consciously aware of the earth's solid presence beneath his feet than he had ever been before.

For the first time in his life he felt completely alive . . . completely human . . . as if the chains had been forged so long ago from his own fears, his doubts about his identity and even his humanity, that they had become stronger than iron. Neither the Shogun's pronouncement, nor his recognition by the other ronin as someone worthy of the term "samurai," had been enough to set him free.

Samurai meant "*one who served.*" The ronin had served their lord even after death, not just out of *giri*—dutiful obedience to a system that, for all its power, was completely soulless. They had also done it because of *ninjo*—the awareness that there were some things only an individual soul and heart could be moved to protect, defend, strive for, even die for—and most of those things could not even be seen, let alone controlled, or enforced: *Justice. Honor. Love.*

Giri *and* ninjo . . . *Order and Chaos . . . the ever-changing balance-points on the ever-circling wheel of life.*

The past few weeks seemed more real to him than all the shadow-years he had spent before then, simply surviving. And finally, kneeling at last by Lord Asano's grave, he had realized that there had been a purpose for his survival after all . . . and that he had fulfilled it. *Lord Asano's soul was free . . . and so was his daughter.*

And so was he. At long last he was at peace with himself and life, enough to surrender to hope, and believe that every ending truly did lead to a new beginning . . . and he would enter his unknown future accompanied by Lord Asano's blessing.

He turned and quietly walked away from the grave, granting Oishi privacy for his own final moments shared with the spirit of their lord.

Oishi watched Kai walking alone toward the castle, surprised to see that his back was straight and proud, and his limp less obvious than at any time since his battle with Kira's demon samurai.

He looked back at Lord Asano's grave, silently thanking his master for the guidance that so many years ago had kept an overzealous, frightened young warrior from drowning a helpless—well, not so helpless—but equally terrified boy.

It was so easy to kill . . . he knew now just how easy it was . . . and how impossible to bring those who were dead back to life. His hand rose unthinkingly to his wounded shoulder as he remembered his fight with Kira at the fortress. He had felt possessed by demons, not divine vengeance, when he had finally killed Lord Asano's murderer—not bravely or heroically, but with a purposeful brutality he doubted even wild beasts were capable of.

He remembered questioning why the Way of the Warrior even existed, when in a battle to the death—whether one-on-one, or with armies of thousands pitted against each other—survival came down to trading another man's life for your own. Warfare made a lie of any moral code, but especially one that demanded the perfection of *Bushido*: "No honesty on the battlefield," Sun Tzu had said. And *compassion? Justice? Honor*? They had no more place there than honesty did.

And yet, when any war was finally over—and the actual attack on Kirayama Castle had not lasted a day, let alone a year, or a lifetime—the survivors still had to return home to their families, to friends, and to total strangers who lived in a world where day-to-day life for most people was as far removed from where they had been as heaven was from hell.

Bushido's code of honor was not intended to teach men how to survive in battle—any more than a warrior's training was meant to teach him that a dog's death was more honorable than a meaningful victory.

Bushido was a roadmap: something meant to show a man the way home, after he had been in the wilderness too long; to guide a warrior back to his humanity, to help him remember which things were really worth fighting for, and how to live in peace again.

A map was a reminder that even a sheet of paper had two sides.

Justice and valor, courage and compassion, courtesy, respect, honesty, loyalty . . . honor. Those described an enlightened being—or one who came close to enlightenment. But even in times of peace, it was impossible for most human beings to live up to such standards. If samurai were to consider themselves worthy of their place in society, then in times of peace—when the best sword was one that stayed in its sheath—they needed to define honor in a different way, and set an example by the good that they did, not the harm.

Oishi bowed again in homage to his friend, his mentor, his lord, who had pointed him toward the way of seeing clearly—toward living with true respect, honesty, and courage, not just posturing and pretense.

But even as he thought it, Oishi remembered what Lord Asano had confessed to him at the very end, as they walked together toward the Great Hall: that he had never really understood what Buddha meant about the true worth of every human being. That he had failed Kai. That his daughter had always understood it, instinctively, but because he had not, she had never dared to tell him she loved Kai—and so he had failed her, too.

Oishi had denied it, and meant every word he said.

But now he realized that Lord Asano had seen clearly through the open window of enlightenment, at the very end. Even though it had been too late for him to change anything in this life, at least he would be guided in the next by that insight. . . .

And now, Oishi undestood, the window of opportunity had opened just as he too looked in the right direction, and he had seen the Eye of Buddha gazing back at him: seen, just in time, the insight he been meant to carry into his own future . . . and he owed Kai gratitude for that, as well.

It occurred to him to wonder how Chikara, like Mika, had seemed to realize Kai's worth instinctively, when he had not been able to see it at all. During the time he had spent with his son during their journey home to Ako, he had been surprised and impressed by the mature understanding that was already beginning to fill the void left by a boy's naïve illusions of the glory of battle, which Chikara had lost forever.

Chikara's greatest wish had been to prove himself as a warrior and as a man in his father's eyes; he had done it admirably. And yet Oishi could not help but realize that his son was still not even as old as he had been when he had almost drowned Kai. He wondered what more Chikara might accomplish, if he was free to live his life until its natural end.

And Riku. . . .

Oishi had prayed—like Kai, like all his men—that he had learned the lessons in this life that would allow him to travel one step further in the next, one step closer to true enlightenment.

And yet he was leaving Riku behind, leaving her with nothing but sorrow. He was taking from her not just the happiness of their life together—but their only child, as well. *What right had he had to do that to her?*

He had sacrificed everything to achieve the goal that had been his ultimate challenge, as well as his ultimate duty, in this life . . . even his own family. Duty to his lord had always ruled his thoughts; that was what it had meant to him to be a samurai. Only now, when it was too late, was he filled with regret at the realization that if he had only been more self-aware, he might have found a better balance between *giri* and *ninjo,* one that would have let him express his love for his family, and his very real duty to them as well, in the same way Lord Asano had.

Riku had always accepted how things were without question or complaint. And yet when he witnessed the communion of souls between Kai and Lady Mika on their journey back to Ako—one that scarcely even needed words; one that words could not describe—all he had been able to think of was Riku's face when they parted. He felt as if he had been as blind to Riku's rightful place in his heart as he had been to Kai's humanity.

He had seen the lesson there to be learned . . . but too late. When he returned to the castle he would try to express his feelings to Riku, and to Chikara as well; even though any words that he might say to them now would only be seeds sown too late in the year. . . .

Reaching out in his need to the part of Lord Asano's spirit that lingered here, Oishi bowed deeply and prayed, hoping that Ako's lord might still be watching over his men for what little time remained, and somehow grant a final boon . . . not to him, but to his loyal wife.

A new day—the final day—illuminated the courtyard, where white mats had been laid out in rows among the blossoming cherry trees, a bittersweet reflection of love and duty.

In their separate rooms within the palace, the forty-seven men who had sworn to avenge their lord, to free his spirit and then follow him on his journey into the unknowable future, donned their white clothing and prepared to keep their final vow as samurai.

Dressed all in white, Kai came softly into the hall where Mika stood alone, gazing out through an open doorway at the rows of white mats beneath the blooming trees. He saw the slight tensing of her body that told him she knew he had entered the room, but for once she did not turn immediately to look at him.

Realizing why, he stopped where he was, waiting for her to acknowledge him. She was dressed once again as he had remembered her for so long, as Lady Asano, wearing the glorious colors of the newborn day. Her layered robes were plain and unadorned, but they were dyed in colors that shaded from gold and peach to magenta and crimson. Today she wore over them a man's sleeveless surcoat bearing the crossed hawk feathers of the Asano *mon,* embroidered in gold on the red silk—the colors of Ako, and of life. It was a bold declaration of her position as regent, rightfully restored, along with the honor of her father and her ancestors—and also of her eternal gratitude to the honorable, unshakably loyal retainers of Ako who had made those things possible.

Her beauty still transfixed him, as it had when he was only a boy, although it had never been the vivid colors of her clothing, or even the fine-boned beauty of her face that had captured his heart like a wild bird, and begun a love that had sustained him through the years. It had been what he had seen in her eyes from the first moment they found his: the recognition of one old soul for another. A resonance so deep that for all those years there had never been any need for promises, barely even the need for contact. Simply to see those eyes, that beloved soul gazing back at him, had been enough.

Love was not something that had made him want her, so much as something he had always felt without wanting: like a magic pool it had shown him depths of peace, and joy—a joy that had burned away life's pain.

At last Mika turned to face him, her eyes reflecting the gentleness of his gaze, although beneath their surface he saw the strength of her will, which had always been something he had loved about her too . . . even as he realized that in this moment it was barely strong enough to keep her emotions under control as she crossed the room to him.

Looking up at him, she said softly, "Before he died, my father told me this world was only a preparation for the next . . . that all we can ask is that we leave it having loved, and being loved." Her hands rose, trembling with the need to hold him . . . with the knowledge that he had always been so near, through so many years here in Ako, and yet so unreachable.

He stared at her expression, her hands, unable to keep the longing he had held inside for a lifetime off of his face—now that this life of eternal patience was finally about to end. He took her hands inside his; they were cold with more than the morning chill—as if the depths of her body and soul were still half frozen from a year when her existence had been a living death. And now . . .

Now there was only time enough left for one vow. "I will search for you through a thousand worlds, and ten thousand lifetimes, until I find you." Willing her to believe that he would never fail to recognize her the moment their eyes met—just as he had this time—no matter what fresh form her soul wore.

"And I will wait for you, in all of them. . . ." Her voice broke. She threw her arms around him and pulled him against her; they held each other for the last time with all the tenderness and passion they had been forced to deny since that spring day, so long ago, when a young girl had kissed a boy and run away, never dreaming it would be for a lifetime.

The wind rustled through the cherry trees, sending down a shower of petals as Oishi led his men out into the courtyard, where forty-seven white mats awaited them. The forty-seven men dressed in white took their places one at a time, with stoic dignity. Kai was the last to enter the courtyard; his face remained composed, even as he saw Mika already in her place among the observers, seated with the Shogun and his dignitaries. Dressed in her brilliant silks, she stood out like a glorious blossom among the somber outfits of the *bakufu* officials, as if she meant for her appearance to be a defiant affirmation of her belief in the eternal rebirth of the spirit and the better world awaiting the doomed men before her.

Yasuno moved over slightly, with a nod of acknowledgment, so that when Kai kneeled he would have sufficient room to do it without betraying his injury. Kai glanced away from the observation stand and Mika, seeing the guards in black and gold who ringed the courtyard, both to keep order in the crowd that had come to witness their final moments, and to act as seconds.

There were no *tobari* enclosing the space where the ritual was to occur. Mika had given the people of Ako permission to attend, which was unusual to begin with, and from the size of the crowd, it was clear that people had come from much further than just the castle town. Despite its size, the crowd waited in respectful silence, as if they were in a temple, and many of them wore the white of mourners. The courtyard was so quiet that Kai heard only rustling leaves, and somewhere a bird singing; the sky was as pure a blue as he had ever seen it, infinite. . . .

At Oishi's signal, the forty-seven samurai kneeled down as one, placing their death poems on the small table waiting before each of them, where a *tanto* already lay. As one they bowed, paying their last respects to the Shogun, and to Lady Asano.

The Shogun looked out from the observation stand at the forty-seven men, witnessing their proud, disciplined acceptance of the sacrifice they had willingly vowed to make. There had been no other way, within the confines set by human law—by his law—for them to live and act freely, even for so brief a time, with no constraints except their own sense of moral justice.

He knew the terrifying pull of something stronger than either society's will or fear of the law; he was the Shogun. Yet even he did not have absolute freedom to do whatever he wished.

He understood why there would always be some individuals who broke away from their predestined path, even knowing the path they chose for themselves led to the edge of a precipice. But whatever their reasons for defying the law might be, and whether the law itself was just or not, society could not function smoothly . . . the Tokugawa *bakufu* could not survive . . . if he showed leniency toward such behavior.

And yet, looking again at the reverent expressions on the faces in the crowd—on the faces of his own samurai—he knew that even he had never witnessed anything exactly like this before. No matter how flawed or ordinary the lives of these men might once have been, he realized that because of the courage, the honesty, and the unshakable sense of justice they had demonstrated in the end, he had seen the true expression of the samurai ideal for the first time. He realized that no one else here today would forget they were seeing it, either.

This was not going to fade away and be forgotten next week . . . next year . . . perhaps not ever. He glanced at Lady Asano, wondering exactly why she had allowed the people of her newly restored domain to witness the *seppuku* of the men that she and all of those people seemed to believe had saved them from Lord Kira. What kind of object lesson did she hope the citizens of Ako would take away from a sight like this?

As Shogun, he was the living symbol of the spirit those men kneeling before him embodied—as well as the symbol of the laws they had defied. He would be judged by history along with them. . . .

Their leader gave a signal, and the forty-seven men picked up their daggers, responding as if all their minds and his were one, united.

"Wait," the Shogun said.

The men stopped, their weapons poised in midair.

"Oishi Chikara," the Shogun said. "Step out."

Chikara looked up in stunned confusion, glancing from the Shogun to his father, to his grief-stricken mother watching from the crowd. His father stared at the Shogun as well, with nearly as much concern.

As Chikara rose uncertainly to his feet, the Shogun looked toward Oishi. "You may have defied me, but I will not deny our country your bloodline," he said. "Your son shall live to serve it, as you have done, with honor."

In the crowd, Riku's hands, which had been pressed together in prayer, rose to her face as if she was stifling a cry.

Chikara stood still, looking toward his father—his commanding officer—for orders, asking silently for permission or denial, torn by a decision he was unable to make on his own.

Oishi looked back at his son, his own expression trapped between emotions, as the leader who had acknowledged a sixteen-year-old boy's right to take a man's vow, a blood vow that carried a samurai's responsibility to see it through . . .

and as a father whose son had barely lived long enough to begin learning what being a man really meant.

Oishi glanced at Riku, suddenly remembering his final prayer at Lord Asano's graveside . . . realizing that somehow his lord had answered it, and his loyalty had been gratefully repaid.

He nodded to Chikara, giving him his permission to leave the field. With a final glance at the tears of gratitude on his wife's face, he turned back to the Shogun and bowed, seeing in his mind Riku's face overlain by the smiling face of Lord Asano.

Mika watched from her place in the stands as Chikara bowed a last time to his father, and then walked in a daze away from the other men, toward the crowd where his mother was waiting. The guards let him pass through, and she rose to her feet, reaching out to embrace him. Mika looked away from them, her heart aching with gladness and sorrow as she looked again at Kai.

Kai kneeled, motionless, like the men around him, his face serene, his white garments blending into a greater whole, making him only one of many—a part of the many who were now his friends and comrades. *He was where he belonged,* she realized. *Where he had longed to be, ever since he had found his way to Ako* . . . accepted at last, no longer either alone or despised, but finally in the company of his equals.

All at once there was nothing in her field of vision but the beauty of his tranquil face . . . the face of a *tennin,* the angelic boy she had once imagined had come into her life because he had lost his way on his journey back to heaven. She had always known that someday the time would come for him to continue that journey, wherever it led him.

In his eyes, gazing back at her, she found the image of herself as he had first seen her: the gentle face of a young girl more lovely than any being he had ever imagined, suddenly appearing at his side to watch over him . . . the memory of her sweet child's voice singing him a lullaby, even as her nursemaids tried to pry her away . . . of her running after him like the laughing spirit of spring through the beauty of Ako's fields and forests . . . a stolen kiss. . . .

And after all these years, the eyes of love, still filled with the same wondering recognition. Kai glanced down for brief moment, touching the poem he had written, before he raised his head to share a last look with her, one that told her his final poem had been written for her alone.

Oishi glanced away from Mika, where she sat by the Shogun's side still gazing at Kai until the end. He looked back at Kai, at all the others, and nodded his head once more. Once more, they raised their daggers, waiting for his final sign. The people watching—even the Shogun's guards—bowed their heads in respect.

Kai looked up, along with Oishi, Yasuna, Hara, and all the rest, taking in a final breath of the sweet air, a final view of the sky, the beauty of Ako . . . *the proof that some things were worth dying for* . . . to carry them through their final moment.

Oishi gave his last command, and as one they closed the circle.

A restless wind moved through the cherry trees in the courtyard; a whirl of petals, white through crimson, filled the air and settled softly, like snow, as the wind passed on . . . marking an end and a beginning, as they had in every springtime since the first. As they would continue to do through an endless cycle of renewal, into a future known only to the gods . . . to whom a closed circle and an eternal spiral, seen from one end, were not indistinguishable.

EPILOGUE

Japan, 1702

Mika stood again on the bridge that spanned the river, with a poem in her hands and inexpressible loss in her heart, just as she had done a year ago. Only a year . . . and yet it seemed like a lifetime that she had been gone from Ako, not knowing what had become of the ones she loved, or even what would become of her. Only knowing that her father's spirit remained here, chained to his grave by injustice, grieving for what had become of them, and what would become of Ako.

Now all of her questions had been answered . . . and still, somehow, she found herself standing on the bridge above the unquiet river as if no time had passed at all, more alone than ever.

Slowly, she unfolded the paper that held Kai's poem, forcing her hands to remain steady, afraid that the paper would be tugged from them by a sudden gust of wind, taken from her as suddenly as Kai himself had been, and Oishi, and all the other brave men who had sacrificed their lives to set right wrongs that no one else had even dared to acknowledge.

She looked down at the lines on the paper, gazing first at the calligraphy, as clear and careful as her father's, yet with an artless grace about it that better suited the hand of a *tennin*. She traced every curve and line with loving eyes, before she could bring herself to look through the surface of its beauty into its heart, allowing the forms of *kanji* and *kana* to resolve into words—Kai's parting words, for her alone:

There is a place beyond life and death
Where the skies are cloudless and the rivers clear.
Remember me, and I will find you there.

The poem was signed "Kai," the name she had given him when he first came to Ako, so long ago. Instead of following samurai tradition, he had not chosen a new name that his spirit would carry after death, life's ultimate rite of passage.

She stared at it in surprise. It was said that if the name someone carried in life was so much as whispered, the soul's rest would be disturbed. But—

"Kai . . ." With eyes closed she breathed his name, barely even a whisper. She opened them suddenly, blinking.

He had kept his name intentionally. Her vision blurred; she rubbed her eyes clear, so that she could read his poem again, and again . . . remembering his vow to her, and hers to him. It had not been meant to disturb his rest, but to comfort them both. . . .

She took a deep, tremulous breath, staring up into the sky, the depths of blue—the perfect reflection of peace.

She looked down again after a long moment, holding the peace inside her as she held Kai's poem close against her heart. Then she folded the paper carefully and tucked it into her *obi,* where it would stay close to her heart always, from now on. Kai was gone from this world, but no one, not even the Shogun, could touch the part of his spirit that still remained with her, held safely in the arms of her soul. She felt the wind settle and saw the river's surface grow calm, until at last it lay as still as a mirror, reflecting the sky, surrounding her with peace . . . but no comfort.

Returning to Ako, coming home, had been the dream that had sustained her throughout her long exile in Kira's mountains. And yet, even though the view from this bridge was as beautiful as she had remembered, she felt as if she saw it through the eyes of a stranger. What had once been her life, her entire world, seemed as unfamiliar now as if she had never belonged to it. The river might appear to lie at rest, but beneath its quiet surface a deep current was forever flowing toward the sea. . . .

Life, too, was a river of no return.

Change left nothing untouched. Even if she brought her father's garden back to its former beauty, it would not bring back her father. And Ako Castle would never be her home again without him . . . without Oishi, without so many of the others who had brought its silent spaces to life. *Without Kai.* The last year, and especially the memory of today, had left indelible scars that would distort her every cherished memory forever.

First her father, and now her father's most loyal samurai, had gone beyond the suffering of this life, taking Kai with them . . . leaving her behind, along with whatever hopes and dreams they had held for their own futures.

Her hands began to tremble, her knuckles whitening as they closed over the bridge's rail. What was left for her here, that still had any meaning—?

Ako. Ako was still here, she told herself fiercely, *and now she was its protector.*

Ako domain was her heritage, and her responsibility. How dare she even question her reason for living, when so many good people had died to protect it? *She would live to make Ako a reflection of the ronin's belief in the things her father had valued, and in her.* . . . That was the vow she made to them now, and to herself as well.

The men who had saved her life, and her father's soul, had been only human, imperfect and vulnerable, not legends or gods. But they had willingly served as the eyes, and hands, of heaven: What they had done would be remembered . . . not just in Ako, or in her heart alone, but in the hearts of everyone who heard their story . . . because what they had done had been done selflessly, for the sake of others.

She knew the people of Japan would honor such men forever—men whose belief in what was right and just had been stronger even than the fear of death . . . for justice and selfless courage were as rare in times of peace as they were in times of war.

She stood straighter, lifting her head as she gazed out at the view again. From now on she would be facing a battle of her own against great odds, one that would last many years, in order to make her vision a reality. Those she had lost but would always love would become her strength: her hands, her eyes gazing back at her from the mirror. And time would fly like an arrow if she stayed true to her vow, the way the men she would be honoring had done.

She touched the Asano *mon* embroidered on her sleeveless jacket: the *taka-no-ha,* the hawk feathers that symbolized the House of Asano and its samurai retainers, ronin no more. On a day like this, when the air was so clear that she could look all the way to the sea, it had always seemed to her that the depths of the sky held eternity. That if she looked deeply enough into the past, her spirit could reach out to the spirits of her ancestors, and as their souls crossed, like the feathers on her *mon,* she would ask them for their blessing.

And if she looked forward, into the future . . .

Her hand rested on the place by her heart where Kai's poem lay. The ones she had cherished most would help her to remember those things in life that were worth living for until her own vow was fulfilled, and she too was finally set free.

And then, somewhere in the infinity of blue, two spirits would cross like the feathers on her *mon*. As a diver might glimpse a pearl in the shadows of the sea, she would look into the eyes of a stranger, and discover her heart's reflection in his soul . . . and she would know that at last her own soul had truly found its way home.

As a result of the actions of the forty-seven ronin,
Lord Kira's lands were seized and the province of Ako returned
to House Asano by order of the Shogun.

To this day, thousands of people across Japan still gather
to pay tribute to the forty-seven ronin and their example
of courage, loyalty, and honor.

OWARI

ABOUT THE AUTHOR

JOAN D. VINGE has been described as "one of the reigning queens of science fiction" by *Publishers Weekly.* She has won two Hugo Awards, one for her novel *The Snow Queen.* Other novels include *Catspaw, World's End, The Summer Queen, Tangled Up in Blue, Psion,* and *Heaven Chronicles.* Vinge also has written film adaptations, including the original, bestselling *Return of the Jedi Storybook.* Her other film adaptations include *Ladyhawke, Mad Max Beyond Thunderdome, Lost in Space,* and most recently, *Cowboys & Aliens.* Born in Maryland, she grew up in San Diego, California, and lived for some years in the New York City area. She now splits her time between Madison, Wisconsin, and Tucson, Arizona.